# Son of
# VENICE

For Dreeen —
who traveled Through
China + had adventures
like Marco Polo!

Dori Jones Yang

5-1-2013

Text Copyright © 2012 Dori Jones Yang
Jacket art copyright © 2012 by Dori Jones Yang
All rights reserved.

Son of Venice, A Story of Marco Polo

Book cover design by Kathy Campbell
Printed in the United States of America.
ISBN: 0-9835-2723-7
ISBN-13: 978-0983527237
Published by East West Insights
www.eastwestinsights.com

# Son of VENICE

## Dori Jones Yang

## A Story of Marco Polo

EAST WEST INSIGHTS

# EMMAJIN'S FAMILY TREE

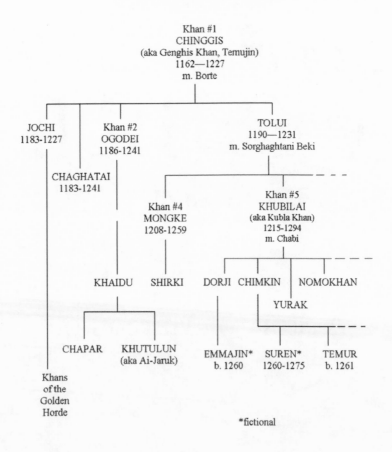

Khan #1
CHINGGIS
(aka Genghis Khan, Temujin)
1162—1227
m. Borte

JOCHI
1183-1227

Khan #2
OGODEI
1186-1241

TOLUI
1190—1231
m. Sorghaghtani Beki

CHAGHATAI
1183-1241

Khan #4
MONGKE
1208-1259

Khan #5
KHUBILAI
(aka Kubla Khan)
1215-1294
m. Chabi

KHAIDU     SHIRKI

DORJI  CHIMKIN     NOMOKHAN

YURAK

CHAPAR     KHUTULUN
(aka Ai-Jaruk)

EMMAJIN*     SUREN*     TEMUR
b. 1260     1260-1275     b. 1261

Khans
of the
Golden
Horde

*fictional

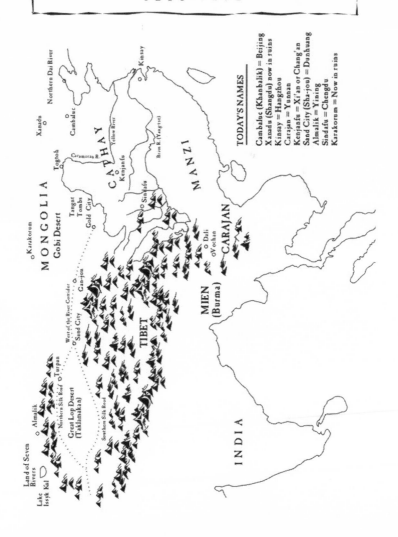

# MONGOL EMPIRE
# UNDER KHUBILAI KHAN
## 1260-1292

TODAY'S NAMES

Cambaluc (Khanbalik) = Beijing
Xanadu (Shangdu) now in ruins
Kinsay = Hangzhou
Carajan = Yunnan
Kenjanfu = Xi'an or Chang'an
Sand City (Sha-jou) = Dunhuang
Almalik = Yining
Sindafu = Chengdu
Karakorum = Now in ruins

Northern Dai River

Xanadu

Cambaluc

CATHAY

MONGOLIA

Karakorum

Togtoh

Caramoran R.

Yellow River

Kenjanfu

Burm R.(Yangtze)

Kinsay

MANZI

Tangut
Tombs

Gold City

Sindafu

Dali

Vochan

CARAJAN

Gobi Desert

West of the River Corridor

Sand City

Gao-jou

TIBET

MIEN
(Burma)

Almalik

Turpan

Northern Silk Road

Great Lop Desert
(Taklamakan)

Southern Silk Road

Land of Seven
Rivers

Lake
Issyk Kul

INDIA

# Part I:
# Together

# Chapter 1
# Marco: The Shaman's Warning

This was not how I envisioned my final day in the capital city of the Mongol Empire, ruled by the Khan of all Khans. Since my arrival a year earlier, in May of 1275, I had been admitted into his imperial presence many times, honored to serve him. My name, Marco Polo, was hailed at court and throughout the city of Cambaluc, in this exotic land of Cathay. Now, here I was chasing after a petty thief.

My dignity dissolved as I ran through the bustling streets of the foreigners' district outside the city walls, my heart pumping, my arms swinging, and my feet pounding the packed dirt. I pride myself in being a fast runner, but this barefoot rascal took advantage of his small size, ducking under a horse, whipping around a cart, veering into an alley. As a grown man of twenty-two, my size slowed me down. In the market, the string of wooden beads this boy had snatched from me would be worthless—yet it was precious to me. I had to retrieve it, to present to my lady.

The narrow alley stank of horse droppings and was darkening in the dusk of this spring evening. For a moment I lost sight of the imp. Then I saw a swatch of blue under a vendor's cart and leaned down to check. Like a scared rabbit, he sprang out and darted away again, nearly knocking a woman down before slipping through the open door of the courtyard of an inn, one of many set up for foreigners.

I chased him in. He hesitated, looking for another door. In that instant, I loped across the yard and grabbed him by the neck of his high-collared robe. He tried to wriggle away.

"Give it back and I'll let you go," I commanded in Mongolian, hoping this child would understand. He had no idea what a luminary I was.

He glanced at me with mischievous eyes and dropped the wooden beads onto the dusty ground of the courtyard. I scooped them up with my left hand, checked to see they were unharmed, and let go of the boy's collar. He dashed back out into the street.

"Must be something valuable," commented a nearby man in laconic Turkic.

I looked into his face, bearded like my own but with nut-brown skin and brown eyes. "More valuable than rubies," I responded in Turkic, one of the many languages I had learned on my travels. I held it up for him to see: a simple string of sixty wooden beads with a wooden cross hanging from the bottom. He smiled.

*Deo gratias*, I thought as I looped the beads over my neck and tucked them under my shirt. This rosary was the only thing I had left from my mother, who had died when I was a child back in Venezia. It had protected me on my three-year voyage to the far corner of the earth, to this city called Cambaluc, capital of the huge Mongol empire, which stretches from the rising of the sun to the setting thereof.

Just this evening, I had decided to give the rosary away, as the most treasured gift I could imagine. I was about to embark on the return journey home, but I wanted these beads to protect someone else now—a lady, Princess Emmajin.

Slam! The wooden doors to the street crashed shut just as I turned to leave the courtyard. Two huge Turkic men stood by the closed gate, staring at me with menace. I wheeled around on my feet, and behind me were two more thugs, including the man who had smiled. Now he held a dagger.

It was the oldest game in the bazaar: hire a small boy to snatch something, then lure a rich merchant off the streets into a courtyard, where you can rob him for all he's worth. Why had I fallen for it?

"Latin dog!" said the first Turk. "Hand over your robe, Marco Polo."

Sometimes there are disadvantages to making a name for yourself.

The leader grinned. I noticed he had several missing front teeth.

I took off my outer robe and handed it to him. That left me wearing only a thin garment of gray silk. He immediately slit open the hem of my robe. No jewels fell out. A common trader's trick was to sew the most precious gemstones into the hem of your cloak. Luckily, I had left my heavy cloak—the one with the jewels sewn into the hem—back in the courtyard of our inn, with my father and uncle and our twenty packhorses.

The Turk slashed my robe again, this time the collar, also a common place to hide jewels. None were there. But he grabbed the coins in the pocket.

Slowly, I backed away, in the direction of the wooden gate.

"Grab him!" the leader shouted. One of the other rogues jumped on me and tried to pin me to the ground. I slipped to the side, struggling to get away, but he held my arms. Another ruffian kicked me in the shins, and the third slammed my shoulders back against the paving stones. Two of them started to pummel me.

I fought back as best I could. But I am not a large man, neither tall nor stout. And I was outnumbered. This, I thought, is not a story I would ever want to tell anyone.

"Stop!" I shouted. "I am under the Khan's protection!"

They stopped beating me. The Turk laughed. "They all say that. Keep on." One ruffian slammed me in the ear.

"Please!" I begged. "I can help you!"

Two of the brutes pinned my arms but ceased beating me. The leader knelt by my side, holding a dagger to my neck. I held as still as I could, my eyes bulging.

"Hand over the gems," the man said.

"I don't have any with me," I answered. I knew I needed to use my brains to get out of this scrape, but the courtyard was spinning.

"Then finish him." The leader stood up, and the *criminali* started pounding again. One blow split open my eyebrow, and blood trickled down to my eyes.

"Wait!" I shouted again, feeling desperate. "I'll take you there!"

The leader held up his hand, and the pounding stopped. He raised one eyebrow.

My storyteller instincts kicked in. "Our horses are packed, ready to leave tomorrow, as you've heard. You know well how it works. We've sold everything large and have mainly smaller items, jewels and spices and silks. My father and uncle are old men now, over forty; they will do anything to save my life. I am the future of the family, heir to the Polo family trading business."

Now I had his attention. While this wasn't exactly true, I was not averse to truth-embellishment, especially to save my life. But I would never lead them back to the courtyard where my father and uncle were sleeping, unsuspecting, with only a few guards and horse boys. What could I say? I had to use my wits, to think quickly.

"May I sit up and explain?" I asked, to buy time.

The leader nodded, and the ruffians dragged me into a sitting position on the paving stones. The three of them surrounded me so I could not escape.

I needed to think up an escape plan, to distract them with a story that would convince them to spare my life, yet get me to a safer place. My mind spun.

My plan that evening had been to visit a Mongolian shaman who sold various healing concoctions. I wanted to obtain some medicine for my uncle, who had been sick the entire year we had spent in this country, coughing from deep in his lungs. Recently, he had improved enough to travel, but I wanted to make sure he had the best drug for pain and for sleeping.

"There is a lady," I began. What was I saying? There was a lady, my lady Emmajin, but I didn't want to tell them about her. What might convince thugs like these? "This lady is imprisoned in a tower by an evil..."—not an evil Turk, that wouldn't do—"an evil king. A terrible king who wants to dethrone the Great Khan."

Their eyes widened. It was treasonous to even talk of dethroning the Great Khan.

"This king," I continued in a low voice, as if telling a secret, "wants to force the lady to marry his son. His son is wicked, cowardly, and lacking in all virtue. The lady refuses to marry him. The lady is..." Quick, Marco, think! The lady is what? "The lady is a granddaughter of the Great Khubilai Khan."

Woops, that was a little too close to Emmajin, but the more I mentioned the Great Khan, the more I had these four thugs in thrall to my story. I sat a little straighter, and they pulled away from my side, more fascinated than ready to kill me.

"Yes, the Khan's own granddaughter," I continued. "Beautiful she is, with a face white as the full moon and rosy cheeks from riding across the grasslands."

The leader's dagger hand fell to his side as he leaned in to listen. Like Mongols, Turks were men of the grasslands, nomads who lived in tents and rode horses, so their lovely maidens all had rosy cheeks.

"She would rather die than marry that scoundrel! But, as the Great Khan's relative, she could not spill her own blood." This, I knew, was a rule. "So she resolved to eat poison, to take her own life."

One thug grunted. But the leader of these Turks was no dimwit. He sat back on his heels and scowled. "We are not here to be entertained by a tall tale," he said. "Take us to your father's courtyard and give us your jewels, or we will slit your throat."

One of the muggers grabbed my arm again.

"You don't understand," I said quickly. "This is no story. I need to go rescue that lady. If you stop me, Khubilai Khan will have you executed."

The leader snorted, as if mocking the idea of Marco Polo as hero. "Which is it? Die now or take us to the jewels?"

By now, a plan had formed in my head. It just might work. "Let's go," I said. They pulled me up to a standing position. "I'll take you to my father's courtyard. Follow me."

———◆———

What is it about a commanding voice and a good story? These four men, all larger and stronger than I was, showed me deference as they followed me out into the alley and down to the main street of the foreigner's district. Of course, they surrounded me so I could not escape. I held my head high and did not try to slip away. After all, my storytelling skill had helped me gain the confidence of the Great Khan himself. Perhaps it would work on these Turks.

I strode with purpose down the main street, acting as if these men were my bodyguards. At the first intersection, I turned right instead of left and walked straight north, dodging my way past puddles and dung and beggars. As orderly and broad as the avenues were inside the city walls of Cambaluc, this district outside the Western Gate was nasty, crowded, and foul-smelling. The four Turks kept close. It was getting dark, and the streets were emptying out.

Finally I arrived at an unpainted wooden doorway in a long, blank wall.

"Here it is," I said. The leader looked wary. Apparently he did know a little about us Polos, the only Latins in town, and this was not where he had expected me to take him. But he was not quick enough to object.

I knocked on the door. A short Chinese man answered. His narrow eyes flickered with recognition when he saw me, but he looked with suspicion at the four Turks.

"Old Wang," I said, using a respectful form of address. "These are my friends. Is the master in?" I pretended to stroke my beard, signaling my real meaning by a throat-cutting gesture only Old Wang could see.

He hesitated a moment and then let all five of us in. He bolted the door behind us.

The Turks looked suspicious. This courtyard was not filled with packhorses, ready to depart the next morning. It was small and empty. "Where are the jewels?" asked their leader, reaching for his knife.

On the far side, the sweet smell of incense wafted out from a sitting room.

"Hah!" With a shout, a tornado blew out of the room.

My heart seized up, but I recognized that this was the shaman, the Mongolian healer and spirit intermediary whom I had met the last time I bought medicine.

He was tall and frightful. On his head he wore a round hat with black strings hanging from the brim, covering his face. Feathers stuck out from the top. Long strings of beads, bones and shells, as well as tasseled ropes and furs, hung over his leather robe. He had a dark beard and mustache, and his hair was long and loose. In his left hand, like a shield, he held a round, skin-covered drum, and in his right, a wooden stick with a rounded head.

"Aaaaaiiiiiiyah!" the shaman bellowed. After leaping into the courtyard, he stood still as he stared at us. I froze in fear, and so did the thugs. From between the black strands, his eyes glittered with a mad, trancelike look, as if he'd been staring at the moon above the courtyard walls.

The shaman lifted his drum, which he held in front of his body like a shield. He used the wooden spoon to pound the drum in an irregular rhythm.

"Owwwooooo," he howled.

My heart beat wildly, with the drum. The thugs seemed mesmerized, too. Their leader quickly sheathed his knife, as if recognizing a greater power.

Then the shaman began to whirl. As he twirled, the strands of silk and fur and beads streamed out from his shoulders, first one way, then the other. They clanked and tinkled as he spun.

I had seen another shaman dance like this once before. The Turks, I guessed, had also seen a shaman dance. They had similar traditions. We all stood, rooted to the spot, watching the performance in fascination and awe. No one leaves during a shaman's dance.

The shaman began shouting words in Mongolian. Although I could speak it fluently, I caught only a few of them at first. "Tengri," I heard—the name the Mongols use for God of Heaven. Something about spirits of wind and fire and moon.

"The lady!" he shouted. "The one with the heart of a warrior!" He twirled full around, and the snout of a mink on the end of a long strand of fur nearly hit me, as if eager to bite my cheek. I ducked.

The lady? Is that what he had said?

"Great danger!" he shouted. "Daaangerrr!"

That word I did hear clearly. Did he mean Emmajin?

"Traitors!" he shouted. "Capture! Defeat!"

He seemed so deeply in his trance that he was not aware who was listening. Was he predicting doom for my lady Emmajin?

"Thugs!" he said finally. "Criminals! Thieves!" He swirled closer to the leader and his thugs. "The Khan commands, kill them now!" His voice rose to a fever pitch.

"Evil!" he shouted, pointing at the leader with the wooden drum stick. "Eeeevilll."

My body was stiff, and my eyes were so wide they might never close again. The thieves, too, seemed frozen and afraid.

"Kill. Kill! Kill!" his voice started low, then got louder as he pushed toward the four Turks.

The leader of the Turks ran to the gate, unbolted the door, and rushed out into the street as fast as he could. His colleagues followed. Old Wang bolted the door after them.

At the bang of the gate the shaman stopped still, panting heavily and breathing loudly. His eyes narrowed as he seemed to see me for the first time.

"Why did you bring evil into my home?" he demanded. "Why did you come?"

I closed my eyes, relieved that the thugs were gone. My plan had worked; I was out of danger. I could breathe again. "To get medicine, Master," I answered quietly. "For my uncle, Maffeo Polo."

The shaman stayed a moment longer in his threatening pose. Then the spirit seemed to gradually lift out of him, curling up like smoke into the sky above us. The moon had risen, casting an eerie glow over the courtyard.

After a few moments, the shaman lifted his headdress off his head. A man stood before me. Tall, to be sure, with black paint on his cheeks and wild hair. But just a man, now, the otherworldly spirit gone out of him.

"Master," I said. "Greetings."

His eyes softened as he nodded, acknowledging me.

Old Wang came up beside him and took his headdress.

The shaman led me into his sitting room, and Old Wang poured us each a cup of a thick green Chinese drink called tea. He also brought me a simple outer robe and warm wet cloths, which I used to wipe the dirt and blood from my face. Old Wang applied a small poultice of herbs to my eyebrow, and I felt better.

"You frightened them away, the evil ones," I said. I had never seen this shaman in a trance before, but I knew that shamans usually did not remember what happened during trances. So I told him the whole story.

He laughed heartily. Then he pointed to the wooden beads, still looped around my neck, still connected to the cross. "That has power," he said. "It protected you."

I smiled, happy to believe that my mother's rosary had power in this part of the world. I suspected it was instead my quick thinking and his wild dance that had protected me. My uncle had often told me my greatest weapon was my silver tongue.

*"Deo gratias,"* I said, adding, "Thanks be to Tengri, God of Heaven."

The Master smiled and took a sip of tea.

When I told him why I had come, he brought out a large wooden trunk with his supplies of medicine. I picked out the right drug for my uncle, a powerful medicine called opium, and Old Wang packed it for me in several small leather pouches. I promised to return the next morning with payment, but he waved his hand as if it did not matter.

Before I left, I asked, "Master, who was the lady and what danger does she face?"

The shaman shook his head, unable to elucidate his own prediction of doom.

---

When I left, the shaman sent one of his burly guards to protect me. I had to get to Emmajin as soon as possible, to deliver my gift before our departure the next morning. My father, uncle, and I would be traveling in the same caravan, returning to the West with our goods, but Emmajin, on an official imperial mission, would be surrounded by guards and officials. I wasn't sure how often I might be able to see her during our journey to Roma.

We headed further north, along the outside of the city walls, to a plain I knew opened wide to the north of the city. There, I had heard, some of the Khan's troops had mustered. Among them, I hoped, would be Emmajin.

But I'm jumping into the story too quickly here. Allow me to introduce myself properly, as a gentleman. My name is Marco Polo. I'm a Venetian first, a Latin, a merchant—or, more precisely, a merchant's son—a traveler, an adventurer, a lover of stories, a lover of languages, a lover of beautiful women, and one lady above all, who captured my heart. She is Venus, goddess of love. She is Diana, goddess of the hunt.

In reality, she is Emmajin, a princess of the Golden Family, granddaughter of the Great Khubilai Khan. She is gracious, gallant, and glorious. As beautiful as Guinevere, as alluring as Isolde, this lady became a fierce warrior like the Amazons of Greek legend, fighting with valor in the Battle of Vochan. But recently she had decided to sacrifice her military career to embark on a noble mission of peace. Khubilai Khan had entrusted her with a letter to deliver to the Pope in Christendom, to establish relations of friendship and cooperation between her people and mine. I wanted her to succeed, and I also wanted her to think of me, every day on this journey, no matter how infrequently I was permitted to see her.

She should, by all rights, have no reason to favor me, a foreign merchant from a distant land. In the minds of the Mongols, merchants rank far below warriors and artisans, and even below herders and farmers, who produce goods rather than just trade them. And yet she had bestowed her favor on me.

As I rushed through the crooked streets, my worries deepened about the shaman's predictions of disaster. What had he meant? In his post-trance state, he had not been able to clarify what kind of danger threatened my lady—or even if the warnings were meant for Emmajin. But it seemed obvious to me that they were. I needed to warn her—but of what danger? I also wanted to reiterate my undying devotion to her—but what would be the right words for that? And I wanted to get a sense of how often it might be acceptable for me to see her, during the journey.

Given the dangers ahead, I was glad I had decided to give her my mother's rosary, for protection. But she would need more than that. How else could I help her? I needed to get to her tonight, whatever it took.

The moon crept over the Western hills, fat and yellow and full, low over the horizon. I was sorry to leave Cambaluc, the name we Latins used for the glorious city the Mongols called Khanbalik. A sense of magic pervades the place where you fall in love; the skies seem bluer, the blossoms brighter, the moon clearer. I knew I would forever remember this place as marvelous, the place where I met my beloved.

Ahead, soaring above the streets, I could see the three-story turret that marked the northwest corner of the city wall. Each level had a tile roof with curved eaves, in the Chinese style. The city wall was, I knew, heavily fortified to protect the Khan's capital, although no enemies had ever come close.

As the guard and I approached the tower, I could see the tents of the soldiers who had gathered north of the city wall. I had heard that Emmajin would travel with only a small armed escort. In recent days, I had learned that several divisions might be traveling west at the same time.

Standing on a slight hill, I saw that the plain was dotted with many rows of round white tents, called *gers* by the Mongolians, and hundreds of horses were tethered, saddled and ready to go. I counted ten tents in each row, and I could not see the end of how many rows stretched out to my right. It seemed like hundreds. With five men in each tent, that meant we would be traveling with thousands of soldiers. They could not all be escorting one princess. What could this mean?

This vast army was clearly preparing to march west, toward my homeland. Had the Khan tricked us? Was he sending a full army to attack my homeland after all? Was Emmajin's mission as an emissary of peace just a tactic, a distraction? If this army camped outside Roma, the Pope would not have any choice in how he responded.

How could I ever find Emmajin in this sea of military tents? I found a horse boy and asked him where the army was headed.

"West," was all he could answer. But he had heard that the army's commander was the Khan's fourth son, General Nomokhan, and that the Khan's grandson Temur would be traveling with him.

Temur. Wherever Temur was, I knew, there I would find Emmajin. She had grown up with her cousins Temur and his elder brother, Suren, who had died in the Battle of Vochan.

Increasingly troubled, I headed to the spot where Temur's tent was said to be. Just outside the North Gate of the city, I discovered three large tents—round and domed and white, in the Mongolian style, but far larger than the typical *ger*. The royal banner fluttered from each, and embroidered bands on a blue background circled the top edge of the round walls. Clearly, these were meant for royalty.

One tent was larger than the others, and I assumed it belonged to Emmajin's uncle Nomokhan, the military commander of this army. The other two, side by side, would be for Emmajin and her cousin, Temur. I smiled to see they were the same size, even though Temur was the eldest grandson, while Emmajin was a girl. With such a grand ger, the Khan and the army were treating her as an imperial emissary, giving her rank and dignity not normally granted to a woman.

But which tent was hers? I stopped for a moment to look at them, to see if one lacked some banner or marking. Even though I was wearing a hood, my foreign face attracted attention, so I could never slip easily through a crowd of Mongolians.

"What is this man's business here?" a soldier bluntly asked my bodyguard. The Mongols did sometimes hire foreigners from the West, including Russians, Persians, and Arabs, to serve as officials, so the soldier treated me with deference.

Understanding his question, I responded directly, in Mongolian, saying, "I seek Princess Emmajin. I am delivering a message to her."

"Marco!" Her voice flowed through me like water. I turned and saw her standing behind me, my lady, more stunning than ever in the moonlight. She laughed with delight. "Come in," she said, pointing to a nearby wooden door.

Relief flooded through me as she led me into one the two identical tents, where three servants were cleaning up from an evening meal and stoking a small fire. Could it really be so easy to find her?

I asked the shaman's guard to wait outside and then followed Emmajin to the back of the ger, where she sat in the host's seat, a wooden camp stool, and gestured for me to sit at her right, the spot for honored guests.

"Airag for my guest," she said to a servant, who quickly brought me a bowl of the Mongols' favorite drink, fermented mare's milk. I accepted the bowl with two hands, and we both drank the milky liquor before speaking. I aimed to look confident and dashing, but my hands shook a little, and it took effort to keep from spilling the airag. I had not seen her for a long time; had she changed her mind about me?

Emmajin sat only inches away, and her beauty emanated from her in waves. At last, I was alone with her. For the rest of my life, I wanted nothing more than to spend time with her, alone, for hours, days, months. Might I drink and talk with her every night on this journey, as I had on our previous trip?

My nose filled with the warm air of her perfume. I had not seen her for nearly thirty days, but it felt like years. She had sent a messenger to me, explaining that she could not see me before the journey. If others knew of our close relationship, that might jeopardize her role as ambassador for the Khan. My eyes drank in the sight of her two neat braids, her high cheekbones, a hint of a dimple, her elegant eyebrows, now arched in question as she contemplated my face.

I watched her eyes, hoping for a sign. These days I had been filled with worry, wondering what she thought of me. Was there another reason she had refused to see me these last thirty days? She could not possibly love me as much as I loved her. But maybe she did. I had been sure that I would be able to tell, from her manner, if only I could find her alone.

For once in my life, I was at a loss for words. Carefully, I put down the airag bowl, reached into the front of my robe and pulled out the leather pouch. She took it from me.

"A gift?" she asked, with a smile.

The pouch had two gifts inside. She pulled out the first, the strand of wooden beads, and held them up. From the bottom dangled a metal cross.

"Is this for praying? My father has a similar one," she said. Her father, I knew, was a Buddhist, living in a monastery.

"These are Christian-style prayer beads. We call it a rosary, for praying to Santa Maria," I said. "We say one prayer for each bead."

She cocked her head. Would she think this an odd gift? I knew she was not in the habit of praying, either Buddhist or Christian prayers. I wasn't sure she knew who Santa Maria was.

"It belonged to my mother, whose name was also Maria," I continued. "I want you to take it with you, for protection on this perilous journey."

"Oh, no," she said. "It has protected you this long. You should keep it."

Her eyes showed a gentleness that I remembered from my mother. A lump in my throat kept me from speaking, though I made a gesture to her to keep it.

I leaned forward and reached for her hand, the one that held the rosary. "Emmajin Beki, you may need more than this to protect you. I have just heard a dire warning—," I began.

Just then, a loud noise at the wooden door distracted our attention. A man barged into her tent without permission.

It was Temur, her cousin. Tall and thin, he had a handsome face with wide-set eyes. His hair was in the typical Mongolian style of braid loops, hanging behind each ear.

"Emmajin! The guard told me you had—" He stopped when he saw me, and a look of disgust crossed his face. "What's he doing here?" I quickly dropped her hand.

She compressed the rosary in her fist and slipped it back into the pouch, with the other gift—which I had not had a chance to explain. "Come in. Sit down," she said to her cousin, as if he were a guest, too. I hoped she would not open the second gift in front of him.

Temur strode across the tent and towered over us, seated on stools. "What is your business here?" he asked me. I had served, after all, as an emissary for his grandfather, the Great Khan.

I stood up, since no man should sit in the presence of royalty, if they are standing, and bowed my head, showing deference.

"Prince Temur, greetings. I came to wish your sister-cousin a good journey."

To my relief, I noticed that Emmajin tucked the leather pouch into her sash. Temur frowned at me, his eyebrows meeting above his high nose.

"You should not be alone with a foreign man," he said to Emmajin. Temur was a year younger than Emmajin, but now that he was sixteen, a fully grown man and a soldier, his voice carried a note of uncertainty as he addressed her. His protectiveness reminded me of his elder brother Suren, who had tried to keep me from Emmajin before. "You do not want to look bad in front of the other soldiers."

Emmajin stared him straight in the eye. "I am not under your command, Temur," she said gently but firmly. "But I value your advice."

Clearly, the two of them were working out a new way to relate to one another.

The tension in the air was thick as mutton fat. Temur's attitude confirmed my worst worry, that others in the royal family would try to keep us apart. Had she heard my warning? I had planned to tell her more, but I did not want to speak of this in front of Temur. It was time for me to leave.

"Prince Temur, I wish you a good journey, also," I said, bowing and making my move to leave. "May Tengri protect you both and keep you from harm."

He grunted, stepped aside, and let me pass. I looked back at Emmajin, who regarded me with a look I could not quite read. Was it longing? Annoyance? Or curiosity? Did she hear my warning?

I rejoined the shaman's guard. As we walked through the army camp and back around the outside of the city walls to the inn, the moon went behind a cloud.

In order to spend any time with Emmajin at all, I would need to befriend Temur. The best way to do so, I decided, was to impress the army commander, General Nomokhan. Perhaps I could do what I had done with the Khan himself, entertain him with stories. My mind whirred with possibilities.

# Chapter 2
# Emmajin: Swan Lake by Moonlight

On the fourteenth day of Fifth Moon, declared auspicious by the personal shaman of my grandfather Khubilai Khan, several regiments of the Mongol Army prepared to depart from Khanbalik—and I was among them, the sole woman. To mark our departure, the Great Khan himself planned to review the troops and give us his blessing.

Early that morning, I slipped the rosary beads and the leather pouch around my neck, and let my fingers linger on them, even as I wondered why Marco had given them to me. But I had to hurry and dress for the departure. Although I was no longer a soldier, I had to wear a military uniform. I picked up the first layer, a thin tunic made of smooth, firm silk—so tightly woven that arrows could not pierce it. On it was embroidered the insignia of the army, a sign I had worn with pride for many months.

As I pulled it on, I sighed. After much struggle, I had finally earned honor among my family and my people, as a warrior. Now I was embarking on an even higher mission: to deliver a letter from the Great Khan to the leader of a distant land called Christendom, regarding peaceful cooperation. For the first sixteen years of my life, I had thought the only way to achieve stature was as a warrior on the battlefield. Now, at seventeen, I had accomplished that but also discovered a better way to earn respect: as an emissary of peace.

After securing the tunic with a thin sash, I donned the outer del, of summer-weight brown fabric, slightly longer than the tunic, worn over matching brown trousers for easy riding.

I should have been filled with joy, but instead I felt conflicted. Temur had been so severe when he found me talking to Marco. I had hoped to see a lot of Marco on this voyage. Would I be able to?

Marco Polo. Why did my heart flip every time I saw him? He held no rank at all, and clearly Temur looked down on him. My stature with the Khan and his army, so hard won, might be at risk if I let others see me with Marco Polo. Yet I could not stop thinking about him. I wanted Marco's attentions *and* the respect of my people, and I wasn't sure how I could have both. It seemed impossible.

How bold, how thoughtful Marco had been to dare to come to see me in my tent the previous night. The sight of him had warmed my heart: his round green eyes, his full beard, his reddish-brown hair. The sound of his distinctive laugh always pleased me. How I had missed him these last thirty days, preparing for this trip! A year earlier, when I had first met him, those same features had seemed strange to me, foreign. But after getting to know him well, I now found them charming. Marco Polo, world traveler, had opened my mind to larger ways of seeing the world. Marco Polo, storyteller, had elevated me in the eyes of the Great Khan by telling the story of my bravery in battle. Marco Polo, citizen of a distant land, had allowed me to see a better way forward than war.

Marco was not good at archery or swordsmanship, skills I valued highly and developed myself. But he was skilled at speaking—in contrast to me. I stumbled over my words. He was knowledgeable about the people and places of the world, while I had been on only one short journey. Plus, he was courageous and clever in ways that had taken me many months to discover.

Last night, after Marco had left my ger, Temur had stayed a few moments. "Emmajin, be careful. You have to maintain your dignity and virtue. If anyone sees you alone with that foreigner, your reputation would be ruined."

Temur's comments annoyed me. "That man knows a lot," I had snapped back. "I'll need his help to learn about his homeland. How else can I carry out the Khan's mission?" Plus, I thought, Marco knows far more than you do, Temur, about matters of the heart. Of course, no Mongol soldier cares about matters of the heart.

My cousin gave me a hard look and then shrugged his shoulders. "Never forget that you're traveling with six thousand men," he said. "Men talk, especially about women."

After Temur had left, I could not sleep. He had a point. I needed to be circumspect. Once I delivered this letter to the Pope in Rome, I might be free to do as I chose—but not before.

I wanted time alone with Marco, yes. But not if it jeopardized my mission for the Khan or belittled me in the eyes of my family and the Khan's army.

That night, as I got ready for bed, the leather pouch had fallen to the floor. I remembered that Marco had mentioned a second gift. So I opened the pouch again. Beneath the beads was a smaller leather pouch. Inside was a flaky black powder, wrapped in silk. I recoiled from its strong, sickly sweet smell. What was it? It must be a medicine he bought, somewhere on his travels. But for what ailment? I wasn't sick. It struck me as strange. Whatever ailment it cured, I hoped I would never encounter.

I took Marco's mother's wooden beads, similar to a Buddhist mala, well-worn with prayer, and wrapped them around my hands. They felt warm and smooth, and I fell asleep recalling tender moments with Marco.

Now, early in the morning, I tucked Marco's rosary—and the Khan's letter to the Pope, sealed in a protective sleeve of leather— under a doublet of leather armor that I slipped over my head. Then I straightened the leather flaps that covered my thighs. Last, I put on my leather boots and a metal helmet, with two streamers of sable fur flowing from the top.

I decided to stop thinking of Marco and focus on this moment, my departure and the Khan's blessing. After all, I had worked hard to earn this glorious commission.

———————

That morning, in the pale light outside my tent, I saw that two large bonfires were burning before a raised dais where the Khan would sit, just outside the North Gate of the city. The officers of the departing army were lined up on the far north side of the fires. The crisp smell of burning wood filled the air.

My uncle Prince Nomokhan was in charge of the departing troops. He organized about fifty of his top commanders and their top aides to greet our ruler.

Although I held no official rank in the army, I belonged with other members of the Golden Family, arranged by rank and generation. So I stood next to my cousin Temur, in the row behind General Nomokhan, who was a younger brother to both my father and Temur's father. I was sure no Mongol woman had ever done this.

Next to the tall, thin Nomokhan stood another high-ranking officer, thick and sturdy with a full beard emphasizing the squareness of his face.

"Who is that?" I whispered to Temur.

"That's Prince Shirki. Don't you know?" Temur answered quietly.

I didn't know, but I recognized the name. Shirki was a first cousin of my father; Khubilai Khan's nephew. This square-faced man had a reputation of being proud and fierce, the commander of the army that defeated several southern Chinese cities. Highly experienced in warfare, Shirki's presence told me the Great Khan expected that this army might engage in battle.

Battle. That thought discomfited me. Uncle Nomokhan himself had told me that he was leading the army only as far as Almalik, a fortress at the edge of the Western Desert, to beef up the Khan's forces against possible rebel attacks. After that, I would continue on, with a small armed guard, heading for the distant city of Rome, to deliver the Khan's letter to the Pope. The three Polos, with their caravan, would travel with us.

But was the army preparing to fight? Against what enemy? I wondered. Khubilai Khan controlled all the territory between here and the Far West. Who might attack us along the way? Or was the Khan expecting to use the army to conquer Christendom? In that case, the letter of peace and cooperation, and my whole mission, would be moot. Was I being misled by my own grandfather? Had I been sent as a decoy? Stranger things had happened at court. I needed to find out the truth.

As the morning sun rose in the eastern sky, I shifted on my feet. Now was not the moment to question the ruler's objectives.

The Great Khan arrived on horseback. With solemn ceremony he was carried on a litter up the steps to the dais. He sat on the wide throne that had been prepared for him, high above us, flanked by two poles flying the Imperial white horsetail standards, swishing in the breeze like real horses' tails.

From this distance, all I could see was a wide bulk of a man, dressed in yellow silk, but I knew well what my grandfather looked like: his thin, pointed beard and mustache, his thick ears, his narrow eyes that could look either stern or smiling. He had become Great Khan on the day of my birth, seventeen years ago. As the ruler of the Mongol Empire, he kept his dignity and distance before all, but I had seen a somewhat softer side of him, the wise ruler who offered mercy to the defeated boy emperor of China. My grandfather had assigned me the task of spying on the foreigner Marco Polo, and later he had commissioned me to deliver a letter to the leader of Marco's homeland. If

Christendom agreed to cooperate with the great Mongol Empire, there would be no need to invade it.

I had not read the Khan's letter, but I could guess its contents. If the Pope simply acknowledged the superior rule of the Great Khan, the Latins could continue living and worshiping in their own way. All they would have to do was send occasional gifts as tribute, and their country would be safe from the Mongol Army. Surely, I thought, that would ensure peace. I hoped I could explain this clearly to the Pope. Speaking was not my best skill.

The Emperor stood up, and the soldiers fell silent. I noticed that his stance was firm, on steady feet, which had not so long ago been swollen and wobbly. That made me smile. Marco Polo had found a cure for the Khan's ailment in the bile of scaly creatures we called dragons. Apparently it was working.

Nomokhan shouted, and we began a time-honored ritual—the blessing of the army prior to a long journey.

Slowly, in quiet rhythm, in order of rank, we marched between the two fires, directly toward the dais. Shirki, I noticed, followed immediately behind my uncle Nomokhan. Although Shirki was older and more experienced, Nomokhan was son of the reigning monarch and thus outranked him. Shirki held his shoulders straight with military dignity, and his square jaw was clenched tight.

This ritual of marching between two fires symbolized purification. I could see the air wavering above the fires, and I felt a sense of cleansing as I walked between them. How glorious it was to take part in this ritual!

When we got to the front, we lined up in two rows. Then, responding to another shout by our commander, we all kowtowed in unison before our Great Khan. I fell to my knees, then dropped my forehead to the ground, stood up and repeated twice. The kowtow symbolized respect, obedience, and unity.

"Rise!" the Khan shouted after we fell to our faces the third time.

We stood at attention while Nomokhan slowly walked up the steps to stand before his father. I hoped the Khan would look at me, to give some signal of his support for my mission, but he did not. Instead, he proceeded with the ritual and gave his imperial blessing to our commander. He dipped his fingers in a bowl of airag and then shook drops of it in the four cardinal directions and on the head of General Nomokhan.

The ceremony sent a thrill through my bones. I was a fifth-generation descendent of Chinggis Khan, our Great Ancestor who had unified the Mongols and begun the conquest of the world. From birth, my cousins and I had been taught that his blood ran in our veins, and that we later generations were charged with the completion of his mission from Tengri, God of Heaven: to complete the conquest of the whole world.

As a child, I had assumed that meant military conquest. But then I myself became a soldier and fought in a battle, where I watched my beloved cousin Suren die of his wounds. That wrenching experience had forced me to develop different ideas. Now, armed with the Khan's diplomatic letter, I hoped that the world could be united under this khan without any further fighting. Perhaps that was a naïve hope. Nonetheless, I held it dear.

A courtier handed Nomokhan one of the poles with the Khan's white horsetail standard. This showed that the Khan was passing the right of command to his fourth son. After taking hold of the standard, Nomokhan walked backward down the steps, still facing our ruler.

From behind the ranks where we were standing, servants had brought our horses to us. Nomokhan mounted his, and the rest of us did likewise. Then, holding aloft the white horsetail standard, the general rode out between the two fires again. Two by two, with a great shout, we followed. Riding between these purifying fires, I felt higher, more virtuous, somehow. We were the troops of the Great Khan, Khubilai the Wise.

---

We rode straight north, away from the capital, out of my hometown. My horse, Baatar, ran in rhythm with those around him, moving smoothly from a walk to a lope then a gallop. I was leaving behind my mother, my father, and my sister, but they could get along without me. I was so confident of returning that I did not look back.

With leather reins in my hand, my horse's creamy mane flying in the breeze, and the familiar stiffness of the wooden saddle beneath me, I closed my eyes for a moment, luxuriating in the sunlight. I could feel my heart beating as one with some six thousand hearts around me, all of us inspired to go forward in service to the Khan and the Empire.

The energy of horses and men swelled around me in the early morning air, throbbing through the muscles of our horses and rising to something grander than any human spectacle. Yet I also sensed an undercurrent of danger, a nameless power surging through those men, aimed at instilling fear in others. I tightened my hand on Baatar's reins but leaned forward to give him his head.

Behind our army, traveling with us, would be Marco Polo and his small merchant caravan, lost in the dust of this grand army, but not forgotten by me. Surely I could find a way to enjoy both the delights Marco offered and the glory of serving the Khan.

After a short time, we slowed slightly, to an easy lope. Temur, riding next to me, flashed me a look of concern. He had been very attentive to me, as if trying to protect me as his brother Suren had done. But he was no Suren. A jolt of pain jabbed me; I missed Suren, my closest childhood friend, who had ridden off next to me on a different adventure, six months earlier. Suren would have grinned, instead.

Temur and I had become closer these past thirty days, as we prepared for this trip. His brother's death had shaken him, and he seemed to feel guilty about challenging Suren and trying to make him look bad during an archery contest the previous year. But our relationship was still tense. Although he was a year younger, he had assumed a level of superiority that irked me.

"Emmajin!" Temur's voice pulled me from my thoughts. He had maneuvered his horse close enough to talk as we slowed, going up a slight hill.

I braced myself for a fresh round of advice.

But Temur surprised me. "I want you to meet Prince Shirki," he said.

I nodded. Prince Shirki. I recalled his straight shoulders and dignity during our sending-off ceremony. Temur's eyes glowed when he spoke of Shirki.

"He's a fine man. I have been assigned to be his aide," said Temur, shouting over the sounds of the hooves around us. "You will like him."

So that was Temur's role on this journey. Only sixteen, Temur was young and inexperienced but anxious to learn. Now that Suren was dead, Temur was the eldest grandson of Khubilai Khan. He needed to learn quickly and prove himself worthy of promotion. Instead of making him work his way up from the lowest rank, that of ordinary sergeant for a squad of ten soldiers, he was assigned to work as an aide to a high-ranking official. It made sense.

By sunset of the second day we reached Kalgan, the well-fortified city just below the mountain pass that marked the border between Cathay and Mongolia. We camped outside the town, which swarmed with merchants loading up their camel caravans for the long journey along the trade route to the West, which foreigners called the Silk Road. Here, I found out later, Marco and his father changed out some of their packhorses for camels.

After setting up our tents, Temur escorted me to meet Shirki, who was sitting on a low stool near an outdoor fire wiping dirt off his leather boots. I was looking forward to the encounter.

"Here she is, General, my cousin, Emmajin Beki," Temur said with deference. Although Shirki was seated, his broad shoulders and graying hair gave him an aura of authority. I hoped Temur had told him good things about me.

Shirki glanced up at me and examined me with his eyes. I had seen this look before and it had become easy to read all that was in it: Is she a real soldier? Or a pretty girl here to keep the soldiers happy? Why is her grandfather indulging her? I was glad I was still wearing my long-distance riding clothes, a simple brown del that hid my figure.

His square face showed no sign of approval or disapproval. He returned to wiping his boots without speaking to me. He should have stood up, to show respect to the Great Khan's granddaughter. He should have looked me in the eye and addressed me. But he didn't. After months in the Mongol Army, I should not have been surprised. He outranked me as a high-level military officer and would not be impressed by a woman, especially one who had quit the army less than eight months after joining it. Still, I wished he had greeted me by name. It would be hard to win his approval.

"Emmajin fought in the Battle of Vochan," Temur said, obviously trying to give Shirki a better impression of me.

Shirki nodded and grunted. Clearly, I was irrelevant to him. So was my mission of peace. He had, I noticed, a dark mole on one cheek. Slowly, he finished his task and put his boot to one side. Then he stood up, ignoring me, and looked at Temur.

"Tomorrow we enter Mongolia," Shirki said to Temur. "Have you ever been to the ancestral lands?"

Temur puffed his chest a bit. "Every summer we go to Xanadu."

Shirki laughed. "Ah, Xanadu. That's all you've seen of Mongolia?"

Xanadu was, in fact, all I had ever seen of Mongolia, too. With its marble palace and planted gardens, it was not the open grasslands of our ancestors. "Prince Shirki, were you born in Mongolia?" I asked, hoping to gain his respect.

He turned to me and examined my face solemnly before responding. "Yes, of course. I was born in the capital city, Karakorum. All the Golden Family lived there then."

His pride in his heritage stung me, as if challenging my side of the family. It was my grandfather, Khubilai, who had moved the capital out of Mongolia and into Cathay, northern China, closer to his power base and an easier place from which to rule the lands he had conquered. Not all Mongols agreed with this decision, I knew, but I had never heard anyone openly question it. Shirki did not. But neither Temur nor I pressed him.

I was eager to leave China and experience my true heritage in Mongolia, which I had heard much about as a child. Northern China, Cathay, was a settled land of farmers, arrogant people who thought they were superior to us, with their ancient history of dynasties, literature, philosophy, and wealth. Although Chinese people look similar to Mongolians, with black hair and eyes, they speak a totally different language and have a different way of living. Our ancestors, the Mongols, lived in the lands north of China as tent-dwelling herders and horsemen. Our ancestors had always lived on the edge of Chinese civilization, with little power, raiding their cities for whatever goods we needed, until some sixty years ago, when Chinggis Khan and his army began the invasion of China. Now, everything was reversed, and we Mongols ruled most of China. My grandfather had adopted much of the best of Chinese civilization, while keeping many of our Mongolian traditions.

The following morning, we finally rode up over the Kalgan pass, leaving Cathay and entering our ancestral homeland. As we crossed into Mongolia proper, homeland of our ancestors, Temur and I stopped at the crest of the pass, staring wordlessly to the north. I felt a catch at my throat.

I closed my eyes. I could sense, for the first time, a direct connection to our Great Ancestor, Chinggis Khan, who had united the scattered tribes of these grasslands, created a Mongol nation, and headed West on a great mission of conquest, creating the largest empire in history. These grasslands stretched from here all the way west across the great continent, almost to Marco's homeland. My heart swelled with the pride of being a Mongol, on top of the world. Suddenly my attraction to Marco seemed absurd; how could I fall for a man who was not Mongolian?

"I'll race you to Rome," Temur said, with a wicked grin. He leaned forward and his horse took off.

———————

After several days of hard riding, we camped near a pristine lake. Shining in the brilliant late-afternoon sunlight, the lake sat in the midst of a huge flat grassland, with several rivers running into it. I had never seen such a handsome lake, edged with lush green reeds, with so many varieties of game birds. Most stunning were the snow-white swans, with huge gorgeous wings, adorned with round eyes like those of a peacock, but of a resplendent golden color. Although the lake had another name, I decided to call it Swan Lake.

Here we would rest for a day, our first day off. Finally, I hoped, I might have a chance to find Marco and ask him about the strange gift—and about the warning he had started to give me. During the long rides, and at night when I lay down to sleep, I had been wondering about this. What had Marco meant, giving me that strange medicine? I overheard that his small caravan of merchants, which had lagged behind us by half a day, would be camping near the eastern end of the lake.

Temur asked me to go hunting with him and a small group of soldiers. Although I had considered staying behind, searching for Marco during the rest day, when most soldiers had left camp for the hunt, the temptation was too great. As a child, I had not been allowed to hunt, since girls were forbidden. But now that I had fought in battle and earned their respect, these soldiers were honored to hunt with me.

Early the next morning, riding with a small group of hunters, I felt happy and free. The plains around the lake abounded with cranes, partridges, pheasants, and other game. The birds were so plentiful and tame that they were easy to shoot, and it was clear we would eat well for days.

The young soldiers laughed and cursed and raced as if I were one of them.

"We have heard of your prowess," one soldier said. "Everyone says your archery is the best."

"Show us!" shouted another.

Temur grinned, as if knowing that I could not resist. He handed me his bow to use.

His bow felt wonderful in my hands. Although I had grown up doing archery daily, I had not touched a bow and arrow in nearly a month. Temur and several of these men had watched, at the seaside, when I made the dramatic gesture of laying my bow at the Khan's feet. That gesture symbolized my decision to leave the army and pursue peace. But archery was my best skill, and I was eager to stretch my arms again.

I scanned the sky, examining the birds. One type of crane was small, with beautiful long red and black feathers hanging from the sides of its head. It flew very quickly and was much harder to shoot than the others. Several of the men had expressed frustration when they could not hit it. I had no idea if it was tasty or not, but decided that shooting one would impress these men.

My first shot was bad. My lack of recent practice was obvious.

Then I saw one of the beautiful small cranes take off from the reeds near a small lake, flapping awkwardly at first, then soaring high.

It was a great distance from me, a shot most men would not take, since the chance of missing was too high.

I pulled back the bow, aimed it straight up, then quickly lowered it to just the right angle and released the arrow, all in one smooth motion.

It soared over the distance, high at first, then arced down at the perfect angle.

Thwack! It hit the mark. A perfect shot.

"Aaaaaaah!" The soldiers cheered around me, duly impressed, as the bird tumbled to the ground.

It felt good to be shooting again. This is the real Emmajin, I thought, not some peace-maker or lovelorn lady. This is the work I have trained for, all my life. My true skill. What was I doing, going on a diplomatic mission to the Far West? Why had I laid down my bow?

I love archery. I love hunting. I am a Mongol, a member of the Golden Family, an heir to Chinggis Khan. How could I ever have imagined that being with Marco Polo was worth giving up this beloved way of life?

As the bird was being plucked, three young soldiers approached me quietly. "Excuse me. Is it true?" one asked me.

The second soldier looked on eagerly, as if he had dared the first one to speak. The third looked embarrassed.

The first soldier continued awkwardly. "Do you, um…do you carry with you a pair of balls you cut from an elephant?"

I regarded him with alarm. His eyes were round and innocent. The other soldiers were listening, eager to hear my answer. Where had they heard such a tale?

His earnestness made me smile. "No," I said. I should have lied, I thought, and told them what they wanted to hear. But as easily as Marco could stretch the truth in his stories, I could not let this tall tale stand. Even exaggeration for the sake of entertainment made me uncomfortable. I had been raised to abhor lying.

The soldier's question made me remember the raw fear I felt at the Battle of Vochan, when the huge elephants had charged at us, frightening our horses. I had, in fact, aimed my arrows at an elephant's private parts, to try to stop him. After the enemy killed my cousin Suren, I had gone into a mad rage, killing every enemy I saw. For this, I had been lauded as a battle hero. I shook my head at the memory.

The third soldier shouldered the first away. "Dumb ox," he said to his colleague. "She keeps them in a locked box. She would never show them to us." It was pointless to deny it; the men already had accepted it as the truth. This is the way legends begin, I thought. Marco would be amused.

Their admiration bordered on reverence. This is what I had dreamed of, as a girl back at court—achieving the respect of Mongol men and soldiers.

Back in my tent, alone, afterwards, I relived the feelings of the day. What was important to me? It was not just a matter of being loyal to my people and my Khan, it was also about being who I really am: a warrior, an archer, an athlete, a person of action. This was the life I loved.

Who was Marco Polo to me, really? Temur was right when he tried to keep him from me. I could see how foolish I had been. If anyone knew the truth of how close Marco and I had been, I might have lost my standing at court. And I had also risked losing the essence of who I was, a Mongol, an archer. I could not let my fondness for Marco dilute that. I needed to tell him that it was not right for me to see him alone again.

———

"Emmajin!" Suren's panicky voice woke me with a start.

My muscles were rigid and I was dripping with sweat. Images of the Battle of Vochan had been pulsing through my head. Horses panicking, elephants bellowing, my mace smashing someone's face, the tip of a broadsword penetrating Suren's throat.

"Suren?" I said. But no one was there.

My heart was racing. I lay still in the dark, trying to calm my-self. It was just a dream. The battle was over. But after that I could not sleep.

After lying awake, deep into the night, I couldn't take it any-more. I knew of only one person who could calm me down after such a nightmare. I got up from my sleeping fur and wrapped myself in several layers of clothing, which covered my braids. I did not want to be recognizable as a woman or as Emmajin.

I easily stepped over the snoring guard and went out alone, walk-ing along the lake in the full moonlight. I headed toward the eastern end of the lake. I wasn't sure how far away Marco was camped or even how far I was permitted to wander.

Seeing Marco would calm me, I thought, and telling him to keep his distance would strengthen my resolve.

An army dog barked when he saw me, and then another. I froze. I didn't want any of the night guards to challenge me, walking outside my tent in the night. But Mongol dogs bark a lot at night, so no one came out of a tent to check. I walked quietly on.

Finally, near the eastern end of the lake, I saw the packhorses that belonged to the merchants, and their tents nearby. Their guards seemed to be asleep. I knew Marco was inside one of them, sleeping. But which one? Just knowing he was near was already calming me down.

I chose to walk closer to the water. Like all Mongols, I loved the land and distrusted water; Marco was the opposite. In his hometown of Venezia, the streets were waterways, and their livelihood came from ships and water routes.

The water of this lake, much stiller than the sea, reflected the stars and the moon, round and bright, just past full. Mesmerized, I stared at it. A breeze created small ripples on the surface. The image of the moon—so solid in the sky—wavered in the water.

Somewhere, in the distance, came music. Someone was playing the Mongolian horsehead fiddle. Its low, deep notes resonated inside my bones. Its voice seemed mournful, expressive, poignant. Something lost. Something that might have been but could never be.

When I heard feet crunch on the gravel behind me, I recognized the sound of his steps. Trained to be on my guard, I normally would have whirled around, to see who was approaching. I was bundled up, dressed like a man, but of course he knew.

Still, the footsteps stopped several paces behind me. He did not come close or touch me. Of course, he would not.

I waited. For what? The horsehead fiddle crooned on in the night air.

Marco. I had come out to tell him I would not see him any more. I had come out to tell him I was a person of action, an archer, a warrior. That seeing him was against the very core of my being. That I was a Mongol at heart. That I could never see the world through his eyes. I blinked back tears.

I remembered the feel of his lips on mine, in what he called a *bacio*, a kiss, unknown in Mongolia. The stiff edges of his mustache, the soft curls of his beard. The light touch of his hands on my skin. Slowly, I turned toward him.

Yes, it was Marco. The moonlight illuminated his face, framed by a beard.

*Marco.* I had missed him so much! I resisted the urge to run into his arms.

It was dangerous for him, too, to consort with the granddaughter of the most powerful ruler of the world—especially surrounded by the Mongol army.

He stood still and waited for me to move.

Finally, I walked slowly toward him. The words I had practiced ran through my mind. *I couldn't contact you because...I can't see you again...This is the end...*

When I got close enough to see his face, I stopped. His green eyes seemed dark, but I could see a look of love and longing. He sighed, as if the mere sight of me would get him through another month.

"Messer Marco," I said, using his title and adopting a formal tone.

He stiffened and lowered his head slightly.

The horsehead fiddle shifted to a different tune, lighter and sweeter.

I remembered the feeling, just after the battle, when I had thought Marco was dead. Frantically, I had searched the bloody battlefield, convinced I would find his body.

I remembered the feel of his hand, holding mine high above his head, facing the Khan and his approving soldiers, after telling an exaggerated version of my battlefield prowess, trying to use his words to help me achieve my dream.

I remembered his distinctive laugh, his witty words, his charming storytelling, the tales of romantic love from his homeland.

Most vividly, though, I remembered the last time I had seen him, when we sat on the beach together on a moonlit night like this one, then entered the sea together and joined as one.

Unbidden, my hands reached out for him. He took them.

My feet stepped forward, and he embraced me.

Words failed me, as they often did. Words seemed so unnecessary.

His arms were warm, and his hair smelled of spices. Despite our thick clothing, I could feel the shape of his body pressed against mine. My body, as if starved for a month, pushed hard against him.

I pulled back my head to look into his eyes, which were sparkling, a little star in each. All the doubts and hesitations I had felt came rushing back into my mind. But his lips were too close now. A year earlier, I had never heard of a *bacio*, but now I wanted one, badly.

Under a full moon, in plain sight of so many tents, we were visible to anyone who might look this way, at this time of night.

"My lady," he said. "You may be in great danger."

"Danger?" Were there guards awake, watching?

"I saw a shaman, the night before we left Khanbalik, a true Mongolian shaman. His words were hard to understand, but he referred to 'a lady' and shouted words like traitors, capture, defeat, murder. I don't know what he meant, but I had to warn you."

My heart pounded, hearing these frightening words. Everyone I knew took the words of a shaman seriously. "Did he mean me?"

"I'm sorry. I don't want to frighten you. He might have meant someone else, but who? Maybe by sending this warning, he meant we should find a way to prevent it."

"Traitor? Defeat?" I repeated. "It doesn't make sense. I'm on a mission of peace." I wondered if the Khan had heard this shaman's prediction—and if so, why he hadn't warned me.

Marco hugged me more tightly. "I won't let anything bad happen to you."

I nearly laughed but didn't. As if Marco could prevent any of these terrible things.

"The night before we left Khanbalik," I said, "you gave me a pouch of smelly black powder. Is that medicine?"

He pulled back, still holding my upper arms. His look turned serious. "It is. It's a very expensive medicine that I found in the markets of Carajan. It comes from poppies."

"But I'm not sick," I said. "What's it for?"

He pursed his lips. "I got it from the shaman. I thought it might help you someday, in case something terrible happens."

I felt a chill run up my spine.

"A very small amount will help if you are ever in pain," he continued. "A larger amount, about this much"—he held his fingers a short distance apart—"will put someone to sleep for a long time."

What was Marco thinking might happen to me? I was safe with the Khan's army.

"Any amount this big or larger"—he held his fingers farther apart—"will kill."

My mouth opened, but the question would not come out. When might I need to kill someone? It occurred to me that Marco Polo, with his great imagination, had envisioned scenarios that had never crossed my mind.

"Please remember," he said, with urgency.

"Grazie," I said at last, using the word he had taught me for thank you. "I hope I will never need it."

He smiled. "I pray you will not."

"And your mother's prayer beads?" I asked.

"For protection, on your journey," he answered. "I know the cross means nothing to you, but we Latins believe it keeps us from harm."

I nodded. "Thank you. I will return them to you after delivering the Khan's letter to the Pope, in Rome."

I could feel the tension going out of his body. I lifted my face as close to his as I could. I drew closer to him. Finally, I felt the softness of his lips on mine.

For a long moment, we melted into one.

Then a dog began to bark.

I stiffened and pulled away, looking over Marco's shoulder. I could not see movement of any man, but a dog was approaching us.

The horsehead fiddle music stopped.

"Marco, you..." How could I say this? "You know this is danger-ous for me, meeting you in private. We cannot see each other like this again."

His arms tightened around me. "Once we get to Rome, will it be different?"

I, too, had tried to imagine what might happen, once I delivered the Khan's letter to the Pope. "Perhaps."

"That gives me hope," he said.

He took my hand from his cheek and kissed the tips of each finger. His kisses sent sparks of warmth through my frigid fingers. Then he folded my hand, kissed the top of it and held it to his heart.

Another dog began to bark. The first dog stopped just a few yards away and barked even louder. Someone shouted from one of the tents. A tent flap fluttered and the sound of boots told us that someone was coming out. We pulled apart and saw a dark figure coming in our direction. Swiftly, I slipped away, walking along the edge of the lake.

Marco turned to the dogs and knelt in the sand, holding out his hand. The dogs growled and snapped at him. The man headed toward him, ignoring me.

I reached a small tree and crouched behind it, hiding from sight.

The man shouted something at Marco, and he answered in Mongolian. I took advantage of the distraction and ran further along the lakeshore, reaching a grove of trees. I waited in the grove a long time, till Marco and the man began walking back to their tents, followed by the dogs, which calmed down and quieted.

The tips of my fingers brushed against my cheeks and lips, remembering the pleasure of his touch. But then I balled up my hands into fists. It was so easy for me to forget myself when I was with Marco.

Stupid Emmajin. I hit the sides of my legs. Where was my brain? I knew the risks of seeing Marco. I had resolved to stop seeing him. So why had I come?

I was fighting a battle, I realized, but not against Temur, not against the world. It was a battle inside myself. That part of me that has always longed to be respected by the Khan and his army was warring against that side of me that came out in the middle of the night seeking Marco.

As I walked back to my tent, I looked up. A cloud had passed over the moon.

# Chapter 3
# Marco: Stories, True and False

As Emmajin slipped out of sight after our moonlit rendezvous, the man we heard, a guard, confronted me, brusquely asking where I had been. I told him that I had gone out to take a piss. "What man were you talking to, and why did he run away?" the guard asked me. Two dogs were yapping at our knees.

"A soldier, drunk," I answered. "He asked me how to get back to the army camp." My storytelling had become so effortless I did it without thinking about the line between tale-telling and lying. Both involved telling the listener what he needed to hear. Sometimes that bothered me, but twisting the truth was a useful skill. To give Emmajin time to get back undetected, I detained the guard with a few questions about the planned departure the next morning.

By the time I pulled back the flap to enter my tent, I felt sure that Emmajin was safe. But I was not. Inside the tent, the darkness was stiff with tension. Both my father and my uncle were sitting upright, on their sleeping furs. Even in the dark, I could sense my father's anger before he spoke.

"That was the worst thing you could have done," my father said. He had an uncanny way of knowing what I had been doing.

"I went out to piss," I said. In the few beats of silence after I spoke, I could hear in my own voice a lack of conviction that confirmed their suspicions. They had heard me lie and tell the truth often enough to know the difference. It was pointless to deny I had seen Emmajin.

"Marco," said Uncle Maffeo, who often sided with me. His voice was stern but steady. "Marco, don't flirt with danger. All three of us could be thrown into prison. Our goods could be confiscated. We could live out our last years with no freedom and no hope of ever returning home to Venezia."

I had considered the risk to myself, how I could be punished as a lowly foreign merchant for daring to seduce the Khan's granddaughter. But I had not thought of the danger I might cause my father and uncle. The vision of my cherished uncle, stripped of his ready smile, quick wit, and dignity, wasting away in a Mongol prison, hit me harder than my father's harsh words.

My uncle continued. "I know what it feels like when your head is turned by a beautiful smile. This lady may enjoy dallying with you, but as a member of the Golden Family, she will never be allowed to choose you. Her family is loyal to the Great Khan and the Mongol Empire. Do not let yourself be fooled."

These were points I had considered myself, many times. Why should Emmajin put her affection for me above her loyalty to her family?

I went to Uncle Maffeo, sat next to him and put my hand on his shoulder. "I promise. I will be careful," I said.

"You'd better!" snapped my father.

My uncle smiled sadly at me.

———

As I tried to sleep, I could not help thinking about Emmajin's face. The soft contours of her high cheekbones. The dark depths of her eyes, filled with longing. And, of course, that kiss. Her lips were wide and smooth and insistent, and her body had pressed against me ardently. I could not give her up forever, that I knew.

The only hope we had, Emmajin and I, lay in the far future. We had to stay apart during these months of travel, but each day we were traveling farther from the strictures of court. And halfway through the journey, the army would stop at Almalik, and we would travel on, with only a small armed escort. Her mission was to go to Rome and deliver the Great Khan's letter to the Pope. If the Pope responded well, then Latins and Mongols could live in peace, without the danger of war. After that...That distant time was what my fantasies focused on. My desire was not for a mundane marriage but transcendent love.

Meanwhile, during these endless months of travel, there was one thing I could do: try to earn the respect of Emmajin's family, especially of Nomokhan and Temur. Shaken by the shaman's prediction of danger, I also needed to warn them so they could protect Emmajin. With their army and guards, they could do far more to keep her safe than I could. It was an immense task, a vital one. Could I win their trust and admiration by using the one skill I had that the Mongols valued, my storytelling ability?

Growing up in Venezia, I was known as a boy whose father had disappeared, beloved as a trickster and manipulator, a teller of lovely lies and terrific tales, a lad with many companions, always laughing and joking, always attracting a pack of youngsters, roving the streets, charming my way onto gondolas, pointing to palaces and amusing my friends with bawdy stories about the local nobles. I knew it was against the Ten Commandments to bear false witness against my neighbor, but I was confident that even Jesus knew the value of a good story.

Yet, when I came here, to Cathay, the Great Khan Khubilai showed me the value of this skill—and showered me with his favor. This imp of Venezia became Story-teller to the Khan of all Khans, who was the most potent ruler in the world since the time of our First Father Adam—more powerful, even, than the Pope.

This great Lord called me a "young gallant" and invited me to speak before His Majesty and his men at his magnificent palace. Surprising him with my fluency in the Mongol tongue, I told him of lands I had traversed, of novelties and strange things I had seen and heard, of divers people and astonishing customs, as well as the tales of my homeland, the romances of Christendom, of knights and ladies, of battles and dragons, of valiant heroes and shifty traitors, of quests and grails. I told the Khan of combats, challenges, wounds, courting, loves, torments and all manner of unending adventure, in words as grandiloquent as I could muster in the Mongol tongue.

And I, a man who could not shoot an arrow or wield a sword, kept company with the mighty. He became partial to me and treated me with distinction, so that even his own Barons waxed envious. It went to my head.

I began to think that I deserved such honor, that a princess might be charmed by my wit. So I had felt reluctant to leave the Khan's court, where I had risen from nowhere and flown with the eagles, where the most noble lady of the land wore my scarf into battle. I had dreamed that the Khan would grant me an appointment to high office; after all, he had appointed many other educated foreigners, especially Mohammedans, to powerful positions. Why not me? That status might allow me to woo my lady openly.

But that dream had crashed when Emmajin arranged what she thought would please me: this mission of hers from the Khan to the Pope. It was noble and high-minded of her, but it pulled me back into my role as traveling merchant. My father and uncle were glad for the opportunity to return to Venice with full packs, under the protection of the Khan, but I felt ambivalent.

Emmajin might be dreaming of the freedom she would have in Venezia, far from the supervision of her family. But I knew how narrow-minded people were back home, how disapproving of foreigners. So I was less confident. I wasn't even sure the Pope would respond positively to the Khan's demand for sovereignty and tribute. Many Latins still abhorred the Mongols and called them Tartars, as if they came from the Roman hell of Tartarus. Few people in Christendom comprehended just how powerful—and tolerant—Khubilai Khan really was.

Still, I hoped that Emmajin and I might find time, in the sunny grape arbors of Italia, to live out my ideal of love beyond all bounds.

For now, during this first part of the journey, traveling with the army, I would have to keep my distance. But I could at least try to win the trust of her uncle, the general. If he came to trust me as did his father, Khubilai Khan, I might be able to at least spend more time openly with Emmajin. Yes, that's what I had to do. No more clandestine meetings in the moonlight.

---

The next evening, after our long ride, I appeared at Prince Nomokhan's tent and asked to speak to him. A guard pulled his knife and challenged me, as if I were a common thief. Just then the general emerged from his tent.

"Prince Nomokhan," I said with a respectful bow, "may I have a word with you?"

He looked at me with blank eyes. "Who are you?" he asked, impatiently. Tall and straight-backed, he towered over me.

"Marco Polo, a merchant from Venezia," I explained, wondering how he could forget me. "Perhaps you heard me entertain the Great Khan with stories?"

Nomokhan grunted, clearly not impressed. He had heard my stories, I knew it.

"My father and uncle know the Pope in Rome. We are traveling with the Princess Emmajin to help her deliver a letter from the Khan to the Pope." I had not expected the need to explain who I was. Hadn't the Khan informed his own son about the reasons we were traveling with the army?

The general glanced away, as if eager to get on with the more important business of guiding his six thousand troops. I knew I had only a few moments.

"A shaman in the capital," I said quickly, and those words brought his gaze back to my face. "A Mongolian shaman gave a prophecy, which I heard. He mentioned the lady with the heart of a warrior, and said she might be in danger."

Nomokhan's eyebrows shot up and he regarded me steadily with penetrating dark eyes. "Which shaman?"

I told him the name, and he seemed to recognize it.

"What exactly did he say?"

"He said the words traitors, capture, defeat."

The general flinched. "The Great Khan's personal shaman said no such things."

I backed away, slightly. "I just wanted to inform you," I said.

He dismissed me with a gruff nod and turned to leave.

"Prince Nomokhan, sir," I added quickly. "May I entertain you and your men with a story one night, during this long journey?"

He looked back over his shoulder. "We shall see. We have little time for amusements." He strode off.

At least I had reported the shaman's prophecy. But it seemed he had not really heard. And what if Nomokhan himself was the traitor? This thought had not occurred to me before. I wanted to get the word out to other high officers, so they would know to protect Emmajin. The best way to speak to them would be through a story.

The next few days we rode so hard there was no time at camp for anything but sleep. But finally, a messenger summoned me: Nomokhan wished me to entertain him and his men that evening with a tale. But it was not to be a long one.

So I needed to think of a story, not too lengthy. Nomokhan had dismissed the shaman's warning. What tale could I tell that would not anger him but would get the message through to him and his men? I recalled the shaman's words: traitor, defeat, capture. And a lady in great danger.

The most famous traitor I could think of was Judas Iscariot. But his tale would mean nothing to these men, who didn't know the story or the importance of Jesus Christ. What about Brutus, who betrayed

Julius Caesar? No. He assassinated an emperor, not a good topic for the Khan's men. Sindbad the Sailor's tales were more about adventure than treason. Most chivalric tales I knew were about battles and lady loves or quests for the Holy Grail. The Trojan War? The Song of Roland? The Templars' battle against Saladin? St. George and the dragon? Percival? Sir Gawain? King Arthur and Lancelot?

Aha! I thought. Mordred! He was a traitor. I tried hard to recall the particulars of what stories I had heard. I might need to use my imagination to embellish them for this audience.

That evening, General Nomokhan gave me the opportunity I had requested. He and his top officers gathered inside his large tent for a meal. After they ate, the general invited me in to begin. He sat on a wide thronelike chair, representing imperial power to these military men of the Mongol Army.

Nomokhan could not have looked more different from his father. Khubilai Khan was wide and broad-shouldered, with a round face and small eyes. The general was tall and angular, with a long, thin nose and close-set round eyes.

Beside Nomokhan sat Shirki, another member of the Golden Family. I was not sure how Shirki was related, but as an older man, he emanated authority, even though he was shorter and sturdier, with graying hair.

Next to him sat Temur, tall and so good-looking he would have turned many a pretty head if he had lived in a society that allowed romantic freedom. As it was, his wide-set eyes and high cheekbones were wasted. He probably had a betrothed waiting for him back in the capital.

My lady Emmajin was present, too, and it took great effort to keep my eyes from staying on her only. Though dressed in a solid dark blue del, with a yellow sash, she was like a ray of sunshine in this sea of gruff, grim faces.

Altogether, about forty people gathered in Nomokhan's tent to hear my tale. Most, I guessed, were high-ranking military officers.

"Honored general, Prince Nomokhan! Prince Shirki. Prince Temur. Princess Emmajin. Officers of the Great Khan's army! I salute you!" I began. "Tonight I will tell you a tale commonly known in my country, a story that, we believe, took place some eight centuries ago, in the darkness of history, on an island called Britannia."

That word seemed to confuse my listeners, so I quickly thought of another way to say it. "A land you might call Britanistan."

Ah. Nomokhan and his men nodded. This name made more sense to them. Anything ending with -stan sounded like a country.

"Britanistan was ruled by a great king called Arthur. That is," I responded again to their blank stares at this foreign name, "Ah-Turo Khan." With more familiar names, they seemed to enjoy the story more. Khan meant king; Great Khan, or Khagan, meaning emperor, was the title only Khubilai could use. So, of course, I used the simpler form, khan, for the ruler of this small and insignificant country.

"Ah-Turo Khan was a wise ruler, much admired and loved by his people. He lived in a lofty and well-fortified castle and had an army of knights, highly trained in bow and sword and spear. In his castle, Ah-Turo had a large round table, where he sat with his top officers and asked their opinion."

Some of Nomokhan's officers shifted uncomfortably in their seats.

"Advisers," said one man.

"Yes, advisers," I replied, correcting my wording. "Ah-Turo Khan made all the decisions, but he sought out excellent advice. His wife was young and pretty, with long hair that shone like gold. Her name was Guinevere—that is, Guenna-ferra." They nodded. In my hometown, this was a strange name, too. Of course, to these men, hair that shone like gold was also outlandish.

"But Queen Guenna-ferra had no children. So the good khan Ah-Turo had no son to succeed him."

Several of the men laughed. "Why didn't he take other wives?" Temur asked.

I hesitated. Mongol khans and their sons each took four wives and many concubines, so they had dozens of children and hundreds of grandchildren. It was one aspect of Mongolian custom that I did not admire. It offended my ideals of romantic love.

"Taking a second wife is against the laws of the Religion of Light," I said, using the Mongol term for Christianity. That would have been explanation enough, but I added, trying not to look directly at Emmajin, "Besides, in my homeland, we believe a man can only truly love one woman in his lifetime."

Guffaws burst out all around—as if these Mongol men could not imagine a more ridiculous notion. Normally, I like it when my stories evoke laughter, but not this time. To them, Arthur was a fool. It was a khan's responsibility to have many sons and perpetuate the line, to ensure stability. Romantic love was not considered important.

Emmajin's eyes caught mine and she gave me a small, secret smile. She alone appreciated this sentiment. That softened the impact of the men's mocking laughter. I struggled to regain control of my audience. "Ah-Turo Khan also had a nephew, the son of his sister. The boy's name was Mordred—Madhu. The king loved this young man and personally trained him to be a knight.

"When Mahdu was nearly fully grown, Ah-Turo Khan had to go away, to fight a war across the sea. Another king was trying to grab away his lands. Ah-Turo took most of his cavaliers and rode off to the seaside, where they boarded ships. They fought many a battle against that wicked enemy, over many years."

When they heard the words war and battle, Nomokhan's men leaned forward, eager to hear more. I should have tossed in a battle scene then. But I didn't.

"While the king was gone, the king's nephew decided he liked being a sovereign. He sat on the throne, took over the castle, and demanded that everyone call him king."

Nomokhan's men let out shouts of ugly words I won't translate. Everyone hates a traitor. All the men seemed interested and engaged except Prince Shirki, who narrowed his eyes and watched me carefully.

"So treacherous was Madhu that he even tried to take the king's wife, Guenna-ferra."

Oooh. The men hurled even worse insults now—at Mordred, not at me. I stole a glance at Emmajin, who was frowning at this ugly image. From our time in Xanadu, I knew that she loved tales of adventure, strong women, and romantic love.

"Guenna-ferra refused his evil proposal. At first, Madhu locked her in a tower prison. Then he claimed that his uncle had died in battle. He announced a date for the wedding. But his people, who loved Ah-Turo Khan, did not believe him, because Madhu was himself raising an army to defend the castle—clearly planning to fight against Ah-Turo when he returned.

"Finally, Ah-Turo returned home. But Mordred's guards prevented him from entering his castle. They told him that Mordred was king now."

"Traitor!" shouted one man. "Pig!" shouted another. This was the response I had hoped for.

"Ah-Turo Khan collected his men around him and prepared for battle." At this point I shifted into words I used to describe almost every battle. "They approached the castle walls, and Mordred's men came storming forth valiantly to meet them. Both sides were well equipped with swords and maces and shields, with bows and arrows. The battle began, and furiously the one host dashed to meet the other. The earth was thickly strewn with the wounded and the slain! Many a man fell there; many a child was made an orphan there; many a lady widowed; and many a mother plunged in grief for the rest of her days."

I had them now. This audience of Mongol warriors loved a battle scene.

"As the sun set on that dreadful day, Ah-Turo faced his nephew, sword in hand. Long hours the fight raged between these two foes, king and traitor. Finally, the king used his spear with skill, staking his nephew to the ground. Mordred's life force was ebbing, but he used his sword to wound his uncle, the rightful king.

"Mordred breathed his last. The good King Ah-Turo, holding his wounded side, rushed to see his lovely bride, Guenna-ferra, in her fearful tower. His queen wept with joy. He took her in his arms. They celebrated with grape wine—and airag. They killed a fat sheep and ate mutton for days."

Nomokhan and his men smiled and nodded. Every good Mongol tale ends with plenty of mutton and airag.

"Good! Good!" some of the men shouted. This was the way Mongol listeners showed their approval, not with clapping.

Temur turned to Emmajin and smiled, as if to say he understood now, why she had liked my stories so much.

"But," I continued, softly. "Ah-Turo Khan never recovered from his wounds. Two days later, the spirit of Ah-Turo fled to the Land of Avalon, never to return."

My voice, which I had raised and lowered, louder and softer, stopped. The men remained silent, staring at me in shock for a long time, as if unable to comprehend this tragedy. And yet, as military men, they understood tragedy better than the rest of us. Every story has a happy ending if you choose to end it right after a joyful scene— and a sad ending if you go on.

Nomokhan had been as engaged as any, but now he acted as if the story had been nothing but idle amusement. "A sad tale, well told," he said. "Let us go then," he said to his men. "We need sleep if we are to get up early to ride tomorrow."

Afterward, I thought about the general and his reaction. Unlike his father, Khubilai Khan, who loved and appreciated great story-telling, Nomokhan seemed to think it an indulgent waste of time.

The story had been successful, but not as much as I had hoped. I could not tell if I had won over Nomokhan—or Temur—or Shirki, who had kept that stony expression during most of the tale.

Nomokhan did not invite me to entertain him again. But perhaps he was tired. I hoped his men might request my tale-telling again.

Also, I hoped my message had gotten across. *Protect the lady! Beware of possible traitors.* But I sensed that Nomokhan did not take seriously advice from an entertainer like me.

Over the next few days, endless days on horseback under the hot sun, I could stand it only by turning my mind to Emmajin. I felt connected to every lover who had ever written a poem or sung a ballad about longing for a loved one. I thought of Lancelot du Lac, who held a true, pure love for the king's wife, Guinevere. And I thought of Tristan, who also loved a king's wife, Isolde. I had once told Emmajin part of that story, how Tristan kept his distance from Isolde after she married his uncle, the king. Tristan knew his duty was to his uncle, who had raised him as a son. What I did not tell her is that Tristan and Isolde often met, in the night, beneath a tree in the royal garden, to act on their love. I also did not tell her the dire consequences that followed.

I had to force myself to be patient. I needed, I wanted, to get my mind on something else.

I began to spend more time with the horse and camel boys. These men, closer to my age than my father's tended to the pack animals at the beginning and end of each day's journey. The army had hundreds of horse boys, locally called mah-foos. Our small merchant caravan had hired six mah-foos, and they not only cared for our horses and camels but guarded our merchandise. Two had traveled with us since

Persia. The others we had hired in Khanbalik, and they chattered with each other in Chinese, a language I spoke only a little. Fortunately, they could also speak Mongolian.

One mah-foo, Wei-ming, was especially talkative. Younger than the others, he had thick black hair, which he tied back with a single leather strip when he worked. His eyes crinkled when he laughed, which he did often, with loud guffaws that infected all around him. He told stories I could never tell the Khan, full of salacious details and rude words, so that he was often surrounded by raucous laughter. I loved spending time with him and the other mah-foos after the evening meal.

One evening, after a long day in the saddle, Wei-ming came to unsaddle my horse after I dismounted. His face, usually grinning and joking, looked grim and worried.

"Master, a private word with you," he said quietly, when the two of us were standing between horses, away from the others. "A rumor is circulating among the soldiers. A nasty one."

I stiffened and looked to the horizon, where the setting sun looked like a huge orange ball over the distant grasses. The rippling surface of the stream glowed reddish in the late-day light.

"They are making it up, I am sure," he continued. "They give details they could not possibly know."

I put my hand on my horse's neck to steady myself. I thought I knew what he was about to say, that someone had seen us by the lake with the swans. But I did not speak, forcing him to continue.

"They say that you, that you and the princess..." This man who told his own bawdy stories with ease had trouble speaking this sentence to me. "In the ocean, actually, they say."

A shock ran through me. The ocean. That was more serious than the simple embrace at Swan Lake. That night at the ocean, a month earlier, I had been sure we were alone. Perhaps someone had seen us return together from the seaside and invented a story. After a month with no rumors, I had thought we had gotten away with it. Most of the Khan's men had been so drunk I had thought they would not notice or remember.

"Who started such a rumor?" I adopted a tone of stern righteousness. "It is insulting to the princess."

Wei-ming breathed out, as if relieved, although I had not denied the rumor. "Who can say? Once rumors start, they spread like wild fires in the grasslands. The soldiers are laughing about it, and mocking the princess, around their campfires. The worst thing is that Temur has heard, and he is furious."

Temur. I had thought my story would help win his trust, but this rumor would destroy that. Though only sixteen, Temur, I suspected, was hard as iron. And now he was red hot.

"I have great admiration and respect for the princess," I said.

"Yes, of course, I know you do," Wei-ming said quickly. "I am only reporting to you this rumor, so you will know what the men are saying."

"Thank you for telling me." I tried to act confident, but I had no idea what to do about this.

Stories, true or false, have power. And once denied, a rumor seems more credible than ever. Particularly if the rumor is true.

# Chapter 4
# Emmajin: Life and Death at Togtoh

I first heard about the rumor from Temur. He barged into my tent, early one morning, when I was just rubbing the sleep from my eyes, still sitting on my sleeping fur.

My young cousin looked down at me with a face that showed a volatile mix of anger, resentment, confusion, and concern.

"Did you?" he asked.

"Sit down," I said, in my best elder-sister voice. "What are you talking about?"

He sat down near me with a thump, then rubbed his forehead, as if trying to push away the hangover from too much airag.

"What's bothering you?" I asked.

"That foreigner, the Latin storyteller," he said, with an overtone of disgust. "You can't really admire him. Do you?"

I wasn't sure where this was going. Was Temur reacting to Marco's tale of Mordred, which had drawn mixed reactions? "Why do you ask?"

"The soldiers talk about him. About you and him."

"Oh." I acted as if this were a familiar but stupid rumor.

Temur examined my face, looking for the truth.

"That's what men do, didn't you tell me?" I said. "When there is only one woman among them, they talk about her behind her back."

Temur nodded once.

"Temur. You've known me all your life, better than any of them. Tell them who I am."

He shook his head. "You've changed. I don't know who you are."

I stared at his wide-set eyes. He was a grown man now, with thoughts and judgments of his own. I was sure he had never felt what I had, that magnetic attraction to someone you could not live without. But he was right: I had evolved into a new person since he knew me as a girl at court. Still, I gave him the same look I used to give him when I was twelve and he was eleven. "I haven't changed. You're just listening to different people."

He was silent a moment before speaking again. "Someone said he saw you, beside that lake with the swans, late at night. Embracing him!"

Mentally, I kicked myself. When you're traveling with six thousand men, you can't expect to be alone, even in the middle of the night. Since that night, I had vowed to keep my distance from Marco, but maybe it was too late.

"And another man," Temur continued, almost breathless with distress, "says he saw you another time, a month ago, near the Khan's hunting camp by the sea. He saw you come back with that foreigner, late at night, laughing."

"What man would dare to say such a thing?" I challenged.

He examined my face closely. "Bartan."

Bartan! This was a soldier who had challenged my role in the army from the first day. "And you believed him?" I persisted, trying to keep him off balance. "Temur," I said, taking hold of his lower arms and looking straight up at his eyes. "You need to stop listening to such rubbish."

For a moment, I saw a miserable, confused young man, and then his eyes went stony. "If Nomokhan hears of this," he said, "you will need to explain."

As I got ready for the day's ride, my hands were shaking. It was easier to talk back to Temur than it would be to face my uncle No-mokhan, the commanding general. Unlike Temur's father, Nomokhan was an uncle I barely knew, one who had been off on military missions when I was growing up. He was stern and harsh. Even his wives feared him, I knew from the women's gossip at court.

But how could I answer such charge? To deny it would be to lie. To admit it would mean losing the respect and status I needed to carry out my mission. Might I be sent home in shame?

That day, riding across the grasslands, I noticed that most of the soldiers would not meet my gaze. A few younger ones, ones I had never met, stared at me. When I turned to them, they gawked at me for a moment, as if evaluating my beauty and character, then looked away. It was chilling. The sun bothered my eyes more than usual, and my stomach grew queasy. Nerves, I supposed.

Nomokhan rode far ahead of me, so I could not see who was talking to him. I rehearsed, in my mind, what words I would say to him when he asked about the rumors. I remembered Marco had told me, with that distinctive laugh of his, that lying is a form of storytelling. But Mongols teach their children that lying is wrong, against the sacred laws of the Yasa, handed down to us by our Great Ancestor. Besides, I wasn't any good at it. Once, as a child, I had lied to protect myself, but I had not gotten away with it.

Even if I did lie, what story would I tell? Other men, too, may have seen Marco and me by Swan Lake that night. And who knows who might have seen Marco and me return from the seaside that earlier night, at the Khan's hunting camp. I had been so intoxicated by my experience with Marco in the waters of the sea that I had not really cared what others might see or say. But I also knew that most of the soldiers, that night, were drunk on airag. Everyone knew that.

Looking back, I kicked myself for getting carried away with Marco, especially that night by the ocean. Had I been drunk on praise, after Marco glorified me in his story to the Khan? Still, no words could adequately describe that wonderful feeling of joining with Marco in the sea. It had been sublime.

Now there was no way to defend myself except by lying. As for the Swan Lake incident, I would say I had slept through that night. And about the seaside, I decided that I would say I had gone straight back to my tent, after the dinner where Marco told the story of the Battle of Vochan. A maid had traveled with me and could vouch for that, I would say. Fortunately, that maid was far away, back at court in Khanbalik. I would give a false name, so that it would be difficult to find her, if anyone sent a message back to court. Then I would go on the offensive, saying that all the men were drunk that night. I would say that thousands of soldiers, traveling in male company, will spread any rumor to keep themselves entertained. To these young men, stewing in their own juices, I was a famous person, a princess of the imperial court, and spreading wild stories about me was to be expected.

But the very thought of telling falsehoods brought bile to my mouth.

That evening, I chose to eat alone in my tent, rather than around the fire with Temur and his friends, where I normally ate. I told them I was not feeling well, which was partially true. I wasn't sick, exactly, but I felt unsettled.

---

After dinner, a messenger appeared at my tent door. Nomokhan wished to see me, at once. Dread washed over me, and I rehearsed my story as I walked to his commander's tent. It seemed that everyone was watching me. I welcomed a slight breeze that cooled my face and steadied my nerves.

The commander's tent was four times larger than the ordinary gers where soldiers slept. It was a round, domed ger, pure white on the outside, lined with colorful banners inside, big enough for an assembly of leaders to meet.

The general was sitting on a stool at the far side of the tent, a tall man with a hard-set jaw and narrow-set eyes on a too-thin face. When I entered, I bowed my head, but then straightened my shoulders and lifted my chin. He gestured to a wooden stool to his right, where I sat down. Aside from a few servants, we were alone.

A servant handed me a bowl of fresh airag, and we both drank before talking. The milky, fermented drink curdled in my stomach.

In the context of the ugly rumors, I had to concentrate to steady my hands as I held my airag bowl. How did this man feel about me being in the army, a woman? I had heard that he was very strict and upright.

"How many guards do you have at your tent?" he asked me, bluntly.

"Last night, just one."

"I will assign three more."

I wanted to contradict him, to say I didn't need guards, but something in his stern manner stopped me. Maybe I did need guards, to keep myself in check.

"You are traveling with six thousand men. All of them are hungry."

I nodded. So this is how Nomokhan viewed me, a royal princess who needed protection, an annoying task. "I have a dagger," I said.

He snorted. "I will see to it that you do not need to use it. Any man who violates my order and bothers you is to be executed."

The knot in my stomach twisted. Did he mean Marco?

He hesitated before his next sentence, and I braced myself. "You have your mission from my father, the Great Khan. But I have another for you."

A frown line deepened between his narrow-set eyes.

"You have heard of Princess Khutulun, commonly called Ai-Jaruk?" he asked.

"Yes, of course," I said, confused by this unexpected shift in the conversation. A year earlier, in Xanadu, I had heard Marco tell the story of Ai-Jaruk, Bright Moon of the Desert West, daughter of a distant Mongol clansman. She had insisted that all suitors compete with her in wrestling, and would not marry any man unless he could defeat her. A huge, strong woman, she had bested them all and earned the right to join her father in battles. Like me, she had chosen to fight rather than marry. Her story had inspired me.

"You may have a chance to meet her."

My heart surged. "I would be honored," I stammered.

"You know that her father is Khaidu?"

Frankly, I had not been clear about who her father was. Ai-Jaruk was such a legend I had not thought of her relations with the rest of the Golden Family.

"Speak of this to no one. Do you understand?" he asked, with an edge of agitation. I nodded. "Khaidu has been troublesome lately, claiming territory for himself. Worse, we have just heard that he has blocked the road to the West, refusing to let the armies of the Great Khan pass through."

I gasped. Blocked the road to the West! If that was true, my mission could not succeed. Our troops would have to open it back up. Would that mean fighting against other Mongols?

My uncle nodded, as if acknowledging the severity of the potential crisis. "This is open disobedience. When we reach his territory, I will demand that he stand aside and let us pass. But he may not listen. He has his own army, strong and well-trained. We want to make sure he does not use it against us. We know that he has a soft spot for that fierce daughter of his. Perhaps he will be more cooperative if you befriend her."

Befriend Ai-Jaruk? It was beyond my wildest dreams. In my eagerness, I dropped the military formality. "Of course! What would you have me do?"

Nomokhan frowned again, as if trying to quash my enthusiasm. "This is a military secret. Prepare yourself. We will see."

The assignment was vague. But it filled my heart with joy. I would get to meet the famous warrior woman. Instead of quizzing me about the camp rumor, Nomokhan thought highly enough of me to give me an assignment, one that no man could fulfill.

After I left Nomokhan's tent that night, I walked with straighter shoulders, both relieved and pleased with my secret assignment. It raised my status in his eyes, showing that he thought I could be useful and not just a girl who needed protecting.

Traveling at a fast pace, on well-fed horses, it took fewer than twenty days to reach our first stop, Togtoh, in the province of Tenduc. For several days, the land had been getting drier, and our horses kicked up dust as they galloped across hard-packed yellow clay soil. By contrast, Togtoh was an oasis of green, spread out along the river.

Looking down from a hill, I sighed in wonder at the sight of the mighty River Caramoran, which bent sharply to the south here. Flowing through flat land, it stretched wide, moving slowly from far in the west, cutting across the land with a broad band of muddy yellowish brown, looking like its Cathayan name, the Yellow River. On the far bank stood dry cliffs, striped in shades of yellow and orange and brown. On the near bank stood a broad swath of green trees and grasses, refreshing to my eyes after the endless tawny plain. Scattered among the green trees along the river, behind a sturdy city wall, were the white tents of Togtoh, hundreds of them. At their center stood two large white tents of the local kings, their distinctive green banners ruffling in the breeze.

Here lived the families and courts of the dual kings, King Ai-buqa and King Kun-buqa, faithful vassals of the Great Khan. As brothers, they headed the tribe of Onguts, followers of the Religion of

Light. They were Turkic people who had intermarried with Mongols so much that they could speak our language as fluently as their own.

A company of Ongut troops rode out to meet us, led by the two kings, holding aloft their green banners. We dismounted, and Temur and I stood together as Nomokhan strode toward the two kings and greeted them as kinsmen. Both Ongut kings had wives from the Golden Family. Ai-buqa's wife, Yurak, was my father's sister—and hence also a sister of Nomokhan. They even had the same mother, Empress Chabi. Aunt Yurak greeted her brother with warmth, handing him a *khadag,* a white silk scarf, the traditional goodwill gift of greeting.

Standing with the straight back of royalty, my aunt Yurak looked like a younger version of her mother, the Empress Chabi, short and stout, with a wide round face. She wore a royal headdress in the Ongut style, with loops of agate. After greeting her brother Nomokhan, her cousin Shirki, and her nephew Temur by giving them *khadag* scarves, she turned to me, smiling with that same tiny mouth I had come to know in my grandmother. Aunt Yurak looked at me with benevolence and approval and used her two hands to offer me, too, a silk scarf of greeting.

"Emmajin Beki, daughter of my brother Dorji," she called me. Just seeing her kind face, I was flooded with goodwill toward her, and I received the scarf with two hands. Under the scarf, she caught my hands and held them for a moment. "Welcome," she said. I sensed an unusual gentleness in her eyes.

The Ongut kings invited all the Khan's top commanders and royal family members to a feast in the royal tent of Ai-buqa that night. They served us the delicacy of fresh lamb, plus fatty sheep's tail and other favorite Mongol dishes, as well as game meats from their hunt. Before the meal, before we could even touch the food, they bowed their heads in prayer and thanked God for the food, ending "we pray in the name of Yesu the Savior." For many generations, this had been a tribe of Christians.

At the meal, I sat next to Aunt Yurak and the other women of Togtoh. Back at court, during my childhood, I had felt scornful of royal women. My father had been absent for much of my childhood, always off at some Buddhist monastery, pursuing his own dreams. My mother, feeling rejected, had withdrawn and had not been able to protect me or my sister when others at court spoke of my father with scorn. My sister, Drolma, had turned to the ladies of the court, learning embroidery and making friends and alliances with other women who might help her. But I had turned away from the women and tried to excel at manly things, at archery and racing and wrestling.

Of the women at court, only my grandmother, Chabi, had won my admiration. Behind the scenes, she influenced her husband, Khubilai Khan, to show mercy to the defeated emperor of China and his mother and grandmother.

Aunt Yurak had the same kind face and manner as her mother, my grandmother Chabi. But my first impulse was distrust. Perhaps she just wanted to get to know me so she could gossip about me at court. Surely she would resent me for the freedom I had, for the stature I had attained, for the ability to rise above the betrothal talks and take on a mission to the West for the Great Khan. I hoped she would not hear the sordid rumors about me. If she did, I was sure this married queen would judge me harshly.

---

We stayed at Togtoh for five days, resting and refreshing ourselves and our horses. The merchant caravan, too, tarried in the caravanserais of Togtoh.

To my displeasure, I was expected to spend time with the women of the court, while Temur and the others went hunting. This annoyed me. Is this what my life would be like if I were married?

The following morning, Aunt Yurak invited me to go to the archery range to observe how well her son used bow and arrow. He showed great skill at archery.

No one asked me to demonstrate my own skills, which were far superior to any I saw that day. Yurak never even mentioned my reputation as a fine archer. I couldn't wait to get out of this place and regain the celebrity status I enjoyed among the men of the army. That is, if they had forgotten about the rumors. Every time I saw someone looking at me, I wondered.

After watching the archery, Aunt Yurak invited me to join her in her ger, a place decorated with bright carpets, smelling of lambskin and mare's milk, of confidences and deep discussions. She sat regally on her wide throne-like chair but tucked her legs up under her body comfortably, like a cat.

A slave woman brought us airag and cheese, in the usual Mongolian gesture of hospitality. Instead of ignoring her, as was customary, Yurak introduced her to me as if she were an equal.

"This is Nasreen," she said to me. "Nasreen, meet my niece, Emmajin Beki."

For the first time, I looked this slave woman in the face. From a few slight wrinkles around her eyes, I guessed Nasreen was older than I was, but she retained much of her beauty, so she was not very old. She had light brown eyes and covered her hair in a blue head scarf, in the manner of Turkic people.

"Emmajin Beki, ma'am," she said, bowing her head slightly and holding out a plate of cheese.

I nodded back and took a cheese square, unsure how to address a slave. Back at home, at court, we never spoke to slaves, except to give orders. What did my aunt expect of me?

Aunt Yurak filled my awkward silence. "Nasreen is Kirghiz," she said. "Her people are from west of the Gobi Desert, in the Heavenly Mountains."

The Heavenly Mountains! I had never heard of such a place. I examined the slave's face again. Her eyes were rounder and more deep-set than those of Mongolians, and her manner was quiet, confident, calm. How did she become a slave? I wondered.

But my aunt quickly changed the subject, talking about her childhood memories of my father, her brother. He was, she recalled, painfully shy but also very kind. She leaned toward me when she talked, and I felt at ease.

Her approachable attitude emboldened me to speak my mind. "It must have been hard for you," I said, "to leave the excitement of the Great Khan's court."

She laughed, with a high, feminine lilt like her mother's. "Life is simpler here in Togtoh," she conceded. "I like it. But you forget that I did not grow up in the court of the Great Khan." Her father, Khubilai, had been a minor prince in the old Mongolian capital at Karakorum when she was born. She had grown up in Xanadu, then a minor provincial town where Khubilai ruled over a small territory.

"I was fifteen when my father became Great Khan. But I missed the coronation celebrations!" she said. "Just two months earlier, I had to leave to go west to marry Ai-buqa." So she had been traded away in marriage and missed out on all the privileges of being the daughter of the Great Khan. I shook my head in pity, but she laughed merrily. Suddenly I wondered if she had been a good archer, too, as a girl. Might she have joined the army, if given the opportunity?

"So you never lived at the Imperial Palace in Khanbalik?" I asked her.

"I went back once, to visit, when my son was three years old. You don't remember? I saw you then. You were probably about ten. Everyone talked about you."

"What did they say?"

She laughed. "They said you were a girl with the spirit of a boy."

Here was a woman who had taken the path I had scorned, marrying the man chosen for her. When my parents tried to find a husband for me, I had sabotaged their efforts. What I had wanted was to control my own destiny, to achieve status the way men did, by showing valor in battle. Now I had given up warfare, but I still aimed to achieve honor by serving the Khan—as an emissary to the Pope, or by befriending Ai-Jaruk. Marriage, it seemed, was a form of slavery.

Yet this aunt of mine, Yurak, did not seem enslaved at all. She tossed her head back like a mare when she laughed, showed pride in her son, and collected women around her for friendship and conversation.

———

The next day, Aunt Yurak asked me to take lunch with her.

At lunch, she told me something I had never known before: that the Great Ancestor had entrusted four of his daughters with the rule of kingdoms while their husbands went far afield to fight with his army. One of those daughters, Alaqai Beki, came here, to marry an Ongut king. Instead of simply keeping quiet and raising his children, she was given a title, "Princess Who Runs the State" and ruled this entire region on behalf of the Great Ancestor, Chinggis Khan. So he had entrusted women, his daughters, with high positions and great honors.

"You see, Emmajin," Yurak said with a smile, "you are the latest in a long line of strong Mongol women."

A warm feeling filled me. All my life, I had felt I was fighting against the odds, trying to do things no other woman had ever done. Now it seemed I had a team of female ancestors who were cheering me on.

Remembering my new secret mission, I asked her about Ai-Jaruk, the daughter of Khaidu. To befriend her, I needed to learn more about her.

"Ai-Jaruk!" Aunt Yurak tossed back her head and laughed in that light voice. "You and she could not be more different."

This was not what I wanted to hear. From the stories I had heard, Ai-Jaruk was a powerful wrestler and had defeated her suitors, winning the right to fight alongside her father as an unmarried woman. "I have heard that she is strong," I said, somewhat defensively. "She's an excellent wrestler. Her father allows her great freedom."

Yurak regarded me in silence for a moment. "Yes, I have heard that, too," she said. "Men make fun of her because she is big. But perhaps they are threatened by her power and independence."

"I hope to meet her someday," I said.

My aunt cocked her head, as if unsure how much I knew about Khaidu and his attitude toward the Great Khan. "Perhaps you will," she said. "I believe she would see an equal in you."

Flattery works, with me. I flushed and looked away. The slave Nasreen was watching me from across the room. I liked my new mission, to befriend Ai-Jaruk. Long before I got to Rome, perhaps I could do something to bring peace between the Great Khan and his difficult cousin, Khaidu of the Desert West.

I also asked Aunt Yurak about her new religion, Christianity. When I got to Rome, to meet the Pope, I would need to know more about it.

My grandfather, the Great Khan, tolerated a wide diversity of faiths within his empire and never tried to force people to change their beliefs, as long as they accepted him as their supreme ruler. Our Mongolian ancestors had worshiped Father Sky—Tengri—and Mother Earth, through shamans, but the Khan was fascinated by more developed religions. He encouraged scholars and priests to debate in front of him and to try to convince him that their religion was best.

Yurak's mother, my grandmother Chabi, had raised her as a Buddhist, and Yurak had been interested in religion as a girl. When she married into the Christian Ongut tribe, she had thrown herself into learning their Turkic language and their foreign religion.

Marco had tried to explain Christianity to me, but I had never understood it. His concept of God was different from what I had learned of Tengri, who was the God of the Sky, Eternal Heaven, the One who gave Chinggis Khan the mission of uniting the world. We Mongols had shamans but no holy books. Perhaps Aunt Yurak, coming from a similar background, could explain Christianity in a clearer way.

What she said was this: Each of us has both a body and a spirit—that is obvious. Our spirit is like a little piece of divinity in us. If you dip a goblet into the river, the water in your goblet is separate from the river, but it is the same essence. Likewise, our spirits, trapped in this body for this lifetime, are of the same essence as God, whom she called the One Sacred Spirit. Therefore, we can pray and God will hear us, because a piece of God is inside us. God not only created the earth and the heavens but knows all and loves all of us individually. God is bigger than any of us can ever understand.

Through Buddhism and other ancient religions, God tried to reveal God's true nature to us humans. But we humans just didn't understand. So God took human form and came to us as a man, Yesu. Like a bodhisattva, Yesu sacrificed his life to save us. His teachings hold the key to life's central question: how to escape the eternal cycle of birth, suffering, death and rebirth. In his life, Yesu was a model for compassionate love. By learning from the Christian sutras, we can figure out how to live the lives we are meant to live, understanding God's will and helping others.

In her words, spoken with the passion of a convert, Christianity made sense and appealed to me. Instead of focusing on how life is suffering, unreality, something to escape from, as Buddhism taught, Christians taught that life can be good. The point of helping others is not so they can achieve personal enlightenment, but so that the world will be a better place.

For the first time, Marco's religion seemed appealing.

"What do you know about the Pope?" I asked her.

Aunt Yurak let out that light laugh again. "Nothing, I'm afraid," she said. "That's a totally different branch of Christianity. We have a patriarch in the West somewhere—Baghdad, I think. But we never hear much about him. He leaves us to practice as we please."

I wondered what her religion taught about sex, but I didn't dare ask. "What about lying?" I asked her instead. "What does your religion say about lying?"

My aunt cocked her head to one side and looked at me closely. "It says you shall not bear false witness against your neighbor. That means you should never falsely accuse someone of wrongdoing."

I paused a minute, to let this sink in. Not 'you shall not lie' but 'you shall not bear false witness.' I tried to fathom the difference.

"And what," I continued, "does Buddhism say about lying?"

My aunt's small mouth registered a smile. "You seem very interested in lying."

I blushed. "I'm curious about religion," I stammered. "I mean, about the different teachings of each."

"Buddhism," she said, with a knowing smile, "teaches that good thoughts lead to good words, which lead to good actions."

"And bad thoughts..." I finished the sentence inside my head. Was I thinking bad thoughts, trying to protect myself from ugly rumors? Was it wrong to protect someone you loved? Had my actions with Marco been bad actions, misdeeds? At the time, they had not felt bad. They had felt delightful.

My own thoughts about religion were muddled in the extreme. Was there something between good and bad, between lying and truth? Or was everything black or white? I had heard, somewhere, of a teaching that there is always some black in the white, some white in the black. What religion was that?

My aunt was staring at me, as if trying to figure out what was going on in my head. This aunt, who had done everything her family had asked of her, could never understand my dilemma or condone my bad thoughts. What was right was what the family said was right, and dallying with Marco was not right in the eyes of my family. Aunt Yurak was family and would certainly condemn me if she knew what I had done.

I blushed. "My father is a Buddhist," I stammered, trying to deflect her attention. "I visited him at a monastery and he tried to explain it to me. My grandfather the Great Khan seems to think that all religions are valid."

She smiled, as if well aware that I was changing the subject. "Yes, all religions can teach us how to live, how to make good decisions. But it's important to choose one. I admire my brother Dorji, and anyone who is on the path. I have chosen a different path, that of my husband and his people. The Religion of Light resonates with my heart."

Her manner was sincere and open, and my heart reached out to her. But my mind warned me that I could not trust her completely.

---

On the night before we were to leave, Temur told me that Nomokhan wished to see me, urgently. The minute I walked into Nomokhan's tent, I could see that his thin face was stiff with anger. He shot me a look of disdain and disappointment, and I felt a pang of fear. Clearly, the rumor had finally reached him.

Still, he pointed to the seat to his right, traditionally the seat for honored guests. I bowed, then straightened my back and sat down next to him. A servant offered me airag.

Nomokhan was silent so long I wondered if he expected me to break the ice. But I stayed silent, too. The hot summer air hung thick inside his tent.

Finally he spoke.

"Emmajin Beki. The Khan trusted you. I trusted you," he began. "Now some of the men are saying you are not a maiden."

What a way to put it! His words made me switch from guilt to anger. A maiden? Were my services to him or the Khan worth nothing if I was not a maiden?

Still, I felt sick. I pursed my lips and looked him boldly in the face. I tried to remain calm and recall all the words I had rehearsed. "What ugly stories have you heard?" I asked. From my earliest days, I had known that a girl needed to keep herself pure, to be seen as valuable to her future husband. Anything else was scandalous, fodder for the gossips, and against every religion known to man. I wasn't sure exactly what it meant to be pure, but hugging Marco in the waters of the ocean surely went over the line.

"That you had carnal relations with the Latin merchant, the story-teller."

I opened my mouth but no words came out. What passed between Marco and me was none of his business—and certainly nothing as crass and ugly as he implied. I had not expected my uncle to be so blunt.

Nomokhan's voice was cold. "If this is true, there is no point in you continuing on this journey."

I hated this attitude of his. How would this affect my ability to deliver the Khan's message to the Pope? Or to talk to Ai-Jaruk as an equal? None of the male soldiers were chaste. Yet I could not say this. Nomokhan had control of my future. My very loyalty to the Khan seemed to be at stake.

"As a maiden, and a princess of the Golden Family," I answered, at last, "I am not used to hearing such language."

Nomokhan leaned back, as if sorry, but did not apologize. "We must clear this up at once." Then he nodded to one of his assistants. "Bring them in."

The assistant went to the tent flap and brought in three men: my cousin Temur, the veins on his face red and popping with anger;

Bartan, the thick-set soldier who had started the rumor; and Marco Polo, his face stony and pale.

A flush of nausea washed over me. I wanted to catch Marco's eye, to see a flash of defiance or an impassioned connection with me. I wanted to reach out to him, to protect him. But he did not look directly at me.

They all bowed to General Nomokhan, and Temur came and sat next to me. The other two men stood before us. Both looked guilty. In a way, both *were* guilty.

Nomokhan began the proceedings. "Today, we will clear up this matter. One of you two men will be punished. The other will never speak of this again."

I knew Marco well enough to recognize the flutter of fear that crossed his forehead. Bartan stood, feet apart, looking aggressive. I had to swallow hard to keep bile from flooding my mouth.

"Bartan, soldier of the Great Khan. Tell me what you have heard."

A heavyset man with a square jaw, Bartan shifted slightly. I glared at him, daring him to look me in the eye. Son of a Mongol military official, this man had challenged me to a sword match when I first joined the army. He had always seemed hostile to the idea of a woman in the army and eager to make me look bad.

Fortunately, I had dressed in my most royal manner possible, wearing a high-collared, embroidered purple del that I had planned to wear when meeting the Pope. I even wore a Mongol lady's hat, with strings of pearls hanging from the sides in loops, like necklaces, over my chest. This gave me a feminine dignity and emphasized my royal lineage.

Bartan cleared his throat. "I mean no disrespect to the Golden Family."

Good start. He seemed reluctant to continue.

"I wish to know exactly what you saw and what you heard," prompted the general. "This is a matter of great importance."

Bartan kept his eyes away from me, which took effort since I sat beside Nomokhan. "At the Khan's hunting camp," he began, "after the foreigner told the tale of the battle, later that night, I was near the sea. I saw the foreigner come back to camp from the seaside. He was walking with the royal lady."

"Was the moon full?" asked the general.

"No. It was a new moon."

"So it was dark. Are you sure it was this royal lady?"

His eyes flashed toward me. "Yes."

"And what were they doing?"

"Talking and laughing. Touching."

Nomokhan let a moment of silence pass as the words reverberated in the air.

"Did you see them having carnal relations?" my uncle pushed relentlessly.

"No. But they were both...wet."

I cringed, remembering how Marco and I had walked into the sea up to our chests and embraced there.

"Wet? From the sea?"

"I don't know."

"What else did you see?"

"Nothing. She seems very friendly with that foreigner. Always talking to him. Seemed very happy when he praised her. After his story, the foreigner took her hand and held it high, right there in front of our Great Khan. Shameless. This is our princess. That man should keep his dirty hands off her."

The air was charged. My insides were tight. Marco put his hands behind his back, as if to keep me from even seeing them.

His life was at stake. If Nomokhan believed he had touched me, besmirched my virtue, Marco could be killed, that very night. On the road, with the army, the commanding officer's word was law.

"Messer Marco Polo," my uncle continued, turning to him with more respect than Bartan had showed. "Emmajin Beki has already told me about that night. Now, let us hear you respond."

Normally, Marco was good with words, but now, with his life at stake, words seemed to fail him. He swallowed hard and stared at the smooth dirt floor in front of Nomokhan's feet. He had no way of knowing what story I had told my uncle.

His eyes darted up to my face, as if trying to read my expression. I felt mostly fear. But I saw in his forest green eyes the same fierce protectiveness that I felt. In that brief moment, in that smoldering gaze, our hearts connected. His fear seemed to abate.

Finally, he spoke. "That night, at the Khan's hunting camp, beside the sea," he began, as if telling a story, but his voice cracked on the word 'sea.' "At the request of the Khan of all Khans, I related the story of the Battle of Vochan. I told of the valor of Prince Suren, who died in that battle. And of the glory of Princess Emmajin, who also fought hard for the Empire."

The contrast was huge between Bartan's harsh half-sentences and Marco's flowing words in charmingly accented Mongolian.

"Pleased with my service, the Great Khan honored me and my father and uncle with goods of surpassing value, to take back to our homeland."

Nomokhan shifted in his seat, as if impatient. "And later that night?"

"Later that night..." My whole body could not have been tenser. To my surprise, Marco smiled sheepishly. "After the story, the princess returned to her tent, as expected. I was relieved that the Khan had approved of my story. I drank too much airag. Many men drank too much that night. I suspect Master Bartan here imbibed, too. I..."

Marco shot an apologetic look at me.

"I know the princess is high above me in status, though I admire her greatly. I would never touch her in any way unwelcome to her. That night, I confess, I..."

He was playing us like a zither, a storyteller in control of his audience. He smiled coyly at Nomokhan.

"General, you are a man, with a man's urges. I hesitate to say anything that might offend the royal princess."

Nomokhan nodded, as if understanding.

"Later that night," Marco continued, "I availed myself of one of the women hired to service the Khan's men. There were many such women. Prince Temur will recall this."

He shot a look at Temur, who looked down in embarrassment.

"For privacy, I took that woman to the seaside, into the water. I would rather not say what happened there. I could not control my urges. I am embarrassed to admit this, in such honored company. That was the woman this soldier saw. A crass, lowly woman. Not a princess from the Golden Family. Any suggestion that the royal princess Emmajin has anything but the highest character and virtue is libel and a crime against her honor."

Using his silver tongue, Marco had turned the situation around completely, making his accuser look guilty. Fortunately, this was the same story I had been prepared to tell. But Nomokhan had not asked me for my version.

Nomokhan's shoulders eased, as if the tension were flowing out of his body, too. He turned to me. "Emmajin Beki. Which of these men speaks the truth?"

Marco and Bartan both regarded me with desperation. The fate of two men was in my hands. Instead of judging himself, my uncle was leaving the judgment to me.

Both Marco's life and my future required me to confirm Marco's lie. Yet I knew: If I endorsed Marco's version, Nomokhan would harshly punish Bartan, possibly execute him. Bartan should not have spread rumors, but he had spoken the truth. Marco had lied. Should he be rewarded for his lying?

An arrow of pain shot through my head, and I flinched. I shut my eyes tight and consulted my conscience. What would Tara do? She was the goddess of mercy, the bodhisattva my Buddhist father admired. If my spirit was of the same essence as Aunt Yurak's God, could I condemn a man to death just because he called me on my own misbehavior? Yet to admit that Bartan was right would be to condemn myself, to publicly admit to behavior I knew was unacceptable.

I lifted my chin and turned toward my uncle.

"The good soldier Bartan was mistaken," I said. "The woman he saw with the foreigner Marco Polo was not me. He should not have spread false rumors. But I hope you will forgive him, if he apologizes."

My uncle frowned, as if unable to understand why I would ask for leniency for a man who had tried to destroy my reputation. But he turned to Bartan and asked, "Do you wish to apologize to the Great Khan's granddaughter?"

Bartan's face contorted. Insisting on my guilt would get him nowhere with his commanding general. He paused for a moment before speaking. "I apologize for any falsehoods I have stated." But not for any truths.

Nomokhan stood, and both men dropped to their knees and bowed their heads. "Both of you, leave now. I charge each of you to speak to no man about this matter, ever again."

The two men rose and left.

After the tent flap fell back into place, my uncle turned to me. I could see in his face that he was not totally convinced.

"Emmajin Beki. Many men have heard these ugly rumors. For your own sake, it is important to prove them false. I will ask my sister to examine you. If she confirms that you are a maiden, then you may continue the journey and I will punish any man who repeats this rumor. Go to your aunt at once."

His words shocked me. Prove that I was a maiden? What did that mean?

I stood, with as much dignity as I could, bowed to my uncle and left.

———————

Outside his tent, I paused for a moment, to collect my wits. What exactly could my aunt tell by examining me? What might she report to Nomokhan, and to the Khan's army? I was tempted to find my horse and run off. But that would only confirm my guilt. Trembling with resentment and fear, I headed to her familiar tent. I needed to think of a strategy, but my mind was blank. My fate lay in the hands of Aunt Yurak.

My aunt was still awake, sitting on her couch surrounded by colorful carpets. Her elaborate headdress stood on the floor, and Nasreen was brushing her long, sleek black hair. This made her look much younger, closer to my age. The light of two small torches flickered on her face.

She nodded firmly toward the maidservants, and they melted into the darkness at the back of the ger. "Sit here," she said to me, indicating the padded wooden stool on her right. Her manner seemed stern. It seemed she knew the seriousness of our meeting.

"It is late at night for a visit from you." In a gentle voice, she was forcing me to put my request into words.

I swallowed hard. "My uncle, Prince Nomokhan,…" The words did not come easily. "…has heard ugly rumors about me and…suspects I am not a maiden." I cast down my eyes. I had lied to Nomokhan, but I could not lie to this kind woman.

She said nothing. When I looked up, I saw tenderness and sorrow in her eyes.

"He commanded me…" Surely she knew this. Why was she making me say it? She was reading me. My voice broke. "He commanded me to ask you…to prove that I am…" This woman, this daughter of Khubilai Khan, had done all that was expected of her, marrying the man chosen by her father, leaving her homeland and adopting the ways of her husband. She was strong but not headstrong. She had never demanded to join the army. She had never thought it her right as a princess to choose a lover.

"He wants me to examine you?" she asked pointedly, with a note of disbelief. I nodded. She took another sip of airag. It occurred to me that she might never have done such an examination, that it would embarrass her as much as it would embarrass me.

Aunt Yurak studied my eyes. I rubbed my knuckles and the callous on my right thumb. My private parts were stinging, as if in anticipation of humiliation. What could a woman tell from looking at another woman's private parts? How much of my secret would be revealed to her?

Frankly, I wasn't exactly sure what had happened, that night in the sea. Marco's embrace was exquisite, unlike anything I had ever experienced before. But it had not been painful, and it had not caused me to bleed—at least, as far as I could tell, in the ocean. At court, I had heard that those were the signs of loss of maidenhood. My experience with Marco had been sublime, not the crude sort of thing soldiers like Bartan joked about. I had never found the right words to describe it.

On her couch, she slid closer to me and reached out her right hand. I offered mine, and she took it in hers, soft and warm and small. By going off in the night with Marco, by embracing him, I had broken the rules. Whatever the details, I had not kept myself pure. I did not expect her sympathy. I could feel tears forming, and I blinked them back. It was easier to confront my uncle than to respond to this gentle silence from my aunt.

She placed her other hand on top of mine, and held them to her nose. Her dark eyes glowed with compassion, like two embers. A tear slipped out of my eye, burning a hot line down my cheek. I looked away, at the blurred patterns on the carpet, anything but those all-knowing eyes. She stroked the back of my hand, then turned it over and pressed a spot on my wrist, as if trying to find and cure the source of my heartache.

Finally she spoke, in a small, soft voice. "Who is he?"

My tears came then, unwanted, flowing from my eyes over my cheeks, like a stream over stones. My secret, held inside so long, was out. I did not bother to wipe my face. It was over. This would be the end of life as I had chosen to live it.

She looked down but held my hand in hers, firmly, as if I were about to drown.

Finally I found my voice, soft and low to make sure no one overheard. "No one you know. A foreign merchant. A storyteller."

What soldier weeps? I tried to stop my tears. My nose, too, was running. What would become of me now? Of course she would tell her brother. Then Temur would hear, too. What story would they tell the soldiers? Would they send me home in shame?

With all her talk of religion, surely my aunt would condemn my actions with Marco. I braced myself for a lecture.

My aunt kept rubbing my hand, pulling my fingers straight, as if that were the examination she was called upon to do. She seemed to be absorbing this knowledge, chewing on it as a cow chews its cud. Finally she spoke again. "Are you with child?"

"No!" I spoke with vehemence. "It is impossible. He and I are too different." I had thought this through many times. Like horses and mules.

Shaking her head with a grim smile, she interlocked her fingers with mine. "Emmajin, my dear. It is possible."

"No. You don't understand. I am..."

She cut me off with a commanding tone. "No. *You* don't understand. When did you last have your monthly courses?"

"When I travel, I never have regular...Aunt Yurak, please. These are private matters. I'm not used to discussing them with others." I looked at her with defiance.

"You are safe here in Togtoh. You can stay here. I will take care of you."

My distrust flooded back. She was going to punish me by keeping me a prisoner here. "No. I have work to do for the Khan."

She regarded me sternly. "Do you want to leave with the army tomorrow morning?"

"Yes."

She nodded slowly, as if making a decision. "Nasreen. Come here."

The slave with the blue kerchief emerged from the shadows and stood before us, her head bowed.

"Emmajin, listen carefully," my aunt said. "I will assign this maidservant to travel with you. She is knowledgeable about womanly things. You must tell her clearly if you see any changes in your body. She understands medicine, and she will know what to do."

I did not care about this servant or her knowledge. The words I heard were 'travel with you.' "Aunt Yurak, I thank you."

Yurak smiled. "There is an even better way. Stay here, and I will help you."

"No." I picked up my airag bowl and drained it like a man. "I have a mission. Two missions, actually. I need to get on my horse tomorrow and carry on."

She leaned back. "And if I tell Nomokhan you are not a maiden?"

I put the bowl down carefully. "Aunt Yurak. Please." I dropped my bravado and placed my palms together as I had seen her do in her Christian prayers.

She placed her two hands over my folded ones. In her eyes I saw generosity beyond my understanding. It seemed forever before she answered. "I examined you as best I could. Mistakes are possible."

Her eyes sparkled, but I felt troubled. "What about your religion?" I asked softly.

She took my hands in hers. "Yesu teaches that we should try to bring about the Kingdom of God on earth. Are you committed to that?"

The Kingdom of God on earth? What did that mean? Peace between the Mongols and Christendom? No more wars? Was lying acceptable, if it helped achieved higher ends? Could we each trust our own heart, to decide when lying was and was not all right? My mind was muddled. But slowly, solemnly, I nodded. "I think so."

She gave my hands a squeeze. "You have spirit. You have a fine mind," she said. "I trust that you will do great things. Remember, you are always welcome here."

"Bayarlaa," I said, to thank her for her trust.

I returned to my tent, full of gratitude and amazement.

That night, my aunt Yurak went to her brother Nomokhan and lied. She told him she had examined me and found I was a maiden. She urged him to protect me, as a daughter, on the journey. The next morning, her eyes brimmed when she said good-bye, although I don't know if she was sad at losing me or losing Nasreen.

I was astounded by my aunt Yurak's fierce protectiveness of a niece she barely knew. Perhaps she had been born with a kind nature, inherited from my grandmother. Or perhaps she had developed, living among the Ongut, a strong sense of the wisdom of women. Or maybe, just maybe, she was showing me an active compassion that explained better than words what she had learned from the Religion of Light.

The following morning, I mustered with the troops, ready to resume our journey westward. As we rode out of the tent city of Togtoh, I saw a sickening sight: the head of Bartan, dripping blood, on a stake.

My stomach turned upside down. This was the consequence of my lying. Bad words led to bad actions. I had saved my life, and my high-minded mission. I had saved the life of Marco Polo. I had asked for forgiveness for this man. But I was guilty of murder.

# Part II:
# Apart

# Chapter 5
# Marco: Becoming a Hero

On the way out of Togtoh, I saw Bartan's head on a post, ghostly white. My hands, holding the reins, shook madly. My overly vivid imagination presented me with an image of my own head, dripping, displayed on that post.

After passing by that horrific sight, my stomach revolted. I had to pull back on the reins, get off my horse and go to the side of the road.

Within minutes, I noticed that my uncle had stopped by the roadside, too, doing the same. And a few moments later, beside him was my father. Likewise.

Was it something we ate? Or were they equally affected by the image of what my head might have looked like, if the encounter with Nomokhan had gone another way? For once, my humor was silenced.

My gut hurt so severely, I could barely get back on my horse. I hated being weak and cowardly. But I could not help thinking: Yes, my life was spared. But at what price? Emmajin, I knew, had been cleared of all wrongdoing. But had she seen the head? How had she reacted? I wished I knew.

The mah-foos had to help all three of us. Wei-ming took charge of our horses and camels.

After a few hours, it was clear we could no longer keep up with the Mongol Army. The troops disappeared over the horizon, and we had to stop. I was feeling better, but my uncle was so sick he could not go on, at least not this day.

Wei-ming found a nomadic herding family that agreed to let us pitch our tents near theirs. An old man, two women, and six children came rushing out to greet us. Wei-ming explained our situation to them, and the old man agreed to let us rest in his tent until the mahfoos had pitched ours.

This family lived the typical Mongolian nomadic life, in a ger. A woman pulled aside the tent flap and we followed the old man inside. The ger smelled of dung fire and sour milk. The odors curdled in my stomach, but I willed it to calm down.

Near the center pole of the tent, the fire in the fire pit was only smoldering; in summer a fire was unnecessary, except for cooking. The tent pole shone with sheep grease. Sleeping furs lined the two sides. Straight ahead was a small wooden chest. Two odd-looking dolls hung above it, one male and one female. These figures, I knew, were the images of Father Sky and Mother Earth, the deities in the traditional Mongol religion.

An old man with missing teeth, the head of the household, greeted us with warm hospitality. He gestured to the stools to his right, where the guests of honor sat. His daughter-in-law offered us airag and goat cheese, which we accepted, but none of us could eat or drink much. All I wanted was to lie down and rest on one of those sleeping furs, but we had to go through the motions first.

"My two sons are in the army," the old man told us proudly, speaking Mongolian. "I myself served as a soldier." He showed us two scars on his left arm, where arrows had grazed him. "We conquered the world," he said. "I fought under Subedei."

My father flinched at that name. A surge of sickness shook my uncle. I grabbed his arm and rushed him out of the tent, so that he would not sully it.

The two women followed us, with worried looks on their faces. They spread a fur on the ground outside the tent, and my uncle lay down on it. Still unsettled myself, I lay next to him. My father began pacing.

Subedei, I knew, was the general who had masterminded the invasion of Christendom, crushing Hungary and Poland during my father's youth. As a child, I had heard frightening tales of these 'yellow hordes' that thundered in from the East, plundering and massacring. They had cut off and collected one ear from each person they killed, as a way of counting the dead. We called them Tartars, in those days, and viewed them as cruel barbarians. When I was a boy, ready to do mischief, my grandmother used to threaten me, saying, "If you do that, the Tartars will get you."

Yet this old herdsman seemed to make no connection between our thick beards and those of the men of our race he had helped to kill.

So this was the famous Mongol hospitality I had heard about. Mongol herders, Emmajin had once told me, live scattered, nomadic lives and seldom meet strangers. When they do, they always invite them into their tents and offer them food and drink.

Mongol hospitality, Mongol brutality. Both true. After seeing Bartan's head, it was hard to reconcile the two.

---

After two days, my uncle felt well enough to travel on. The medicine I had purchased from the shaman took the edge off his pain and settled his stomach, but his nagging cough returned. The dust kicked up by the army's six thousand horses had brought back his ailment, the one that had laid him low in Cambaluc. Traveling with only our five horses and twelve camels was easier on his lungs, but he needed rest.

The army, I assumed, was pushing on ahead at its break-neck pace of two hundred *li* per day, and our small caravan fell behind. After trying to keep up during the early part of the journey, one of our horses had collapsed in Togtoh.

We fell farther and farther behind. Although the grasslands were fairly flat—slightly rolling hills—we could not see the army even in the far distance. They had gone over the horizon in the west, Emmajin with them.

Each mile that separated us stung my heart. As I rode, my mind whirred.

My plan now was to catch up with Emmajin at the military fortress of Almalik, at the western edge of the Great Desert of Taklamakan. There, supposedly, the bulk of the Khan's army would stop. At that point, it would make more sense to join our caravan with hers. General Nomokhan would stay with the army at the fortress, rather than traveling on with Emmajin to Christendom. Temur might, too, although I was not sure. I still hoped I might be able to see more of her after reaching Almalik. But that rendezvous was many months and miles away. And would Emmajin wait for us?

As the distance grew between my lady and me, the void inside me filled up with anger. Why had Nomokhan executed Bartan, simply for repeating a rumor? Emmajin had specifically asked her uncle to forgive her accuser. What kind of tyrant was Nomokhan? Bartan had not threatened the chain of command. And why had my offense been so bad, loving the lady Emmajin? She was no man's wife.

Nomokhan was a typical Mongol. The Mongols treated their women badly. They did not deserve a lady like her. They did not deserve this huge empire. Someday, God would punish them.

My thoughts grew more and more negative. I remembered every tale of battlefield brutality ever told me. More than once I had seen stacks of skulls, neatly arranged along the main road along the edge of the desert, to ensure that travelers knew the cost of resisting the Mongol army. Mongol armies had massacred the inhabitants of a city by lining up all the men in several rows, then forcing each man to kill the man standing in front of him. These barbarians did not spare women and children—only artisans, who might prove useful back home.

These bloody images infected my mind during the long days on horseback, following the Black River to the west and then south, and festered.

How had I fallen for the idea that the Mongols were superior, simply because they had conquered most of the world? They didn't even have a written language until Khubilai, the fifth Great Khan, commissioned one. Their native religion, shamanism and sky-worship, was extremely primitive, a joke really, compared to Christianity and even Buddhism and Mohammedanism. The Mongols had no churches, no temples, no sacred texts. They didn't even have their own style of architecture, since they had all lived in tents until recent generations. The great palaces of Khubilai Khan were built in the Chinese style, with curving eaves and great square courtyards.

I could not hate all Mongols. After all, Emmajin was a Mongol. She had been brought up to believe that war was good and military conquest was a birthright to all her people. I admired her archery skills, and she raced on horseback as if she and the horse were one. She had fought bravely. But even she had betrayed me, by gathering intelligence about my homeland's defenses to further the Mongol agenda of world conquest. She could not read or write, or recite poetry, or pray.

She had, it's true, left the army to take on a mission of peace. But now it seemed obvious that the Khan was undermining her, sending six thousand troops to the West, intent on conquest, in case the Pope did not respond well to the letter of cooperation. How could I have believed, even for a day, that the Great Khan of the Mongols would want to establish peace and friendship with Christendom?

The Mongols weren't to be trusted. Khan's letter was probably a hoax.

Uncle Maffeo had been right. How could I ever expect Princess Emmajin, granddaughter of Khubilai Khan, to favor me, a Venetian merchant, over her royal family and triumphant people? She had always been loyal to the Great Khan and the Mongol empire. What kind of person would she be if she just tossed aside that loyalty to be with me, a lowly merchant? Still, in my mixed-up mind, I wished I could do something to truly earn her respect. Following the Mongol Army with a caravan of merchandise did not permit the kind of heroics I admired in the legendary tales.

One day, during our midday stop, my uncle began coughing badly again, and my father decided we should stay for the night. I gave my uncle some medicine and sat with him until he fell asleep in the hot shade of our tent. Then, I had to get out.

Wei-ming and I mounted our horses and went to fetch water from the river. As we rode, I saw a single ger on a hill. It was a typical herder's tent. A flock of sheep grazed nearby. We had not eaten meat in many days, and I decided to approach the herders to see if we could purchase a sheep from them, in exchange for something they needed.

Wei-ming and I rode over to the ger to talk with the nomads.

Before we reached the tent, I could see that something was wrong. A single horse had been tethered too long, so that his feces had piled up, and his water bucket was empty. No Mongol treats his horse that way. The horse whinnied pitifully when we passed him.

As we approached the ger, an unbearable stench hit my nose. I held back, but Wei-ming pulled aside the door flap.

Inside the ger, the odor was putrid. A man and a child lay on the floor, apparently dead, their bodies covered with huge black boils. Horror rippled through me, seeing that hideous, deforming disease. A woman, her body covered with black boils, whimpered, in Mongolian, "Water."

I picked up her empty water bucket and ran out to look for a nearby stream. When I turned to return to the tent, it was in flames.

I dropped the bucket and ran toward the ger. "No!" I shouted, imagining the woman inside, burning to death after all the suffering she had been through. I expected to hear her screaming. Instead I heard nothing but the cracking of the dry felt tent. She must have been too weak to cry out.

"What happened?" I asked Wei-ming, who was watching the fire.

He shook his head solemnly. "The Black Death."

"She was alive, that woman!"

"Not for long. No one survives the plague. We could not have helped her. If you had touched any of those people, you would have gotten the sickness yourself. No cure."

Wei-ming was a gentle man; I knew he would not have burned the tent unless he knew it was necessary. I wanted to scream at him, but I sensed he was right. A lump formed in my throat and began to choke me. Here, in this grassland paradise, a hideous plague had been hiding, all this time. I released the family's horse.

Back on our horses, Wei-ming explained to us about Black Death. "All the people of this region know about it," he said. "Marmots and other rodents spread it. It is why hunters refuse to eat a marmot if they can catch it with their bare hands."

This horrific image filled my mind, for days. I imagined that I had run into the putrid tent, lifted the woman gently, and carried her far away from her dead family, then dribbled water into her mouth until she recovered.

This incident set me to thinking in new ways.

I wished I could become a hero in my own right. It was not enough to be a teller of tales and a lover of beautiful ladies. I longed to be a gentleman who performs feats of chivalry, a knight who rushes toward danger to save the princess, a hero who exposes evil and rights wrongs.

Yet even as these thoughts swelled my head till it was too big for my body, I knew that such ambition was laughable. I knew better than anyone that I was not tall and broad-shouldered, muscular and fit, skilled with sword and bow, a giant among men. My nose was not chiseled but roundish, my eyes not fiercely blue but oddly green, my hair not dark but reddish-brown, my beard not sleek but curly. I had seen, reflected in my lady's eyes, the shock of seeing such a man as I was, so different from the Mongol warriors, with their black braid loops and shaven crowns, their high cheekbones and flashing brown eyes, their arms muscled from archery and their legs bowed from constant horse riding. How outlandish I must have seemed to her!

Yes, it was foolish to think I could ever be the hero of my own story.

———————

"Come, Messer Marco. It will amuse you." Wei-ming, my mahfoo friend, looked at me with concerned eyes.

"I suppose so," I answered. Had I been so glum of late, that I needed amusing?

After endless days of slow travel, we had a rest day in the town of Shingching-foo, and Wei-ming had heard of a smoke-and-fire show that evening. After dinner, we walked together down the main street of town, heading toward the river.

Shingching-foo was not much of a town, but at least it had shops and inns, set in a pleasant plain, verdant with growing crops in early summer. That was a welcome sight after the barren hills we had traversed, following the river from Togtoh to this place.

By the size of the city wall, I could see that this town had once been far larger, a great city, capital of the Western Hsia empire. But after the Mongols destroyed it, fifty years earlier, no one had bothered to do more than ransack earlier palaces and walls for stones to make a few streets' worth of humble, low-slung buildings. Even the city wall was crumbling; there was no need to rebuild it, nothing left to defend.

Evidence of Mongolian barbarity cropped up everywhere. As we walked toward the river, we soon passed through a part of town that had been destroyed. I could still see where the streets had been, laid straight and broad as in Chinese cities, with crumbling walls of packed earth still outlining grand houses that once dominated this thoroughfare.

Wei-ming stopped and stared at one such ruin. "I think this was it," he said.

"What?" I asked, looking out over the dirt mounds.

"My home. I was born here."

This shocked me. We had talked of many things, but I had never asked him exactly where he was from. "I thought you were Chinese," I said, feeling stupid. Wei-ming certainly looked Chinese, and I knew he could speak the language.

His lips tensed. "No, I'm Tangut. This was our land, our capital. For two hundred years, this was a glorious city. My grandfather told me that during his childhood, the Tangut emperor used to ride along this avenue, carried in a palanquin by four servants, accompanied by drums and gongs and banners, on his way to bathe in the river."

I looked out over the acres of ruined homes. "Where is everyone now?"

"Tens of thousands were killed. Many others fled. My father got out before the massacre, but the rest of his family did not."

I tried to imagine the horror and blood that once terrorized these silent streets.

"Chinggis Khan?" I asked.

He nodded, unwilling even with me to speak out loud to blame the Mongols' Great Ancestor revered by the ruling Golden Family.

It wasn't until my father returned home from his travels, when I was fifteen, that I heard anything positive about the Mongols. He and Uncle Maffeo had visited the court of Khubilai Khan, where they were awed by the magnificence of the Khan's palace. Now that I had seen that palace myself, I understood: its wealth and brilliance far outshone anything we had in the West, even the great cathedral of Rome, Saint Peter's Basilica.

After seeing the splendor of Khubilai Khan's palace in Cambaluc, as well as his summer palace and gardens at Xanadu, I too had become captivated by Mongol wealth and power. At court, the Khan was called Khubilai the Wise, revered for his good governance, such as provisions for widows and orphans and grain policies that required storage of grain from good years to help during bad years. He had shown mercy to the boy emperor of Sung China, giving him a title and sparing his life after the defeat of China. Now that the Mongols ruled most of Asia, they had established Pax Mongolica, a peaceful era that allowed traders like me to travel safely from Christendom to Cathay.

But even this peace, Pax Mongolica, was possible only because of Mongol conquests, which were possible only because of Mongol brutality. Outnumbered in almost every battle, Chinggis Khan's armies could never have had such success without the fear they inspired. Emmajin's heritage included both good and bad. So, in fact, did mine.

Walking through these abandoned streets was eerie, and an awful feeling burned my heart. How many tens of thousands of Tangut men, women, and children had been slaughtered by the Mongols? And why? During war, men sometimes do terrible things. But to my mind, nothing could justify such a massacre of innocents.

I was not in the mood for a show of smoke and fire, whatever that was. But Wei-ming hoped to see someone he knew, and he insisted I go with him. So we continued to the river's edge. There we joined a group of locals, some of whom greeted Wei-ming in their native tongue. None were relatives or close friends, but several remembered his family.

They were eating raisins and sweet melons with light green flesh, a specialty of this region, newly harvested. Men and women together, they seemed light-hearted and celebratory, and I asked Wei-ming what the occasion was.

"Today is the sixth day of the Sixth Month," he answered, as if I would know what that meant. He looked a little sheepish. "Please don't tell anyone, any Mongols."

I looked around. "I won't. There are no Mongols for miles around."

He smiled ruefully. "The army passed by many days ago. They camped out by the river and left the town alone." Then he continued in a low voice. "Every year on this day, we remember the glories of the Tangut Empire. We called it the Great State of the White and Lofty."

It seemed sad to me, but this tiny remnant of living Tanguts wanted to recall the lofty achievements of their lost ancestors.

When the show was about to begin, after sunset, we all sat on a hillside overlooking a branch of the river. Two men went out in a small boat. Everyone hushed as they watched.

Boom! The sound startled me, but Wei-ming seemed to expect it. I heard a whistling noise from the boat as something shot straight up from it.

A second boom rattled the evening sky. Then a glorious shower of white drops of fire exploded in the sky, falling in the shape of weeping willow branches over the water.

My breath caught in my throat. What was it?

"Oooooh! Aaaaah!" the people around me shouted.

Wei-ming laughed and yelled with joy.

"Hooray!" people shouted. "Long live the White and Lofty!"

White and lofty it was, but nothing I had expected. I had heard of smoke-and-fire shows, but I had no idea it would be this beautiful and exciting.

Before I could ask questions, I heard another boom. This time, I looked more closely at the boat. A little tube was shooting straight up from the boat. With a second boom, this one exploded into a ball of red sparks that grew larger before fizzling out and dropping into the river.

"Aaaah," I found myself shouting with the others.

The sound, the lights, the happy crowd, all filled me with joy. I forgot about my worries, my anger, even my noble goals. The show continued, with four more explosions, all in red or white but creating different shapes in the sky. The last one was the largest, combining red and white sparks, looking like a giant palm tree over the desert.

Everyone around me seemed joyful, too. People lingered on the hillside, eating raisins and sunflower seeds, unwilling to go home and break the spell.

"You've never seen anything like it, even in the capital?" asked Wei-ming.

"I've heard of such shows, but never seen one," I answered. "But I know a little about fire medicine."

Wei-ming handed me another handful of raisins, plump and yellow and sweet. "You do?"

"Yes. When I was in Carajan, the local people used it for firecrackers, to make loud noises and scare away evil spirits. In fact, I found out about the three ingredients: black powder, yellow powder, and white powder, and bought some at the local market."

"Hmm." Wei-ming cracked a seed open with his teeth and spit out the hull.

"Did you know that fire medicine can be used in battle?"

He looked at me skeptically.

"The loud noise scares men and horses. We used it at the Battle of Vochan, to scare the elephants." I didn't even tell him that this had been my idea, that the battle had been won because of me. I was so used to being the storyteller, not the hero, that I had grown accustomed to leaving out my role in it. That experience had given me my first taste of making a difference. I had, in fact, been a hero, yet I had told the tale of the battle as if Emmajin herself had won it. That taste of pride now made me yearn for more.

"I wish my ancestors had had that," Wei-ming said. "Then we might have defeated the Mongols and kept them from destroying our land."

It wasn't until later that night, after Wei-ming had gone to bed and I was sitting, wide awake by the fire at the inn, that his words came back to me: *We might have defeated the Mongols and kept them from destroying our land.*

No boom went off in the sky, but a spark of light exploded in my mind.

Fire medicine. In battle. The Mongols had this weapon now, thanks to my clever thinking. The Mongol army was rapidly heading west. Officially, their plan was to stop at the fortress of Almalik, to reinforce the troops there and defend the borderlands of the Great Khan's territory. But what if the army went on and invaded my homeland, Christendom?

No one in Christendom had ever heard of fire medicine and the explosions it caused, as far as I knew. Certainly no one had ever used it in battle. Of all the rubies and emeralds in our saddlebags, nothing could be as precious as this: a weapon to protect our homeland. A new weapon, unheard of. Those who didn't have it could not win against Mongol invasion. Those who did might have a fighting chance.

After that, I could not sleep all night. The next morning I would check the local markets to try to buy the white powder. The black powder was common charcoal, and the yellow powder was sulfur. It was the white powder, saltpeter, that I had never seen in Christendom. It came from bat guano in caves. I would buy as much of it as I could carry, along with some sulfur powder, and take them home to Venezia. As merchants, we stuffed our saddle packs with many things; I hoped that no one would question the reason for my stash of saltpeter.

My yearning to be the hero of my own story had seemed foolish at first. But maybe it wasn't. Emmajin was loyal to her family and her people; I should be loyal to mine. If I could help the Mongols win a battle against invaders, shouldn't I find a way to defend my own people? Loving her did not have to mean abandoning my own heritage. Bigger things were at stake than our future together.

Now, I thought, with my understanding of the Mongols and their weapons and methods of warfare, I could be the savior of Christendom.

# Chapter 6
# Emmajin: Quenching Thirst

One evening, less than a month later, after a particularly long and grueling day on horseback, the Mongol Army camped along a stream, near a waterfall. Although most of the soldiers were covered with desert dust, they went to the stream only to drink. Raised on the grasslands, in a dry, cold climate far from the ocean, we Mongols generally do not care for washing our bodies in water.

But I had begun to lose my fear of water. I lingered by the waterfall after the soldiers had left to pitch the tents and prepare our dinner. Nasreen sat by my side on a warm rock near the water's edge. She pulled off her boots and dangled her feet into the clear water of the stream.

"Ahhh," she said, tossing her head back in the last rays of the evening sun.

"That looks nice," I said.

My maidservant smiled and then turned to pull off my boots, too. My feet were hot and sweaty and creased from too many hours and years inside leather boots. Imitating her, I dangled them into the stream, and the cool water felt delightful. For the first time in days, I laughed.

It had been hard for me, since leaving Togtoh. The image of Bartan's head haunted my waking thoughts and gave me nightmares. The man had been executed for lying, but Marco was the one who had lied. And so had I. With Aunt Yurak's help, I had saved Marco's life and my reputation, but at a cost. That had made me think deeply about lying. Was it always wrong? Who had the right to say what was wrong and what was right? I welcomed a relaxing escape from these worries.

Nasreen pulled her feet out of the water and massaged them with her hands. Watching her, I did the same. This simple motion brought delicious relief.

"Do you have a family?" I asked her. I don't know what got into me. In all those years, living at court, I had never asked a servant a personal question. Somehow, rubbing our bare feet together, intimacy did not seem inappropriate.

She glanced at me with surprise, and then lowered her eyes to her hands, rubbing her toes one by one. "I had a husband in Togtoh, and a child, but they both died."

Pain jabbed like a blinding ray of sun into our idyllic moment. I let a beat of silence pass as I pondered this. "What happened?"

She shook her head, refusing to offer details. "Sickness. That's why I started to learn about healing."

At first, I had questioned my aunt's judgment in sending a maidservant to travel with me. I thought Nasreen might not be able to keep up with the fast pace of the army. She rode with the servants, but day after day she appeared at my tent shortly after it was erected. She prepared my meals, kept my belongings in order, and slept in my tent at night. I liked hearing the soft sound of her breathing in the darkness. After growing up with my sister, I had never gotten used to sleeping alone.

Since joining me on this journey, Nasreen had been mixing mysterious powders into my mutton soup each night. In those first few days after leaving, she had answered many of my questions about my own body, issues my mother had never discussed with me. She spoke in a direct way, with no judgments, explaining the facts. I could not believe how ignorant I had been, how little I had known about men and women. I had confided in her, telling her what had happened with

Marco in the sea. She told me it was unlikely that I was pregnant, but she could not tell, from my description. Still, she thought it safer to give me medicines that would ensure I wasn't carrying a child.

This possibility shocked me. A pregnancy would prevent me from delivering the Khan's letter to the Pope, although I still might complete my short-term mission of talking to Ai-Jaruk. My belly was as flat as ever, but Nasreen said that was normal for the first three months. Now I understood why Nasreen knew so much about pregnancy. She had given birth to a child of her own.

"Losing your husband and child—that must have been terrible," I said.

She shrugged. Slaves were not expected to have feelings. Come to think of it, I had never seen a slave express any emotion stronger than impatience.

Although she covered her hair with a kerchief, Nasreen had a lovely face, with rounded cheeks, large eyes, and long eyelashes. My own eyelashes were short and stubby, so I noticed this feature. Her voice was quiet, her movements careful and her presence calming.

"Were you born a slave?" I asked.

She turned and looked at me with hard eyes. "No."

"How did you become a slave?" Now I was curious.

She glanced away, clearly avoiding answering my question. "Look," she said, pointing her finger.

A short way upstream from where we sat, Temur was reaching out toward the waterfall, splashing his face and neck with its fresh water. He was wearing his trousers but his chest was bare, and he seemed unaware of our presence.

My eyes sparkled at Nasreen in conspiracy, and I put my finger to my lips to ask her to stay quiet. Then I stood up and walked as silently as I could, in my bare feet, toward Temur. When we were children, I had seen him bare-chested many times, wrestling and playing in the woods of Xanadu.

"Danger! Water!" I shouted when I was close behind him.

Startled, he slipped on the rock he was standing on, then slid into the pond below the waterfall and landed on his bottom in the shallow water. He shouted as he fell with a huge splash. He looked to see who had disturbed him, and for a long moment I wasn't sure how he would react. He had a larger dose of pride than his brother. Surprise and anger flitted across Temur's face, and I worried that I might have caused him to break an ankle.

In a flash, his hand was around my ankle, and I was sliding into the pond with him. "Danger! Water!" he was shouting, with a grin.

I managed to stay on my feet, balancing with my arms. From the shore, Nasreen grabbed my hand to keep me from falling completely. Temur used his other hand to create a wave and splash me, so that my entire del was wet. Nasreen was half wet, too. Off balance, I fell backward into the water, landing on my bottom and pulling Nasreen in with me.

The next thing I knew, the three of us were sitting in the pond, laughing loudly and splashing each other mercilessly. Temur dropped his seriousness and acted again like the boy I had known in my childhood. This shallow water seemed far from dangerous, and after a parched all-day ride through the desert, it felt divine.

Nasreen, who had always been so quiet and cautious serving me, suddenly seemed free and happy. Once she was completely wet, she moved to a deeper part of the pond and began swimming. This astounded me. I had never seen anyone swim.

"How did you learn that?" Temur asked her.

"My cousins are fishermen," she said, "living by a deep lake. When I was a child, we often swam with them."

Her cousins? From her childhood, when she was free.

Temur and I looked at each other, both of us amazed that we were frolicking in the water at all, let alone with a slave woman.

"She's not like other slaves, is she?" Temur said.

I nodded. I laid my head back against a rock and let the water stream over me. It felt good, this easing after the constant tension of the fast-paced journey, the scrutiny of my personal life, the harsh judgment of my uncle, the prophecies of danger. I needed this moment of relaxation as much as a parched rider needs a drink of water.

Temur left first, and Nasreen and I stayed on the rocks till the warmth of the sun went out of them. Then we slipped back into our tent in the darkness so no one would see our clothing sticking tight to our bodies.

That night, for the first time in months, I slept well.

The next morning, I woke up with a heavy feeling in my belly. As soon as I stood up from my sleeping fur, I realized that my monthly courses had begun.

"Oh!" I said as I saw the blood. It seemed heavier than usual—though I had no set pattern when I traveled.

Nasreen rushed over. She smiled slightly, as if she had accomplished her mission.

"Was it the medicine you gave me that caused this?" I asked.

She shrugged humbly. "Maybe." She immediately found a clean pair of trousers for me, as well as a cloth to wear that day, and took off the soiled trousers to wash. It was good to have a maidservant to handle such things.

After she left my tent, I almost cried. My biggest worry had vanished.

Yet after the initial relief ebbed and flowed, I was left feeling empty. I had nothing of Marco inside me except deep, unanswered questions.

---

The army was moving at a much faster pace now, loping westward and then southward, over the flat land along the Caramoran River, and then turning northwestward again, following a corridor between two ranges of mountains.

My horse, Baatar, was always exhausted by the end of the day, as was I, but fortunately, the grasses were thick and green and the water plentiful along the riverbank.

During the long daily rides, when we were moving too fast to allow for conversation, I was haunted by fears about my future.

As Baatar's hooves pounded the dirt road, I wondered. What would happen, after the army reached its destination, the fortress of Almalik? I thought a lot about Ai-Jaruk, what I might say to her to convince her father to cooperate with us. What sort of woman was she, really? Had she ever loved a man? Had she found a way to love a man without having him take away her liberty?

And I wondered about the second part of my journey, after Al-malik, when I would be traveling with only a small armed escort and the Polos' caravan. I would see Marco daily, and there would be no No-mokhan or Temur to stop me from spending as much time as I liked with him. What did I really want, then?

It was easy to chafe against those who kept us apart. But once we were together, what would that be like? Would Marco expect to sleep with me? Would he try to control me, as other men did? Could a royal woman have a concubine, a man who pleased her and then went away? That idea was stunning but it didn't appeal to me.

After we reached Marco's homeland, what might happen then? The Pope would treat me with respect, I was fairly sure of that. After all, I represented the most powerful ruler of the world. But after that meeting, then what? Would Marco try to get me to marry him, to live in a wooden house on a road made of water, to dress in heavy velvets, to eat fish and drink grape wine? I loved the idea of traveling to foreign countries, observing the strange customs of others, visiting with kings and queens of Christendom, watching knights joust in tournaments. But what rules did they have for women? Would Marco expect me to live by those rules?

So much about what made Marco attractive was the fact that I couldn't have him. What if I could have him, alone, all day, every day? Aaah, I thought. That would be wonderful. But only if we were alone, with no one—from East or West—to dictate our behavior.

I sighed. An impossible dream.

***

After splashing together in the pond, Temur and I began to relax around one another. Sometimes he rode with me, and he often came to sit outside my tent, after dinner, chatting amiably. He became more confident that he was winning the trust of both Shirki and Nomokhan, and that made him less tense. Once we realized Marco and his caravan would not catch up, Temur stopped acting protective around me.

Lonely without Marco, I was glad of Temur's company, and we began to have in-depth conversations about the larger issues of the day. From Shirki, Temur had learned much about the Great Khan's overall plans for conquest, and how some of the khans to the west were not obeying. It felt good to hear him confiding in me about military secrets. Temur was, I suspected, smarter and more capable than his elder brother Suren, who had been light-hearted and playful, without much depth of knowledge. I would never have admitted that while Suren was alive.

One thing I didn't discuss with Temur was the danger that Marco had warned me about. Temur never referred to Marco's story about Mordred, so he probably thought it was light entertainment. But I knew Marco had been trying to get across a message about danger to me, and a possible traitor. And I spent long hours pondering this. I wore the rosary beads around my neck, next to my heart, every day.

My cousin admired Shirki, but I thought Shirki the most likely potential traitor; his loyalty to Khubilai Khan might not be as strong as that of Khubilai's sons and grandsons. But Shirki had proved his commitment over fifteen years already and fought bravely in many a battle. Might the traitor be Nomokhan himself? After his harsh execution of Bartan, I disliked my uncle, but why would he, the Khan's fourth son, have reason to be a traitor? My uncle had no interest in me or my mission to deliver a letter to the Pope, but that did not make him evil. He had, after all, asked me to take on an important role, befriending Ai-Jaruk. Might the traitor be Khaidu, Ai-Jaruk's father? We didn't need a shaman's warning to be wary of Khaidu. I continued looking closely at other military officers, too. One thing I knew for certain: the traitor was not Temur. He always had my back.

One time Temur mentioned that he might want me to serve as his adviser some day, when he was given more responsibility. As the Khan's eldest grandson, he was being groomed for high office. This nipped my pride, since he was younger, but also appealed to some part of me, since it showed that he valued my opinion. It also showed me that he didn't expect me to drop out of this man's world to get married and raise children.

One evening, after a rest day, Temur and I had more time than usual to talk.

"What is it about that Latin you liked so much?" he asked me bluntly.

I was surprised Temur had asked this question, that he had even been thinking about Marco Polo. The easy response would be to brush off the question with a joke. But Temur was regarding me with genuine curiosity and seemed open to hearing a real answer.

"You heard him tell a story," I said. "He's fun to listen to, don't you think? And he has traveled all over the world."

"Yes," said Temur, knitting his brow as if trying to imagine how this would make Marco alluring to me. I knew that Temur considered Marco 'too foreign,' a low-status merchant who was not accomplished in any of the manly arts.

What else? When you're strongly attracted to someone, it's hard to put in words the reasons why. "He thinks in a different way," I continued.

Temur listened, as if trying to figure out why *different* might possibly be *appealing*.

"In Marco's homeland, they have a concept called courtly love." I wondered if I was going too far, expecting Temur to understand this. After all, it had taken me a long time to fathom it. I should have told Temur about Marco's brilliant strategy on the battlefield instead. But suddenly I wanted to try to explain this foreign notion of romantic love to someone from my own culture. "Marco also called it *love from a distance*. A man admires a lady and reveres her, giving his whole heart to her."

Temur's face reflected the struggle of his mind, trying to grasp this. "From a distance? How strange. And giving his heart to a lady?" he asked.

I laughed. It did seem absurd, when said in Mongolian. "One true love, for life."

Temur looked at me as if I were crazy, but he seemed intrigued. I couldn't think of one example of this among all the Mongolian stories I had heard, although there was a Chinese story about lovers who died together and their souls turned into butterflies. That wouldn't appeal to my cousin.

"Someone you think about all the time," I said. "They have many stories about this in the Far West. Some warriors pledge their loyalty to ladies and go off to do battle in their honor."

"Warriors go to battle to fight in honor of women?" He looked at me as if I'd told him that the earth was full of stars.

"Someone who means more to you than any other person. Someone you couldn't live without."

"You mean, if they died, you'd..."

I nodded, although I wondered. What if Marco died? Would I be able to live on?

"Do you mean, like Yang Guifei?" Temur asked. I had not heard this story, so he told it to me. "One of the Chinese emperors of the Tang Dynasty was obsessed by a woman who was another man's wife. He had to have her, so he took her as his imperial consort, even though others objected. When she angered him, he sent her away, but he couldn't eat or think until she came back."

"Yes, a little like that," I said, pleased to hear there was such a story.

"Her relatives planned treason against the Emperor. He had to kill all of them. Including Yang Guifei."

"Oh," I said. This didn't sound like Marco's kind of courtly love.

"Too much love for a woman distorts a man's thinking," said Temur. His usual tone of scoffing cynicism was emerging.

"And too much love for a man?"

"Likewise," said Temur, shaking his head. He hesitated and then asked me, "Do you want to marry this man, this Marco Polo?" His voice had a hard edge.

Shocked that he would even ask, I hesitated. "It's not about marriage," I said. "Romantic love is higher than that, purer. It's about excitement and mystery, a deep connection. Idealistic. Free. Daring. Intense. All-consuming. Spiritual. Abiding."

Suren would have laughed at me, but Temur seemed to be trying hard to digest all these words and make sense of them. It was indeed a foreign concept, this Western idea of romantic love. I thought I caught a glimmer in his eye, as if he conceded the appeal of it.

"If it's love at a distance," Temur said, "does that mean you have no desire to be close to him?"

Aha. Here was the contradiction. I had not figured this out myself. And I certainly did not want to admit these feelings to Temur.

What started as love from a distance drew me in, with a strong desire for love close up. For touching.

"I can't explain it," I said at last, shrugging. "You either feel it or you don't." Temur, I was certain, would never feel this way.

"Well, you have love from a distance now," Temur said. "It's a good thing he's not traveling with us any more. It's safer for you."

This was the old Temur, protective and controlling. At least he had tried to understand.

Nasreen came out of the shadows to refill our cups. She did not look me in the eye, but she glanced up at Temur. I sensed she had been listening to our conversation, and I wondered if she had understood any of it. Surely a slave could not understand such things.

---

The land, flat for so many days, began to fall away. One day, the brown earth sloped down into a deep, wide valley. The sun grew hotter, as if the earth itself were burning. A few scraggly trees gave way to greater greenery, and suddenly we were surrounded by lush vineyards, so gorgeous that they refreshed my spirits. Local men, with brown skin and round eyes, waved from their donkey carts, and the women, in head scarves, smiled with wrinkled faces while they lifted water from wells. For there were wells everywhere—dotting the hillsides, in rows.

This was Turpan, an oasis in the heart of the Western Desert. Although there were few rivers, green crops spread far and wide in all directions. Over thousands of years, the ingenious people here had built and maintained a complex system of wells and underground tunnels for irrigation.

As the land sprang to life with trees and bushes and vines, my spirits lifted. The soldiers around me, silent for much of the journey, began to talk and laugh.

Our horses headed down into the basin, and the sweet fragrance of grapes, ripe on the vine, wafted up. In the hottest month of summer, the grapes hung heavy from wooden trellises that stretched out from both sides of the road. The local people hummed under their breath and smiled easily. With sun-kissed skins and friendly eyes, these people, known as Uighurs, seemed a whole different race from the dried-out, hungry-looking men we had seen along the desert highway.

After countless thirsty, dusty days on horseback, I was ready for a break. Turpan seemed to be a land of magic, hidden in the midst of the desert, untouched by war, drought, fatigue, envy, or despair. This was the first place on our long journey that seemed worth visiting. The sun, our scorching foe during the trek across the desert, shone friendly here, angling low from the western sky, making the grapes shine like amethysts. Across the valley, the Flaming Mountains glowed red in the sunset.

Temur seemed to catch the spirit of this place. He leaned forward and spurred his horse on. We raced downhill like children.

We stayed at a well-appointed hostel not far from a big lake, called Moonlight Lake. At dinner that night, Temur sat at the head table, with Nomokhan and Shirki and the idikut of Turpan, a large, wide man with a wispy white beard and a black skullcap finely decorated with colored beads. The idikut had chosen to cooperate with the Mongol overlords, so he continued to rule from Kharakhoja, a sprawling city in Turpan.

We had arrived just at the season for the grape harvest, a time of celebrating happiness and love and plenty. Children rushed about the dining room, chasing each other and laughing, undisciplined. Sitting along the wall, a young woman nursed her baby, and a young man leaned over and spoke to her tenderly.

The servants presented us with more kinds of grapes than I had imagined could exist: grapes of emerald green, agate purple, pearl white, and ebony black. Then they poured several kinds of grape wine, some deep red, some pale yellowish, in delicate cups made of thin, translucent marble, called "night-glowing cups."

These Uighur people of Turpan were kind and hospitable, wine-drinkers like Marco's people. They had, I learned, converted to Islam but still were known for their love of dancing, singing, and grape wine. The best of East and West met here. Might Marco and I settle in this place someday, far from both his people and mine?

Nasreen, I noticed, chatted easily with the servants, who seemed to understand her native tongue, although she spoke a different type of Turkic.

A Uighur servant girl offered me a glass of grape wine. The ruby-red liquid looked thin and clear, nothing like the milky-white mare's milk of airag, and the smell made me wrinkle my nose. I took a sip—my first taste of grape wine. It filled my mouth with a sharp, acidic taste. Loud noises like cymbals clanged in my ears, heating up the skin of my face. I closed my eyes and thought of Marco's distinctive laughter.

After dinner, a young man and a young woman performed a dance for us, acting out the harvest-season custom of presenting grapes as tokens of love. Their bodies swayed toward each other, and the girl smiled and flirted. They were well-matched, their eyes the same round shape, their skin the same shade of brown. My body relaxed after the stiffness of days of travel. I longed for Marco. I longed for love.

Temur, holding a wine cup, caught my eye and gave me a smile, full of mischief. It reminded me of the boy who wrestled with me as a child and the man who splashed me by the waterfall.

The banquet lasted late into the night. Yet even when it ended, I did not feel sleepy. "Let's walk," I said to Temur.

Not far from the banquet hall was a grape arbor, and Temur and I plunged into it. The grape vines wound up trellises and hung low over our heads, so that we had to duck, walking through. The grape wine made me feel light in the head, and I laughed like a girl. Temur, too, seemed affected by the wine; he moved and talked more freely.

The moon shone full. I missed Marco with a physical ache. If only he were there, my joy would be complete.

Temur picked a small green grape and popped it into my mouth. The sharp sweet taste exploded on my tongue, and energy and freshness flowed through my weary body.

"The grapes of Turpan," he said, with a smile.

I felt full of gratitude, as if he had given me the taste of life. I was so glad to be traveling with my cousin, who was as close as a brother to me. Temur, I thought, represented the best of Mongol manly virtues: skilled at archery, wrestling, and racing, he was smarter and more sensitive than most Mongol men I knew. Maybe even smart enough to be a worthy successor to Khubilai the Wise.

Suddenly, Temur's arm curled around my waist, and the next thing I knew, I was crushed against his chest in a full-body embrace.

All my senses went on high alert, and my mind cleared.

"No!" I said, pushing him away. What was he thinking?

"I thought you liked this sort of thing," he said, holding on a moment too long.

I scraped his arm off me and backed away. "Not from you!" I said. We were cousins, and such relations were forbidden.

I turned around and began running through the arbor, back to the road. When I paused for breath, I realized that he had not pursued me. Feeling a little sheepish, I walked briskly back to my room at the inn. Nasreen, who should have been there, was not. So I pulled the door firmly closed and got ready for bed myself.

I lay in the dark, awake, alone, for a long time. I had trusted Temur and relaxed around him. Now I would have to be on my guard.

The next morning, a soft sound awakened me. I opened my eyes and saw Nasreen creeping into the room, in the early morning light. Her hair was mussed, and the kerchief was in her hand.

"Where have you been?" I demanded.

She gave me a soft smile. "My apologies, mistress. Did you need me in the night?"

At breakfast, Temur had an unfamiliar grin on his face and watched every movement of Nasreen as she served me.

I felt sick. What had Temur heard me say? This was not my idea of romantic love. Had my talk with Temur fueled this desire of his? Had my rejection made him grab out for whatever woman was available? Love was not the same as physical pleasure. Was it?

But Nasreen, oddly, seemed happy—even though, as a slave, she had no choice.

# Chapter 7
# Marco: Danger Ahead

Gold City was not well named. Aside from a line of willow trees along the river, the town was dirty and dusty as a camel after a month in the desert. A row of miserable wooden shops lined the main street. An aging wooden temple sagged on a barren hillside. Beggars hobbled along the roads. My uncle told me that gold had been discovered in the nearby hills, a few centuries ago. Clearly, all the gold ever mined here had been carted off to richer locales, and any man who profited from it had fled as well.

We found the only inn in town and rented a room there, hoping for a decent meal and fresh water for a bath. I was pleasantly surprised with a huge bowl of beef noodles, tender and tasty. But the bath was warmed-up river water, murky and unappealing.

After eating and bathing, I took off to roam the local shops, none of which looked promising. Aside from the typical lineup of millers, smiths, ropers, and cartwrights, most shops had aging baskets of dun-colored minerals or metals or produce, equally unappetizing. The shopkeepers sat in the back and swatted flies. I decided this place should be called Lazy City instead. Dullest city on the Silk Road.

It was hard to imagine myself a chivalric hero in this dirthole. Regarding the town with dismay, I reminded myself of my noble task, saving Christendom from the evil designs of the Mongol hordes. I chuckled at my own words. I did take myself too seriously sometimes! But such romantic dreams were what sustained me, especially in hellholes like this. Once I got back to Venezia, I would need to create lavish, lush language to describe this godforsaken town.

I asked around and then located one shop that offered the white powder I was seeking, saltpeter. The shopkeeper, a skinny man wearing the distinctive white cap of the Muslims, had stashed it behind several barrels of cooking oil, since no customers asked for saltpeter except for firecrackers at Chinese New Year.

"Where does it come from?" I asked the vendor.

"Caves," he grunted, "in Sichuan. Warmer there."

I bargained hard and bought his entire stock of saltpeter. That got the vendor talking. Using increasingly animated gestures, he told me about the proper proportions for firecrackers, fireworks, and even thundercrash missiles.

When I asked about "smoke and fire show," his dark eyes lit up. He showed me the equipment needed for it: tubes made of packed paper and string and a mortar, which was a short iron pipe, open at the top, with a small hole at the bottom for a fuse. The mortar was used for launching the tubes high into the air, safely away from the people watching.

I bought all the tubes he had in stock, twenty of them, each with a long fuse rope coming out the bottom and a stick coming out the top, to make it fly straight. Inside these hollow tubes, the vendor had told me, was more of the fire medicine powder, loosely packed, plus some 'stars'—bits of metal salts that would turn into bright colors as they burned. The tubes were plugged with clay. I asked the vendor for details about how to create the effect I remembered: a burst of colored sparks in the sky above, falling in lovely patterns. But I also asked him about how to create the thundercrash missiles; they seemed more useful for warfare.

Once he had my money, the vendor gave me a serious lecture about the dangers if something went wrong with these fireworks. "Get too close," he had said, "and it could burn you badly. Maybe blow off your hand. Maybe kill you. Maybe kill your friend. Maybe set big fire."

The launcher, the twenty tubes, and the white powder would take up a lot of space in my saddlebags, I knew. We might even need an extra packhorse. But I could imagine the shrill delight of Venetian ladies, seeing the smoke-and-fire display in the skies over the Grand Canal. And the white powder might, from what I knew, prove more valuable than any of the other goods we carried in our caravan.

Back at the hostel, my uncle's health was slipping again. His cough had returned and he was too weak to get off his sleeping fur the next morning. My father, as usual, was nervous about this, but my uncle always seemed to recover from his illnesses, so I was not too anxious. There was no point in two of us worrying.

The delay meant that the distance between Emmajin and me was growing. I assumed she would wait for us, once she reached the military outpost where the army was headed. It would probably take two months to get there, at top speed.

On our third day in Lazy City, in the late afternoon, my father went off searching to buy a particular medicine made of crushed deer horns, panacea for all ills. Wei-ming and I were playing the Mongolian game of knucklebones in the courtyard when we heard the sounds of the arrival of a new caravan, this one of Persian merchants.

*Good,* I thought. I was always eager to meet new people and pepper them with questions. Besides, I hadn't had a chance to speak Persian in over a year. My Persian was getting frayed.

Ten men showed up at the inn, dusty and hungry, demanding hot bath water and food, just as we had. Wei-ming rushed off to the stables to guard our horses and packs as the Persians' horse boys unloaded theirs. Mah-foos from other caravans often had sticky fingers.

When the traders were waiting for their rooms, I began talking to one of the youngest Persians, who looked about my age.

"How long have you been traveling?" I asked him.

He looked at me hard, as if taking in my reddish hair and light eyes and trying to place my accent.

"I'm a Latin," I said, responding to his unasked question.

He nodded. His black beard was thinner than mine and he had a narrow, high nose. "Nine months. And you? Where are you going?" he asked.

"We're heading back home to Venezia," I said, surprised that his journey had been so short. "It took us more than three years to get from home to Cambaluc. We stayed there for a year."

He laughed ruefully. "You haven't heard? The road west is blocked."

"Blocked?" His news took me aback.

"We were heading home, too, but we couldn't get through, so we're heading back to Cambaluc now. What a disaster."

"What happened? A mudslide?"

"No. You've heard of Khaidu? He's got an army out there, and he's decided not to let any caravans through, at least not this year."

Khaidu! Of course I had heard of him, on our journey out from Venice. He was the Great Khan's cousin, and he had his own army in the Desert West. His daughter, Ai-Jaruk, fought by his side. Everybody knew that Khaidu hated Khubilai Khan and thought his side of the Golden Family should have inherited the throne of the Mongol Empire. "I had heard rumors," I said. "But surely there must be a way to get through. He's a Mongol, after all, a member of the Golden Family."

The young Persian's mouth drew into a grim line. "We spent three months in Almalik, hoping for a breakthrough. The Mongol commander there is furious that the road is blocked. Khaidu may be a cousin of Khubilai Khan, but he's acting more like an enemy. His army is now bigger than the Great Khan's forces at Almalik."

So this was why Khubilai Khan had sent six thousand troops to the West! "Are they fighting?"

"Not yet. The Great Khan's men are still talking with Khaidu, trying to reason with him. Twice we heard promising news, but the commander could not convince Khaidu to open the trade routes to the West. "

"A big force of the Mongol army is headed toward Almalik," I said. "Six thousand soldiers. That should convince Khaidu to open the trade routes."

The Persian nodded. "I saw those troops about ten days ago. Traveling at great speed. Headed by the Khan's son, Nomokhan. We may wait here in Gold City for a month or so, to see if Nomokhan and these extra troops can break Khaidu's grip and reopen the Silk Road."

Finally I understood! The Khan had known this all along, of course. That was why he had sent the six thousand troops to the West! It had nothing to do with Rome.

"And if they can't?"

"Well!" He shook his head. "The alternative is not appealing. We would have to travel all the way back to Cambaluc, then try to get on a ship and go back by sea."

I whistled. "Now that would be a long journey!"

"Yes, and dangerous. We Persians can ride camels for months across deserts, but the thought of even one night on a ship makes us sick."

I nodded. We Venetians are used to traveling by ship. But I had never heard of anyone traveling from China's coast all the way to Persia. Was it even possible?

"Hassan! Come!" one of the Persians yelled. My companion nodded at me and rushed off.

I went straight to my uncle and sat near him as he slept. When my father returned, we shook my uncle awake and I told them what the Persian had said about the closing of the trade route to the West.

"What can we do?" I asked.

This was a crisis of major magnitude. We had to decide: Should we keep moving? Or stay where we were? Or turn back and return to the capital city, Cambaluc, where our journey had begun six weeks ago?

My father, Uncle Maffeo, and I had long, heated discussions about this. I argued that the Khan had sent Nomokhan and an army of six thousand soldiers for this very purpose, to ensure that the trade routes to the West remained open. The soldiers had pushed ahead of us; by the time we reached Almalik, the Silk Road might be reopened. I wanted to keep going, to get to the fortress of Almalik. That was where Emmajin would be.

My father thought we should turn back. If the land route was closed, we should not waste any more time traveling west. Instead, we should explore options of returning home by sea.

My uncle, coughing heavily by now, settled the question. For the moment, he could not travel either east or west. He needed to rest. He believed we should stay in Gold City, with the Persian caravan, and wait for news from the Desert West. So we decided to stay put.

That night, I tossed in bed. My Emmajin was galloping further and further away from me, and I had to wait indefinitely in this god-forsaken dust bowl, with its surly shopkeepers and murky water.

Over the next month, Gold City began to wake up. More and more merchant caravans, large and small, Turkic, Arabian, Persian, and Russian, arrived in the riverside town and stopped their journeys. Some, like us, came from the east, heard about the closure of the trade routes, and realized it was useless to keep going west. Others, like the Persian traders, came from the west after getting stuck at Almalik. No one had met up with any caravans that had come from the Far West, allowed to pass through Khaidu's lands. There must be, I imagined, a town like this to the west of Khaidu's territory, where caravans traveling east had stopped to wait also, unable to go any farther.

The concentration of traders from many countries in one place was stimulating and made for great fun. Those with lutes and flutes and horsehead fiddles began to play for us, and I saw many a lively dance. Men in boots kicked out their heels and tried to teach me the vigorous dances they had learned from childhood.

But they distracted me only for a short time from thinking of Emmajin. If the Mongol army fought against Khaidu, would Emmajin fight? She had laid her bow down before the Great Khan, symbolizing her decision to give up warfare. But she was a born fighter. In my gut I knew, if it came to war, she would fight. To reach the Pope, to make peace with the West, it might be necessary to fight to reopen the trade routes. And this fight would be Mongol against Mongol.

I tortured myself with images of Emmajin arming herself for battle.

---

One day, a small caravan arrived from the Khan's capital, Cambaluc. Five Mongolian men, dressed in silks with sashes of cloth-of-gold, arrived from the east. They spoke to no one.

But Wei-ming, my ever resourceful mah-foo, befriended one of their mah-foos by offering him fine airag. The two discovered they were distant relatives; Wei-ming's cousin had married the other mah-foo's aunt. They stayed up late, drinking, and the other mah-foo told Wei-ming something he should never have mentioned.

The next morning, when my uncle was sleeping and my father was drinking tea with the Persian traders, Wei-ming asked to speak with me privately. His dark eyes flashed, as if he were harboring a secret.

We walked away from the inn to the riverfront, where we strolled along the water's edge, under the willow trees. Wei-ming kept looking back over his shoulder and would not open up until he was sure no one could overhear us.

"They are on an urgent mission, those Mongolian officials," he began. "They left early this morning, rushing to the west."

"What did he tell you?" I asked.

Wei-ming glanced over his shoulder again. "He was not sup-posed to say anything."

"And?"

"Those men are officials from the Great Khan's court. They are very worried. Not long after we left Cambaluc, with Nomokhan's army, they found out that Shirki's wife and children had left town, disappeared!"

That was strange. But what could it mean? I nodded for Wei-ming to continue.

"Shirki is a nephew of the Great Khan. His father was the previ-ous Great Khan, Mongke, Khubilai's brother. He thinks his branch of the family should inherit the throne."

Wei-ming looked at me as if I would immediately grasp the implications of this, but I didn't. "What does it matter, that his family left town?"

"That's what I said, sir. But the mah-foo told me. The Great Khan's men captured one of the former servants in Shirki's household, and tortured him till he confessed." He leaned toward me and whis-pered. "Shirki and some other officers plan to betray the Great Khan and his son Nomokhan. They are traveling with the Khan's army, but once they get to Almalik, they plan to switch sides. The servant said that they plan to steal away a lot of the Khan's troops and align them-selves with Khaidu."

"Switch sides!" This news shocked me. So Shirki was the traitor. Who else might be a traitor, among those six thousand men? What would it mean for Nomokhan, and for Temur—and for Emmajin?

Wei-ming shook his head solemnly. "Exactly. It appears that Nomokhan has no idea. They are carrying a sealed message from the Khan, rushing to warn him of these plans before it's too late."

"But the Mongol troops are traveling quickly, up to two hun-dred li per day. By now they are many weeks ahead of us. How can anyone catch up?"

"He complained, the mah-foo did, that they are galloping all day every day, as fast as they can push their horses. They switched to fresh horses here in Gold City, so they can push on at the same pace."

The bottom fell out of my stomach. Emmajin was in danger, in grave danger. This, clearly, was what the shaman had predicted.

If Shirki was willing to betray the Great Khan, why would he value the lives of the Khan's son, grandson and granddaughter? Might Shirki take them prisoner? Hold them for ransom?

Or might Shirki and his secret supporters turn and fight against those troops still loyal to the Great Khan? Temur was in line for the throne, standing in Shirki's way. Was Nomokhan powerful enough to stop this traitor? And what troops might follow Shirki? I realized that I knew very little about the Mongol Army, about the loyalty of any given group of soldiers.

The shaman's warning seemed vividly real now. Traitors. Capture. Defeat.

The more I thought about Wei-ming's news, the more I agonized. Did Emmajin know of these rumors? Did Temur? Someone needed to warn them, to tell them to take precautions.

It might not be too late to alter Fate.

That night I could not sleep, so agitated I was. How could I linger in Lazy City with my father and uncle when Emmajin was in danger? I was tempted to rush on, to try to catch up to her, to get to Almalik when the officials got there. Yet what could I do to help her if I did?

Should I, could I, leave our merchant caravan and hurry ahead to warn her? How could I possibly gallop fast enough to catch up?

Yet the more I thought about it, the more it seemed that was the right thing to do. The only thing to do.

Emmajin had asked me to keep my distance from her. But she didn't know about this danger. I had to find some way to catch up to her and warn her.

# Chapter 8
# Emmajin: Khaidu's Demand

That afternoon, when everyone in Turpan escaped the blast of the summer sun by napping in the hostel, Nasreen had put wet compresses on my head to cool me down, then started to rub my feet.

This vigorous foot rubbing was a habit she had begun from her first days with me. It was part of the healing techniques she had learned, and she knew of various spots of my feet that corresponded to different ailments of the body.

The air lay thick around us, sapping all my energy. I was lying back on my elbows, and she was rubbing my feet when I asked her bluntly:

"Did you spend the night with Temur?"

Her hands stopped briefly then continued the gentle massage. She did not look up or answer, but she was blushing.

"Did he force you, against your will?" I persisted.

A slight frown crossed her forehead and she gave a quick shake of her head, as if saying 'no' to herself, not to me.

"Nasreen! Talk to me! You're *my* slave, and you don't have to do what Temur asks." I was angry. Temur had plenty of women to use for such purposes; he should have kept his hands off my maidservant.

She looked up to me with a combination of strong emotions I found hard to read. I thought of her husband, who had been taken from her by sickness, and her family, who had been taken from her by force. Most of her life was beyond her control.

"Temur was wrong to ask you to do that," I said. "You know that, right?"

This time she gave me an elder-sister look, from an experienced woman to a younger one. "Not entirely, Your Highness."

I leaned forward and put my hands on hers, which were still rubbing my feet. "Nasreen, for once, talk to me directly, as a woman. Did you enjoy it?"

She looked up at the wood-beamed ceiling and blinked her eyes; her mouth curved into a slight smile.

I fell back to my elbows. At court, as a child, I had heard that carnal relations could be painful and terrible, especially if the man was drunk and the woman was forced. After all Nasreen had been through, how could she find pleasure in such an act when she had no choice in it? I doubted Temur had spoken to her of love. Shouldn't love and sex go together?

"Surely you understand," I persisted. "He's a prince. He takes whatever woman he wants, when he wants. Especially slaves."

She began rubbing harder, pushing her thumbs into the soles of my feet. "Yes, Your Highness."

"A young woman back at court is betrothed to him, awaiting his return. Eventually he will be expected to take four wives and many concubines."

"I could be a concubine," she said.

So that's what she was thinking! That would be a major step up in her status. "At court, even concubines are from good families," I said. "None of them are slaves."

"I hear that the sons of concubines are treated equally with the sons of wives."

This was true, or nearly so. Only the sons of the chief wife were eligible to take the throne, but all other sons were given equal privileges. And Temur could elevate Nasreen to the status of concubine if he chose, even though she was a slave. This seemed unlikely, after just one encounter.

"You want to be a concubine?" I asked, finding this ambition easier to imagine than any love between them. "Then why give yourself to him for nothing?"

"He gave me this." She stopped rubbing and pulled a small silver amulet out of her sash. It was a cheap trinket, something he had probably picked up when he traveled to southern China with the army. On it, ironically, was a picture of the same goddess I prayed to, Tara, the Protectress, goddess of mercy. This annoyed me. Tara was pure, and her image should not be traded for favors.

"At best, you'd be a sex slave," I said harshly.

She gently put the amulet back in her sash.

"Nasreen. You work for me. Aunt Yurak is expecting you to return to her. I won't let him have you."

She began rubbing my feet again. I thought the conversation was over, but a short time later, she added, "You have your freedom. It inspires me. Why can't a woman love whatever man she chooses?"

It was true, I wanted to love whatever man I chose. But I was a princess of the royal court. It had never occurred to me that a maidservant might want the same. Especially if the man she wanted was my cousin, a royal prince. The idea was almost too big, too radical, for me to contemplate.

"I'm ready to rest now," I said. That hot afternoon, I got out Marco's beads and held them as I fell asleep, hoping to clear my thinking. Listening to Nasreen's soft breathing not far from me in my tent, I marveled at what she had been dreaming about, these last months. Her desires seemed as wrong to me as mine did to others.

That evening at dinner, Temur tried to avoid me. But on the way back to our rooms, I confronted him.

"Temur," I said. "Leave Nasreen alone."

"A pleasing woman," Temur said. I got the feeling he was search-ing my face for signs of jealousy.

"She deserves better."

"Better than me? It's an honor for her. I can choose whatever woman I want. Except you, of course." A slight tone of mocking bit-terness crept into his voice.

"You're crazy, Temur. We all know that cousins of the Golden Family, up to five generations distant, are not to marry."

"I didn't ask you to marry me. Are you still pretending you're a maiden?"

I was ready to throw something at him. Did he think I was fair game for any man—even my *cousin*—since I had admitted to loving Marco? "So you have the right to take any woman you want?"

"Yes, with some obvious exceptions. Did you think otherwise? Nothing stops me."

"Then why can't I do likewise?"

Temur laughed sardonically. "Women get pregnant and bear children. That's why the rules are different. Obviously!"

This I had learned the hard way, but it still seemed unfair. "Ai-Jaruk can have any man she wants." I wasn't sure of this, but I had heard it.

Temur snorted. "That's disgusting."

"It's disgusting for you to take any woman you want."

"You're the one who talks about courtly love," Temur retorted.

"The love I talk about doesn't mean grabbing someone random and taking him back to my tent."

"This wasn't random. I've been watching Nasreen for a long time."

Why hadn't I noticed this? Besides, he had been drunk, and he had reached for me first. "That's not love," I said.

"How do you know?"

"Do you love Nasreen?"

"I want to take her scarf to battle. I would die for her." Temur grinned wickedly. Sometimes he was too smart for his own good.

"Don't mock Marco."

"Why not? Don't fool yourself, Emmajin. He wants what I want."

Anger boiled up in me but I couldn't think of an answer. This thought had occurred to me, too, but I had dismissed it. The way Temur said it, it sounded obvious.

"It's just much harder for him to get it," Temur continued relentlessly. "So he needs fancy words and stories."

I refused to take the bait. "I don't want you hurting Nasreen. She's been hurt enough in her life. Did you know she was born free?"

"No. But I'm sure she will tell me."

That made me angry—his certainty that he would continue to see her. And yet I remembered the coy way she had smiled. "Be gentle with her, please?"

Temur's face softened. "She's just a slave. But she's a good woman."

After that, Nasreen rubbed my feet each night before bed and then disappeared for a few hours. She was always there for me in the morning, often humming.

Temur never mentioned her to me, but he seemed less sharp. We resumed our easy talks. I did not want Temur judging my feelings for Marco, so I had to suspend mine about his relations with Nasreen.

After a few days in Turpan, we resumed our journey through the parched plateaus of East Turkestan. We rode along the Northern Silk Road, skirting the edge of the Great Lop Desert, also known as Taklamakan, the place of no return. After that, the road began climbing, and the Heavenly Mountains came to dominate the horizon to our right.

Riding hard all day, every day, I could not stop my mind from spinning. I was tempted to refuse to let Nasreen leave my tent at night. But I decided to let her have this small taste of freedom.

Temur did not mention Nasreen to me again, but I could see his eyes watching her as she moved about. I withdrew from him, but that made me lonelier. Of the six thousand men I was traveling with, Temur was the only man I cared about. He began to spend all his time with his commander, Shirki.

Alone again, my thoughts turned more and more to Marco. What did I really want? Could I, as a royal princess, simply take what I wanted and no more, regardless of Marco's feelings? Marco wanted to spend time alone with me, I knew that. But what else did he want? Or did he, as Temur implied, simply want me in his bed? As more distance separated me from Marco, I began to forget the joy I had felt in his presence.

Now I faced a new quandary. If Khaidu was powerful enough to close the trade routes, if our troops under Nomokhan could not quickly force them open, as I had assumed they would, then I could not complete my mission. So what was I doing, galloping so fast to the West? The two things I wanted most in the world—to be with Marco and to reach the Pope with the Khan's letter and ensure peace with the West—both seemed far out of reach, over the horizon. I felt as though I were riding straight into a huge stone wall.

The first step was to reach Almalik as soon as we could, to bolster the Khan's troops there. That was, in fact, the farthest point in the realm actually controlled by Khubilai Khan. Beyond it were the lands of Khaidu—technically part of the Mongol Empire but clearly not under Khubilai's control.

But after that—what might we face? A battle with Khaidu? Many of the soldiers were itching for that. None more so than Temur. When I had been off fighting the Battle of Vochan, he had been in southern China, but he had yet to fight in a battle. He spoke often of bravery and valor, though he knew nothing of them. I knew, better than he did, that military practice did not truly prepare you for the horrors of the battlefield.

But it seemed wrong to deal with Khaidu by fighting him. He was a fellow Mongol after all, even if he defied the Khan. Our Great Ancestor taught that we should not spill the blood of others in the Golden Family.

The best solution, by far, would be the one Nomokhan had suggested: to find a peaceful way to convince Khaidu to cooperate. I could not imagine what Khaidu was thinking. If his motivation was to topple the Great Khan and take his throne, then obviously we could not work with him. But that seemed absurd. Khubilai Khan's power was at its peak; he had just conquered the Song Dynasty of China. Why would any Mongol choose this moment to defy the Khan of all Khans?

———

Once we confirmed the news that Khaidu had blocked all roads to the West, our troops began to travel even faster. The summer days were long, and each day, we began riding at dawn and did not set up our tents until nearly dusk. There was no time for leisurely conversation by the fire; after meals, everyone fell asleep. Temur rode with his commander, Shirki, so I was alone much of the time. Nasreen continued to serve me in her quiet, confident way—a calming presence but hardly a companion.

I had been thinking a lot about my assignment, to befriend Ai-Jaruk. It would be touchy, I knew, because of Khaidu's belligerence. It might even be impossible now. I doubted I could get Ai-Jaruk to come to me. I might need to go to her, to show I trusted her and her father.

The very idea of meeting Ai-Jaruk both attracted and intimidated me. Ever since I had first heard her story, told by Marco back in Xanadu, I had envisioned that we would immediately form a bond, like sisters. And yet Ai-Jaruk, the unbeatable woman warrior, had done far greater deeds than I had. I had fought in only one battle; she had fought in many. She excelled at wrestling; I was too thin and light. But I had heard she was a fantastic archer; so was I. Perhaps if I took her on in archery, she would respect me.

Finally I came up with a great idea: to stage an archery competition between Ai-Jaruk and me, inviting troops from both Khubilai Khan's army and Khaidu's. Instead of fighting a battle, the soldiers from these two sides could each cheer on their favorite woman warrior. The more I thought about this idea, the more I liked it. Sport, not war, could unite us Mongols. Even if I lost, I might defuse the tension.

Nomokhan would need to endorse the idea and plan for it. He had dealt with Khaidu before, and he would know the best location and timing. So, at one of our rest stops in the midst of the long journey, I approached his large tent after dinner. It was a dark evening, with only a sliver of moon.

Nomokhan's guards let me into his tent, but asked me to sit in a waiting area near the door. At the far back of his large tent, my uncle was speaking loudly to someone I did not recognize at first.

"It's the only way!" the other man shouted. "We must negotiate with him."

I looked at my hands in my lap and tried to remain invisible so that I could hear this conversation. This other man was Shirki, I realized.

"We've tried, again and again," said my uncle. "Now that he's closed off the roads, he is making impossible demands."

"Negotiation is better than war, isn't it?" Shirki asked.

"The Khan will never accept this," said Nomokhan. "Khaidu has no right to rule such a large territory. These lands west of the desert were left to others, and their ruler must acknowledge the Great Khan's sovereignty over all lands of the Empire.

"Besides," continued Nomokhan, "Khaidu can't forget what happened, how power passed to our side of the family. So many of his relatives in Ogodei's clan were killed."

Shirki remained silent for a moment. It was his father, Mongke Khan, who had seized power from Ogodei's clan. I sensed that the other officers were looking at Shirki, waiting for his response. Finally he spoke. "Khaidu just wants respect, a small khanate for himself. There are no big cities in the territory he demands, just grasslands. It's a small price to pay, if Khaidu is willing to reopen the trade routes and assure his loyalty."

"That's the question, isn't it," said Nomokhan. "If we grant him the right to rule this large territory, can we be assured of his loyalty?"

"Yes, I'm sure we can," said Shirki.

I jumped to my feet and barged into their high-level discussion.

"I can help," I said, emerging into the light of the fire they sat around.

All three of the men were taken aback at my interruption.

"I will talk with Ai-Jaruk. Khaidu listens to her." I told them about my plan to stage an archery contest between Ai-Jaruk and myself, somewhere between our fortress and the lands Khaidu controlled, for the entertainment of men from both our troops and his.

The military men listened in silence until I finished.

"Sport, not war, could unite us Mongols." After I finished speaking, silence hung heavily in the air.

"It could work," said Shirki. My opinion of him leaped.

"We will think about this," said Nomokhan. "You may go, Emmajin Beki."

In high spirits, I left. My voice had been heard in the highest councils of war. The solution to this troubling dilemma might just lie in the muscled arms of two women.

---

Finally we emerged from the desert. Riding uphill past fields of summer wildflowers, we crossed over a pass through the snow-capped Heavenly Mountains and followed a ravine down into the pleasant valley of the Ili River.

When the moon was full again in Seventh Moon, we arrived at our destination: the town of Almalik, farthest outpost of the Great Khan's empire. We had left the Khan's capital of Khanbalik when the moon was full in Fifth Moon, so our journey took exactly two months. That was astonishingly fast. Still, we were less than halfway to Christendom.

After so many days of brown desert scenery, the sight of Almalik on the Ili River seemed like a return to civilization. It was a charming green valley, nestled between two brown ridges of the Heavenly Mountains, intensely cultivated with grain fields and orchards. Along the swift-flowing river stood neat rows of fruit trees. Fields were covered with vines growing Hami melons, with sweet green flesh.

We slowed down and took our time passing through the town of Almalik, a large, crowded center for trade and agriculture along a sprawling river valley. Traders approached us with large baskets of melons and apricots as we passed through. I bought a handful of apricots and savored their ripe sweetness.

We proceeded to the garrison on the far side, a large military camp surrounded by a high stone wall, protecting the town and valley from the marauders to the west. In charge of the garrison was General Hantum, formerly Right Minister of the Khan, who had been given temporary command the previous winter, when General Nomokhan returned to the Khan's court. At Almalik, Hantum commanded thirty thousand troops; our traveling forces of six thousand swelled this number to thirty-six thousand.

This garrison was a tent city, with no permanent structures except the high stone wall surrounding it. At its center were four large tents, arranged in the cardinal directions, with the Khan's imperial pennant fluttering from the top of each. Each was rounded, but far bigger and more luxurious than a normal ger, decorated with carpets and tapestries in the colorful local style. The largest one, to the north, was reserved for General Nomokhan, and the south one was for General Hantum. General Shirki took up residence in the western one. That left only the eastern one. Normally, as members of the youngest generation, Temur and I would have shared it, but since I was a woman, Temur chose to stay with Shirki. So I had the huge ger to myself.

Nomokhan and Shirki immediately went into meetings with Hantum, as well as other high commanders. As a prince, Temur was invited to attend; I was not.

The discussion went on for many days, and twice I saw messengers ride out of the fort, to the west, then return six days later. I assumed that meant that Khaidu's camp was three days away.

Every time I saw Temur, his face was drawn and worried, but he refused to tell me what was being discussed at these high-level meetings. More than ever, it bothered me that I, as a woman with no standing in the army, was excluded. After all, Nomokhan and Shirki had listened to my suggestion about the archery contest. Were they seriously discussing it?

In the meantime, I picked up my bow and began practicing furiously. I needed to get back my skills after too many months on horseback. The idea of an archery contest began to seem more and more likely the longer the talks went on. It was the only way. Perhaps Nomokhan had made the proposal and was waiting for Khaidu to accept.

Finally, one afternoon, Temur came to my tent. His manner was intense and his brow creased. I ordered Nasreen to bring him fresh airag. "You have come from the meeting?" I wanted badly to know what was discussed in high councils.

"I have. But I am sworn to silence."

This, I thought with annoyance, was the old Temur, deliberately coming to my tent to tell me he knew something I had no way of knowing, then refusing to tell me what it was. "Well, then, there's nothing to discuss. I'm getting ready for bed now."

He wanted me to beg for information. "Actually, it's important to your future."

"Is it?" I feigned indifference. "Then I'll find out sooner or later."

Now Temur was annoyed. I was refusing to play his game. He shook his head and leaned forward. "It's about Khaidu," he said.

"Has Khaidu agreed to the archery tournament?" I refused to give up hope. Many times I had imagined meeting Ai-Jaruk in this very tent, as regal a setting as could be had in this region.

Temur shook his head sadly. "No. Nomokhan liked the idea. But Khaidu flatly refused. He demands that we go to his camp and kowtow to him."

"What?" The idea seemed ridiculous. Nomokhan and Temur, son and grandson of the Great Khan Khubilai, kowtowing to Khaidu?

"Emmajin, he's more powerful than we thought. A few years back, Khaidu held a meeting of some men of the Golden Family. They declared him Great Khan."

A laugh burst from my lips. The very idea seemed absurd to one who had grown up in the palace of Khanbalik. Khaidu, a nomadic desert ruler, daring to get a few cousins together and declare that he had more right to the throne than the Great Khubilai Khan?

"He is a grandson of Ogodei, who was chosen by The Great Ancestor himself as successor." Ogodei's branch had not ruled for more than twenty years, not since my great uncle Mongke had been named Great Khan.

I thought of the thirty-six thousand troops amassed around us, all loyal to the Great Khan. "Khaidu has no power," I said.

"True, Khaidu has fewer troops than we do, but he has a choke-hold on the road to the West. We can't even send a messenger to Persia without Khaidu's approval." Temur's dark eyes exuded a hard intensity.

I stood up and stepped closer to Temur, matching his intensity. "This is my moment, Temur. Tell the generals that I will speak to Ai-Jaruk and get her father to cooperate. Everyone says he respects his daughter. Nomokhan has already asked me to take on this task. It is the best hope we have."

"His daughter!" Temur laughed, ruefully stepping back. "They are trying to set up a meeting now—between Nomokhan and Khaidu. You and I won't get to go. But they will be talking about you."

"Talking about me?" So perhaps the archery tournament would go ahead.

Temur looked at his hands. "I don't know the right way to say this, Emmajin Beki. There may be a role for you, to ensure peace with Khaidu. But it's not what you think."

I frowned. "What role then?"

He tapped his fingers on his thighs, as if nervous about letting me in on a secret. "Khaidu has laid down a condition. He will talk to Nomokhan only if he promises to give you over to Khaidu to marry his son."

His words hit me like a blow to the stomach. Royal daughters and granddaughters were often traded as brides to strengthen alliances, but I had assumed I was an exception. After all, Khubilai Khan had permitted me to join his army. And I had proved myself in battle. I stared, hard, into his eyes.

"Our grandfather, the Great Khan, would never allow such a thing."

Temur shook his head. "The Great Khan is far away. Nomokhan is in charge here. His task is to gain Khaidu's cooperation. He'll do whatever is required."

I hoped that Temur was bluffing. Maybe he was jealous of me, now that I was about to play out a prominent role assigned to me by Prince Nomokhan, negotiating with Ai-Jaruk. But Temur's face was serious. "Is that what you want, Temur Oljaitu, for me to be traded off as a bride to the Khan's rival?"

"Of course not! I'd rather fight! That's what I've been arguing for. It's wrong for him to trade you as a bride, like a bribe."

A battle with Khaidu no longer sounded bad. "Well, then," I said. "Go back and make sure he listens to you."

Temur looked at me as if he had expected me to gasp and faint and plead. If he was going to show off his influence and access to power, let him prove it. Dismissed in this unexpected way, Temur got up and left.

I saw him out, then sat down, hard. Despite my act of indifference, my skin was hot as if I had a fever.

Nasreen came to me with a wet cloth and wiped my forehead. I could tell from her eyes that she had heard the news.

"It can't happen. It won't," I said.

"If it does, I will go with you," she said.

My heart swelled with her generosity, but I shook my head vigorously. "No! Neither of us will go."

She wiped my face and regarded me with the look of a fond compassion, an older and wiser woman who knew that most women had no choice in their future. I had had a remarkably good run, she seemed to say, able to control my fate far more than most women. Now it was about to come to an end.

Nomokhan could not, would not, trade me as a bride. The Great Khan would never approve this. I was so visible, an important symbol, the first woman to join the army. I was an equal of Ai-Jaruk's, if not her superior; I was not a lowly sister-in-law. Besides, the Khan had assigned me the mission of going to Rome.

But for Khaidu it would be a coup—demanding and getting the Khan's favorite granddaughter, a warrior, as bride for his son. Had I been fooling myself, thinking that I would be treated differently from any other royal princess?

If this was true, then it was Nomokhan who was the traitor, as foretold by the shaman. The Khan was fond of me, but my fate did not figure large in the list of important imperial issues. Uncle Nomokhan was the one who put me in danger.

I put my forehead in my hands. I had tried so hard to earn the respect of my family. If you are loyal to country and to your ruler, they should be loyal to you. Yet of course this thought was naïve. If No-mokhan traded me to Khaidu, I would lose my freedom, control over my life, any future with Marco, my role as a soldier and an ambassador, and my status with the Great Khan. Everything at once.

Had it all been a pipe dream? When you scratched the surface of any Mongol man, perhaps of any man at all, women didn't count.

---

For the next several days, the generals continued to meet for long hours of discussion. I sent a message to Nomokhan, requesting an audience, but received no response. I dictated a letter, explaining how I planned to carry out Nomokhan's assignment to befriend Ai-Jaruk, given the new developments. I could bring Khaidu to our side, by talking to Ai-Jaruk. Still, Nomokhan did not respond.

I felt a growing sense of desperation. I needed a plan. Finally, one night, I decided. I would force my way into Nomokhan's tent and make them listen to me.

But the next morning, I found out it was too late. As soon as I stepped out of my tent into the pale light, I heard the news: General Nomokhan had just left Almalik, riding off with Shirki down the Ili River valley to the west. They were going to meet with Khaidu, to negotiate a final settlement. That was a bad sign for me. Temur did not go with them. It was considered too dangerous.

Rumors swirled around the garrison. General Nomokhan's mission was supposed to be secret, but everyone seemed to know. No-mokhan had arranged to meet with Khaidu at a designated site half-way between Almalik and Khaidu's camp—at the junction of two rivers. It would take them each a day and a half to get there.

By agreement, Nomokhan took with him only one thousand troops, since the plan was to meet and talk, not to fight. He would present the Great Khan Khubilai's demands: that Khaidu declare loy-alty and join his troops with ours. Khaidu must allow safe passage through his territory for our troops, for messengers and for all trading caravans. In exchange, Nomokhan would offer—what? In the camp, no one seemed to know. But I knew. It made me sick.

The only way out was to flee. I had to go back to the east now, to find Marco.

I ran back into my tent and began to collect everything I owned. Nasreen looked at me with alarm. "Pack up," I said. "We are leaving now." She obeyed.

Just then, Temur came to my tent. He looked defeated. "It is done. Our uncle is taking a message to Khaidu."

"I won't do it," I said. "I am leaving. Now. I'll go back east. The Great Khan will agree; this cannot happen."

Temur shook his head. "Nomokhan left orders. Your tent is to be carefully guarded. If you make any trouble, General Hantum is authorized to lock you up."

So. I was a prisoner among my own people. My own family. My own army.

I rushed out of the tent door, not thinking, ready to run to my horse, to begin riding, anywhere, away from here.

Immediately, a guard stopped me, holding his sword sideways to block my way. When I tried to push past him, he held my arms and would not let me pass. "Apologies, royal princess," he said. "I have to follow orders."

I fell to my knees and wept.

———————

That evening, Temur came to my tent, to eat a simple meal with me. We ate in silence. Nasreen served us both mutton soup and hovered nearby. Temur watched her but said nothing. Had he spoken to her about her future? Would she remain loyal to me, as she had promised? Or might Temur give her a better offer?

Temur seemed to quake with suppressed frustration and anger. I knew he wanted to protect me, to prevent what was about to happen. He had just not figured out how.

It occurred to me that we would not have many such meals together in the future.

Just as we finished our meal, the sound of voices erupted outside our tent door. A man was arguing with our guards. Temur jumped up and drew his sword, facing the door. I scrambled for my sword. Our uncle was gone; who might wish us ill?

The voices were garbled and unclear, growing louder. My guards were shouting, insisting that no one was allowed to enter. I froze in fear, at the back of the tent, watching Temur go to the door. Had someone come to drag me away? What danger faced me now?

Temur burst out of the tent door, shouting, "Who dares disturb us?"

The tent flap fell back into place before I could see the commotion on the other side. But I could hear Temur's voice: "What? You again?"

I drew my sword and dashed to the tent entrance, pushing aside the tent flap. Outside the doorway, in the dark, I could see a thrashing of men and hear the metal clashing of swords. It seemed there was a single intruder, not a group of armed men. In the moment it took for my eyes to adjust, Temur had disarmed and downed the assailant and had his sword pointed at his throat. I was impressed.

"Important message from the Great Khan! You must listen!" the prisoner shouted. To my shock, I realized it was Marco's voice, although higher than I had ever heard it.

Marco! My heart leaped. How could he possibly be here, in Almalik, at the very edge of the Khan's territory, at this very moment when my future was in jeopardy?

"Temur, stop!" I used my sword to try to stop him, but the tip of his blade nicked the skin of Marco's neck and a tiny spurt of blood popped out.

Temur used his hip to shove me aside. "It's that foreigner, the scum. Whatever reason he's come, it's too late."

# Part III:
# Decisions

# Chapter 9
# Marco: Heroic Warning

Pinned to the ground, knife to my throat, this was not how I had envisioned my reunion with Emmajin—or my role as hero arriving to the rescue. During many long days in the saddle, making a perilous journey, I had imagined myself as a cavalier, Galahad or Percival, galloping in on my steed to save the day and rescue the princess. Now here I was, dusty and dirty from the long journey, my hair greasy and stringy, staring into the eyes of a prince who hated me.

I clutched at my neck and struggled, but the guards pinned my arms. "Prince Temur!" I shouted. "I've come on the Great Khan's business. Kill me if you will, but first hear His Majesty's message!"

Temur snorted. "The Great Khan would never send *you* with a message!"

"Hear him out!" Emmajin's voice sounded almost as strangled as I felt.

Her cousin pulled his knife back and placed its tip on my chin. "Speak, dog."

I coughed, half expecting to spit blood. "I traveled with the official messenger of the Khan. He went directly to Prince Nomokhan's tent. But the message cannot wait."

"What messenger?"

A crowd was gathering around us, and someone shouted. "It's true. A swift messenger from the court has arrived. He is reporting to General Hantum now."

Temur leaned closer to me, keeping his dagger pressed on my chin, and hissed: "If you're lying again, this is your last day."

The Great Khan's grandson sheathed his knife and stood up. "Guards!" he commanded. "Keep this foreigner here till I return." He strode off toward another large tent in the compound, to hear what the messenger had to say.

In a moment, my lady Emmajin was kneeling at my side, her calloused fingers gently touching my neck. Dressed in a del of summer-sky blue, she pulled out the end of her sun-yellow silk sash and pressed it against my wound. I thought of Isolde the healer, caring for Tristan.

Emmajin's arm at my back, I sat up, then stood as she guided me into her large tent. The guards stopped at the doorway but kept watch. I sat on a stool by the fire pit as her maid used a clean cloth to wipe the blood away. Fortunately, the wound was only superficial. Her servant brought forth a balm and applied it gently to my neck.

Worry clouded Emmajin's exquisite face, and I could not tell if my lady was glad to see me or not. I remembered the first time I had observed her close up; she had banged her nose against her horse's neck and it was bleeding profusely. Her nose had healed perfectly, in a straight line with no hint of a break. *Deo gratias*, she looked safe and well.

"Why are you smiling?" she asked.

Because I feel overjoyed to see you, I wanted to say. But I knew better than to say this, at that tense moment. She was right. This was not the occasion for a smile, so I set my mouth firmly. "The messenger brings grim news," I said.

Her hands dropped to her sides, and she cocked one eyebrow, waiting.

I looked around and noted that the guards and Emmajin's maidservant were far away, by the door. "Prince Nomokhan is in great danger," I whispered.

Her brows hardened. "Meaning what?"

"Is he here? Is he with Shirki?"

"Why? What is the message?" She seemed brusque now. After months of traveling with the army, her soft side was invisible.

"It's about Prince Shirki," I said, *sotto voce*. "He plans to betray Khubilai Khan and Prince Nomokhan. He's the traitor."

"Shirki?" Emmajin frowned. "Shirki is the Khan's nephew. He is loyal."

I glanced again at the guards, remembering all too well how actions observed and words overheard can lead to trouble. "After you left, Shirki's entire household moved out of Cambaluc, in the dead of night, and headed for Karakorum. There might be time to stop him."

Her maid walked over and handed me a bowl of airag, the traditional way of treating a guest. I shifted uncomfortably, not wanting her to hear anything I might say.

Noticing my nervousness, Emmajin commanded Nasreen to sit by the door. When the maid was out of hearing range, my lady turned to me. "Go on."

I knew that her cousin Temur was close to that traitor, Shirki. What I didn't know was how close my lady might have grown to both Temur and Shirki, in the months they had been travelling together.

As I sipped the airag, my eyes drank in every detail of Emmajin's beloved face: her intelligent eyes, her full lips, the wisps of black hair that had fallen out of her braids. "The Khan captured Shirki's master-servant and tortured him till the truth came out. Shirki ordered his family to quit Cambaluc because he anticipated danger for them."

Emmajin sat in silence, as if thinking this through. A frown fluttered across her smooth ivory brow. No man loyal to the Great Khan would expect his family to come to great danger in the Khan's capital. "What does he plan to do?"

"No one knows. But if Shirki went away with Nomokhan, far from the garrison of Almalik, it could go badly. How many of the Khan's troops went with them? Are they all loyal to Nomokhan?"

Emmajin swallowed hard, as if battling deep misgivings before discussing troop movements with a foreigner. This time, she whispered. "Only one thousand soldiers went with them, by agreement. Khaidu was to bring one thousand, too. Shirki insisted that half of the Khan's troops be from his own regiment."

"Half the Khan's troops that went with Nomokhan are loyal to Shirki?"

My question hung in the air. I could almost see the implications racing through Emmajin's mind. Nomokhan and Shirki, camped in the wilderness tonight, would the next day meet with Khaidu. If Shirki threw his support to Khaidu, the two of them could easily kill Nomokhan and take charge of his troops.

I could see my own fear reflected in her eyes.

A crash of pottery broke the silence, and we both looked toward the door. Her maidservant had dropped a bowl and spilled airag on the boot of a guard. The ensuing hubbub gave us a few more minutes to speak.

"This is what the Khan's messenger is reporting?" she asked me.

"I believe so. Do you want to hear it from him?"

Emmajin sat back and straightened her shoulders. She looked up, as if examining the smoke hole in the ceiling of the round tent. I was surprised to see a flicker of relief.

She sighed. "Nomokhan was planning to make me marry Khaidu's son."

My breath caught in my throat. "That can't happen!"

She slowly shook her head. "Not now. But now Nomokhan's life is at risk. He could be killed."

"Or captured." This scenario had occurred to me. If Khaidu imprisoned the Great Khan's son, Khaidu could hold him for ransom, making outrageous demands.

"Shirki might come back here to the fortress and take control of the Khan's troops," she said.

This had not occurred to me. "How many troops are here?"

Her voice dropped again to a whisper. "Not quite 40,000." Four tumens of the Khan's troops, a major part of his army, might be turned over, in effect, to Khaidu. An alliance between Shirki and Khaidu might give them enough armed manpower to turn fully against the Great Khan.

"It would be open war," I said.

Emmajin's lips tightened. "That cannot be allowed to happen."

I put down my drinking bowl and leaned forward on the wooden stool. "My lady," I began. My mind scrambled for the words I had practiced during long hours in the saddle. "Come away with me, now. The road to the West is blocked. We cannot stay here; this fortress is not safe. If we head back east, we could hide in the Heavenly Mountains. Then later, while everyone's attention is on the battle, we could head west, just the two of us, taking the Great Khan's letter to the Pope..."

She laughed. She actually laughed at me. "O, Marco. Is that what you call a plan? Hide out in the Heavenly Mountains while the Mongol soldiers fight the worst traitor in Mongol history? You want me to crouch in a cave while my fellow soldiers die in battle?"

*Come away with me. Please.* That's all I wanted to say to her.

This time, Emmajin lowered her voice, till I could barely hear it. "A man lost his life because he saw us together, alone. You want me to ride out of this fortress with you and hide in the mountains?"

My proposal sounded ridiculous, the way she said it. When I had said it to myself, and to my horse, it had not sounded absurd at all.

She pressed on. "Is that my destiny, you think?"

"What is your destiny?" I dared ask, in a small voice. Obviously, her destiny did not include a Latin lover.

She looked off to the smoke hole in the ceiling again. "I don't know. I used to think it was to deliver the Khan's letter to the Pope, to ensure peace between your land and mine. Recently, I've thought

it was to befriend Khaidu's daughter, the warrior Ai-Jaruk. Uncle Nomokhan thinks my destiny is to marry Khaidu's son; I hope that's not
it. Now you think my destiny is to run away and live in the wilderness."

I pleaded with my eyes. Tristan and Isolde did, for three years, I
thought but did not say. If you chose me, we would...

At that moment, Temur burst into the tent and strode over to
Emmajin. His words tumbled out. "I just heard the news. General
Hantum is organizing a contingent of troops to catch up to Nomokhan
before he meets with Khaidu."

Temur had donned a suit of leather armor and seemed older now,
a commander as confident as any of the Khan's top men. "I'm going to
talk to him now," Temur continued. "I want to lead that contingent. I
must leave as soon as possible."

Emmajin stood up. Though not wearing armor, she too exuded
regal authority. "I will go, too. All Khaidu asked for was me."

My heart flipped. This was her answer to my plea? Had she even
heard me?

"No!" Temur's braid loops shook with his head. "You are not a
soldier now. You must wait here." For once, Temur and I were on the
same side, though he didn't know it.

She spoke in a calm voice. "Uncle Nomokhan commanded me to
speak to Khaidu's daughter. The time has come."

The two cousins, standing face to face, both strong-willed descendants of Chinggis Khan, looked alike at that moment: straight
noses, wide-set eyes, steely gazes.

"Emmajin," Temur said, almost pleading. "It's too late. There
may be fighting."

"I will not lounge behind these fortress walls."

I could contain myself no longer. Now Emmajin seemed to be
living in the land of legends. Valor was great in stories, but not worth

it when her precious life was at stake. I jumped up. "No! You could be killed."

Temur and Emmajin both turned toward me.

"You!" Temur's voice dripped with scorn. "You have no right to know any of this! Who else have you told?"

"No one! Of course."

Temur's eyes narrowed. "Guard!" he shouted.

Another guard entered the tent. Several must have been waiting outside.

"*Principessa!*" I spoke to Emmajin in Latin, hoping she would remember enough from our lessons. "Do not go with him. It is *periculosa.*"

I could tell from her eyes that she understood my meaning.

"What is he saying?" Temur demanded.

I could not read her mind. But she seemed to be contemplating two possible futures. Her eyes locked on mine, and she answered, slowly. "You're right, Temur. I choose to stay here." It barely sounded like her voice.

My heart surged as I read deeper meaning into her statement.

Temur looked at her, then at me. "With *him?* Is that what he wants? Is that want *you* want? When Nomokhan is in danger?"

Emmajin was looking straight into my eyes, as if into my soul. She had chosen me. She would not ride off into danger. A surge of astonished pleasure flooded my heart.

Temur looked from Emmajin to me and back again. "No. I won't allow it. I've changed my mind. You will ride at my side."

My objection got stuck in my throat. I could see in her brow, that she felt conflicted, tempted to stay, tempted to leave with him. My heart spun.

Prince Temur turned to the guards. "Take this foreigner away. Watch him day and night. Do not let him leave Almalik under any circumstances. This is an order from Prince Temur and hence from the Great Khan himself."

A guard took my arm and began to lead me away. I was too stunned to speak.

"Marco!" Emmajin said, just as I reached the door of her tent. Her eyes were brimming with turmoil. "Thank you. You have shown loyal service to the Great Khan."

Temur, too, nodded his head in reluctant acknowledgement.

I smiled grimly. Thank you? and a nod? Before locking me up like a potential traitor? I had risked my neck to save their lives, to prevent their betrayal by one of their own. Yet they could barely choke out a thank you.

Emmajin's shoulders fell slightly, and she smiled back, a look that mixed gratitude with apology. In Christendom, a princess would have swooned and fallen into my arms, weeping with thanks. At least, in the tales I had heard. Was this just the difference between life and legend? Or were Mongols fundamentally different from people in my part of the world?

Too many months on the road, separated from her, and I had forgotten the very nature of Emmajin. Given a choice between my embrace and a bold gesture to save the Great Khan, of course she would choose her people.

I had meant to save her life. Now she was preparing to ride off into the jaws of danger.

# Chapter 10
# Emmajin: The Battle at Ili River

As Temur and I walked to the general's tent, my heart was pounding so loudly I could barely hear. I felt like I was walking in a fog. Marco was here! What a miracle. He had shown enormous bravery by rushing here to warn us of this possible traitor in our midst. Yet Temur had treated him terribly. What was it that Marco had proposed? Things were happening too fast. I needed to think clearly, but everything was a blur.

Marco had come for me, to warn me, to keep me from danger. Yet Marco and I had not had time for a proper reunion. These past months, I had tried to put Marco out of my heart. Temur and I had grown closer, and he kept reminding me my primary duty was to the Khan and the Mongol Empire. My cousin's words had made sense, and I had begun to question my attraction to Marco. But just seeing Marco again, in person, hearing that charming, deep voice so close to my ear, had turned my head, yet again. I longed to see his green eyes wrinkle into a smile and hear that distinctive laugh. Was that disloyal?

My feet were walking away from Marco, but my heart was straining towards him. His proposal, to escape with him to the wilderness was totally unreasonable, ridiculous even. He imagined outcomes that never occurred to my more practical mind. All my military training, all my upbringing and values prepared me to jump up and ride into danger. I had to do everything in my power to prevent Shirki's treachery. There might still be a role I could play by conferring with

Ai-Jaruk. Yet leaving Marco, so soon after he arrived, brushing off his plea, seemed hard-hearted. The right choice was obvious, but it felt dead wrong.

"What if this message is a trick?" General Hantum asked us a few minutes later. When Temur and I entered his tent, he was examining a map with another officer, a burly, one-eyed man. Hantum did not unseal the message from the Khan; it was for Nomokhan's eyes only, but the messenger had revealed its contents to Hantum because of his role as commanding officer. Hantum's wind-roughened face remained calm but I could tell his sharp mind had been spinning. "Our enemies could be using it to try to draw the main strength of our troops out and away from the fortress."

Much wiser and more experienced than either Temur or I, General Hantum still seemed glad to talk over his plans with members of the Khan's family, young as we were. He told us he had decided to keep the bulk of the Khan's troops in the safety of the fortress of Al-malik, firmly under his control. To warn Nomokhan as quickly as possible, though, he planned to send one thousand troops immediately, ordering them to leave that very afternoon and travel lightning fast, to deliver the Khan's secret message to Prince Nomokhan in person.

Hantum showed us the route on the map. The fortress of Al-malik, where we were, was on the Ili River, which flowed westward through a valley onto an open plain. He knew that Nomokhan and Shirki had planned to travel west along the river, a journey that took a day and a half, with the goal of meeting Khaidu at the confluence of the Ili and Charyn Rivers by noon on the following day. Hantum wanted to send one thousand troops along the same route, leaving that night and riding as swiftly as possible. He hoped there would be enough time to catch up with Nomokhan at the meeting site by noon. It was a risky and high-stakes mission. There was a chance they would not arrive in time.

"I will lead the expedition," Temur insisted. He had waited so long for this moment of bravery. It reminded me of my excitement—and Suren's—before the Battle of Vochan. If Temur had experienced battle, as I had, he might speak less confidently.

"My prince, with all respect: You are still young and have never commanded troops," Hantum replied. "I have chosen to put one of my most trusted men, Captain Buri, in charge of the troops."

Hantum gestured toward the one-eyed man who stood next to him, who bowed toward us. "Royal prince," said Captain Buri. I knew Buri just a little; he had a reputation of being solid and loyal, like an old dog.

Temur flinched but could not countermand the general's orders. "Either way, I must be the one to deliver the message to my uncle."

General Hantum hesitated, looking Temur over as if sizing him up, trying to decide if this prince was man or boy, loyal to the Khan or potentially loyal to Shirki. Temur shifted uncomfortably. As a prince, he outranked this man, but in the army he was a subordinate. Temur, tall and bold, towered over the old general, but Hantum had undoubtedly seen many reckless young men dash into battle unprepared. In Nomokhan's absence, both Temur and I had to obey General Hantum.

"You may go with them," the general said. "But you are to follow Captain Buri's orders until you reach your uncle."

Temur nodded. "What if we arrive too late? What if Shirki has already acted?" *Shirki.* The very name made me angry. I had no great love for my uncle, who was ready to trade me like a sack of wheat, but if Shirki betrayed him, all chance for peace was lost.

"If General Nomokhan is not able to give orders, then the troops must follow the orders I send. If any soldier has betrayed us, I authorize Buri to pursue the traitor and any troops he has taken with him."

Buri nodded. I sensed he would be dogged in pursuit of any traitor.

Temur seemed to relish being consulted in the planning of such a momentous event. "Many soldiers are loyal to Shirki. If Shirki and Khaidu join forces, that would be a disaster." Young as he was, Temur had the tone of a man learning to command.

"A disaster indeed," the general said. "That cannot be allowed to happen."

My emotions were in turmoil. Temur had insisted on going. Should I insist, too? Part of me was tempted to stay here, in safety. My mind was torn, but I had to speak up. "My uncle assigned me a task, to speak to Ai-Jaruk to secure her father's cooperation. Is it too late for me to play that role?" I asked.

Hantum regarded me levelly. "May I speak frankly, Emmajin Beki? We don't know exactly what has happened, or what is likely to happen. This is not the moment for talk between women."

Blood pounded in my temples. I hated being dismissed as a mere woman. But I tried to hold back my anger and speak with the dignity of a member of the royal family. "No one knows the mind of Khaidu. Maybe he does not want to join with a traitor. His daughter can reason with him. I must speak to her."

Hantum stroked his beard, a long thin one, and regarded me deeply for the first time, as if surprised that I had a brain. Buri did not even glance at me, as if gazing at a royal princess would be disrespectful to the Golden Family.

I jumped in again. "I am trained as a soldier and I have fought in battle. If there is any chance that I could play the role assigned to me, I would like to do so." There. At least I had spoken.

"Circumstances have changed. The princess must stay here, in safety," Hantum decided. "I am sure that would be the Great Khan's wish."

Part of me was relieved to hear him give this command. Staying here would give me a chance to spend time with Marco. But another part of me, a louder voice inside my head, rebelled against being ordered to stay behind when so much was at stake. I glanced at Temur.

My cousin seemed to read meaning in my hesitation. I knew that he wanted me to be the heroine of Vochan, not a weak woman who dallied with foreigners. He defied his commander's orders. "Uncle Nomokhan asked me to take responsibility for her," Temur said. "She is experienced in battle; she will come with me."

Hantum shrugged. It seemed as though he considered it a matter within the royal family, and he did not want to interfere. "As you wish," he said.

My heart twisted. But my pride would not allow me to stay behind. I wanted to be with Marco, but that could wait till I returned. Perhaps I would be gone only a few days. If I succeeded in averting this disaster, perhaps Khaidu would reopen the trade routes, and Marco and I could continue on our journey to the West. Plus, my bravery would raise my status with the army and the Khan. So I merely nodded. In fact, I savored the idea that I would play a role in stopping this treachery.

Within an hour, Temur and I were fully armed and on horseback, galloping west with Captain Buri, at the head of one thousand of the Khan's troops. Once again, I had wrapped my breasts in a thick cloth, donned the uniform of the army, and taken up my sword and bow. There was no time to say good-bye to Marco. But I put Marco's rosary around my neck with the little medicine pouch attached, for protection.

As my body leaned over Baatar's neck and rushed off in the night, my thoughts swirled. I was riding west on the type of high-stakes mission I once dreamed of. I had made up my mind and insisted. Yet I still felt conflicted. If we prevented the defection, we might maintain peace and reopen the trade routes; but I did not want to fight in another battle. Talking to Ai-Jaruk might prevent fighting, but she had a reputation as a warrior, not a peace-maker. I had given up war at the peak of my fame as a war hero. Then that fine reputation was tarnished by Bartan's accusations. Now I would have a chance to regain my honor—if I averted war, or if I fought with valor.

But my mind kept returning to Marco. I had made this decision, to rush off into danger, in haste, without seriously considering the alternative. Marco had offered me another choice: to run off with him to the wilderness. I would be a nobody, out there in the mountains, a coward who fled from danger. Yet I would wake up every morning next to Marco. Marco who made me laugh and forget my worries and obligations. Marco who saw past my bravado and my title. Marco who loved me for who I was, not what I did.

Marco offered me nothing, really. Escape, quiet, togetherness. What I yearned for was adventure, action, respect, glory. Yet the very unthinkability of Marco's vision attracted me.

But now, dressed as a common cavalryman, I was racing away from Marco, possibly toward battle, perhaps even toward death. On the surface, I was one with the one thousand horsemen around me. But inside, I had already begun to change. These men did not see the world as I did.

I rode between Temur and Buri, the field commander. The imperial messenger, though exhausted from riding straight from Khanbalik for more than a month, at a fast pace with no more than six hours' sleep each night, had to come with us, to deliver the Khan's sealed message to Nomokhan. Only the Khan's direct orders would convince Nomokhan of the impending danger. What might he do with that information?

The sky was clouded, so that even the moon, five days past full, did little to light our way. As we quickly passed through the Ili Valley, the river grew wider, and the valley broadened out into a plain. The sweet orchard smells of Almalik gave way to the dry, brittle smells of grassland in Eighth Moon. The cool night air chilled my cheeks.

As the night wore on and the eastern horizon behind us began to show pink in the predawn light, the rhythm of pounding hooves made my head nod with fatigue. I had never galloped through an entire night. In the darkness, I remembered the shaman's prediction: Danger. Traitor. Defeat.

The sun rose behind us. As daylight broke, we could see the trampled grasses where Nomokhan and Shirki and their one thousand horsemen had thundered through just a day earlier. This was the Land of Seven Rivers, a broad grassland of rolling hills fed by rivers that tumbled out of the imposing Heavenly Mountains behind us and to the south.

Toward midday, the land began to rise again. The Ili ran on in a vale below us. Would we make it by noon? The sun crossed its midpoint and began to fall, until finally, I could see, on the ridge of a hill, a line of soldiers flying the Great Khan's banners.

As we approached them, I looked down into the river valley. Far below, in the triangle where two rivers met, stood a cluster of our soldiers on horseback. Nomokhan had taken half of his one thousand troops down to the river and left the other half on the ridge, overlooking the valley where he was to meet with Khaidu.

From the ridge, I could see the white horse that bore Nomokhan, holding the horsetail standard. His tall thin figure was easy to spot. Next to him was a short, stocky man in metal armor—certainly Prince Shirki. It was a historic moment. The two princes, both of the House of Tolui—sons of two brother khans, Khubilai and Mongke—lined up to meet with Khaidu, of the House of Ogodei.

Shirki was far below me but within bowshot. I could take him out if I had to. "Khaidu has not arrived yet. We have been waiting since midday," the captain of the ridge-top troops told us.

"Then we are not too late!" said Temur. "A messenger has arrived from the Great Khan. We must get the message to Prince Nomokhan as soon as possible."

A wave of relief washed over me. Perhaps it was not too late to avert treachery.

With a shout, Temur and the imperial messenger began rushing down to the valley to reach Nomokhan. My instinct was to join them. But Captain Buri ordered me to stay on the hillside, with him and the rest of the troops.

Suddenly Buri shouted and pointed. I looked up, across the valley, to a hill beyond, in the west. Along that far ridge, outlined in silhouette by the lowering sun, a line of mounted soldiers appeared, all at once. Dressed in light green, the color of the grass on the steppes, they stretched along the ridge as if they had been hiding behind it for some time, organizing themselves so as to appear as numerous as possible. They carried banners of green with a symbol on them, which I could not see clearly.

Khaidu and his troops. It was not a huge army, but clearly he had brought more soldiers than the one thousand of our men who had traveled with Nomokhan and the extra thousand who had arrived with us. Watching from horseback at the top of the eastern ridge, I strained forward as if to reach out to them across the valley.

Khaidu's troops were far enough away that I could not see individuals, but at the center I did see three black horsetail standards held high, and I imagined that it was Khaidu himself, his son Chapar and his daughter Ai-Jaruk, holding back their snorting horses. I strained my eyes, trying to glimpse Ai-Jaruk for the first time.

The messenger was halfway down the hill, racing toward Nomokhan. If Shirki did not defect, then the two sides could meet as planned, and Nomokhan could carry out his talks with Khaidu.

More than half of Khaidu's troops stayed on the hillside, and a smaller group of Khaidu's men, including those with the three black horsetails, slowly began to ride down into the river valley—at a pace that suggested goodwill, coming to talk not to fight. The metal of their armor glinted in the late afternoon sunlight as they advanced toward Nomokhan's troops, which fell into line, formally waiting, on their side of the river.

I squinted to try to make out the two soldiers on either side of Khaidu. Normally, his son, higher ranked, would ride at his right side. Both seemed large, but the one on his right seemed slightly smaller than the bulky one on his left. Impressive, I thought. Khaidu allows his daughter to ride at his right. I stared hard at that figure on his right, thinking: finally, I have set eyes on the famous Ai-Jaruk, who defeated all suitors at wrestling and earned the right to fight as a warrior in battle. I imagined an instant connection, like lightning, between us. Did she look up at me on the hillside? She would have no way of knowing I was there. How much had she heard of me?

My chest tightened as I watched Temur and the Khan's messenger speed down the hillside. Temur, my cousin, companion of my childhood. The danger of the situation hit me like a blow to the chest. I had already watched his brother die. Temur and I had become much closer in recent months, although our relationship remained turbulent. If anything happened to him, could I breathe again?

Khaidu and his companions reached the river's edge and began to splash across the smaller tributary to meet with Nomokhan's troops on the other side. Would the messenger and Temur reach Nomokhan before Khaidu did? What was Shirki doing? Would he guess the warning the messenger brought?

The late afternoon sun, still above the western hills, cast a brilliant light on the entire scene, making it sharp and vivid. Baatar stomped his hoof beneath me.

"On alert!" shouted Buri.

We pulled our horses into formation, our bows at the ready but pointed skyward. I waited shoulder to shoulder with Buri.

This was meant to be a meeting among allies. But allies are not always reliable. So both sides had backup troops on the hillsides, armed and alert.

Khaidu splashed across the river with his small cohort, and they stood in formation, directly opposite Nomokhan and his brown-uniformed troops. Nomokhan kept turning his head back and forth, from the messenger speeding down the hill to Khaidu crossing the river. I could only imagine the confusion in his mind.

Temur and the messenger reached the Khan's troops and passed through with a flurry and a ripple, finally reaching Nomokhan with the message from the Great Khan.

Nomokhan the Tall, towering above other men, took the message, broke the seal, and unrolled it. He read it quickly, then looked at Shirki, the short and stocky man at his side. Shirki shouted. A soldier behind them tossed a lasso around Prince Nomokhan's waist, jerking him off his horse and to the ground. A lasso, the kind used to herd sheep. No soldier carries a lasso. This was obviously one of Shirki's men who had planned for this moment.

Shirki shouted an order, and many of the troops rallied behind him. A few soldiers loyal to Nomokhan scrambled to form a circle around their leader.

I lowered my bow and aimed directly at Shirki. But in the dust and turmoil, I could no longer see him clearly. What if I hit Nomokhan by mistake? I glanced at Buri, who also seemed confused. None of us loosed our arrows. We could not fire into our own troops.

In the chaos, I could not see my cousin. How many troops were loyal to Shirki? How many would follow his orders if Nomokhan fell? The Great Khan's troops below by the river, near the action, had not been able to see what happened as clearly as I could, watching from the ridge top. They swirled in confusion.

Buri sheathed his bow. "Traitor!" he exclaimed. "Advance!" All our mounted soldiers, standing at the ready on the hillside, fifteen hundred strong, let out a war cry and began streaming down the hill. We had to free Nomokhan.

Baatar, trained as a war horse, surged ahead with the other horses, and my body leaned forward out of instinct. The dry air sliced my cheeks as I galloped down. A disconnected feeling came over me, as if I were watching the scene from the sky. I looked at my soldier self, rushing into battle and thought: What is she doing? I hated one man, Shirki, for destroying the chances for peace. And another, Khaidu, for provoking this needless confrontation. But I felt none of the bloodlust I had felt advancing against the Burmese at Vochan.

Instead, conflicting emotions wrestled within me. Those were my people, below on the plain, all Mongols. What valor is there in killing your own kind, fellow soldiers you have traveled with for months on end? My loyalty to the Great Khan, inbred since birth, made me want to stop the betrayal. But my uncle Nomokhan had been prepared to trade me away as a bride. Temur was in danger, and I could not stand to see him cut down as Suren was. Yet how could I protect him? It was not a cause I wished to risk my life for. Yet there I was, rushing into an ill-conceived, unplanned battle.

I could see, across the way, that Khaidu's backup troops, too, were charging down on the western side of the valley, a churning river of green. Normally, we would have been shooting arrows as we rode, but we could not shoot into the midst of our own troops.

Khaidu himself, flanked by his warrior son and daughter in the valley, stopped and stood still, as if waiting for the outcome of the fray between the grandsons of Tolui.

Khaidu's backup troops stopped when they reached their leader. Dressed in green, with a distinctive style of armor, they would have been easy to recognize in a fight. But they kept back. Even as the scene blurred past my eyes, I wondered what Ai-Jaruk would think, watching men from Khubilai Khan's side of the family fight each other before her eyes.

Just as the two parts of my mind had been warring against each other, now Mongols were warring against Mongols. We Mongols have been united for three generations; had that just come to an end?

Ironically, Khaidu might not have betrayed anyone. One of our own officers, Shirki, had done so. The Great Khan's commanders did not seem to know what orders to give or what leader to follow.

We must capture this traitor, Shirki. But it was not so straightforward or easily done. Once we reached our own troops, they were thrashing about in disarray. It was unclear who was on which side. We were all dressed in the same brown uniform. None of us was trained to fight against other soldiers dressed in the Great Khan's colors. It seemed that some troops, loyal to Shirki, had captured Nomokhan.

I sheathed my bow and drew my sword as we neared the Mongol Army troops. Some were running away. Others were fighting each other. I worried that our rightful commander Nomokhan, roped on the ground, might be crushed in the melee.

With the flat side of my sword, I shoved back soldiers of the Khan and pushed toward the center of the fighting. Temur himself was clashing swords with Shirki. Nomokhan was now on his feet, but his arms were tied tight with a rope. I rushed forward to cut the rope. But a soldier loyal to Shirki stopped me, blocking me with the broad side of his sword. Filled with rage, I slashed at him, ready to slash his limbs off. But he parried with his sword, and the sound of metal against metal clanged in my ears.

A swift movement in the air caught my eye, and I saw a lasso fly past. It looped over Temur's head, then tightened around his chest. His sword fell from his hand, his arms pinned to his sides. His eyes bulged. He fell from his horse.

It was up to me now. I wanted to save both Nomokhan and Temur. "Release them!" I shouted. I charged ahead.

Just then, I heard a shout from Khaidu and saw that his troops were beginning to move in. Cleverly, they surrounded the Great Khan's troops, pinning us against the two rivers.

I charged straight at Shirki, the traitor. He wore full metal armor over his chest and arms, plus a leather neck guard and leather flaps over his legs, and a metal helmet.

Wildly swinging my sword, I hit not Shirki but his horse, jamming my sword into the animal's neck. The horse screamed, jerked, and slowly fell, with Shirki on his back. Shirki jumped off just before the horse could crush him. He swung the flat side of his heavy sword at Baatar's front knees. Baatar crumbled and fell forward, and I had to move swiftly to slide off my horse's back.

I landed on my feet, gripping my sword and swung it wildly at Shirki. He parried and then swung again, broadside, as if aiming to stun me. I slashed upwards and cut his right arm just below the armpit. If only I had had more strength, if only I had kept up my training, I might have cut his arm off. Blood gushed out, and he clutched at the wound. His sword clattered to the ground.

Now his eyes were even narrower and I could see the hair of his mustache bristling as his mouth firmed into a grim line.

"This one is also from Khubilai's house! Seize her!" he shouted.

I swung my sword again and sliced open his leather neck guard. Under the black of his beard, I could see the vulnerable skin of his neck. I raised my sword, ready to plunge the point straight into his neck. Shirki raised his left elbow to parry my blow.

Just as I began to plunge my sword toward him, I felt a flurry of movement above my head. A lasso fell over me, and I raised my sword to cut it before it tightened. But I was not quick enough. The rope tightened around my arms. With a jerk, it lifted me off my feet. Blood pulsed into my eyes. My elbows dug into my waist. My fingers released my sword to the dusty ground.

Hooves and armor and spatters of blood blurred my eyes as my feet bounced along the ground. The rope bit into my upper arms, and my lower parts scraped painfully against the rough, trampled grass.

Finally, my body landed with a thump against another body—that of Temur, bound but alive. My head landed on his chest, and he leaned his head over mine, as if to protect me from further injury. I could feel his heart hammering wildly.

Temur's hands were already lashed behind his back, as were those of Nomokhan. Temur and Nomokhan were propped back to back. Someone roughly propped me against them too, then lashed my hands behind my back and my feet to each other.

A circle of horsemen stood around us, men of the Khan's army whom I recognized, companions of Shirki's. They kept us from being trampled as the skirmish continued.

Suddenly, Buri, the one-eyed captain who had traveled with us, charged through the circle, on foot. With his dagger, he cut the rope that bound Temur's feet. He had come to rescue us! Buri the Loyal would be hailed as a hero, back in Khanbalik.

Temur staggered to his feet. Buri slashed open the rope that bound my feet and freed me. I tried to push myself up. The one-eyed man moved around to free General Nomokhan.

The short, squat shape of a soldier loomed behind Buri, his sword held high.

"Captain Buri!" I shouted. "Behind you!"

But it was too late. The soldier's sword crashed down on Buri's helmet, knocking him off balance. Buri swung his sword as he fell to the ground, hitting the attacker across the legs. Before my eyes, not three feet in front of me, the traitor swung again, chopping off Buri's head. His one-eyed head spun off to my left, and the blood from his neck spurted like a fountain, drenching my boots. His body lay at my feet, like a loyal hound.

Buri's desperate charge was the last initiative from the troops loyal to the Great Khan. Clearly, Shirki had laid his plans well, ensuring a well-armed coterie of men at the center. Soon the fighting was over. Our feet and hands were bound again.

We were prisoners, Nomokhan, Temur and I. The son, grandson, and granddaughter of Khubilai Khan, bound like sheep. If it had not happened to me, I would have declared it impossible.

So quickly I barely knew what was happening, Shirki handed us over to Khaidu, Khan of the Desert West. He exchanged a few words with Khaidu, which I could not hear. I wondered how much communication there had been between the two of them and how they could possibly have planned this.

Then with a shout, Shirki grabbed the Khan's white horsetail banner, which Nomokhan had been carrying, and began to cross the Ili River, which was wide and shallow. Most of the Khan's troops, seeing one of their commanders with the familiar banner, followed him. In the confusion, they had probably not fully realized what had happened. Only a few, loyal to the traitor Shirki, had known in advance. The rest, unable now to follow Nomokhan, followed the horsetail banner and the soldiers in brown because they did not know what else to do. They crossed the river and headed north.

Khaidu dismounted and stood over the three of us. A stocky, wide man, he had a look of surprise on his broad, flat face. Shirki had handed him a gift of inestimable value, a gift he had apparently not expected. He recognized Nomokhan but had to ask who Temur and I were.

"A woman?" he asked, staring at me. "This is the princess?"

I looked him straight in the eye, with what dignity I could muster. This was the father of Ai-Jaruk, beholding the Princess Emmajin.

"Put them on horseback. See to it they don't escape," he said. "We return to camp."

Someone placed me on a horse and lashed my feet to the stirrups. I looked around, trying to locate Ai-Jaruk. Surely she would not allow them to humiliate me this way. But I could not see her. Instead, I saw another of Khaidu's men binding Temur to a horse in the same way. I could not see Nomokhan.

Soon all of us were riding south, in the midst of Khaidu's men. I had lost my chestnut stallion Baatar in the fighting, and I never saw him again. I don't know if he lived beyond his first wound or died in battle that day. Perhaps I am too sentimental, but I left a part of my heart, a part of my childhood, on the battlefield that day when I lost my valiant stallion. And for what? It seemed senseless.

Surely, some of the Khan's soldiers would straggle back to Almalik, and General Hantum would send a backup force west to try to rescue us. But by the time they reached the confluence of the two rivers, I knew, we would be long gone. They could only guess what had happened to us. I hoped they would quickly pursue Khaidu and rescue us.

No legends of valor would ever be told about this short, inglorious battle at Ili River. It had no heroes.

I had made a choice in haste, to come on this expedition, for all the right reasons. With a sense of invulnerability, I had not considered carefully what might go wrong. Like Shirki's decision, which would change history and end any semblance of Mongol unity, my decision would change my life forever, in ways I could not predict. It was irreversible, and I had to live with the consequences.

# Chapter 11
# Marco: A New Partnership

After Emmajin rode off with the soldiers, I felt as though the world had gone black, that the sun would never shine again.

Two guards led me, stumbling between them, across an open military training ground, past several rows of round white tents where the soldiers slept, to a mud-brick hut near the thick wall that surrounded the garrison. I could barely stand in this small cell, and, though its floor was covered in fresh straw, it smelled of goats.

I collapsed in the corner, exhausted both from the lengthy, fast-paced ride of the past month and also from the deep, bitter disappointment of my reunion with Emmajin. During long days in the saddle, I had envisioned an embrace, tears of gratitude, confusion about the news, consternation about the need for a quick decision to leave with me—a host of reactions from the Khan's granddaughter. I had not imagined Temur's knife to my throat, his sneer, his suspicion, or—worst of all—her decision to ride west toward danger instead of east with me. And I certainly had not expected to be escorted to a goat stable, where armed guards would watch me, day and night.

As soon as the guards slammed shut the wooden door, my anger took over. In a burst of energy, I strode to the door and pushed it open. The guards reacted immediately. The shorter, thicker one pushed me back inside, and the other banged the door shut. Then the two of them pushed against it with their weight, yelling crass words at me. I pounded my fists against the wooden door and the mud walls and shouted back at them. How could they treat me this way? It was unconscionable. I hated my guards. I hated Temur. I hated Emmajin.

These Mongols—what were they made of, cattle dung? Tartars, that was a better word for them, guardians of the underworld, lower than Hades. They loved tales of valor, but they couldn't recognize true heroism when they saw it. They had no sense of high-mindedness or nobility. I shouted every rude and crude insult I knew in Latin, Venetian, and the four Eastern languages I had learned on this journey: Arabic, Persian, Turkic and Mongolian. But the guards held the door tightly closed until I stopped pushing. At least it was not locked. Still, I was a prisoner.

In a corner of the shed, I put my head in my hands. I had put so much effort into racing across the barren landscape to get the news to Emmajin, that I had no energy left. I had attempted something daring, something larger than life, and I had succeeded in reaching the Khan's granddaughter before she faced peril. To no avail.

Gloom settled over my spirit, and I could barely lift myself off my sleeping fur for days. My sense of humor, wit, charm, light-heartedness—all dissolved. Two guards followed me each time I went out to relieve myself. Food was brought to me; I was not permitted to wander about the garrison or talk to anyone.

Had I really expected Emmajin Beki to abandon her people and run off with me, to hide in the mountains until the fighting was over? How often I had envied Tristan and Isolde, who spent three years in the wilderness, living off wild berries and love. Now I kicked myself for believing stupid myths. This was real life. This was the present-day Mongol Empire. Legends were fabricated by men like me, scrubbed-up versions of the truth, designed to entertain, not to imitate. Why had it taken me so long to realize this?

Inside my shed, the heat roasted my flesh till it dripped and stank. My cell had no windows, just a solid wooden door with a thin crack beneath it. The summer sun in this dry climate beat down on the roof, and the air burned in my lungs. After a few days, I talked the guards into keeping the door open, if I promised not to come out. Otherwise, I might have suffocated.

The Great Khan Khubilai, I felt certain, would never have treated me this way, especially after I had risked my life to warn his people. The farther I traveled away from court, the more I appreciated how civilized the Great Khan was, compared to the men of his army. Khubilai listened to wise counselors and learned from all the world's religions how to be a fine ruler. These military men were more like the earlier generations of Mongols, crude and barbaric.

While I waited for Emmajin to return, I began to observe my two guards, thinking of how I might describe them later, if I lived to tell the story. They were classic types: one short and dark with a thick beard, and the other tall and beardless with a smashed-in face. I began calling them Mutt and Roach.

For days I heard no news at all about Emmajin and Temur, and what was happening in that meeting with Khaidu. My imagination created all kinds of scenarios, from skilled diplomacy to full-scale war. My lady could handle herself in battle, that I knew, but there were always risks.

Then one day, when I was out for my morning relief, a smattering of soldiers came rushing back into the garrison, without a leader. They came through a back gate and were greeted by much shouting. Normally, I would not have witnessed such a scene, but my guards had not known in advance.

"Woeful news!" they shouted as they entered the garrison.

"Where is your commander, Buri?" one soldier shouted at them.

"Gone to the ancestors!" said one soldier. Another yelled "They cut off his head!"

"And Prince Nomokhan?" An officer arrived, with the more important question.

"Gone! Taken!"

"Taken by whom?"

"By Khaidu!" one man shouted.

"No, by Shirki!" said another.

Despite the heat, my heart froze in my chest, and I could not swallow or speak. I looked behind the soldiers, straining to see Emmajin returning with them, but there were no more than twenty of them, and she was not among them.

"Prince Temur?" Roach asked. "Emmajin Beki?"

"Tied up like sheep!" one said. "All of them."

"Taken by Khaidu," said another.

My heart heaved. Emmajin—captured and in danger! Just as the shaman had predicted. My own captivity, with an unlocked door and two lazy guards, seemed mild compared to what Khaidu might do to his prisoners. Khaidu had a terrible reputation, and he hated her grandfather the Great Khan.

Two of the captains were led off to report to General Hantum, and the rest stayed to talk to the crowd that gathered around them. I pushed to get close enough to hear.

When they calmed down a bit, the soldiers told us the sorry tale. After the treachery at the confluence of the rivers, some soldiers went north, some south, some west. Most of the Khan's soldiers had followed Shirki, because of his high rank. But these few had witnessed his perfidy and chosen to return to the garrison.

"Where is the princess? Which direction did they take her?" I asked at last.

At the sound of my voice, Mutt and Roach suddenly remembered their duty, to guard me. Roach grabbed my arm and dragged me back across the courtyard to my goat shed. I struggled mightily against him, eager to hear more, but in vain.

This changed the balance of power in the region, and might change history as well. It was open rebellion, a slap in the face of the Great Khan, if not a dagger in the back.

What did it mean—for the Khan, for the Empire, for Emmajin, for me? If only Emmajin had come with me, fleeing to the hills east of here, as I had suggested.

That night and the next, I thought until my brain hurt. What should I do? My princess was the prisoner of an enemy khan. But this was no tale, it was real. And the evil khan was no dark knight but Khaidu himself, a ruthless Mongol rebel.

Maybe this would be my chance to become the hero of my own story, to right a wrong, to prove my loyalty to the Great Khan, to come to the aid of the lady I loved. But how? Where might Khaidu have taken his prisoners? Clearly, his camp would be well-guarded and he would ensure that no one from the Khan's garrison could find it.

I did not envy General Hantum. Left in charge of the Khan's garrison, he had to make a decision, how to respond. He could not wait for orders from Khanbalik. Yet there was so much contradictory information. Hantum could not leave the fortress undefended, yet if he tried to pursue all the traitorous groups, no one set of soldiers would be strong enough to face a determined enemy. All Almalik fell into turbulence.

One morning, I overheard my guards talking about a big meeting that was about to take place. All soldiers were expected to attend, to hear the General's decision.

"What about us?" Mutt asked his partner. "Can we leave our post?"

"You stay here," said Roach. "I'll go to the meeting to find out what's going on."

"No," Mutt responded. "You stay and I'll go."

"This prisoner is no longer important. Prince Temur gave the order, and he has been captured! Everything's changed now."

In the distance, a single man began shouting, and I could hear a crowd gathering.

"Stop!" shouted Mutt.

Apparently Roach took off. Mutt came to check on me, and I pretended to be sleeping. He closed the wooden door, and I heard a latch. But I knew how to open it. I waited, and sure enough—Mutt left, too. This was my chance. Quickly and silently, I set to work packing up my belongings—not much: my traveling robe, a change of clothing, and the few precious items I had in my saddlebags, including the white powder and smoke-and-fire rockets. They might come in handy.

When I pushed open the wooden door, no man was in sight. The summer sun was bright at midday, and though the heat was thick and dry, the fresh air was so much better than the still air inside my prison cell.

Carrying my belongings, I walked swiftly across the open yard of the fortress. The sound of the crowd and the shouting man came from far to my right. I was curious to hear what Hantum had decided, but instead I veered the other way, to the left.

First, I went to the horse corral. Most of the mah-foos were sleeping, but one was very accommodating and helped me find Amadeus, the horse I had acquired in Gold City before leaving my father and uncle with Wei-ming. I tossed the saddlebags on Amadeus's back and mounted. The mah-foo did not question my right to ride off on my own horse. Apparently he had not heard that I was being held prisoner. I told them I was just going into town to buy some provisions and would be back before sunset.

To get to the fortress gate undetected, I rode in a nonchalant way, unhurried but determined, as if attending to business. The main gate faced east, toward the town. The guards here had not abandoned their posts, but they did not bother about a mounted man leaving the fortress. Their duty was to prevent anyone from entering, not from leaving. So I nodded at the guards and rode right out, as if I did so every day.

No jail break had ever been easier.

The town of Almalik sprawled about the outside walls of the fortress, a dusty frontier settlement whose merchants clearly relied on trade with the army stationed there. The moment I rode out the gate, several young men and boys accosted me, asking me to buy their apricots, grapes, sisters. Not far from the gate was a large outdoor market and I went there. I dismounted and held Amadeus by the reins. I could not walk into the main marketplace leading my horse, but the merchants were eager for a sale. I told a boy what I wanted, and he ran into the bazaar to find a merchant for each of the items, and the merchants came out to me with their wares.

Using the few copper coins I still had, I bought enough food to last me for ten days of travel: dried meat, hard Mongolian cheeses, a leather flagon of mare's milk, as well as a sack of fresh apricots and grapes. I also bought more saltpeter, the white powder used to make fire medicine, just in case.

I had one more transaction to make—a big one. I was pondering how I could do it and still guard my horse and supplies when I saw a familiar blue head scarf.

Could it be Emmajin's maidservant, off on her own?

"Nasreen!" I shouted, still unsure.

She turned her head and I could see that it was the right woman. She was fingering some apricots. Her eyes registered a quick flash of fear, as if I were catching her doing something wrong. She recognized me, and her eyes went into servant blank.

"Messer Marco," she said, dipping her head.

"I need you to watch my horse and supplies for a few moments." I knew she was used to hearing commands, not requests.

She took the bridle without asking questions, and I chose to trust her.

"Wait here," I said. "Let no man touch my horse or bags." She nodded solemnly.

I went into the tent of a master merchant who was more than willing to change one of my smaller jewels for the coins used in this part of the world. Earlier, I had taken the jewel out from the hem of my coat, where my father had hidden in, back in Cambaluc. The money-changer wanted to exchange it for the Khan's paper money, but I refused, as I wasn't sure whether it would be accepted west of here.

I tied the rope of coins to an inner sash under my robe, then reemerged into the sunlight of the market. Sure enough, Nasreen was standing there faithfully, holding my horse's reins. But she did not hand them over immediately.

"Where is the master going?" she asked, more boldly than I would have expected. It seemed she had noticed the ten-day supply of food in my saddlebags.

One curl escaped the scarf and framed her face. Her deep brown eyes held a look of more than curiosity. I did not want anyone in the fortress to know where I was headed.

I hesitated, then lied. "I am heading back to the east, to rejoin my father."

Her eyes hardened as she searched my face. "The lady is in danger," she said. "She is west of here, and south." So Nasreen had heard the same rumors I had.

I said nothing.

"West," Nasreen continued. "That is the direction of my homeland, land of the Kirghiz people." Nasreen was a slave. Her mistress had disappeared. I knew she respected Emmajin, though I did not know how much loyalty she felt.

"You have family there, in the land of the Kirghiz?" I asked, switching from Mongolian to Turkic, which is similar to the Kirghiz language.

Her face softened slightly and she continued in her own dialect, which I could understand because of its similarity to Turkic. "I know nothing of the lands to the east. But if the master were headed west, I could help him talk to the people of that region."

She had read my mind. I looked around me, at the men and boys in the bustling market. Most of them, I was certain, could speak Turkic, and many could probably understand Nasreen's dialect.

"Come," I said. "Let's talk."

We walked to a quieter area, just outside of the busy market area.

Soon Nasreen was sitting on the back of my horse, just behind the wooden saddle, and my bags now held enough food for two people for ten days. I bought a sharp knife for myself and a strong bow and arrows for Nasreen, at her suggestion—mostly for looks, as she admitted her archery skills were limited.

Two people, a man and a woman, traveling alone on a single horse, lightly armed, invited bandits and danger. But we clearly did not have a caravan of goods, ripe for stealing. And we were not as threatening as an army would be. So soldiers would leave us alone, at least until we got to the territory controlled by Khaidu. At least I hoped so.

As we traveled, I reviewed my plan in my head many times. But I did not reveal my plan to Nasreen. I was glad for her company and help, but I did not trust her or anyone. I carried my dagger inside my boot so the slave woman could not reach it.

# Chapter 12
# Emmajin: Meeting Ai-Jaruk

Khaidu's camp sprawled across a high river valley below the Heavenly Mountains, with a commanding view of the Silk Road curving through the Land of Seven Rivers spread out below. Unlike my grandfather Khubilai, who ruled from a grand Chinese-style palace in a walled city, Khaidu lived a traditional Mongolian life. Like my more distant ancestors, Khaidu ruled his ever-shifting kingdom from a large white ger, which he moved frequently, always surrounded by a mobile city of troops and families. Khaidu was khan, or king, of a sparsely settled swathe of land; like other Mongol khans, he was subject to the Great Khan Khubilai. But now, clearly, Khaidu was in open rebellion.

The first spot he picked for his camp, after capturing us, had surroundings of natural beauty that rivaled Xanadu. Eagles soared between red cliffs, and white gers dotted the green valley, while the river rushed downhill with a gaiety that seemed eternal.

To get there, I had to ride a horse with my hands tied in front of me at the wrists. Another rope bound my upper arms to my body, just above the elbows, rubbing my chest painfully. A man also tied each of my knees, just above the boot, to the stirrups, just loose enough that if I fell off, I would dangle awkwardly. He put the reins in my hand, but I had no freedom to direct the horse, since Khaidu's men surrounded me as I rode. It took all my energy just to stay on my horse as it galloped in pace with its brethren. Though no man touched me, I felt violated.

Khaidu's men spoke Mongolian but with an unfamiliar accent and none of the Cathayan words we often used. They sprinkled their Mongolian with words I did not know. I guessed they were Turkic, since these Mongols lived in lands inhabited by Turks.

When the road went uphill, I caught sight of Temur, bobbing on his horse ahead, amidst another band of men. I could not see my uncle, Nomokhan. My captors all had swords at their sides. But with bound hands, I could not have grabbed one or held onto it.

As the sun set to my right, sending its last brilliant rays over this bloody, awful day, my mind gradually came out of its state of numb shock. I was a prisoner in the hands of Khaidu. So were Temur and Nomokhan, princes of the imperial house of Khubilai, the Great Khan. All my life I had assumed the power of the Great Khan would protect us, but now we were beyond the limits of that power.

What kind of man was Khaidu? If he expected to ransom us, he would not mistreat us. Yet here I was, with ropes cutting into my wrists. Obviously, I could not stand before Khaidu with dignity and make the case for peaceful cooperation. Khaidu had asked for me as a bride for his son, and Mongols of old had a tradition of stealing women for brides. That thought was too ugly to contemplate. The only hope I had was that Ai-Jaruk would release my bonds and treat me as a sister-cousin.

I looked for Ai-Jaruk among Khaidu's men, but could not distinguish her. After so many years of admiring her from a distance, soon I would have a chance to meet her—but not under the circumstances I had imagined.

The sun disappeared behind the shadowy western hills, and we continued riding as ominous darkness fell. After not sleeping the previous night, my mind grew woolly and I nodded off in the saddle as we rode. I longed to lie down and sleep.

It occurred to me that I should look for landmarks that would guide me back to Almalik, if I should escape. But in the dark, with clouds obscuring the moon, I could not see many signs. I could hear a river nearby and could tell we were headed uphill. Because the sun had set on my right, I knew we were headed south.

At daybreak, we arrived at Khaidu's tent city. The gers were different from ours, the roofs more steeply pitched, the sides circled with decorative bands of sun-faded red and yellow, and tent flaps decorated with motifs of plants and animals. These gers were not lined up, military-style, but scattered among the high grass and stones. As we entered the camp, I smelled urine. Nomadic Mongols use nature as a latrine, and those habits work well only when the group is small or on the move.

When our horses stopped, a soldier untied my knees and led me to a ger, messy and smelly. There a guard tied my feet together again and secured that rope to the center tent pole. He let me drink water and eat a strip of dried meat before retying my hands behind my back. Then he sat and watched me, his hand on his dagger.

Sleep washed over me. I dreamed that I was still on horseback, bumping and jostling, but that I was riding Baatar, faster and faster, till we took off like a bird and began flying. I had long wanted the freedom to fly in a direction of my choosing, and now I had no freedom at all.

That day I did not fear for my life. If anyone had wanted to kill me, it would have happened during the fighting. But we in the Golden Family have a strict rule: We do not shed the blood of others in our family. On the rare occasions when it has been necessary, the one to be executed is rolled up in a carpet and trampled by horses, so his blood is not shed on the ground. But that treatment is only for traitors. Like Shirki.

There was a good chance we would be rescued. After all, General Hantum had planned to send ten thousand troops after us, to the confluence of the two rivers. I hoped that they were pursuing Khaidu, trying to free us. But they may have been distracted by Shirki's troops, which had galloped off in the opposite direction. I hoped Shirki would not show up in Khaidu's camp. If he did, I would be tempted to strangle him.

On the second morning, a woman entered and spoke to my guard: "Khutulun Beki wishes to see this prisoner. Bring her at once."

I had no time to arrange my hair or clothing. The guard untied my feet and pulled me to a standing position. Khutulun Beki, Princess Khutulun. The name seemed vaguely familiar.

Men stared at me as I stumbled on stiff legs through the tent city. I was led to a grand tent decorated in the local style, with bands of blue and green highlighting the roof line and the tent flap. Inside was a blaze of color—bright carpets on the floor, strips of carpeting hanging along the curved walls, banners of felt with complex patterns of embroidery, silk scarves and feathers and tassels hanging from the ceiling. At the north end was a stack of blankets, carpets and pillows piled up on chests.

In front of that, on a throne-like chair, on embroidered silk cushions, sat the largest woman I have ever seen. Her shoulders and arms were massive and muscular, her breasts large and flowing into her bulky middle, and her legs like tree stumps planted on the carpet in front of her. Her nose was flat, splayed across a wide face, and her eyes sat far apart, thin slits above broad high cheeks. Her hair was pulled back harshly in a bun behind her neck. At first glance, I thought she was a man, but she wore elaborate braid coverings and a woman's hat with a peaked top.

"So you are the one who calls herself Emmajin." Her first words stunned me, both because of their harshness and because of the quality of her voice, high and feminine. I had expected a deep tone from such a massive physique.

"Ai-Jaruk," I said in wonder. I recalled the words of Marco, who had told us the story of this woman: *Stunning she was, sturdy and strong, with a round face surrounded by shimmering black hair...*

She laughed, a giggle really, and I could see crooked yellow teeth. "Is that what they call me, in your land, in *Cathay*?" She emphasized Cathay, as if to say I lived in a foreign land. "Ai-Jaruk is my Turkish name. My Mongolian name is Khutulun."

"Khutulun Beki," I said, with a nod of respect. *A great Mongol warrior.* Then the words I had practiced in my head came to my lips. "I have longed to meet you. You are much admired at court."

She laughed again, as if not used to responding to compliments. It was hard to guess her age, but from the stories I had heard I knew she had to be over thirty.

"I was told that Ai-Jaruk means Bright Moon," I said, gazing at her face in wonder. Round and wide as a full moon, it had as many craters.

"And your true name was to be Tara," she said, "because your father has eaten the foreign religion."

"I never liked that name." Girding myself against her insults, I hoped we would quickly find values we shared.

She cackled. "You are so small. You can't be good at wrestling."

I felt small, in front of her bulk. I knew I could never beat her in wrestling, but I wondered how her thick arms could be accurate in archery. "But I am strong," I said. I hoped she could not detect my lack of conviction.

Sensing a struggle of wills, I tried to take the offensive. "Where is my uncle, Prince Nomokhan?" My uncle was the only protection I might have, this far from court.

"Rolled in a carpet, perhaps," she answered, with a wicked smile.

I sensed she was toying with me. "Your father is wiser than that," I said.

"My father is wise enough to get rid of him. Your uncle, the so-called Pacifier of the West, is heading west as we speak."

"Heading west?"

She laughed, enjoying the upper hand. "He's paying a family visit to our relatives in the Golden Horde." Another surprise. A khan from the house of Jochi, the Great Ancestor's eldest son, ruled the distant western land of Russia, as Khan of the Golden Horde—so called because the gers of his *orda* were draped in yellow, the imperial color. But the Khan of the Golden Horde had never been terribly friendly or respectful toward Khubilai Khan. He would probably make difficult demands before releasing Nomokhan.

"And Temur is with him?" I imagined Temur, his hands and feet bound, riding for months to Sarai, the Golden Horde's capital near the Black Sea.

Ai-Jaruk laughed. "Your beloved Temur. I hear your family tolerates incest."

*Incest?* How dare she say such a thing? I was too shocked to speak.

She winked. "A strong woman can have any man she wants, no?"

Rage rose in me, from my heart through my neck, clogging my throat. Ai-Jaruk would not talk this way, at least not the Ai-Jaruk I had envisioned.

"Have you tried a Mohammedan or a Turk?" she continued. "We have quite a few here. They have beards, and they are very virile."

Beards. Had she heard about Marco? I could not believe her vulgarity. "Why didn't your father send me to the Golden Horde, too?" I asked.

"We needed something to barter. We sent the fine horse to the Golden Horde and kept the camel and the goat here."

A ripple of hope broke into my heart. "Temur is here?"

She gave me a snide look. "In the House of Khaidu Khan, first cousins are not permitted to marry, although second cousins may."

This twisted person was trying to provoke me in every way possible. I wanted to inflict pain on her. "My grandfather will see to it that you and your treacherous father are punished," I said.

She laughed, as if relieved that our position as adversaries had finally been established. "We will see who is punished. Eternal Heaven, Tengri, is on our side."

Then she gestured dismissal, and two guards seized my arms and led me away.

She was wrong. Eternal Heaven, I knew, was on the side of Khubilai Khan.

Back in the heat of my ger, I reflected on Ai-Jaruk. Marco had not described her incorrectly. She was sturdy, strong, and, yes, stunning. But I had imagined beauty. A unique feminine combination of beauty, grace, and strength. And of course, dignity and nobility of spirit, a kindred soul who would understand my appeal for peace. Without realizing it, that was the image I had aspired to. That Ai-Jaruk had never existed.

Now I wondered at all the suitors who had failed to win Ai-Jaruk's hand, the suitors she had defeated at wrestling. Surely, with that bulk, she was good at wrestling. But did any of her suitors lose on purpose, once they saw her pock-marked face and heard her sharp tongue? A hundred horses and the humility of one defeat in wrestling would be a small price to pay to avoid a lifetime with such a woman.

---

Shortly after that distasteful meeting, a stack of carpets, blankets and pillows was delivered to my ger, as well as a set of clothing so strange and gaudy I hesitated to wear it. It included a pink dress with long white pleated sleeves, covered by a black del with colorful embroidery over the chest—and a round velvet cap with ribbons, plus silver and coral ornaments for my braids. I thought it a joke, but the man who left them grunted that I should put them on because Khaidu Khan expected me at dinner that night. Fortunately, he also left me a basin of water for washing and a comb.

A maidservant quietly untied my hands and then helped me bathe and dress and fix my braids. With a pang, I missed Nasreen.

Where was she, back at the fortress? And where was Marco? Was he still being held prisoner, too? We might both have been free, in the mountains, if I had followed his suggestion.

But I needed to concentrate on my current dilemma. I assumed Temur would be at the dinner, too. I needed to find a way to speak to him, to plot a strategy for our release. With our hands and feet unbound, perhaps we could speak sense to Khaidu, appealing to his self-interest as well as his pride. I wished I had a silver tongue like Marco's.

That evening, inside Khaidu's grand tent, only a few torches were lit. It took a moment for my eyes to adjust to the dim light. The air smelled of rancid airag and sweaty bodies. Khaidu himself sat on a throne bench covered in snow leopard fur, with his chief wife on his left, three of his sons lined up on his right, and Ai-Jaruk next to her mother, Khaidu's chief wife. They appeared as a solid mass of broad chests and shoulders.

Khaidu, with thick jowls, small eyes, and a wispy beard, reminded me of my grandfather, except that his eyebrows were white and shaggy. He dressed not in silks but in a sheepskin del with wide cuffs. He wore a round-crowned hat trimmed with fox fur and tied below his chin. Although Khaidu was the same generation as my father, he was much older.

When I walked in, Khaidu and his family stared at me as if I were a peacock on display. For one awkward moment, my body nearly betrayed me, so accustomed was I to kowtowing. But I did not. I nodded my head toward Khaidu in respect, then said: "Greetings and respects from your cousin, the Great Khan Khubilai."

The silence lay heavy, like a wet felt blanket. Khaidu's face grew stern, and the faces around him showed fear. But when he spoke, his voice thick and gravelly, he chose not to contradict me. "The Great Khan Khaidu sends his respects to his cousin and his greetings to his cousin's granddaughter."

My back stiffened. He had called himself Great Khan, *Khagan.* That was blasphemy. He was a minor khan, not Great Khan, and he should not get away with such effrontery. Yet his manner was not impolite.

Just then, I heard a noise behind me. The door flap was pulled aside, and Temur strode in, dressed magnificently in borrowed clothing and fine boots, standing tall and broad-shouldered, his hair in neat braid loops, his face regal and annoyed. Temur represented the best of Mongol manhood, dashing and good-hearted, over-protective but for all the right reasons. As his eyes swept the room, he noticed me and nodded, with a flicker of relief.

Temur strode around the central firepit and stood directly in front of Khaidu. He dipped his head in a polite bow, but did not kowtow. Like me, he spoke first: "Prince Khaidu. My grandfather, your liege lord, the Great Khan Khubilai, sends his greetings." Temur's language was deliberately confrontational and condescending.

Khaidu hesitated a moment, for Temur's insolence to seep in, then spoke. "Prince Temur, of the House of Tolui. I did not expect your visit here, but I welcome you."

By saying Temur was of the House of Tolui—the fourth son of the Great Ancestor Chinggis Khan—Khaidu was pointing out that he himself was descended from the Great Ancestor's third son, Ogodei, who had ruled as the second Great Khan. Khaidu believed that the heirs of the House of Ogodei should rule the Mongol Empire, not those of the House of Tolui, the youngest son. Although a distinguished general, Tolui had never been chosen to rule. But Tolui's son, Khubilai, now held the great throne.

Temur stood with dignity, but did not respond.

Khaidu broke the awkward silence. "Please have a seat, next to Prince Chapar."

Prince Chapar. Khaidu's eldest son. I looked closely at him for the first time. Although he was not as broad and thick as the rest of his family, he was no better looking. His face seemed old—closer to my father's age than mine. Surely this was not the man Nomokhan had been thinking I would marry. Khaidu's younger sons moved over to make space on the bench for Temur.

Temur frowned at the seat. "My uncle, Prince Nomokhan, should take the seat of honor. He is a son of the Great Khan and commander of our army."

"Ah, your uncle." Khaidu rubbed his beard, a white fringe along the edge of his chin. "At his request, I have sent your Uncle Nomokhan further to the west, to visit our cousins at the Golden Horde."

"That is impossible! He is commander of the Great Khan's western army."

"I was told that General Shirki is now in command."

"Shirki is a traitor!"

"You of the House of Tolui need to sort out your own differences. We in the House of Ogodei are united, and we invite you to set aside our differences and join us for a meal tonight. Please have a seat."

Temur was clearly confused, as I was. Weren't we prisoners? Since Khaidu was choosing to treat us as guests, Temur took the seat of honor next to Chapar. Ai-Jaruk pointed to the seat next to her, at the women's table, and I sat down. From my seat, across from him, I caught Temur's eye. He seemed to be assessing that I was unharmed. One of his eyebrows rose as he took in my pink clothing. I rolled my eyes, and he smiled. Ai-Jaruk shifted her bulk, as if she noticed the exchange.

"Let me show you traditional Mongolian hospitality," Khaidu said to Temur, as if we knew nothing about our people's traditions. "We have prepared a *beshbakmak*." That, I learned, was a local Turkic word for a table laden with many different dishes, served to welcome guests. The meal included a sheep's head, the most honored dish.

Temur accepted a goblet of airag and waited for the host to drink before he drank. When Khaidu's lips touched his goblet, a single musician struck up a tune on the horse-head fiddle—far from the orchestra that played when the Great Khan drank, but the same honorific custom. It made me sick to see this pretender.

After a few pleasantries, about the weather and the health of the horses, Khaidu asked Temur if his sleeping quarters were satisfactory.

Temur responded with an edge to his voice. "I was tied up and treated as a prisoner. Only today was I treated as a prince of the Golden Family."

Khaidu's thick white eyebrows rose. "It was your father's cousin, Shirki, who tied you up. Now, you can see, it is I who released you from your bonds."

"I am pleased to hear you say it. We will not tarry long here in your camp, my sister-cousin and I."

Khaidu cleared his throat. "I have sent a message to your grandfather this day, stating that you are safe in my care, handed over to me by his nephew, Prince Shirki."

Temur leaned forward. "I would return to Khanbalik with that messenger."

Khaidu smiled firmly and shook his head. "I am afraid you must stay here. There are traitors roaming these territories. I could not guarantee your safety if you left my camp. I have sent a message to your grandfather to that effect."

His meaning was obvious. We would be held until our grandfather responded to the message, which undoubtedly contained some demands the Great Khan would never accept. It could be months before our release.

Temur caught the meaning of Khaidu's words, too. "Are we hostages then? My grandfather will never bargain for our freedom."

Khaidu's voice was patronizing. "Oh, no, not hostages. You are honored guests, cousins of the Golden Family. I am pleased that your grandfather sent you to me." At this point, Khaidu smiled at me, and a shiver ran through my body. My grandfather had not sent me to him. Or had he?

From across the ger, I noticed a similarity between Chapar and Temur, sitting at his side. Both were tall and regal with broad shoulders, though Temur was slimmer. Chapar had the same shaped mustache as Temur but had a rim of black beard around the edge of his chin. And he had weathered skin. All of these Mongols had darker skin than those at court, probably because they lived outdoors most of the time, exposed to sun and wind and winter storms.

As the banquet progressed, Ai-Jaruk acted like a different person, polite toward me, taking her cues from her father. She offered me food, gesturing with her pudgy hand, decorated with coarse silver rings set with turquoise and jade, and explained the dishes that were unfamiliar to me. The food tasted good after days of deprivation. The change in her behavior took the tightness out of my shoulders, but I still did not trust her.

At one point I noticed that Chapar was regarding me with curiosity, as was one of his brothers. When he saw me looking at him, he scowled. I looked away.

After dinner, two musicians performed for us, one plucking a long-necked lute and another bowing a two-stringed instrument. The music was lively and gay. The men, as they got drunk, began to relax and laugh. Two male dancers performed for us, mimicking horses so perfectly I watched in amazement. With a pang of longing for my Baatar, I sent out a prayer to Tengri that he would be cared for. Then I lost myself watching the dance, laughing at the dancers' antics. When it ended, we shouted "Good! Good!" just as the men did at home.

This was, I realized, the pure Mongol lifestyle—a nomadic camp, in tents, with mutton and airag, traditional music and dance. It resonated deeply with me. It felt more authentic than the Mongol lifestyle at the palace.

A burst of familiar laughter hit my ears. It was Temur, responding to something said by Chapar. Khaidu was smiling at both. We were rivals, captor and captive, yet somehow, we were able to relax together, over airag. A sense of hope crept over me. It would not be easy. But maybe it was possible, after all, to fulfill my assignment.

---

The next day, Ai-Jaruk called me into her tent. This time, she offered me a cup of airag and a seat to her right. Her manner was warm and deferential. Despite her coarseness at our first meeting, I hoped she might prove to be the woman friend I had been longing for these many months.

"Your face pleases my eldest brother. He had heard about you, a man's woman, from afar. We did not expect your grandfather to offer you up so easily and cheaply."

My back stiffened. "My grandfather did not offer me up. I am here because my father's cousin, Prince Shirki, betrayed us. I will soon return to the Great Khan's army."

Ai-Jaruk shook her head at me, yet she smiled as if I were a naughty child. "You have so much to learn about us, about the House of Ogodei." Ai-Jaruk leaned forward, and I could smell raw onion on her breath. "The house of Tolui usurped the throne. I doubt they told you the truth about this, back in Khubilai's marble palace. We will never forget what your great-uncle Mongke did when he grabbed the title of Great Khan."

I had done nothing to offend Ai-Jaruk, yet she was sliding back into hostility. "Tell me," I said, trying to convert animosity into friendship.

"The throne should have gone to the son of Ogodei, to Prince Shiramon. You know what happened to him, right? That wretched Mongke drowned him! He did worse to the regent, the widow of the previous Khan. He had her stripped of her clothes, sewn up in a sack and drowned. Then Mongke grabbed the throne." She narrowed her eyes at me, as if I personally had stolen the throne from her people.

I straightened my back and tried to calm my voice. "My grandfather is Great Khan now. If we can all unite behind him, the Mongol Empire will be..."

She exploded. "Khubilai! You think he was chosen at a legitimate khuriltai?"

"Of course he was. It was the day of my birth. He..."

"Hah! That khuriltai was held in Cathay, not in Mongolia. And how many attended from the House of Ogodei, the House of Chaghatai, the House of Jochi?"

I shook my head. Why did it matter if my grandfather had the support of all those obscure people? He was Great Khan now, undisputed. At least, I had thought so.

Ai-Jaruk's eyes, thin and slitted as they were, bulged. "Not one! Only Khubilai's supporters attended that khuriltai. He crowned himself!"

"What a pack of lies!" I said. This was not the way I had heard the story, but part of me wondered if it might be true, at least partly. Could the Great Khubilai Khan have crowned himself, ignoring the wishes of his extended family? If he had, no one in Cathay would dare to speak such damning criticisms openly.

Ai-Jaruk looked down her flat nose at me and sneered. "You should know, little princess from the House of Tolui, that the legitimate ruler of the Mongol Empire is my father, the Great Khaidu Khan! He is the heir of Ogodei, who was chosen as successor by the Great Ancestor himself. Khubilai is a pretender."

Her face, red with her rage, had swollen up wider than usual. Her loud, accusatory voice raised the bile in me, and I wished I could strangle her for her attack on my family. Yet her words raised doubts in my mind. I could see that this might be righteous anger. If I had been born in the House of Ogodei, if my branch of the family had been chosen to rule, only to be supplanted by others, I might be just as furious. This was the way wars started, with righteous indignation.

"And you did not bow before him last night!" she said. "What restraint he showed you. He had a right to strip you and drown you, as your uncle did to my aunt!"

The names and the details of her story swirled in my head. I tried to remember the story as I had heard it from Old Master, the court storyteller. He said Khaidu was a bitter cousin, not content with the lands granted him by the Great Khan, who made war on his relatives and sowed dissension within the family. Now I could see why.

I did not want to engage her in a shouting match. A small spark in the back of my mind still believed that Ai-Jaruk was a woman larger than life, a woman capable of good things. Uncle Nomokhan had asked me to speak to her, with the goal of creating goodwill between Khaidu and Khubilai. I had to at least try.

"Khutulun Beki," I said, in a moderate voice, in sharp contrast to her shouting.

She stopped her raging and looked at me with hostile eyes.

"You are a woman of great knowledge and experience. I have long admired you from afar. You and I are both women of the Golden Family. We are sister-cousins." She opened her mouth as if to speak, but I cut her off. "We are both strong women, skilled in the manly arts of war. You and I, we can change history."

She stared at me. Somewhere inside that massive body, surely, was an earlier version of what Ai-Jaruk once had been, the Ai-Jaruk whose tale had inspired me.

"All this hatred, all this rivalry, all this talk of legitimacy and lack of endorsement—we do not need to live by it," I continued. Her eyes narrowed, but she listened to me. I imagined a younger Ai-Jaruk, one who competed not just for personal victory but to prove something valuable. "You remember, I'm sure, the story of Alanne the Fair, our ancestor. She said her sons could never achieve anything unless they were united. If our men keep fighting each other, the Mongol Empire will fall apart in our lifetime. No Mongol wants that."

"What do you know of such matters?"

"I heard you out. Now do me the honor of listening to me."

She shut her mouth. I sensed that my message was starting to get through.

I moved closer, as if talking in confidence to a friend. "Everyone in the Golden Family knows of the prediction of the shaman Kokchu, in the old days. At the first khuriltai, when Temujin was named Great Khan Chinggis, the shaman announced…"

She finished my sentence, using the same words I had learned as a child of the Golden Family: "…that Tengri gave him the task of conquering the entire world."

I lowered my voice again. "That can happen in our lifetime. The Mongol Empire covers most parts of the world, thanks to the bravery of our ancestors. Only a few countries remain outside our control. Once we gain control over all the world, there will be more than enough territory for all the sons and grandsons of the Golden Family."

She snorted. "You are trying to get me to endorse the usurper Khubilai."

I shook my head. "Khubilai is now sixty years old. How old is your father?"

"Close to fifty, I guess."

"They are our elders. We owe it to them to make this a reality."

"To make what a reality?"

"To unify the Golden Family and complete the conquest of the world."

She sat back, as if stunned by my words and the vision they evoked. She had been so wrapped up in her father's hatred and rivalries that she had not seen the larger picture. For a moment, she was in my lasso.

"Think of it, Khutulun Beki. Two women, from rival houses, could unite all parts of the Great Ancestor's family and achieve his vision. We have no enmity between us. We are not ordinary women; the men in our families respect us. Someday our brothers Temur and Chapar will head our two houses. They listen to us. If you and I join hands, we can do this." I extended both hands to her, palms up.

She looked at my hands, then at my face. Her eyes narrowed. "It's a trick."

"No trick," I said, flipping my hands over and back to show they were empty of anything but this offer of reconciliation.

She laughed, and her crooked teeth showed. "You are nothing but a prisoner."

"I could be more, and so could you." Again, I extended my hands.

"Once my brother Chapar takes you as his wife, your sons will be of the House of Ogodei. You will stop saying such things."

Her words hit me like a whip. Was this the point of capturing me? "Chapar!"

"You did not see how he looked at you? His third wife died recently. He has been looking for a replacement, a younger woman to amuse him and bear more sons. When you join the House of Ogodei, you will see things our way."

I rolled my fingers up into fists. Ai-Jaruk had won the right to remain single. Why should I have to marry against my wishes? "I did not come here as a bride. I was stolen."

"So was Ho'ellen, remember? And she bore the Great Ancestor."

I stood up, as straight and tall as I could. "I am a soldier in the Great Khan's army. I have chosen not to marry."

"You do not deserve the honor, but my father has chosen you anyway, to be his daughter-in-law."

"You had a choice. You challenged each suitor and refused to marry unless one could defeat you."

She smiled and nodded, as if reliving happy memories. "Yes. No one could."

"No one can defeat me, either."

"You? I could knock you over with my little finger."

"In archery?" I asked.

"In wrestling."

"No, in archery. That is how we Mongols won our empire, with archery."

She stared at me for a moment, as if assessing me. I could see that my comments had aroused her competitive nature. "In archery, then. It will amuse my father. If you lose, you marry my brother."

"I will not lose. If I win, I regain my freedom—and that of my cousin Temur—and we return to the court of our grandfather. If I win, you speak to your father and convince him that unity is the only way. I will take his overture back to Khanbalik, and our two houses will be at peace."

She laughed. "That will never happen. You will not win."

But I was sure I could. Such massive arms could not shoot as straight as I could. If she would not agree to reconciliation based on reason, she might agree based on skill.

"You accept my challenge then?" I asked her.

"I never turn down a challenge," Ai-Jaruk said. "But you will regret it."

# Chapter 13
# Marco: Family on the Grasslands

Nasreen was like my trusty squire, and I a knight on horse-back—except that she was a female slave and we were riding on the same horse. Plus, I had no suit of armor, no shining helmet, no splendid sword. Between the two of us, we had only a small bow, a few arrows, and a dagger. Also, of course, a saddlebag full of powder for 'fire medicine' and paper rockets for a smoke-and-fire display, whatever that was worth.

Riding together on Amadeus, we crossed the Ili River at a ford not far from the fortress. The sun shone hot on my back and arms, but not as excessively hot as it had been in dryer lands to the east. The river flickered and sparkled in the sunlight, with many birds and ducks quacking and flying in and out of its reeds and islands. The water level was low in late summer, and some irrigation ditches drew it even lower to keep the surrounding farmland green. In the distance, I could see majestic, snow-capped mountains on both sides: the Borohoro to the north and the Heavenly Mountains to the south, including the tallest peak named Khan Tengri, for the sky god of the Mongols.

It wasn't until we reached the south bank of the river that a thought struck me: I should have found Emmajin's letter from the Great Khan to the Pope and brought it with me! I doubted that she would have taken it with her that night; she expected to return quickly. That letter contained the best hopes for peace between my homeland and the Mongol Empire, the entire purpose of Emmajin's mission to the West. What good would it do if I rescued her and managed to get her safely to Rome, if we did not have that official letter?

I pulled my horse to a halt, and Nasreen, sitting behind me, asked, "What is it?"

Nasreen was a slave, so I did not confide in her. I looked back across the river at the thick walls of the Mongol Army fortress, where I had been held prisoner. Should I go back and try to get the letter from Emmajin's tent? My guards might be organizing a search for me. No, I could not go back, even for a letter as important as that.

I said 'tchoo,' the word Mongolian horses recognize as 'go,' and urged Amadeus into a steady lope.

We followed the road to the west, through the broad, flat Ili River valley. Fruit orchards covered that side of the river. The air smelled sweet with ripe apricots. It reminded me of the sunny countryside outside Venezia in August.

I looked over my shoulder many times. The number of trees diminished, and we rode through open pastureland, with grasses close-cropped by sheep and cattle. We saw fewer dwellings the further west we rode. Flies buzzed everywhere.

Once the Mongol fortress was well out of sight, I relaxed and worried less about being chased. Now I could begin to think about the future.

I had, once again, acted on my impulses and not made a clear plan. I could hear Emmajin's scorn in my head, "Is that what you call a plan, crouching in a cave?"

Now, heading west, I had only one idea of how to proceed: To be captured by Khaidu's men. I had to get to Khaidu's camp, and I knew it would be hidden well from the Khan's army. Of course, Khaidu would be expecting the Khan's soldiers to chase him and try to free the royal prisoners. The roads would be guarded. As an individual, unfamiliar with this land, I could never find him on my own. My only hope was to travel openly and get captured by Khaidu's men, who would then take me to the camp where Emmajin was. Of course, they might kill me before I had a chance to charm them with smooth words. My best protection would be our appearance—a man and woman on a single horse, only lightly armed, not threatening.

Once there, I would talk fast, hoping to convince them to let me entertain Khaidu with a story. My tongue was the only weapon I was skilled at using. What story would I tell that would win Khaidu's trust and help me to rescue Emmajin? Could I distract Khaidu and his men, to give Emmajin and me time to escape?

A lot of the details needed to be worked out. The plan was risky. In some ways, it seemed impossible. All my plans lately seemed to be going wrong. But if it went right, it could be the bold move that defined my life.

Nasreen proved to be a good traveling companion. She never complained, no matter how many hours we spent in the saddle. She quickly figured out how to pitch the small traveling tent I had purchased and knew how to choose a safe spot for it, near a water source but protected from wind and sun against a hillside.

She did not mind if the door flap did not face south; Mongols were obsessed with this, but she, as a Turkic Kirghiz, did not seem to care. I knew little about her people. They looked like other Turkic people—with tanned skin, wavy brown hair, and brown eyes that were rounder than the Mongols' eyes but not as round as our Latin eyes. Like the Mongols, these Kirghiz people lived nomadic lives in domed tents, herding sheep and goats. But they spoke a different language; for instance, they used the word 'kumis' for the fermented mare's milk drink the Mongols called 'airag.'

Nasreen knew how to start a fire and cook, and on that first day she showed that she could use that bow and arrow very capably, by shooting a fat marmot for stew. I dipped into my small collection of precious spices and added a pinch of dried pepper to make it tasty. I had never had a better servant.

On the first night, she pitched our small ger on a hillside, next to a well-used fire pit. No other travelers were visible. While waiting for the marmot meat to stew, we sat by the fire.

Nervous, I picked a long stem of grass and tossed bits of it into the fire, one by one. We had only one tent. I was not in the habit of sharing my tent with a woman. She had been a slave, forced to obey, but she was not my slave. If she was on her way home to her people, perhaps she was not a slave any more at all. In fact, she wasn't.

By contrast, she sat still and calm, staring at the flames and the simmering pot.

"Um, Nasreen," I began, addressing her by name, not the usual Mongolian way of speaking to servants with grunts and nods. "How does it feel to be free?"

She looked sharply at me. "Free?" she said, as if not comprehending my accent.

"Not a slave any more."

"I serve you, master," she said, warily. And it was true that I was giving her food and shelter. "Until," she added, "I am reunited with my mistress."

I stilled my hands. "Don't you want to return to your people?"

"I am not a runaway," she declared. Runaway slaves, I knew, could be punished with death if caught. So this is what she had been thinking as we rode, that she might be captured and punished.

"You left the fortress of Almalik without telling anyone."

Her mouth set in a firm line. "I am going to seek my mistress."

"Your mistress is a prisoner. Do you think she will need a lady's maid?"

"I am sure she needs a lady's maid."

I hated to think of Emmajin in captivity. How were they treating her? Would they make Emmajin a slave, as someone had done to Nasreen?

I turned to Nasreen with curiosity. "How did you become a slave? Were you born in captivity?" Most slaves, I knew, were either captured by conquering soldiers or sold by their poor families in exchange for food. But some people were born to slave mothers.

Her eyes narrowed with a look that told me she had spent years hiding her true self from her masters.

"You can tell me whatever story you like," I said. Sometimes, I knew, it's easier to make up a story. But you can get to the truth that way, too. "When you're on the road, there's nothing that goes better with marmot stew than a fine story."

She smiled briefly, looked away, frowned as if remembering something terrible, then stirred the pot. "It is ready," she said. Her marmot stew was tastier than I expected. She had cut the meat into small chunks to make it cook faster.

We ate for a time in silence, hungry after our long day on the road. As I finished, I realized that Nasreen was gazing at me. "I understand you are a storyteller," she said, as if seeing me for the first time.

"The Great Khan has called me that." I was tempted to practice by telling her the story I planned to tell Khaidu, but I hadn't worked out the details yet. Besides, I was tired and not eager to entertain. I'm not sure what got into me—it was more typical of me to talk rather than listen—but I asked her, "Do you have a story to tell?"

She shook her head and rubbed her elbows inside her sleeves, shivering.

"You were not born in captivity," I said, guessing.

She shook her head, no.

"Somewhere out here, in the Land of the Kirghiz, you were captured," I said, gesturing to the slightly rolling grasslands below us.

She pulled out her fingers and blew warm air on them, then rubbed them together.

I waited. I was not used to waiting for others to speak, but that time I did.

"I was twelve," she began.

So young. "Most Turkic girls are already betrothed at that age," I said, encouraging her to continue.

She nodded, looking away. "True. I was. To an old man, a friend of my father's. I was to marry him at fifteen, but I did not want to."

Many times during the long journey with my father and uncle, I had grumbled about the fact that I had not been given choices in my life. I had wanted to stay in Venezia, to chase the pretty girls. But when I was fifteen, my father returned from his long journey and insisted I travel with him on the next one. I could not imagine how terrible it would be for a young girl to know she must marry an old man. Perhaps her capture had opened new possibilities for her.

"Twelve is a terrible age to be captured," I said.

Again, she looked at me sharply. "True. I was a virgin."

I nodded, shivering at the thought of that fearful day in her life. "Who captured you? Mongol soldiers?"

Her face hardened again. "Yes. They took me to their commander for his pleasure."

Her words slapped my face like a bucketful of cold water. *Twelve years old. For his pleasure.* I searched her face for signs of pain, but she just stared at the fire. The light flickered on her high cheekbones. This was the way of men, the way of soldiers, everywhere in the world. What could I say?

"It grieves my heart to hear that," I said at last.

She looked at me with surprise. She picked up a long stem of grass and smoothed it flat. Then she nodded, ever so slightly. "I had always thought my father would protect me. But he was away, with the flocks, when the soldiers came to our tent. My mother was out with the horses, milking a mare."

She glanced at me, and I nodded for her to continue.

"My younger brother, Danat, was playing with a lamb near the tent, and when I saw the soldiers coming, my first thought was to save him. Sometimes they take boys as young as ten and force them to become soldiers. I pushed him back into the tent and ordered him to hide under a sleeping fur. Then I took my baby sister outside with me and held her, hoping they would think I was a young mother and not hurt me. She started crying and I could not calm her."

Nasreen's voice was clear and vivid, and I was mesmerized by her story.

"There were ten of them, the soldiers. I could barely understand their accents, but I knew they were Mongols. We had heard stories of Mongol soldiers galloping through our Kirghiz lands and conquering great nations in the West.

"Two of them jumped off their horses and came over to me. 'Meat,' said one. 'Kumis,' said the other. I put the baby on my hip and went inside the tent. A soldier pushed his way in and grabbed the wooden bucket of kumis that was by the door flap. Hoping to distract them so they wouldn't see little Danat hiding under the sleeping fur, I reached for a bowl of cheese squares we had been eating recently, and another soldier seized it from me and took it outside. It was summer, so we had no meat. When we got outside the tent, I could see that the soldiers had grabbed two full-grown sheep, our finest ewes. They slit the sheep's throats and emptied the blood on the ground before strapping them on the back of their horses, behind the saddle.

"Just then, my mother reached the tent, huffing and yelling, demanding that they go away and leave us alone. One of them grabbed her by the wrist and slapped her face, and she spit at him as she struggled to free herself. 'You Mongols, you barbarians, you think you can just take what you want. We need that food for our family,' she said.

"It happened so fast, after that. One of the soldiers grabbed me, and the baby fell off my hip. 'That's right,' he said, leering. 'We take what we want.' The baby was on the ground, probably bruised, crying like crazy. I wanted to pick her up, but the soldier pulled me back. Then he lifted me up, tossed me over his shoulder like a sheep, and carried me off to his horse. I started screaming, and my mother was yelling, but a soldier was holding her back, and I wasn't strong enough to free myself. The soldier tossed me on his horse, mounted, and rode off. I cried and tried to wriggle off the horse, but he was holding me too tightly. He was laughing, loud and hard, as he urged his horse to a gallop. I fought and squirmed, and my mother chased us on foot, and then on horseback. But she couldn't catch up. I was hoping I would fly off the horse and hit the ground and die, rather than be captured. But I lived."

She stopped speaking. I expelled the breath I had been holding. Deep sorrow filled my chest, and I wished I could comfort her or take away the pain. My own stories, the ones I had told the Khan, seemed trivial by comparison. Quiet, compliant Nasreen had had this story bottled up inside her. What other untold stories had I never heard, from slaves and servants everywhere?

Her calmness amazed me. I had railed against the unfairness of God's world when I was held for just a few days, at the fortress. How did she stay so serene? Why did she not get up and scream at the world and its harshness? I sensed that her hurts were deeper than any I had ever felt. That she had learned, over the years, to hide her pain, while I had taken all my passions and poured them into the grandiose stories I told. My passions were exaggerated, and hers were understated but equally strong.

I must have been gazing at her in awed silence, because she plucked a stem of grass and threw it at me to break the spell. "Every slave has such a story," she said.

"The Mongols are brutal," I finally said, not sure what else to say. I had heard stories of wanton killing by Mongol soldiers on the battlefield, in earlier generations, but it had never occurred to me to understand the cruelty of captivity and slavery.

She looked at me thoughtfully. "There are brutal men in every tribe," she said. "And good men, too."

I remembered a comment I had overheard from one of my guards, who said he had seen Nasreen coming out of Prince Temur's tent one morning. "Some Mongols are kind," I agreed, wondering if she had loved Temur or merely served him.

"My mistress is kind," she answered. "I admire her. Do you?"

Now she was the one probing. I did not want to reveal to her my feelings for her mistress, Emmajin. So I turned the focus back to Nasreen, trying to get her to admit to loving Temur. "Did you find, among the Mongols, a man to love?" I asked.

"Love? What do you mean when you say 'love'?" she asked.

This reminded me of one of my first conversations with Emmajin in the gardens of Xanadu, where I had told her our Western ideas about romantic love. These people, Mongols and Kirghiz alike, did not think of love in the same way we Latins did. If Nasreen had not been a slave, I might have said my usual, 'Ah, forgive my poor language ability,' but I did not. Instead, I shrugged, as if it did not matter.

Nasreen examined my face, then spoke. "My mistress spoke often of you."

"What did she say?" I said, too eagerly.

She laughed, as if denying sweets to a child. "A servant never reveals what her mistress says." I wondered if she was trying to figure out what her mistress saw in my thick, curly beard and round, green eyes.

"I thought of her often, when we were separated," I said. "Every day. Every hour. Every minute."

She laughed nervously, as if unused to hearing masters speak such deep feelings. Then she sighed, and I suspected she understood more of romantic love than she let on. Had she been married? I wondered.

"I believe," I said, "that for every man and every woman, there is but one true love." The last time I had said this, to a group of Mongol soldiers, I had been mocked.

Nasreen frowned and looked up. The setting sun lit up the clouds on the horizon, turning them bright orange. "I disagree," she said. "I see love in a different way. But I am older than you. Perhaps you will see things differently at my age."

"I am twenty-two," I said.

"And I am nearly thirty," she responded. "The love that matters most is love within the family."

"There is another kind of love, between a man and a woman," I said. "Surely Mongols and Kirghiz people know what it means."

She smiled, as if acknowledging my point. "The human heart is universal."

It occurred to me how immoral slavery is, that such an intelligent woman as Nasreen could be confined to a life as a maidservant. In a better world, she might be a teacher of girls or a respected elder. God is good, I thought, but life is not fair.

Nasreen got up and took the pot off the fire, saving the rest of the stew for the next night. Watching her work, I sat by the embers of the fire, reluctant to go into the small tent we had to share—especially after our tension-filled talk of love. After sunset, the night air was cool and a breeze was ruffling the edges of her head kerchief. I could see that her hair was wavy and dark.

After she finished, she stood before me. "I am tired," she said, "and wish to sleep now. I prefer that..." She hesitated, as if unused to stating her preferences to a master.

"I am not your master," I said. "Only your traveling companion. Have no fears. I will not touch you."

She did not smile, just solemnly nodded a grateful acknowledgement. Then she went into the tent. Later, as I stretched out my sleeping fur near hers, I realized that I thought of her as an elder sister or a young aunt. Full of stories not yet told. I could learn a lot from Nasreen.

The next morning, the air was crisp, and a strong wind was blowing across the grasses. I half-expected that Khaidu's troops would have found us overnight, but they did not. Surely this would be the day they would detain us.

Nasreen and I resumed our journey. I felt sure we were being watched from hilltops. Perhaps two people riding on one horse posed no threat; perhaps Khaidu's men were looking for an army. Still, I kept a constant lookout for Khaidu's soldiers.

Beyond the hilltops, to the south, were snow-capped mountains, which became clearer as the road edged south across rolling hills and grasslands. Several times, the road forked, and I would hesitate. Nasreen, holding on behind me, would point, usually to the south, with quiet confidence, and I would head that way. After her story the previous night, something had changed between us. I knew of her intelligence and honesty, and I trusted her. She seemed more open and relaxed, as if she trusted me now, too.

At sunset, we again stopped and pitched the ger, this time among a patch of stubby trees. Nasreen made a fire and heated the leftover stew, which she had carried in a leather pouch.

After dinner on this second day, I decided to confide in her. Perhaps she could give me some ideas. I told her my plan for rescuing Emmajin once we got to Khaidu's camp. My plan involved storytelling and a smoke-and-fire display, if I could get it to work. She seemed skeptical, but she listened, without comment at first.

During the long hours in the saddle I had mapped out a story to tell to Khaidu. I told this story to Nasreen, and she gave me some ideas about how to make it better.

"And afterwards?" she asked me. "If you do succeed? They will chase you. How will you get away? Where will you go?"

"I really want to go home, to Venezia, with Emmajin Beki if possible," I said. "You may not know this, but the Great Khan had asked her to take a letter to the leader of my homeland with a promise of cooperation. Emmajin Beki dreamed of making a difference this way, and I wish I could help her achieve that."

A flicker of recognition ran across Nasreen's face, but then she suppressed it and stared at me blankly.

"Now that letter is probably lost," I continued. "That's too bad, because if she could deliver it to the Pope, he could not help but be impressed by her—not just by her beauty but by her status as a grand-daughter of the most powerful ruler on earth."

Nasreen picked up the empty pot and took it to a nearby stream to wash it. When she returned, she rubbed her hands over the embers of the fire to warm them up.

Watching her move, I wondered if it had been a mistake to confide in her. I continued. "It's a risky plan, I realize that. Khaidu's men would chase us and try to capture us. If they did, Khaidu would quickly execute me and continue to keep her hostage until her grand-father agreed to his terms." I shook my head. Being hailed as a hero after my own death did not appeal to me.

"What of Prince Temur?" she asked. "And Prince Nomokhan?"

Aha, I thought. Did I detect some emotion on her face? "I was hoping they could escape on horseback while I was distracting Khai-du," I said. "If they escape and return to the fortress at Almalik, per-haps they will tell the Khan the story of how I rescued them."

She suppressed a laugh, as if listening to the impossible plan of a younger brother.

I suppressed my annoyance. It was true that my plan was far-fetched. But what else could I do? "I wish I knew this territory," I said. "I'm not even sure how to get to the West, except to follow the setting sun."

She looked at me steadily. "I know this territory," she said. "My people live here."

But instead of feeling reassured, I felt a shiver of fear. I had been open with her, trusted her. Was she just using me to get back to her people? Would they help me, or would she tell them of my plans? I wished I had not spoken so openly. The stakes were high. But the calmness in her eyes had quieted my fears.

---

On the morning of the fourth day, a path led off to the left, heading straight for the snow-capped mountains. From behind my saddle, Nasreen nudged me in that direction.

"Are you sure?" I asked. The other road, straight to the west, seemed more well-trodden. I turned back to see her eyes.

"Yes," she said, with certainty. It seemed wrong, but I chose to trust her.

The trail, which had been flat, became steeper as we climbed through hilly country toward the mountains.

As we rode, I thought of my discussions with Nasreen. Was my hunch right, that she loved Prince Temur? Did she think she was riding to the rescue of a young man far above her in status, a Mongol prince of the Golden Family? Was that any more absurd than me, a Latin storyteller and merchant, riding to the rescue of the Great Khan's granddaughter?

Finally, on a ridge, we saw some horsemen approaching. I clenched my teeth. Was this it, then, the moment I would be captured by Khaidu's men?

But these two men looked more like local herders. From their hats and colorful clothes, Nasreen told me they were from her tribe, the Kirghiz. They wore tall white embroidered felt hats with black brims and black cloaks with thick metal belts.

"Remain silent," she said. "I will speak to them." Her body tensed.

My back tightened too, and I wondered if she would betray my secrets.

As the men came closer they called out something. I could barely understand their local dialect, but I could read their body language. As far as I could tell, the conversation went something like this:

"Who goes there?" they called.

"My husband and I are traveling to his homeland in the West," she responded.

"And why does he not speak?" the older man asked.

"He is from another land and does not speak our Kirghiz language."

"You speak like a local. Who are you?" asked the younger man.

At this point, the horsemen had approached close enough that I could see their faces. They had darker skin than Nasreen, probably from spending most of their lives outdoors, with similar wavy dark hair and long straight noses.

"Tell me!" the younger man said. "Who are you!"

She hesitated. "Danat?" she said, as if she could scarcely believe it.

No translation was needed for what came next. She jumped off the back of my horse and ran to one of Kirghiz herders.

"Brother?"

But the young man stiffened.

"Danat, it's me, Nasreen! You're alive!"

Here was the younger brother from her story!

"Nasreen?" he said, looking down from his horse, as if he could not believe his eyes.

If it were me, seeing my long-lost sister, I would have jumped off my horse and embraced her. Wouldn't a brother, whose sister had been captured by soldiers at the age of twelve, be overjoyed to welcome her back?

The older man got off his horse and strode toward her. He glared up at me. "Who is this man? Are you one of them now?"

Was he really more concerned with tribal honor than with re-union? As if a female slave has a choice in such matters!

"Uncle?" she said to the older man.

"Come with us," the older man said. He got back on his horse, and Nasreen came back to me. She mounted my horse, sitting behind me, and we followed the herdsmen.

"Is that really your brother? Do you want to go with these men?" I asked. She tightened her grip but did not respond. It seemed unreal.

Just over the next ridge, we could see a single ger, a herder's tent, with a line of smoke coming out of the dome. I could feel Nasreen tense up behind me, almost shaking—with anticipation? Or dread? I could not read her mind.

Were we riding into a trap?

Outside the tent, an older woman was walking, bucket in hand, and two small children were frolicking nearby.

"Mama!" Nasreen shouted. When we got close enough, she slid off my horse and raced to the old woman, her arms out. This time, they did embrace, and it seemed they would never let each other go.

I dismounted and stood holding my horse's reins, at a distance. I had never imagined I would see this family reunion. Had she known where the family would be at this time of year? Or was it coincidence? Had she abandoned the search for Emmajin and deliberately led me off course?

The older man yelled and pointed at me. "No, he is not my husband," I heard Nasreen say. "But he is a good man. He helped me."

Finally, Nasreen came to my side, with a smile on her face.

"I am home, thanks to you," she said. "Come in and enjoy Kirghiz hospitality."

I bowed in the Latin fashion, one hand behind my waist, one in front, in gratitude. Our food was running low, and I was hungry. I was also relieved that her uncle was not inclined to kill me for being with his niece. So I followed her inside the family home.

The family's Kirghiz-style tent looked much like a Mongolian ger—a dome on top of a round frame. Although made of felt, this tent seemed more gray than white, and it stood a bit taller than I expected. Once inside, I could see why. The roof poles, arranged overhead like the spokes of a wheel, were bent at the lower end, so they fit more smoothly into the walls. This allowed the roof to rise higher than a Mongolian ger.

Also, the dirt floor was covered with a few small carpets, not in the elegant Persian style but patterned with what had once been bright colors. Over one bed hung a beautiful hand-embroidered fabric, ornately decorated with flowers and curved designs, not new but still brightly colored—clearly the family's prized possession. Each simple stool had a seat cushion, also decorated with fine stitching. Sunlight from the roof hole shone into the tent, and a small fire burned in the center of the floor.

Nasreen, the slave I had once considered quiet, would not stop talking to her mother and her brother, Danat. Her familiar voice made the strange dialect easier to understand. The uncle and I sat silently on the men's side of the tent, drinking kumis. Nasreen watched in joy as her mother and sister-in-law bustled around the tent, in constant motion, getting dinner ready.

Danat went out and killed an aging sheep for us, a rare treat to have meat during the summer, when most herders eat only dairy products. I remembered the sheep slaughtered by the Mongols before they stole Nasreen.

Smiling, I tried to take in every detail of this amazing story I was watching. These people were not as demonstrative as Latins would be, reuniting after such a long absence. Family relations among the Turkic people were beyond my comprehension.

After dinner, Nasreen's mother pulled out some special liquor, also made of mare's milk but clear like water and very intoxicating. It seemed this was something special they served only to celebrate memorable occasions. The old woman poured some in each of our bowls and we drank to the family reunion. Although their dialect was hard to understand, I listened while Nasreen told her family about her years in captivity.

Then her brother, Danat, told his wife the story of the day Nasreen was captured: How she had insisted he hide under a sleeping fur, how the bad men had come into the tent, but he had stayed silent. How he had regretted, his whole life, that he had not done something to save his sister. How much he appreciated what she had done to save him. The longer he spoke the more I understood of his thickly-accented dialect.

As the evening wore on, Nasreen explained to them who I was, and why I had come. She told them I wanted to find Khaidu's camp, that Khaidu had taken prisoner someone important to me; she did not tell them who it was.

"Khaidu's camp?" her brother said. "I know where they are. We all know."

Khaidu's army had passed through a few days earlier. They were headed straight toward the mountains, through a well-known pass. On the other side of the pass, Danat explained, was Issyk Kul, a massive, deep saltwater lake. He suspected that Khaidu's army was headed toward that lake, a protected place that was easy to defend from pursuing troops.

"I can take you there," said Danat. "It will take only three days."

I eagerly accepted his offer.

That night, listening to the breathing of this family around me, I realized how much I had learned from this woman I had nearly overlooked. For once, I had listened, and this was my reward: Her brother would lead me to Emmajin.

I had been so eager to tell Nasreen what love was, and so convinced that she and her people didn't understand it. But now I could see: At its best, love is selfless. It means thinking of others before yourself. Sometimes it means letting go. As a girl, Nasreen had protected this brother of hers, saved his life, and the cost was being captured and forced to live as a slave. That was love, too, as I had never before understood it.

# Chapter 14
# Emmajin: The Contest

Early the next morning, I awoke to the sound of dogs barking and men shouting. Although I was no longer tied up in my tent, two guards sat by the entrance. One guard told me I was to get ready for departure. Men were busy taking down gers, removing their felt coverings, detaching the spokes of their roofs, flattening and rolling up their latticed sides, placing them on carts.

My guard held the saddle and helped me mount, as if I were a child or an old lady.     Ai-Jaruk rode up to me, and I asked her why we were moving camp.

"Why do you think?" she answered. "Your people are in pursuit. A folly. We know this region better than they do. They will never find us."

"What of our archery contest?" I asked.

"It will have to wait until we are set up in the new camp."

In the distance, I saw Temur, too, on horseback. I waved at him, and he nodded somber encouragement. He, too, was surrounded by guards. I regretted my harsh response that night of his embrace; he was a young man, and he had been drunk on grape wine, in the moonlight, responding to male urges. Temur would make a good leader someday, if he ever got back to court alive.

Just as we were leaving, I noticed a commotion. Temur had spurred his horse and steered away from the group, heading downriver. I spurred my horse to follow, but my guard quickly caught the reins.

Still, hope surged in my heart. Temur was a fast rider. Once he escaped, he could return to Almalik and come back for me with a detachment of troops. He carried with him the future of the Empire.

But it was not to be. A group of Khaidu's men caught up with him, surrounded him, and brought him back. After that, his hands were tied and his horse was securely tethered to another's. I was treated similarly. The leather thongs cut into my wrists.

I had plenty of time to think about my decision to challenge Ai-Jaruk. She kept her horse close to mine as we rode up the river and high into the cloud-shrouded mountains, continuing all day for three days. The higher we rode, the more my anxiety rose. The hillsides loomed dark green, with tall fir trees wedged onto steep mountain sides in tight patterns. At higher elevations, the stream rushed madly, choked by rocks as it charged downhill. Above us rose the peaks of the Heavenly Mountains, capped with snow even in this hottest month of summer.

When we came to a pass and could look down the south side, the view caught my breath in my throat. Below severe cliffs spread an inland sea, a huge lake of brilliant blue-green, guarded by two imposing mountain ranges. It was trapped in this land, fed by mountain springs flowing into it, but with no river flowing out.

Ai-Jaruk stopped her horse next to mine. "The locals call it Issyk Kul," she said. "That means 'warm lake.' It never freezes, even in the coldest days of winter."

This woman seemed to have two separate natures, one friendly and one hostile. I never knew which might show itself at any given moment. She seemed inexperienced and inexpert in the art of personal relations.

We wove down the steep trail and then rode single file along a narrow road, squeezed between cliffs and the lake, till we came to our campsite, a broad meadow protected on three sides by mountains and on the fourth by the massive lake. The narrow road was the only way to reach this campsite, perfect for defense.

The lake reminded me of the ocean, but its waves were tame. Flocks of mallards flew freely overhead, landing on the water and swimming in loyal pairs, as if mocking my status as a lonely prisoner. This spot, along Lake Issyk Kul, was the closest to a natural paradise I could imagine. Yet the bright sun on the water made my head ache.

Khaidu had chosen the following day for my archery contest with Ai-Jaruk, to entertain his family and men after the arduous journey. Once he had ensured the safety of his camp, he seemed inclined to indulge his daughter.

That day of the archery contest dawned cool but grew warm and gloriously clear by midday. I wanted to grab the day and take it back to Xanadu. It did not belong here.

All the men, women, and children of Khaidu's court and army gathered to watch our contest. It had been years since they had seen their princess Ai-Jaruk compete, and her usual matches were in wrestling, not archery. Rumors of my prowess had spread through the camp, exaggerated no doubt. Our competition had deep undercurrents: the pride of the House of Ogodei, older and more closely tied to tradition, versus the young warrior from the House of Tolui, seen here as usurpers who had gone soft under Chinese influence. I wished I really did have those elephant balls and their virility medicine.

Khaidu Khan took a seat on a wooden throne in the best viewing spot, and his son Chapar stood next to him. This time Chapar regarded me with cold eyes, and I suspected that he was not the one who had suggested a marriage between us. Perhaps he had his hands full with his other wives and did not want a troublesome one like me. Other princes and commanders of Khaidu's court surrounded him, and soldiers of his army looked on from the sides.

Temur was not among them. I wondered why he had not come. I assumed Khaidu had forbidden it—perhaps because of Temur's escape attempt. Or perhaps to ensure no one would cheer me on. I alone represented the House of Tolui today. Oddly, this thought gave me strength, as if all my absent relatives poured their skills into me.

Before beginning, Ai-Jaruk and I stood side by side and bowed to Khaidu Khan. We were dressed in identical outfits, a red tunic over a white del, with brown trousers and leather boots. But Ai-Jaruk towered over me in height and her shoulders seemed twice as broad. I felt puny and weak, and I knew my arm muscles were out of practice.

The targets were identical to the kind we used at home: a low wall of hand-sized sacks made from sheep gut, the center ones stacked highest. I was allowed several practice shots, to get used to an unfamiliar bow and a new setting. My arms adjusted more quickly than I had any right to expect, as if constructed from birth for the art of archery.

I had stood like that many times, bow pointed straight up, eyes on that low target, arm muscles tense, hands precise, mind focused sharply. The thick callous on my right thumb paid tribute to the thousands of times I had drawn a bow and released an arrow. It was, I had long thought, the epitome of who I was as Emmajin: the archer.

I had never hesitated to show off my archery skills, competing against any man or child. But this time, I stood shoulder to shoulder not with some boy cousin or soldier or nameless competitor but with Ai-Jaruk herself.

Ai-Jaruk, the legend, had given me the strength to try to control my life, to resist an arranged marriage, to develop my skills at warfare, to resist the expectations for a princess of the Khan's court. Expectations that I would move away and bear children for some man from another family.

Ai-Jaruk, the real person, had also rejected these expectations. But now that I saw her in her own setting, a nomadic tent city, where the outdoors was one great latrine, where half her life was lived on horseback, where hardiness and toughness were a necessity of life, Ai-Jaruk did not seem a rebel. By nature, true, she had a man's spirit in a woman's body. But her father had shaped her. He delighted in her victories and boasted of how many contests she had won. In fact, he had treated her almost as a son, refining her toughness like silver in hot flame. She had not grown up resisting her family's expectations; she had exceeded them.

If I had met Ai-Jaruk a year earlier, before I met Marco, I would have admired her skills at the three manly arts: wrestling, horseracing, and archery. I would have listened with awe to her stories of battles fought and contests won. I might even have laughed at the crudeness of her humor, even though I bristled at her father's claim to the throne.

But now I saw that she manifested the worst of Mongol qualities: brutality, arrogance, superiority, spiteful humor. Now that I had tasted the sweetness of courtly love, now that I had pondered the possibilities of peace, Ai-Jaruk seemed simple and crass. I had discovered the joys of being a woman; Ai-Jaruk, I suspected, had not.

I realized, with a start, that I no longer aspired to be like Ai-Jaruk. I looked at her thick arm pulling back the bow. It was not her body shape that repelled me, but her attitude. I hated her sense of superiority, the way she exploited power, the way she lorded it over me as if I were inferior.

Is this the way Mongols were seen in the rest of the world? Those who did not know about the sophistication of the Great Khan's court— did they see us as brutal and heartless, willing to kill thousands in a day, destroying towns and cities and entire civilizations? Did they feel as helpless before the Mongol army as I now felt before the great Ai-Jaruk and her power-hungry father, the pretender-Khan Khaidu?

Was there room for kindness and compassion in the world of the Mongols? I thought of my grandmother, the Empress Chabi, raised in a nomadic camp not unlike this one, now Empress of the World but exemplifying mercy and benevolence. I thought of the Great Khan, criticized as weak for his decision to lower taxes on the Cathayan peasants in order to rebuild the farms that fed them.

No, I did not yearn to be like Ai-Jaruk. What a fool I had been to think she would be like me, like the person I had become, wanting to find a way for peace and wise rule. I lowered my bow and looked at Ai-Jaruk with new eyes, waiting for her to begin.

Our contest was the best out of seven arrows. If I won, I might have a chance at freedom. I was on my own now—far from the protection of my grandfather. Never before had I competed for such high stakes.

The bow I was given to use, curved back on both ends like all Mongol bows, made of composite wood, horn, and sinew, was not as good as my own, lost in the skirmish by the Ili River. But it was not bad.    I ran my fingers along its smooth edge, glad to be holding again this symbol of my power and skill.

As I pulled back the string to test its tautness, I thought: this is a deadly weapon. These people have given me the means to kill. If I were a different sort of person, who would I kill first? The answer was obvious: Khaidu. He was plotting to overthrow the Great Khan of the Mongol Empire. If I killed him, I would save the Empire. But I would be killed immediately myself. This was a moment for heroism. Did I have what it took?

I was careful not to look up at Khaidu Khan, but I remembered exactly where he was sitting, surrounded by his sons and other family members.

Ai-Jaruk went first. Her arm muscles tensed as she pulled back and aimed her arrow toward the sky. I could see a dark stain of sweat under her arms. Why, I wondered, had she challenged me? Did she feel the need to prove herself in front of her father and brothers? Did my presence, and my reputation as a skilled archer, threaten her status as a woman warrior?

Then she lowered her bow and released the string with a twang. Her arrow whizzed through the air and hit the very center sack in the target. The judges all emitted the distinctive cry indicating a perfect shot and put their palms together, showing no distance at all between the target center and the actual hit.

"Good! Good!" shouted the onlookers. Even dour Chapar smiled.

Ai-Jaruk grinned at me. A part of me did not want to be compared with her in any way. Another part wanted to roll her in a carpet and stampede horses over her.

I rotated my shoulders and flexed my arm muscles. By now the sun was warm on my shoulders. A servant, standing behind me, held a quiver of twenty fresh arrows, all for long shots. They were made of good willow, with well-formed iron tips and vulture feathers. I selected a straight arrow and turned toward the target. Then I fitted it against the bowstring, stretched out my left arm, steadied the bow directly before my eyes, and pulled back the string with my right thumb. I noticed a tremor in my hand and willed it to stop. I was young and fit, and Ai-Jaruk was no match for Emmajin of Khanbalik.

I raised my bow, aimed to the sky, then swiftly lowered it and released the arrow. It flew straight and true, hitting the exact center of the target. The judges did not instantly emit their short cry or show their judgment with their hands. Instead, they looked at Ai-Jaruk. She nodded, and they put their palms together to show that I had hit the center.

I should have known then not to trust these judges.

"Not bad," Ai-Jaruk said. Even her compliment rang of spite.

Wiping sweat from her forehead, she turned to the servant standing behind her, picked another arrow out of the quiver he was holding, and checked it for straightness. She rejected it by dropping it on the ground. A second arrow met her exacting standards. She fitted it against her bow and drew back. For a fleeting moment, she looked at me. That distracted her, and she dropped her arms, shaking them as if getting better prepared. At her age, past thirty, did she fear defeat from a younger warrior? I tossed my head and stood straighter.

Her right thumb, calloused like mine, was as large as an apricot. It seemed to me that those bulky fingers would be a disadvantage in such an exact skill as archery. Yet her arms, thick as a horse's legs, concentrated strength and power.

She turned slightly away, as if willing herself not to notice my presence. The back of her del was now wet with sweat. She pulled back on the bowstring, and I thought I saw the string quiver. She stilled her hands, raised her bow, lowered it and shot

The arrow sailed over the target, landing in the dirt behind it. It was long. The judges' cries were mixed and hard to understand. They looked at the arrow, then looked at Ai-Jaruk with anxiety. She nodded, and they showed with their hands the distance the arrow had fallen behind the target. One judge showed the distance of fingertip to elbow. The other two showed a much shorter distance, wrist to elbow.

Ai-Jaruk's arms were too powerful. Her days as a master archer were over.

I flexed my right arm and shook it. I took my stance, holding my bow with perfect archer's posture, my right thumb pulling back on the bowstring. I pretended I was back at home, demonstrating for my cousins. I raised my bow toward the sky, lowered it, and released the bowstring.

The arrow sailed true, hitting the top center of the target, off by only the width of a finger. One judge declared it a direct hit. The other two judges cried out and showed a distance of a hand's width. I wanted to stomp and shout, *Unfair!* but that is the behavior of children. I clenched my teeth, raised my head and looked at Ai-Jaruk with defiance.

Officially, we were tied. One good shot, one bad shot, each.

She spat on the ground and rubbed her hands. Then she went to her quiver-holding servant and whispered to him. He nodded and offered the quiver.

Ai-Jaruk again selected an arrow and inspected it. She found one to her liking and fitted it against her bowstring. I watched her closely, but this time she did not look at me. Just as she loosed her arrow, I heard a noise behind me but I did not look, watching instead for the judges' call. The arrow hit the center of the target. It seemed off by a finger's width to me, but all three judges called it a perfect shot.

Ai-Jaruk grinned at me. I nodded, acknowledging a good shot.

I turned to my quiver bearer. The arrows in the quiver seemed different, not as I had left them. I always select the rightmost arrow first, and two arrows were in that spot. Someone had disturbed my arrows. I looked sharply at the servant, but he kept his face expressionless. Ai-Jaruk was inspecting the curve of her bow.

I selected an arrow, one of the new ones. I did not even need to look down its shaft to see that it was crooked. I dropped it and picked another. It was nearly straight, but not completely. Because arrows are made of willow, many are not completely straight; I knew that. But for a contest, only the straightest should be used. I looked at Ai-Jaruk. The bottom tip of her bow was on the ground, and her right palm secured the top of it. She was leaning against the bow, watching me with dull, lidded eyes, as if bored.

I dropped the arrow and selected another. It too was warped. I dropped it and fished around in the quiver for a straight one. The next one I pulled out was nearly straight, but not up to standard. The crowd grew silent, watching me.

It was obvious that someone had replaced my straight arrows with crooked ones. It was an old trick, one we sometimes played on each other as children. No one got away with it. Could I publicly accuse my captors of tricking me?

I did not want to whine. I selected another arrow, almost straight. I had practiced with such arrows many times. I rubbed it between my fingertip and thumb, as if that would straighten it completely, and smoothed the feathers, good vulture ones.

Ai-Jaruk sighed heavily, as if she suspected me of stalling for time.

As I turned to take my stance, I heard a sound behind me. Another servant was picking up the rejected arrows and putting new ones in my quiver. Or were they putting the rejected ones back? I did not look to see.

I fitted the arrow, took aim, and shot. I could feel in my arms that it was a perfect shot, but the arrow landed to the left of center. All three judges showed with their hands the same distance, a hand's width. It was the arrow, I was sure. I clenched my jaw.

I was down one. I wondered if I could win this contest at all. If not, then what? Was there anything else I could do, with dignity?

Ai-Jaruk made a show of selecting just the right arrow and shot again. Again, her powerful muscles overshot the target, by just a hair. The judges had to report it long.

This time, it seemed, all the arrows in my quiver were crooked—some slightly, some grotesquely so. No judge would allow such arrows in a public match in Khanbalik.

I picked them out, one by one, and dropped them on the ground.

"What's the matter, princess?" Ai-Jaruk mocked. "Our arrows are not as good as those in Cathay?"

*No, you worthless trash,* I thought. *And in Khanbalik, the true Khan's Capital, we don't cheat our opponents.* But all I said was, "I am looking for a straight one." As I looked, I tried to control my rage.

Finally, I found a straight arrow. I took my stance and aimed. An image bounced into my mind, that of Temur crossing the finish line ahead of me on a white racing horse given to him by the Great Khan. It was a race I should have won. Pulled taut, my arm muscles quivered. I had been cheated of victory before, but it would not happen this time. I steadied my arms and shot. The arrow, filled with my righteous anger, flew true and hit the exact center. After a slight hesitation, the judges called it a perfect shot.

We were tied again. My eyes flashed defiance at Ai-Jaruk. I, Emmajin Beki, would defeat her, even if she cheated. Her future was not at stake.

She laughed. "Good shot," she said. "What do you think of this little archer, Chapar?" She turned and looked at her brother. He was standing in the front of the crowd, next to his father's chair. To my surprise, I saw a look of relief on his face. Perhaps he did not want another wife, especially one as headstrong as I was?

A stocky boy of twelve or thirteen stood next to him, probably one of his sons. The boy was gesturing and talking to his mother; I suspected he was questioning the judges' call. He wore a round hat of blue and green silk, with a large red pom-pom at the peak, a ball of red silk with a red silk tassel hanging from it.

If I lost this contest, I would answer to Chapar's chief wife and have to take orders from that spoiled boy. But I was not going to lose. I would show them that we Mongols of the court lived by fairness and higher rules.

Ai-Jaruk shot another perfect shot. She was indeed a formidable archer. Every shot of mine had to be perfect in order to defeat her.

I looked in my quiver. All the remaining arrows, it seemed, were warped. I picked them out and rejected them, one by one. Each time I dropped an arrow, I felt a surge of anger. Anger, I knew, was anathema to good archery. I had learned that as a child; when I made Suren angry, I could always defeat him. I had learned to notice when someone was baiting me and to swallow my anger. I could feel the blood pounding at my temples. I pressed my fingers against my temples, to calm my nerves.

I heard Ai-Jaruk's derisive laughter. "I thought she *liked* competition," she said.

Calmer, I walked to Ai-Jaruk's servant and selected an arrow from her quiver.

"What are you doing?" my opponent demanded.

I inspected it, then walked back, taking my stance. It was a good, straight arrow, but it landed short of the target, by an arm's length. The judges jumped forward with a cry, all showing the same distance with their hands.

"Ohhhh." Ai-Jaruk's voice sounded as if her child had disappointed her.

Again, I was down one.

As Ai-Jaruk selected and fitted her sixth arrow, she glanced at me with a look that implied she was showing me how it should be done. She shot again. Her arrow seemed at least two fingers off target, but the judges declared it a perfect shot.

Blood surged into my face. "That was off center!" I cried.

Ai-Jaruk feigned surprise. "All three judges declared it a perfect shot. You question their expertise?"

It was getting to me, the judges' unfairness, the crooked arrows, the biased crowd, her jeering face. I could feel my breathing speed up. *Calm down*, I told myself. *You are a better archer than she is. She is deliberately baiting you.*

With only two shots left, I needed a backup plan. My first preference was to defeat her in a fair contest. It seemed that was now impossible. What else could I do? My mind whirred. My sixth shot was perfect, but I was still down one.

Ai-Jaruk's seventh shot sailed over the target, again. She frowned when the judges ruled it long, but it was obvious to all.

In her scowl, I saw, suddenly, what she had to lose. Over many years and many victories, she had won what I long pursued: the respect of the men of her family. She had defeated many men at the most manly of sports, wrestling. To have a woman defeat her now would be humiliating—especially a woman from the hated House of Khubilai. My life was at stake. But so was her standing among her people.

I breathed easier. My next shot, my seventh, had to be perfect. If I missed, I would lose.

Only one arrow was left in my quiver. I pulled it out. It was not straight. I dropped it on the ground and looked defiantly at Ai-Jaruk. She nodded to her servant, who brought over five arrows. He held them out, across his two forearms. These were finely crafted of willow, but they were a little short. I glanced up at Ai-Jaruk to see if she knew this. Any good archer can tell the slightest difference in the length of an arrow.

I could shoot a short arrow. I just needed to aim it a little higher and pull the string a little tauter. I selected the longest and best of the arrows.

The crowd quieted. Ai-Jaruk leaned on her bow and watched me intently. Then I took a long look to my left, at Khaidu, sitting in his chair surrounded by his family. I beheld the broad flat cheeks of Khaidu's wife, the wispy beard of Khaidu Khan, the square bearded chin of his son Chapar, and the moon face of Chapar's son. They were all traitors to the Great Khan, scheming to steal his throne, covetous of his power and might, envious of my beauty and skill. I wished I dared to send the arrow straight through them all, stacking them up as dead men. Next to his father, the stocky boy with the ridiculous pom-pom glared at me with an insolent, haughty look. Behind the boy was a wooden post, the kind used for tying up horses.

I rubbed the short arrow with my fingers, judging its exact length. Then I fitted it to my bowstring. It was vitally important that I hit my target exactly.

I raised my bow to the sky, keeping my eye firmly on the target. To hit it exactly with a short arrow, I would need to aim beyond it.

But as I lowered my bow I swiveled to my left in a smooth, rapid gesture. I let loose at just the right moment. Chapar's eyes grew large and he moved quickly to his right, towards his father, as if to protect him.

But my arrow flew to his left, straight at that red pom-pom on his son's hat. At this short distance, it quickly found its mark. It smashed into the red ball, making the boy's hat fly back, and impaling it on the wooden post behind him with a loud thwack. It could not have been a more perfect shot. I was lucky the boy did not duck. Instead, his eyes enlarged with fear.

Chapar turned back and grabbed the stocky boy into his arms. The hat dangled by its red pom-pom. It seemed Chapar and Khaidu and everyone else watching realized at once that I could easily have killed any one of them.

The person standing closest to me, Ai-Jaruk, tackled me. My chin hit the ground and then my chest. She sat on my back with her immense weight, nearly crushing the breath out of me. The weapon flew out of my hands, and someone grabbed it and took it out of my reach. Two servants rushed over and pinned down my arms and legs.

Faced into the dirt, crushed by my adversary, I felt wonderful.

Several pairs of leather boots surrounded me. At a gruff command, Ai-Jaruk lifted her weight off me, and the servants flipped me on my back, though they continued to pin down my arms and legs. I was looking up into the faces of Khaidu, Chapar, and Ai-Jaruk, all glaring at me with shock and alarm.

I began to laugh. With my perfect shot, into a crowd, killing no one, I had shown a far higher level of skill than Ai-Jaruk. Even by imprisoning me, even by cheating away my victory, they had not broken me.

Chapar kicked dirt in my face to stop me. I choked but kept laughing.

"How dare you attack the heir to the House of Khaidu?" Ai-Jaruk said.

"Is the child hurt?" I asked. "You can see that we of the House of Khubilai do not harm our relatives."

"Swine!" said Chapar.

"Silence!" commanded Khaidu.

I stopped laughing, curious to hear how he would deal with me. He could, of course, order me to be killed for my insolence. I recalled what Ai-Jaruk had said about how my great-uncle had killed a woman of her family by tying her up in a sack and tossing her in the river. Curiously, at that moment, I didn't even care.

"You cannot get away with this," Khaidu said to me, still sprawled in the dirt. "Which would you prefer: immediate execution or marriage to my son Chapar?"

"Immediate execution," I said, without hesitation.

"Then you shall marry Chapar," he pronounced. As he turned on his heel and walked away, I caught sight of Chapar's square face, which reflected horror.

# Chapter 15

# Marco: Fire in the Sky

Every good story needs an element of surprise, but Nasreen's pronouncement was one I had not predicted.

"I'll go with you," she told me.

She and I, after a day of rest, were talking with Danat about how I should proceed. The summer evening air was fresh and clean, and we sat on stools outside the family ger, drinking the last of the airag. It was her first full day as a free woman united with her family of origin.

As the crow flies, Danat had told me, we were not far from Khaidu's camp, but the mountain trails were steep and winding. He said it would take three days to get there.

Nasreen was giving me a steady gaze strikingly different from the blank look she had often adopted as a slave. Her story had just reached its happy ending; I could think of no reason for her to go on with me in this perilous venture.

"No. You should stay," I advised her. "You've found what you were looking for. You have no unfinished business with the Mongols at Khaidu's camp."

"You'll need my help," she insisted. Her certainty reminded me of the shaman and his predictions. How could anyone foresee the future?

"Danat will help me find the camp," I said. "Once there, I'll figure something out. Besides, how could you help?"

Nasreen persisted. "Most of the servants at Khaidu's camp are probably local people, Kirghiz like me. I can find out where the prisoners are being held. Servants may tell me things you could never find out."

"Danat could do that," I said.

Her gaze darted toward her brother, who was sharpening his knife on a stick.

"Danat will show you the way," she said, "but I doubt he will go into the Mongol camp with you. He does not speak Mongolian. You said yourself you can barely understand him when he speaks our dialect. Besides, he has no reason to care. He never met the prince or the princess. He hates all Mongols."

The word 'hate' made me cringe. "Do you hate all Mongols?" I asked her.

"Of course not."

Something in her flashing eyes made me ask her directly: "Is it because of Temur, that you want to go?"

She looked away, avoiding my gaze. "The prince is a good man, and I admire the princess greatly. Both of them treated me well. They should not be prisoners."

So I let her come—not that I could have stopped her. I felt relieved and grateful when the three of us took off together, early the following morning.

Nasreen's mother wailed as we left. After the long-awaited reunion, she did not want to let her daughter out of her sight. Nasreen held her hands for a long moment before mounting and assured her mother she would return soon. I hoped she would.

Danat led the way, with his sister behind him on a gray horse, and me bringing up the rear on Amadeus. We headed up a steep mountain path, and several times we had to dismount and walk. This man never hesitated when the trail branched.

Danat was even quieter than his sister, a tall and solemn man, and I could not read him well. He was helping me because I had helped his sister escape, but he had not warmed up to me, as her mother had.

On the first night, still on the north side of the mountain range, we camped under a rocky overhang, near the edge of a cliff that fell steeply below us to a rushing stream. The trees here were pines, thin and scraggly. This high up, the wind in the ravine blew much colder than on the rolling hills below, where Nasreen's mother had remained with the uncle and their sheep and goats.

We had one tent for the three of us, the small one I had brought. As we pitched the tent—hard to do on the rocky trail—Nasreen's brother regarded me with suspicion, as if looking for a sign that I expected his sister to warm my bed.

"I will sleep here," I said, tossing my sleeping fur on the men's side of the tent. Nasreen carefully laid hers on the women's side, and Danat put his between us, at the head of the tent, where the master normally slept. This seemed to placate him.

While Nasreen and Danat went off with their bows and arrows to find some dinner, I lit the fire and thought about my plan. There was one aspect I needed to practice.

I wasn't sure how the two of them would react. I didn't want to alarm them. But it was vital that I test out my new acquisition.

They returned with a small mountain goat, big enough for one meal for the three of us, albeit tough and chewy. I watched as Nasreen expertly gutted and skinned it. She tossed chunks of bloody meat into the boiling water, and I added salt, pepper, and a touch of ginger, to soften the gamey flavor.

After we ate, I tried to get Danat to speak.

"Danat, what do you know of these Mongols, this Khaidu?"

Danat glanced at me and picked his teeth with his finger. Nasreen jumped in to translate. My Turkic accent was as incomprehensible to her brother as his Kirghiz speech was to me. Danat growled out a short reply.

"He says he knows nothing of the Mongols and doesn't care to," Nasreen said.

"Do Khaidu's men often camp near the lake?" I asked.

After translating, she answered, "Mongols hate water."

That I knew, from my year with the Mongols. We Venetians love and respect the water, but the Mongols, raised on the grasslands far from the ocean, fear and distrust any large body of water. I thought of Emmajin, who had finally agreed to wade into the ocean with me, despite her deepset fear. It had been a huge symbol of her trust.

"They don't use boats?" I asked. "Do the Kirghiz use boats on this lake?"

"It's a deep lake," Nasreen translated her brother's words. "There's a Kirghiz fishing village at the eastern edge of the lake. We have cousins who live there."

"Danat," I said, finally. "Nasreen, will you translate this for me? Tonight, I need to practice something. When I get to Khaidu's camp, I will try to convince them to let me entertain Khaidu and his men with a story. Then, afterwards, I plan to create a show that will distract the khan and his men. This involves a display of light and fire in the sky, with great noise. I do not have experience with making this kind of show, so I need to practice. I need to do it now, before we get to the other side of the mountains, where Khaidu's men might see it. I don't want you or Danat to be alarmed. Can you trust me and watch as I practice?"

Danat frowned deeply as Nasreen translated, but I waited till I saw him nod at me before I began. She expressed her brother's only question. "Does it sound like thunder?"

I smiled to myself. These men of the grasslands, even the fiercest of warriors, feared lightning and thunder—perhaps because of the danger of unstoppable wildfires. "It makes a loud noise," I said solemnly, "but not the same sound as thunder."

I went to my saddlebags and got out the items I had purchased in the markets of Gold City and Almalik. First, I mixed three kinds of powder: white, yellow, and black, to make a small quantity of 'fire medicine.' This I had learned from a tribe of people in the hills of Carajan, southwest of China, during a journey the previous year with the Khan's troops. They used this 'fire medicine' for centuries to make loud noises during happy celebrations, and I had helped the Khan's troops use it in battle, to frighten elephants.

But this time I wanted to recreate the effect I had seen in Shingchingfoo with Wei-ming as fireworks—shooting bright streams of sparks into the sky, which then fizzled out into smoke before falling to the earth.

I got out the launcher, a short iron pipe, open at the top, with a small hole at the bottom for a fuse, and the twenty tubes, each with a long fuse rope coming out the bottom and a stick coming out the top. Each of these tubes, I recalled, was loosely packed with more of the fire medicine powder, plus some 'stars'—bits of metal salts that would turn into bright colors as they burned. The tubes were plugged with clay.

I wanted to save as many as possible of the tubes to put on a show for Khaidu. I decided to set off two or three to practice. I could not risk making a mistake in front of the man who had Emmajin in his clutches.

The vendor's warning came back to me, about the dangers if something went wrong. "Get too close," he had said, "and it could burn you badly. Maybe blow off your hand. Maybe kill you. Maybe kill your friend. Maybe set big fire."

Concentrating, I threaded the fuse into the mortar and measured out the three powders in the proportions I had learned. I packed it down as tightly as I could, then fitted a paper tube on top of it, with the long fuse underneath and the stick on top. I angled the mortar so that the device was aimed not straight up but at a slight angle. I wanted the little rocket to fly over the ravine, with the sparks dropping into the stream, not directly over our heads.

The brother and sister regarded me with curiosity at first, though Danat still had deep frown wrinkles on his forehead.

"When I light the fire, you will have to stay back, against the rock wall behind us. It's very important, because it could be dangerous," I told them. Nasreen translated.

Danat plastered himself against the wall, as far away as possible but still within sight. Nasreen looked over my shoulder, watching each step of the preparation. I had to insist that she stand back with her brother.

I adjusted the tube so it fit snugly in the mortar. My hands were shaking slightly. Fortunately, it had rained during the day, so the bushes in the ravine were not too dry.

After checking to make sure Danat and Nasreen were out of harm's way, I thrust a stick into our campfire till it caught fire. Then I lit the fuse under the mortar.

I ran back and joined the others. The three of us half-crouched there, our hands over our ears.

Nothing happened. The fire on the fuse had not caught properly.

I tried again, re-lighting the fuse. This time I stayed nearby just long enough to ensure the end of the rope caught fire. I ran back and joined the others, covering my ears. This time Danat and Nasreen did not cover their ears, although I told them to.

BOOM! The noise was deafening, and Danat cried out in alarm, covering his ears too late. The tube shot up in the air, not quite at the angle I expected, but close.

I watched as the fire on the tube's fuse worked its way up the rope. Then—

BOOM! With a second roar, the tube burst, high in the air, and brilliant red sparks burst out in an elegant sphere—flying straight up or out at first, then arching into lovely trails of color over the ravine. The stars burned out before hitting the ground, but I ran to the edge of the ravine to make sure nothing had caught fire.

Perfect! After all my worrying, I couldn't believe I had made it work on the first try.

Nasreen and Danat looked at me as if I were a master magician. They were speechless. Nothing in their life's experience matched the fiery beauty of this display.

I laughed with joy. They responded, smiling and laughing, too. Then Nasreen peppered me with questions about how the fire medicine worked, what the ingredients were, how I had learned about this. She and Danat examined the metal pipe, which was intact though blackened, and the other tubes and fuses.

"I need to try once more," I said, more confident now. "Are you ready?"

"Oh yes!" Nasreen cried. "Do you have other colors?"

I picked out a tube marked 'white' and started the process again. This time, both of them watched my every move: how I mixed the three powders, placed the fuse and the powders in the metal mortar pipe, packed them down, then fitted the paper tube into the pipe, with its long fuse curled under it. The stick on the top had bent slightly, and I had a hard time trying to straighten it, to make sure it would fly straight.

"You must stand back again. You really must. It's dangerous," I said. Nasreen stood back against the cliff, but Danat lingered near me.

"Let me light it," he said.

"No. I need to practice getting it right," I replied. "Please. Stand back."

The mortar had moved slightly, so I tried to set it back at the same angle as before, digging a little hole for it in the rocky dirt.

Once I was confident, I lit the end of the first fuse, then rushed back against the cliff. Danat wouldn't come all the way back to where Nasreen and I were crouching, with our hands over our ears. He insisted on standing closer to the mortar, to get a better view.

BOOM! The little rocket shot out of the mortar. But this time it did not go as planned. Instead of heading high into the air over the ravine, as the other had, it shot out to the side, toward Danat. It brushed against his arm, setting his del on fire, and then angled crazily over toward some bushes near the trail's edge.

Danat screamed in pain. I rushed to Danat and knocked him down, smothering the fire with my body. He was more frightened than hurt. The accident had only caused a brush burn on his upper arm, although the sleeve of his del was ruined.

BOOM! The second explosion went off behind me.

"Marco!" Nasreen screeched.

I turned to see white sparks bursting out from a bush, scattering crazily all over the trail and nearby bushes. One spark hit our tent.

I ran to the tent first and smothered the tiny fire there. Then I grabbed my sleeping fur and used it to smother the larger fire on the bush. Nasreen grabbed her sleeping fur, too, and ran around putting out the smaller fires. I struggled with the bush fire, which was hard to extinguish because of the shape of the bush. Finally, worried about damaging my sleeping fur, I pulled back and just watched the bush burn. It was small and not close to other bushes, so the fire did not spread.

All three of us were breathing heavily from fear even after the fire died out.

Among the medicines in my saddlebag, brought as merchandise, I found a salve cream for Danat's burned skin. He cursed in Kirghiz as Nasreen smeared it on his arm.

I examined the mortar, which was angled to one side. Either I had not placed it properly or I had not straightened the stick well enough. I wasn't sure which.

The vendor had been right to warn me about mistakes. They could be serious.

It took a long time to calm my companions enough to let me try a third time. But I had to. I could not, in good conscience, set off fireworks in Khaidu's large army camp without making sure I knew how to do so safely.

BOOM! The third rocket shot off perfectly, high into the air over the ravine. And BOOM! A shower of green sparks rained down like the branches of a weeping willow.

Yes! I could do it right. I sighed with relief.

I hoped none of Khaidu's guards were close enough to hear the loud noises. I cleaned up and packed my gear back into my saddlebags.

We sat up talking late that night. The explosions had opened Danat's lips. He talked a lot about how much he hated the Mongols, about the devastation Khaidu's men had wrought on Kirghiz lands, about friends of his whose sisters had been stolen. He loved my fireworks and wanted me to burn down Khaidu's camp on purpose.

"No," I insisted. "I don't want to start a war. That would be even worse for you and your people."

---

The next morning, we followed the steep trail up ever higher, until around noon, when we reached the pass. This seemed to be a trail no army would ever use—too narrow and steep. Finally, shortly after the pass, we could see over to the south side of the mountain.

Below us, spread in dazzling glory, lay an amazing deep blue lake, nestled amidst snow-capped mountains. I had never seen such a huge inland lake. I could see mountains on the far side, but to the west it was so long that I could not see the end of it. Although we were at an altitude that required heavy coats, the late-summer sun was shining brightly on the surface of the lake, giving it a brilliant sapphire luster.

"Lake Issyk Kul," said Danat. The word meant 'warm lake' because the saltwater lake did not freeze over, even in the depths of winter.

My heart quickened. Down there, in that deep valley, alongside that gem of a lake, was Emmajin. Soon I would see her, perhaps rescue her. At last.

We could not see Khaidu's camp at first. But after riding a while further, Danat pointed to a spot on the northern shore of the lake where there was a lot of smoke, from cooking fires. I could even smell the smoke on the breeze.

Danat stopped his horse. "I go home now," he said, wrinkling his nose as if he could smell the stinky Mongols below. "Come, Nasreen."

"No, I will go on," Nasreen said. "Rest assured. I will come back when my work is finished."

The two of them locked gazes in what looked like a power struggle. She had spent many years away from home and was not in the habit of obeying her brother's commands. After getting to know Emmajin, I knew better than to try to force a strong-willed woman to do something different, once she had made up her mind. I also knew better than to intervene in a family squabble. Secretly, I was pleased that Nasreen wanted to go with me. I had begun to think of ways she could help.

Finally, Danat shrugged his shoulders. We had a last midday meal together, and then her brother mounted his horse again.

"Thank you," I said to him, in my best Turkic. After he rode off up the trail, I turned to his sister and said the same to her, this time in Mongolian: "*Bayarlaa.*"

After her brother left, Nasreen spent a few minutes cleaning up. I followed her to the stream, where I sat on a rock as she washed the pot.

"What is the real reason you didn't go home with your brother?" I asked.

Scrubbing the pot in the stream, she did not look at me. She hesitated and then answered, "You told me once about one true love."

I waited, listening.

Finally she looked up at me. "Is it possible to love someone whose status is far above your own?"

I smiled. "Look at me."

She did not smile, but looked off downstream. "He will probably never love me as I love him. But I want to make sure he is free."

I understood. Nasreen and I suffered from the same ailment. It made no sense for us to try to rescue a prince and a princess of the House of Khubilai. But we had to try.

"Also—I have something to show you," she added. She gathered up the pot and spoon and bowls and we headed back to the small traveling tent.

Nasreen went into the tent and came out, holding a small package wrapped in cloth and rope. She handed it to me, using both hands, as if giving me a precious gift.

Carefully, curiously, I opened the package.

Inside was the Great Khan's letter to the Pope.

I closed my eyes for a moment, holding the letter to my heart, overcome by relief and hope. Perhaps there would be peace between the Mongols and Christendom. Perhaps Emmajin's mission would succeed. I thanked Nasreen again, from the bottom of my heart.

The next day, we wound our way down the mountainside and approached the small fishing village at the eastern edge of Lake Issyk-Kul. Nasreen's brother had given us the name of his cousin, a fisherman. After some bargaining, the fisherman agreed to sell us one of his small boats, with two pairs of oars.

I loaded my saddlebags into the boat, and Nasreen put her small bag there, too, along with her bow and arrows. The villagers gave us as much information as they could about the location of Khaidu's camp, on the northern shore of the lake, protected by mountains on three sides. Approaching it by water seemed the only way.

Nasreen and I set off on our quixotic quest.

# Chapter 16

# Emmajin: Uniting Two Great Families

Immediate execution or marriage to Chapar? I had decided, and my choice had been overruled.

Not long after I had been dragged back to my tent, too shaken by elation and exhaustion to think clearly, a maidservant entered with another set of too-colorful clothing. "For your betrothal banquet tonight," she explained.

I was shocked. Could they be serious, after what I had done to Chapar's son, shooting the hat off his head? Could Chapar possibly agree to go through with this sham wedding? Why would he want to? I decided that Khaidu must be trying to teach me a lesson in humility. Or was there more to it?

"No," I said in anger. "I demand to see my cousin Temur."

She put down the clothing and scuttled out.

Shortly afterwards, my tent flap moved aside, and the massive bulk of Ai-Jaruk entered my ger. She plopped down on a bench near me.

"What's this, my little sister? Pouting?" Ai-Jaruk asked.

I recoiled at her condescension and the whiff of sweat that reached my nose. But I was surprised by the look in her eyes. Instead of the jeer I expected, I saw there a look of hope. Could she somehow be pleased that I was going to join her family?

"You cheated," I said.

Her eyes registered a flash of anger. Then she nodded. "It was important that I win. For your sake." As if she had won so that I might have the opportunity to stay in Khaidu's camp.

"Where I come from, contests are won fairly." I tossed my words like knives.

She looked at me with amusement. I remembered that race, back at court, where Temur had beaten me only because the Khan had allowed him to ride an imperial racehorse. How many contests in the Golden Family had been predetermined?

"Your last shot missed the target," she said, her voice dripping with sarcasm.

"You probably cheated against all those suitors, too." I wanted to make her angry, but this comment made Ai-Jaruk smile benignly.

"Maybe you'll be as good as I am, if you keep practicing," she said. "Since you're staying, I can help you."

I wanted to spit in her face. Was she putting her considerable weight behind this ridiculous wedding? "I demand to see my cousin Temur. He will not approve. No marriage can happen without the approval of my family."

She searched my eyes, as if looking for a sign that I would like to stay there in Khaidu's camp, with her. For the first time, I sensed a hint of sympathy, a softening of her attitude. But I could not fathom the reason for it, except perhaps that she wouldn't mind my company as long as I accepted her right to dominate. Could it be that Ai-Jaruk was lonely, not fitting in with either the men or the women of her tribe? Perhaps I was the first woman she had met who was like her in any way.

"As you wish," she said. "Let's go now."

As we walked to Temur's tent, I imagined my life as Chapar's fourth wife. Every morning I would wake to the stench of urine in Khaidu's mobile camp, not sure if that day we would stay or decamp. For years I would wander about the deserts and grasslands of this distant Turkic region, far from both Mongolia and Cathay. As a daughter-in-law, I would effectively be a slave to Khaidu's foul-tempered wife, who was the head of household. I would be forced to learn to cook, sew, milk mares, make airag, churn butter, make cheese, tend livestock, give birth, wipe the bottoms of small children. Each meal, I would listen to the coarse language and vulgar jokes of these men. Each night, Chapar could do with me as he wished, no matter what my wishes were. Daily, I would see Ai-Jaruk, a constant reminder of the folly of my youthful idealism.

If I had babies, they would be members of Khaidu's clan. My sons would strut about, mocking the House of Tolui. My daughters would learn to emulate Ai-Jaruk, scorning their own mother. I would never see Marco again. The vision of such a life made me want to retch.

I had not cleaned up after the match, and my del still stuck to my back. As I followed Ai-Jaruk, I took note of the route to Temur's tent. She took me past her father's great banquet tent toward a small one on the far side, near the cliff that rose at the back of the camp. Two well-armed guards were standing outside. They followed us into Temur's tent and flanked us, swords at the ready.

Temur was sitting on a bench at the head of the ger, which, like mine, was fitted with colorful carpets and pillows. He was not tied. He leaped to his feet when I entered.

"Emmajin!" He came to me and embraced me. I buried my face in his chest. I had not realized how badly I missed him during these tense days.

"What's happened?" he asked me, drawing back to look at my stricken face.

I could not say the words. It felt as though I had fallen off a horse, mid-race.

Just then, Chapar walked into the tent and pushed his sister aside. He stood face to face with Temur. Their eyes were at the same height.

"What's happened?" Temur repeated, looking from my face to those of Ai-Jaruk and Chapar. I noticed that the two of them had both a sword and a dagger at the waist, as usual, while Temur and I were unarmed.

"Our families will be joined," Chapar said. "The betrothal will take place tonight."

"Betrothal?" Temur said, his words dripping with scorn toward one who would take advantage of a woman prisoner. He pulled me close, as if I were the helpless female I suddenly felt myself to be. I had run out of ideas about how to save myself.

"My father has decreed it," Chapar said, with perhaps a hint of apology in his voice. "You are to attend the banquet." I could not look Chapar in the face, but from his words and tone of voice, it occurred to me that perhaps he might be a decent man, trained from childhood to speak like a prince, now forced to play a role, as eldest son, that Temur might understand. He did not care how I felt, but apparently he was reluctant to marry if my family did not agree.

But he did not reckon on Temur's iron strength. "I do not consent," Temur said, loosening his grip on me so that I could stand by his side and face these usurpers. "No man in my family consents." He knew the rules well enough. No woman could marry without the approval of the men in her family—unless the bride was snatched. And for royal families, bride-snatching was cause for war.

Chapar shifted on his feet, his hand fingering the hilt of his sword. "You must consent. Your uncle Nomokhan has already spoken to us of this possibility."

There was a big difference between speaking of a possibility and contracting a betrothal. If Nomokhan had indeed made a firm promise—and I had no way to confirm it—I could never go back to court. I was truly a pawn in some larger game, with no patronage, no protection.

Temur narrowed his eyes. "Then you will have to go after Prince Nomokhan and get his word."

Chapar gripped the hilt of his sword, the reflex of a man facing an unexpected challenge. But before he could draw it, Temur reached over and grabbed the dagger out of Chapar's belt. At this close range, a dagger was more effective than a sword anyway.

By instinct, I stepped back as Temur flipped the dagger forward, toward Chapar. Chapar grabbed Temur's wrist and turned the point of the dagger down, but it ripped a slice in the front of Chapar's del. The two men, equally strong, grappled, and the dagger's blade flashed in the light streaming in from the smoke-hole in the roof of the ger. I reached for Ai-Jaruk's dagger, but she was too quick. She twisted my wrist down and spun my arm behind my back, pinning me with her bulk. I let out an anguished cry.

Temur and Chapar were more evenly matched, but the guards drew their swords and came forward. In the skirmish, Temur nicked Chapar's hand before Chapar wrested the dagger from him. Temur lunged toward the door, but the guards stopped him. They pushed him back into his chair and pinned him with the broad sides of their swords.

Chapar sheathed his sword with a sharp movement. A drop of blood traced a path down the back of his hand. "It would be easier if you cooperated."

"Keep your hands off what is not yours," Temur hissed.

"Bind him," said Chapar, in a resigned voice. A guard tied Temur's hands behind his back, despite his struggling. "Feet, too!" The guards lowered Temur to the floor, bound his feet, and handed the end of the rope to Chapar. "Get a cangue."

"Temur!" I hated the desperate, vulnerable sound of my voice.

Temur's face was red and bursting with humiliation and anger, as he lay on the floor with his arms bound behind his back. "The Great Khan will hear of this," he said.

"It's too bad you act this way," said Chapar. "My father had saved the seat of honor for you at the engagement banquet."

A servant returned with a cangue, a horrible wooden contraption that he fitted over Temur's neck. The cangue was made from the forked branch of a tree, and he tucked Temur's neck into the fork, so that the thickest part hung down his chest. He took another sturdy branch and placed it behind Temur's neck, using horsehair rope to bind the branches together behind Temur's ears, forming a wooden noose. Then he took Temur's right wrist and bound it to the thick branch on his breast with a leather strap, so that Temur could not use his right hand to free himself. The cangue was an ancient Mongolian way of binding prisoners, one that had been used on the Great Ancestor as a youth, when he was captured by the Taichiut clan. For nomads, it worked better than prisons.

I had never seen a cangue, since Khubilai no longer used it in Khanbalik. It was a hideous way to treat royalty. Horrified, I looked away.

There was no hope of reasoning with these people. Forcing me into a marriage was one thing. Putting Khubilai's grandson in a cangue was a declaration of war.

Temur yelled a curse, but Chapar's face was impassive.

"Come," Chapar said to Ai-Jaruk, and she hurried me out of Temur's ger.

I could think of nothing but saving Temur. I needed to find a way to rescue him from that hideous cangue and from this horrid camp. But how? I wished I had Marco's imagination.

That night they dressed me up and held a dinner they called my betrothal banquet. It was a cruel joke. Normally a betrothal is a celebration of two families, but Temur, of course, was not present, nor anyone else from my family. The mood was festive but felt forced. Chapar in particular looked glum and angry.

At the dinner, my mind went numb. I observed it all as if through a dark fog. Khaidu announced that our wedding would be celebrated with a big dinner the following day. Usually there were months or even years between betrothal and wedding.

Khaidu joked about the look he thought he saw in Chapar's eyes and wondered aloud if his son could keep his hands off me for one full night and day. This wedding, Khaidu said, would unite the House of Ogodei and the House of Tolui. My position as fourth wife to Khaidu's son would not-so-subtly acknowledge Khaidu's superiority.

Khaidu seemed almost giddy at the prospect. Chapar smiled grimly, accepting the teasing of his father and the other men about the prize he was about to receive in bed.

"What a fine horse you will have to ride!" one man said, eyeing me lasciviously.

"Enough!" said Ai-Jaruk, her eyes blazing. I was surprised at her vehemence. "When you have taken your enemy's horse, do you bait it with a stick?"

The men fell silent. Perhaps Ai-Jaruk felt a degree of sympathy. Had she ever been taunted and humiliated like this, as a woman? Whatever her motives, I felt grateful that she made them back off.

The air was cool, the meat was excellent, the airag flowed freely. But my gut was so tight and twisted I could neither eat nor drink.

After dinner, as the dancers emerged, a sharp cramp tightened my belly. I doubled over, and Ai-Jaruk called a servant to take me to my tent. "Bride's nerves," she said.

This time three soldiers stood guard outside my tent, and their manner was much more respectful. Fine carpets had been laid on the floor of my jail-ger, and several new down-filled silk quilts and pillows had been delivered to my prison.

I lay down on the soft quilts and curled around my throbbing stomach. It felt as bad as if I had eaten something poisonous, though I doubted that. I suspected it was a deeper poison, infecting my spirit.

I had tried to convince Ai-Jaruk to work for peace. That effort had failed. I had tried to gain Ai-Jaruk's respect in the archery contest. That turned into a farce, too. Here in Khaidu's *orda*, Ai-Jaruk had power over me. Power mattered more than skill. I knew that now.

Another stab of pain shot through my gut.

I've failed, I thought. All the things I wanted so much to do had come to nought. What made me think I had the right to a life different from any other woman? What made me think I was better than other people? How foolish I had been, pursuing the vain ambition of battlefield glory. How foolish I had been, trusting in people's better nature. If I had sat back and let my parents pick a husband, he surely would be better than this man Chapar. I would be among my people instead of vulgar nomads. Here I was an object of derision. I would never have a man of my own choosing.

An arranged marriage to that man was too awful to contemplate. I had tasted how sweet love could be, at its best. Now I would have to swallow a bitter marriage to a man I despised.

Everything I cherished had vanished. I had lost Marco, Temur, my freedom, my life at court, my status in the army.

There was only one way out. *Death.* That would show them all the consequences of mistreating a princess of the royal family.

I remembered the leather pouch at my breast. *This* was Marco's last gift. At the time I had wondered what it was for. Marco had told me that a high dose could be fatal. Is that why he had given it to me— to use at a moment like this?

I undid the top of my del and pulled out the rosary. Still attached to it was the small leather pouch. I pulled it open and looked inside. My nose recoiled at its sticky sweetness. The pouch contained enough sleeping medicine to kill one person. I could eat it quickly, and I would die. Then I would wait for Marco in the next world.

For a moment, I held the pouch next to my cheek. Marco had touched it. Marco was a prisoner, too, waiting in the garrison at Almalik. Did he know of my capture?

I imagined him racing across the grasslands of Mongolia, through Tangut, past the deserts, past the green valley of Turpan, to the Ili River valley, to bring me the message about Shirki's betrayal. I remembered the look in his eyes as he warned me, in Latin: *Principessa! Do not go.* Yet I had not chosen to escape with him. Why hadn't I defied Temur and obeyed General Hantum, who wanted me to stay in safety?

That old ambition, that pride, that desire to be remembered in legend—I thought I had outgrown it. But it had reappeared, and it had robbed me of the one man who could give me all I ever really wanted or needed in life.

I had been so confident that I could find a way to have both Marco and the respect of my people. Now I had neither. My life had been meaningless. Khaidu and Khubilai would never live in peace. Marco and I would never reach Venezia.

Instead, I was being forced to do what so many women of the Golden Family had done before me: marry a stranger to satisfy some great man's desire for alliances.

Yes, death would be better. It was the only way to preserve my honor, my dignity, and my love for Marco.

The tightness inside me eased. I had made up my mind. I lifted the pouch to my lips. The sweetness fouled the tip of my tongue, and I recoiled. It would take great courage to eat this stuff.

The odor overwhelmed my nose. How could anyone eat this? I poured myself a cup of airag, dropped some of the medicine in it, and drank. It burned all the way down my throat to my stomach. I forced myself to drink it down. Then I curled up again, clutching my belly. I closed my eyes.

Gradually the pain subsided. I lay still, gripping the leather pouch, waiting for the courage to finish it, to ensure a fatal dose.

I could not see a way out. But there must be one. Temur, strapped in a cangue, needed my help. Marco was still alive, somewhere, as far as I knew. That gave me reason to hope.

Sleepiness weighed down my eyelids. I drew the pouch shut. It might prove useful someday. But not now. Not this night. I could get through one more day.

Temur lived. Marco lived. And I wanted to live, too.

---

After a dreamless sleep, I awoke later that night and stared at a patch of sky, visible through the roof-hole, still black and starless, covered with clouds. In the darkness of my prison-ger, on a silk quilt, I lay drenched in sweat. Yet my body felt strangely calm, as if some greater power had quieted the worries that had upset it earlier. I gripped the pouch in my hand, rubbing my fingers over its soft leather. But I did not open it again.

Instead, my mind whirred like the wings of a small bird. I had to rescue Temur and escape. I needed to get back to Almalik, where Marco was waiting. But how?

Khaidu had many thousands of soldiers in his camp. Now that I had competed against Ai-Jaruk, almost every one would recognize me. I had no hope of escaping by daylight; yet the following night I would be Chapar's bride. I had waited too long.

Without a horse, I could not escape. Even riding a fast one, I would need a head start. A woman traveling alone would arouse suspicion. If I could rescue Temur, too, a couple traveling would not look so unusual. Yet how could I free Temur from that cangue, in his tent guarded day and night? Khaidu's horses were well-guarded. Could we get two of the fastest? Perhaps we could disguise ourselves so that we could travel safely through Khaidu's territory and then travel back to the Khan's fortress at Almalik. I didn't even know if Almalik was safe. Shirki might have taken it.

In the dark of the night, I sketched out a plan—a brilliant plan. I would act compliant during the day, as if I had made up my mind to cooperate with the wedding. Then, after the wedding banquet, I would put in Chapar's airag enough opium to make him sleep, but not enough to kill him. I was not certain of the exact amounts; I could only hope the medicine would take effect before Chapar had a chance to have his way with me. I knew the wedding custom: the male friends of the groom follow the bridal couple to their tent and shout their encouragement until they hear evidence that the marriage has been consummated. As Chapar dozed off, I would have to fake the sounds they would be listening for. Once the merrymakers had left, I would remove Chapar's wedding clothing. If Temur's guards were still awake I would offer them airag tainted with opium, too. Staying in my distinctive bridal costume, I would take the groom's clothing to Temur's tent, in the darkness of late night.

Then, I would borrow a guard's dagger, cut Temur free and have him dress in the groom's clothing. We would go to the pasture and ask for Chapar's horse, saying that Chapar and his bride wanted to take a late night ride. Riding two of the fastest horses, we would leave by the only road out—the narrow road east, between the cliffs and the lake. Then we would head north, back to Almalik. At night, in the dark, dressed in groom's clothing, Temur might be mistaken for Chapar. That would protect him.

The plan was risky in the extreme. It could easily go wrong. But what was the worst that could happen? I could be killed. Or I could remain a prisoner. But I was already a prisoner. The Great Khan might pay a ransom for Prince Temur, but not for the fourth wife of Khaidu's son. I preferred being killed by sword or arrow, trying to regain my freedom, rather than marrying the enemy—or taking my life.

In the morning, after a nearly sleepless night, my heart literally hurt. But my mind was calm and determined. I thought of my father in his Buddhist monastery, full of serenity. I thought of Tara, the goddess of mercy, who can see the sufferings of everyone. I thought of Marco, who would tell the daring story of how I escaped.    When dawn began to lighten the overcast sky on the day set aside for my wedding, I folded my quilts carefully. I went over my plans once again and girded myself for the ordeal of the day. I would have to suppress my anger and pretend to go along with this wedding. That would take more strength and bravery than any I had shown on the battlefield at Vochan.

Three maidservants arrived in mid-afternoon, the hottest part of the hottest day of summer. It was the last day of Eighth Moon. The maids used a soft cloth to wipe my body with cool water and essence of rose.

I wished I could talk to Temur, to tell him about my plan. It was as far-fetched as any that Marco might have dreamed up. Temur might scorn it at first, but then he would have helped me refine it. But even if I managed to see him, we would not be left alone. Someone would overhear us. Extra guards would be posted, both for me and for him. It was essential that the guarding be slack that night, that I seem to be agreeable.

The maids dressed me in a long white satin del, with a high collar and loose sleeves, secured with a red sash at my waist. I put my arms through the holes of a long red sleeveless tunic, open in the front, embroidered with gold thread. The maids exclaimed in wonder at my beauty. I didn't ask them what Chapar's other three brides had looked like.

As they clothed me, I felt like another person, a doll they were dressing up for their amusement, a warrior being humiliated. Inside my ger, the air was sweltering. I could barely breathe in the stifling atmosphere.

It was hard for me to imagine going through with a farcical wedding acting modest, with downcast eyes, not allowing anyone to see my spirit, my objections. Yet how many strong-minded women throughout history had done so? The more I protested, the more pleased Khaidu would be at crushing me.

Well, I would not give them that pleasure. I would trick them into letting down their guard. I needed to let them think they had succeeded in turning a spirited horse into a docile sheep.

The most elaborate part of my bridal costume was the headdress. It was heavy and overbearing, a stiff pink hat decorated in ornate patterns with gold-thread embroidery, studded with pearls, and weighed down with two long, thick braids of pearls and coral beads. Necklaces of pearls and jade connected these two braids, looping under my chin and over my breast. Across my forehead hung a fringe of dangling pearls, including one large pearl between my eyes. Although it was the most elaborate headdress I had ever worn, my sister would have laughed at its simplicity compared to those worn by brides at court. There, the gems were emeralds and rubies rather than simple pearls and jade, and the headdresses were so heavy the young brides had trouble holding their heads erect.

While the servants were beginning to braid my hair, I heard a rustling noise outside my tent, and the tent flap opened. Ai-Jaruk entered, already dressed in her wedding finery, with a bulky awkward headdress tipping unsteadily on her large head. After working so hard to calm my nerves, I did not want to see her pock-marked face, sneering at my humiliation.

She came and sat near me, lowering her bulk onto a wooden bench. I closed my eyes and tried to envision an expanse of grasslands on a windless day, covered with wildflowers and scattered sheep.

Ai-Jaruk shifted, as if expecting me to speak. She did not seem to know how to comment on my appearance. "My brother is lucky," she began, in a conciliatory voice. I shot her a hard look. "...to find such a strong woman," she continued. Why was she trying to be nice?

In this outfit, I hardly looked like a strong woman. "Such a good archer," she corrected herself. Stay calm, I told myself. Act as if...

"You will learn to like it here, with us," Ai-Jaruk continued. I could not believe my ears. Was she genuinely trying to make me appreciate this terrible fate? "Think of our Great Ancestor's mother, Ho'ellen. She is honored to this day."

I knew the story well. Ho'ellen had married a nobleman from another tribe, who was taking her home in a cart when Yesugei abducted her and forced her to be his bride. She had cried and screamed curses at him. I remembered the words from Old Master's story: "She set up a loud wailing, and she cried till she stirred up the waters of the Onan River, till she shook the trees in the forest and the grass in the valleys." Ho'ellen later became the matriarch of the Golden Family, mother of Chinggis Khan, the man who united the Mongols and conquered the world. Yet once she had been my age, forced to marry a man neither she nor her family had chosen. How angry she must have been with her new husband. This was a side of traditional Mongol culture I hated.

"You condone bride-snatching?" I asked Ai-Jaruk. Bride-snatching, I knew, was common practice only in the most backward parts of Mongolia. It was associated with poor people who could not afford to pay a bride-price.

Her voice took on a defensive edge. "This is not bride-snatching."

My hands shook and I tried to control them. I recalled my vow to speak calmly. "I was brought here tied in ropes. This jewelry is from your family, not mine. Your family did not provide any wedding gifts to my family, not even a single goat."

Ai-Jaruk set her lips firmly, as if suppressing anger. "If you and Chapar have a son, he would represent the uniting of two great branches of the Golden Family."

I sat straighter and stared up at the smoke hole in the tent roof. I thought of that ugly boy, the one whose hat I had shot off. Would my son look like that? Chapar's son?

"Imagine," Ai-Jaruk continued. "Your son would be a direct heir of Ogodei, the chosen successor of Chinggis. He would also be respected by the House of Khubilai."

"But Chapar has older sons," I said.

"The oldest son does not automatically inherit, you know that. It is the most capable who inherits."

A flash of heat surged through my body, already sweating. Could I have a son who would become Great Khan some day, uniting these two families? What an irony! "Khubilai would never allow it."

Ai-Jaruk grinned. "Your grandfather will not live forever. What if your son is born in Karakorum, the true capital of the Mongolian homeland?"

I was confused. "How could that be?"

"By next summer, we will be there, in Karakorum."

I looked hard into her narrow eyes as the implication of her statement washed over me. Karakorum was the former capital of the Mongol Empire, when it was still based on Mongolia and not in Cathay. My grandfather had moved the capital out of Karakorum, but to many Mongols, that was the true capital of the Mongol Empire, not Khanbalik. If Khaidu was planning to invade and occupy Karakorum, that meant he was finally taking action to usurp power from my grandfather.

"The first baby born in Karakorum, after we return from our victory," said Ai-Jaruk, her voice now seductive. "A son born of the two great ruling families, united at last. Would he not be destined for greatness? What woman would not want to raise a future Great Khan?"

It was tempting. I myself had been the first child of Khubilai's clan born after he became Great Khan. Yet as a girl, I had not been able to claim a birthright. Now, perhaps, my son might inherit the throne. I would have years to shape him, to ensure that he would be a wise ruler and not petty and bitter like the rest of Khaidu's clan. That is, if these people let me raise my own son. It had the odd feel of destiny.

Ai-Jaruk laughed. She had seen my eyes brighten with visions of such a future. "I should not admit it," she said. "But I might enjoy having you as a sister."

Ai-Jaruk was saying this to me. Ai-Jaruk, who had inspired me to join the army.

Ai-Jaruk, whom I had longed to meet. I took a closer look at her: her broad, flat nose, her brushstroke eyes, her hair pulled back harshly from her flat cheeks. Did she want a sister to confide in, to keep her company, to grow old with? Or did she want a younger sister to dominate, to domesticate like a wild dog? She smiled, showing her crooked yellow teeth, as if trying to seem benign and even, yes, friendly.

I nodded back at her with a weak smile, my best attempt at acknowledging her overture to me. I, too, had felt lonely when surrounded by men and women who did not understand me. But I would never have sanctioned this sort of humiliation of another strong woman.

She put her wide, thick hand on top of mine. "You'll do fine today," she said. "Chapar will be happy with his bride."

She rose and began to leave. "Oh," she said, turning just before reaching the tent flap. "My father has arranged special entertainment for your wedding banquet. A foreign jester has arrived, a trickster who can entertain with smoke and fire and loud noises."

My heart leaped. "Foreign? From where?"

"I don't know. Big beard, big nose." She paused, as if reacting to some look of recognition she saw in my eyes. "You know someone like that?"

I commanded my eyes to go hard. "No," I said, too ardently. "I have no interest in such light-hearted things on this day. If you'll excuse me, I need time to get ready."

After she left, the servants continued braiding my hair and fixing it in decorated braid coverings. The news that Khaidu had a plan to usurp power was stunning. But I could think of only one thing: the bearded foreigner.

It had to be Marco.

# Chapter 17
# Marco: Wedding Banquet

The last thing I expected was to arrive in time to celebrate Emmajin's wedding.

Emmajin's wedding! To Khaidu's ugly, middle-aged son, Chapar, as his fourth wife! When I heard this, my mouth filled with the taste of bile. Beautiful, spirited Emmajin Beki, treated like a breeding mare.

I had to act, and much faster than I had planned.

Nasreen and I left the fishing village early that morning, and it took much longer than I expected—nearly all day—for us to row a small boat across Lake Issyk-Kul to Khaidu's camp. I had obtained two sets of oars, but now I wished I had brought along a village fisherman to row for us, too. But that did not fit my plan.

I had bargained hard to obtain a boat big enough to carry five passengers; I hoped that Emmajin, her cousin Temur, and her uncle Nomokhan would be in the boat on the return journey. The Great Khan might reward me richly for rescuing his son and grandson. But if I could rescue only Emmajin, I thought, perhaps we could row in the opposite direction—toward the West.

The water of Issyk-Kul was sky blue in color, exceptionally clear, and I could see small fish swimming deep below our boat. After we pushed off from the sandy shore, the bottom fell off quickly, though. The fishermen told us this was the deepest lake in the world.

The summer sun beat down as Nasreen and I rowed. I had to take off my del and wear only trousers, and even then sweat poured down my chest as the day wore on. Nasreen, seated in front of me on the boat, facing away, glanced back at first but then averted her eyes when she saw the curly hair on my chest. Most men in this part of the world have smooth hairless chests.

Sweat was dripping down Nasreen's neck, too, and of course she could not remove her del to cool down. Nasreen had an especially hard time rowing; her arms simply did not have the muscles she needed. Not that mine did, either. Traveling and storytelling do not develop arm strength. I needed Emmajin, with her archer's arms.

When the sun was at its highest in the sky above the peaks on the south side of the lake, we stopped to rest.

"Here," I said to Nasreen, handing her the leather pouch of drinking water.

She felt how thin it was and looked at me. "It's almost gone."

I nodded. "Go ahead, finish it." The lake water, oddly, was salty and undrinkable.

During our rest break, she began asking some pointed questions about my plan. I had already told her the basics, about how I hoped to soften up Khaidu and his men with my storytelling as they drank heavily at a banquet, then distract them with fireworks. My goal was to find a way to rescue Emmajin, her cousin and her uncle by boat while the whole camp was drunk and distracted.

"What about the camp guards?" she asked. "Won't they be sober and watching, making it impossible to leave? You know how Mongols hate water. How are you going to get Prince Nomokhan, Temur, and Emmajin all to trust the water and fit into this small boat? Don't you think Khaidu might have Kirghiz servants who have boats and would pursue us across the water? How do you plan to get back to the fortress of Almalik, eight days' journey away?"

I did not have good answers. On our journey together, Nasreen had proved herself to be level-headed and practical, just like an older, wiser sister. So I asked for her ideas, and we talked about various options.

Finally, she asked, "What can I do to help?"

We discussed a few possibilities. Most involved her being invisible to the Mongols—almost impossible when we were the only boat approaching their camp.

"You're not afraid of the water?" I asked her.

She laughed. "No, of course not!" she answered. "I can even swim. It's so hot, I'm tempted to dive in. Do you want to see me swim?"

She reached to unbutton her del at the neck. Her hair was plastered to her neck, and I could see the sweat streaming down her face.

"No!" I cried.

But it was too late. She pulled at her sash, and her del fell open. I gasped, but then noticed that she had bound her breasts tightly with a long cloth. So when she dropped her del off her shoulders and wriggled out of it, she was not naked. She also wore loose silk pants underneath, wet with sweat and plastered to her bottom.

I was not used to seeing a woman's bare shoulders, arms, and waist.

I reached into the water and splashed her back. "Don't go in the water," I said. "I believe you, that you can swim." The water was surprisingly warm on my hand.

She laughed and turned back, picking up her oars from the bottom of the boat. "Shall we continue?" she asked, as she dipped her oars in the water.

We began rowing again. I was at the rear of the boat, rowing with my back to the shore, and she was in front of me, with a second set of oars, facing away from me. Although I thought of her as a sister, I could not help staring at the smooth skin of her pale shoulders and watching the muscles of her bare arms.

As we rowed, she asked, "Did you hear about the killer fish?"

I laughed nervously. "Killer fish?" Maybe I had misunderstood her dialect.

"The people in the village told me about it," she said. "Bigger than a man. Pale brown. Huge teeth. It usually swims near the bottom, but sometimes it comes near the shore and attacks men and swallows them alive."

I shuddered. This sounded like the sharks that I had heard about at home, in the Mediterranean. But I did not think this lake big enough for them—and I thought they lived only in salt water. But Issyk-Kul was a saltwater lake. And of course it probably had fish unknown in the West.

Nasreen turned her head to check my reaction. I laughed. "When I was boy, I saw killer fish every day," I said. "I used to wrestle them."

This time she laughed. "Oh. We Kirghiz eat them for breakfast," she said. We both knew we were teasing, and somehow it made our mission less frightening.

"Let's catch a killer fish and show it to the Mongols at Khaidu's camp," I said.

That really made her laugh. "Then offer to teach them to swim!" she said. I wondered where this Nasreen had been these past two decades. She seemed to be dropping the hard surface she used to protect herself, all those years as a slave.

The time passed more quickly in the afternoon. Soon we could see the whitish-gray dots of the tents in Khaidu's camp, and we rowed straight in that direction.

Emmajin was there, amidst those gray dots. I put more energy into my rowing.

Khaidu's guards could not have been expecting anyone to approach over the water, but we were visible from far away, and five soldiers stood on the beach, bows loaded and ready. As soon as we caught sight of them, Nasreen stood up.

"I think I'll investigate that killer fish," she said. With no more explanation, she grabbed her dark-colored del and dove into the water.

Shocked, I held on to the sides of the boat as it rocked. Her wet head surfaced, and she grinned at me.

"What are you doing?" I demanded. But she just swam away, toward the shore but at an angle, so that Khaidu's men might not see her. Her dark shape quickly disappeared into the reeds near the shore. As I watched her go, I guessed that she was carrying out some plan of her own—or expecting to figure out a plan once she got there. I just wished she had told me.

Alone, I kept rowing toward the main beach of the encampment. As a sweaty, bedraggled boatman, I apparently did not strike fear in the hearts of the Mongol guards. They lowered their bows but did not wade in to help me disembark. Instead, the five archers stood in a row, blocking my way.

Behind them, on a gentle slope, were arrayed about one hundred gers, Khaidu's camp. The gers were Kirghiz style, with gray felt coverings and somewhat higher domes than typical Mongol tents, and a few were decorated with embroidered banners or door flaps. Two much larger gers stood higher on the slope, one with a flag flying from the top of the dome. The horses, I could see, were pastured off to the right, where the shoreline narrowed to a thin strip between the water and the cliffs. It was a perfect, safe place for a camp, between high mountains and the deep lake, accessible only by one road on that narrow strip of land, easily defended.

With one last push, I maneuvered my boat onto the sandy beach and steadied it. "Who goes there!" one of the soldiers barked in Mongol-accented Kirghiz.

I stepped out, grabbed the boat's rope, and looked up. One of the soldiers flinched when he saw me up close, with my rounded nose, my green-blue eyes and my curly, reddish-brown beard. I wondered if they had ever seen a Latin, a man from the Far West.

I bowed, Latin-style, with one hand behind me and one in front. Then I answered in Mongolian. "A weary traveler, honorable captain. Have you fresh water to drink?"

They ignored my request and narrowed their eyes in suspicion.

"Who are you? Why did you come here?" one of the soldiers barked. They stared hard at my half-naked, sweaty body.

Despite my parched throat, I reached for the one skill that helped me most: my 'silver tongue.' I tossed back my shoulders and tried to look dignified. "My name is Tristan. I am a Latin from the Far West. I am here to offer my services to the Great Khan Khaidu, as a skilled storyteller."

I knew that Emmajin would have hated hearing me give the title of 'Great Khan' to Khaidu, since only Khubilai rightfully bore that title. Khaidu was a khan in this region, but not "Khagan," or Khan of all Khans. In my travels, I had learned that flattery, in appropriate doses, could be more effective than a sword or an arrow.

The captain narrowed his eyes to a slit as he regarded me. At least they had not seized me as a captive the minute I stood on the shore.

"I will take you to my commander," he said.

I insisted, first, on tying up the fishing boat to a nearby tree stump. No Mongol, I knew, would touch it. I also put on my finest del to meet the commander, so I would not appear to be a common fisherman. All my fireworks equipment was in a leather satchel, which I carried with me.

As I followed the captain to a nearby tent, I noticed that armed guards were stationed outside many of the gers and along the camp's periphery. Servants were rushing around, carrying buckets of water and piles of clothing.

My fluency in Mongolian helped me with the commander, who seemed impressed that I spoke the polite language of the court. Once I entered his tent, he welcomed me in the Mongolian way, offering me the 'honored guest' stool at his right in the back of his ger, as well as a bowl of airag, which I drank from before we spoke of business. I was so thirsty I drank the whole bowl at once.

"Honorable commander, I spent many months in the city of Khubilai Khan," I told the commander. "But I found him to be an insufferable barbarian, and I left as soon as I could. Now I am traveling back to my home in the Far West, and I have come to ask the Great Khan Khaidu for a tablet of passage through these lands. In exchange, I have but one gift to offer him: my skill as a storyteller. I think your great leader will appreciate hearing my tales of what a terrible ruler Khubilai is. Some call him Khubilai the Wise. But at court, when his back is turned, some call him Khubilai the Idiot."

This line made the commander and his men laugh, and I could see their shoulders relax. I told them a quick story—totally fabricated—of Khubilai saying something stupid, stumbling on his feet, and falling off his horse, and I had the guards guffawing and slapping their sides within a few minutes.

"His feet are so swollen he can barely walk," I said. "He leans on two slave girls at all times just to get from his bed to take a piss." The Khan's swollen feet were a taboo subject at Khubilai's court—a disability no one was allowed to mention publicly.

I surprised myself, the way I could switch from loyal courtier to sarcastic fun-maker so quickly. But I had traveled through many lands, and one thing I had learned was how to please my audience wherever I found myself. Everyone loves making fun of a common enemy. I hoped I could let loose in front of Khaidu without Emmajin's eyes widening in shock as I belittled her revered grandfather.

Laughter makes quick friends, and before long the commander had sent me to a higher-level officer, who agreed to forward my request to appear before Khaidu and entertain him with a story.

"Your arrival is well-timed," the commander told me. "Tonight, Khaidu Khan celebrates the marriage of his son, Chapar, to a nubile young maiden we captured recently. She is a granddaughter of this pretender you mention, this Khubilai."

I nearly spit out a mouthful of airag. "Marriage?" For a moment, I lost my ability to act the part I was playing.

The bile taste filled my mouth as I heard him tell the amusing story of the proud young woman who had dared to challenge their Princess Ai-Jaruk in an archery contest. How she had lost (lost? the famous archer Emmajin?) and yet Khaidu was honoring her by accepting her as the fourth wife of his eldest son, Chapar.

"Wait till she gets to know his first wife!" one of the soldiers said merrily. "She'll wish she were a slave to Ai-Jaruk instead!"

They all laughed heartily at that, and I tried to stretch my mouth into a smile.

My heart was spinning like a tornado. This could not be happening. All my clever plans for winning Khaidu's trust over several days and preparing him for the fireworks show sank like a stone in deep Lake Issyk-Kul.

My mind whirred, revising my plan. I would need to act quickly.

"Celebrating a wedding, tonight?" I finally said, when my voice came back. There was not much time. I would have to carry out my plan this night, after the wedding dinner but before the marriage was consummated. "I would be happy to entertain your khan and his men at dinner. But after dinner—I have something that could help you celebrate in an even grander way. A show that will make this wedding the most memorable ever."

---

In the few hours remaining before dinner, I had no time or freedom to wander the camp and find the tents where Emmajin and Temur were kept, as I had hoped. Using flattery, I managed to get the commander to talk about the high-profile prisoners from Khubilai Khan's family. He told me that the young prince had 'misbehaved' and could not be permitted to attend the dinner that evening. Of course, Temur would have tried to prevent this abomination of a wedding.

What humiliation for Prince Temur—to know his cousin was being forced into such a degrading marriage!—and to be unable to stop it.

I wondered where Nasreen was, and how or whether she had slipped into the camp, dripping wet, without detection. I hoped that she was exploring the layout of the camp.

Fortunately, these Mongols, though not used to bathing themselves, allowed me to wash up after my hot, exhausting day of rowing. A servant brought me a bucket of fresh water from a nearby stream, which I poured over my sweaty chest and head. In the way of Mongol khans, they provided me with a fine set of clothing for the dinner, comfortable and clean but nowhere near as fine as the cloth-of-gold emerald and sapphire robes provided by the Great Khan Khubilai at his summer palace in Xanadu.

The sun had just dipped below the magnificent, fir-clad mountains in the west but the hot air still hung heavy when they escorted me to Emmajin's wedding banquet, which had already begun.

The commander informed me that he had received a message from Khaidu, who was willing to let me entertain him at tonight's banquet. I was surprised but pleased to hear that he was willing to trust a total stranger. Apparently my jokes about Khubilai Khan had convinced his minions that their leader would find my humor entertaining.

As I was led to the largest of the tents, up the slope, near the protection of the cliff, I looked around. The tents seemed to be arranged helter-skelter, not in the neat rows as in the Mongol Army—although all doors, of course, faced due south, toward the lake.

It seemed that all the women and children in the camp came out to watch this bearded foreigner pass. Many women wore the colorful head scarves of the local Kyrgyz tribe, and the small children wore almost nothing. I looked deep into the crowds, hoping to catch a glimpse of Nasreen, or a hint of where Emmajin might be. She had probably passed this way less than an hour before, dressed in as much wedding finery as this crude Mongol camp could provide.

The minute I entered the huge tent, the smell of unwashed bodies, overcooked mutton, and fermented mare's milk overwhelmed my nose, and I nearly gagged. The wedding banquet was well under way, with loud voices, crashing music, and the barking of dogs under the tables, fighting over bones tossed from the tables. By the time my eyes adjusted to the dim light inside, I was being led around the left side of the rounded tent, behind the revelers, toward the head table on the north side, farthest from the door.

The head table was set on a raised platform, and I caught a glimpse of a bulwark of wide male bodies, shoulder to shoulder, all wearing pointed white hats. At the table to their left was the women's table, with five or six equally wide women.

In the midst of the women sat one slender, lovely figure—Emmajin. She was staring straight ahead, with an empty look, as if her spirit had left the shell of her body.

My heart nearly leaped out of my chest at the sight of her. Her slim body was dressed in a white satin del with a high collar, covered by a red tunic. But most remarkable was an oversized, stiff pink headdress perched precariously on top of her head like a huge vase, narrow in the middle and wide at the top. It was the most ridiculous hat I had ever seen. A huge peacock feather rose out of the top of it, and the bottom was weighed down with thick braids of silver and pearls and coral beads. Necklaces of pearls and jade looped under her chin and over her breast, like some absurd-looking bird. Her hair was invisible, stuffed up inside that monstrosity. How the Mongols could think that beautiful was beyond me.

The women around her, wearing similar bizarre headdresses, were among the ugliest I had ever seen. An older woman—possibly Khaidu's chief wife?—would have easily frightened children back home, and another wore a scowl so fierce I felt like running. But the largest of all was a younger woman, thick and muscled, who smiled at Emmajin with a look of possession that sent shivers up my spine.

When I caught sight of Emmajin, I stopped still. I wanted to drink in the sight of her, yet I felt nauseated, seeing her in such foul company. Slowly, almost imperceptibly, her head turned till she faced me.

The moment she caught sight of me, a jolt straightened her back, and the crazy hat wavered above her, its feather quivering.

Her presence shimmered in the tent. I held her gaze as long as possible. In that moment, I could see it all: her despair, her defeat, her loneliness, her anguish. After our long separation, I wanted to drink the dark liquid of those deep eyes of hers.

My ears shut out the loud voices around me, and all the crude, crass Khaidu people disappeared for a moment. She saw me, and I saw her, and nothing else mattered. I forced my face into a confident smile, trying to convey the message, "Do not fear! I have come to rescue you!"

The torchlight caught a sparkle of wetness in her eyes.

I looked away. I knew that she needed to act as if she had never seen me before. She lifted her airag bowl to her lips, and then leaned over to comment to the old woman next to her, who quickly looked at me, too. I could imagine her comment, because I had heard it before: "Can that man even speak Mongolian?"—or, as the Mongols commonly said when they saw me, "Does that man even know how to talk?"

I continued walking behind the commander, who was waiting for me near the head table. Khaidu caught sight of us and nodded to the commander. Khaidu raised his bowl, and the room grew silent as each person held his own bowl to his forehead.

My eyes quickly scanned the head table. Sure enough, Temur was not there. I hoped Nasreen was finding out where he was being held.

Next to Khaidu, slightly lower, sat a man I assumed was the bridegroom, Chapar. He looked wrinkled from too many years riding across the grasslands in the hot sun. Chapar too looked ridiculous, wearing a tall peaked red hat, with a wide black brim, a gold knob on the tip and a red tassel hanging down the back. In this very masculine Mongolian setting, he looked like a fop.

At a nod from Khaidu, the commander introduced me, in a loud voice, as Tristan, a Latin traveler from the Far West, an entertainer. I tried not to let my eyes stray to Emmajin's face. I knew she would recognize the name.

I stood before Khaidu and bowed in the Latin way. "I am most honored, Khaidu Khan," I began. I knew he preferred the title 'Khagan'—Great Khan—but out of deference to Emmajin, I could not bring myself to say that. Instead, I deliberately used my foreign accent to swallow the word so that it would not be clear whether I had said 'khan' or 'khagan.'

"And honored Prince Chapar, congratulations on your bride," I continued, nodding in Emmajin's direction without looking at her. "She is the most beautiful I have ever seen!" I bowed to Chapar in my Latin style, which I knew Mongols found amusing. The men laughed nervously. I should have kowtowed, but as a foreigner I might be forgiven. "I tried to snatch her before you got her, but she would not have me." Everyone roared at the absurdity of a bearded foreign merchant trying to snatch a Mongolian princess. I purposely exaggerated my foreign accent for comic effect.

Laughter always bolsters my confidence—at least when I intend it. I spoke up in my most dramatic storytelling voice, with a knowing smile: "As they say in my country, Give me this lovely lady, and I will hold her and serve the khagan forever for her love."

Now everyone in the tent was laughing. Such a request, from the accented voice of a foreign man, was not threatening but absurd. I dared to look at the bride, who was staring intently at her plate, blushing furiously, as she should. Yet I could almost hear her thoughts: *Marco! Stop it!*

The joking served me well. I played the crowd like a well-tuned fiddle, judging their level of drunkenness, their mood, what types of humor would work with them. They were, I could tell, well lubricated from generous servings of airag.

"Tristan at your service," I proclaimed. "I am a humble merchant traveler from the Far West, returning to my homeland after a stay in the corrupt land of Cathay." I heard grunts of approval.

"While traveling in the East, I learned some Cathayan trickery with noise and smoke. The backward people of Cathay enjoy hearing thunderous noises and seeing sparks of fire. It is the latest in entertainment there, and I humbly hope you will find it amusing. If the honored Khagan Khaidu wishes, after the banquet, I will put on a small display by the lake, setting off the fireworks from a small boat so as not to unduly alarm the ladies."

The crowd began buzzing at this, and Khaidu frowned.

"We shall see," Khaidu said. I could tell that he did not trust me yet. I would have to win his confidence by telling a great story.

So I launched into my tale. After more than a year in Mongol territory, my words now flowed from my lips, using familiar Mongolian terms, even puns and inside jokes. I wanted them to forget I was not one of them.

"Long ago and far away," I began. "Or maybe not so long ago or not so far away," I added with a wink, "there lived a corrupt king, drunk on his own power, ruling a land he had no right to rule."

The room went silent. I could not bear to look at Emmajin, who would catch on soon enough. I looked straight at Khaidu Khan instead.

"This king came from a line of noble hunter-warriors, descended from a blue-gray wolf and a fallow deer." This, I knew, came straight from the secret history of the Mongols, a story every Mongolian knew as their ancestral origin. "But this king did not deserve his noble ancestry. After his elder brother died, he called together an assembly of his friends and supporters, who elected him king without consulting the other nobles. When his younger brother challenged his right to rule, the king had him killed."

I could almost hear Emmajin gasp, though I knew she would not make a sound. Such words were blasphemy in her family. I hated offending her, but I had only a short time to win Khaidu's trust. I could not do so over several days, as I had initially planned.

At that moment, Khaidu chose to take a sip of airag. As is the Mongol custom, the music struck up, and we all lifted our airag bowls to our foreheads, waiting for him to drink. Then we could drink, too. I drank deeply, hoping the liquor would loosen my tongue and bolster my courage.

When the room quieted, I continued. "This king, through trickery and murder, became khan of all those who dwelt in felt tents."

I continued. The young king fought bravely in battle against an evil land of arrogant farmers, taking cities by siege. But when the king had consolidated his power, he did what no self-respecting nomadic king should do: He abandoned his home in the grasslands and built a marble palace in a city in enemy country. Then he took on the dissolute ways of the enemy, wearing silks, reading ancient texts, writing poems.

I made Khaidu and his men laugh by telling how ridiculous the king looked, pretending he could read. He learned to recite a Chinese poem about a drunken man who loved the reflection of the moon in the water so much that he reached for it from his boat, fell overboard and drowned. The corrupt king tried the same, going out on a boat, as no decent Mongol would do, and admiring the moon, only to fall overboard. He screamed and flailed in the water until foreign courtiers came to save him. That tale made Khaidu's men hoot with derision.

The corrupt king got fatter and fatter, till he was unable to mount a horse. This made Khaidu's men double over with laughter, since a man who could not mount a horse was as good as dead in the grasslands. The king ate so much rich food that his feet swelled up and he could not walk but had to be carried. The men cheered at this image.

Things were going well. Khaidu was not a smiling man, but I could see amusement soften his stiff face. I tried to drag out the story so that he and his men would get drunker.

Clearly, I was pandering to Khaidu and his hatred of Khubilai Khan. I knew that, Khaidu knew that, Emmajin knew that. But human nature is such that we love to make fun of those we hate and fear.

I stole a glance at Emmajin, and she was not scowling. Instead, she was regarding me with soft, fond eyes. A new wave of confidence washed over me, like cool water, loosening the tension that had tightened my shoulders. I had to find a way to speak to her, to tell her my plan for her escape.

Once the wedding banquet was over, I knew, by Mongol custom the couple were considered married. They did not have a religious ceremony, as we did at home, blessed by a priest. To Mongols, weddings were about families and feasting. The moment was drawing closer where Chapar and his bride would be escorted off to his tent to consummate the marriage. I had to stop that from happening.

When I ended my story, Khaidu's men stomped and shouted "Good! Good!" In the hubbub, I went up to Khaidu at the head table, and bowed to him, saying a few words of respect, amidst the music and laughter. Khaidu's face, normally stern, creased with smile wrinkles. Chapar leaned in to hear what I was saying.

"Now," I said, "I know what our bridegroom is thinking: Shut this man up and let me take my bride to bed!"

The men laughed. I did not dare to look at Emmajin.

"But if he can delay his male urges—just a short time longer!—I have a show that should amuse all of you. It's a smoke-and-fire display in the sky, loud and colorful, the way the Chinese celebrate big occasions. I will set off the display over the lake, for safety. It is a wondrous sight."

I could tell by his reaction that Khaidu had never seen such a thing before. But Chapar had heard of it and was eager to see it. It was his wedding, and Khaidu was inclined to give him his way. I used my hands to describe the way the rocket blasts skyward then bursts into lovely flowers of sparkling lights before falling back to earth. Finally, Khaidu nodded. I had his permission.

"I will go to the lake and prepare. It should be only a short time," I said. He gave me permission to leave.

I bowed, then began to walk out, passing behind the women's table. I was moving clockwise around the perimeter of the tent, as is proper. I had learned such customs at the court of Khubilai Khan, during my stay of more than twelve months in his realm.

The distance closed between Emmajin and me. First I stopped to chat with Khaidu's wife, standing behind her chair. I bowed respectfully and said a few charming words.

I then moved on till I was standing behind Emmajin. I could smell her jasmine perfume. Just then, a group of dancers began to perform, and most people's attention shifted toward them.

She turned in her chair, and I thought I would melt. I bowed to her, as formally as I had to the others, and complimented her great beauty, in formal terms. I maintained an outer appearance as distant and respectful as I had been toward Khaidu's wife, but I'm sure she saw the intensity in my eyes.

I switched into Latin—the language I had taught Emmajin the previous year in the gardens of Xanadu. It was a risk, because I wasn't sure how much she remembered. But I could not speak to her in words that could be overheard.

"Principessa, my lady, my love. You are the bride of my heart," I said in Latin, keeping my facial expression as bland as if I were discussing the weather. She had heard me say these familiar Latin words before. "Do you want to marry this man?"

"No, thank you, I do not," she responded, in Mongolian, as if I had asked her if she wanted another drink. My heart raced, so close to my beloved.

"I can help you get away." I used simple Latin words. "But you must trust me."

She nodded as if agreeing that this was the hottest day of the year. "How?"

"At the end of the fireworks display, there will be an especially loud sound. When others run east, you run west, to the side of the lake. I will wait there in a boat."

The large, muscled young woman was leaning over as if wanting to hear what this strange man was saying to Emmajin.

"Yes, yes, an excellent story," Emmajin said in Mongolian, louder. "Princess Khutulun, this man comes from the Far West, where city streets are rivers of water."

Khaidu's daughter wrinkled her nose. Water in the streets of a Mongolian ger camp usually means trickles of urine. I bowed and addressed her, in Mongolian. "Khutulun Beki, it's an honor. I have heard about your magnificent abilities."

"Enough. Get on with the show," she said.

After that, I had no time to talk to Emmajin alone. I had to pass behind the other women and out of the tent. I needed to find Nasreen. Everything had to work perfectly before Emmajin was forced to join her bridegroom. I had no backup plan.

# Chapter 18
# Emmajin: Choices

Just as he was leaving Khaidu's tent, Marco turned and looked back at me. I gave him a signal—a single nod of my head. He saw it and left.

The sight of his roguish eyes and the mesmerizing sound of his storyteller's voice had lit a fire inside me. I could not even imagine how he had managed to get here, to this well-guarded camp between the cliffs and the lake, travelling alone across enemy territory. And how in the name of Eternal Heaven had he won the trust of the evil Khaidu to be allowed to entertain him at such an important event? Let alone convince these barbarians to allow a show of fire in the sky?

Marco Polo had magic. He had given me hope. But everything had to go just right. If not, I would end this day as everyone else expected, in a marriage bed with Chapar.

Soon after he walked out of the tent, the men began teasing the bridegroom and agitating to follow us to our bridal tent for the consummation. But Chapar temporarily silenced them by standing and holding up one hand.

"Later, my friends," he said. "First, let us go to the lakeside and see what this foreigner has promised: colored blooms of fire in the sky."

Khaidu led the way out of the tent. I could not help noticing that Khaidu, though similar in age to my grandfather, strode steadily, without assistance, on normal feet. I felt a pang of pain for my grandfather, whose swollen feet were the butt of jokes.

A light breeze was a welcome balm after the stifling banquet tent. I trudged to the lake, surrounded by the women of Khaidu's family. The huge, heavy headdress made walking awkward; I had to hold my back straight and stiffen my neck to keep it balanced on my head. One slight nod to the side and the whole thing could tip over, wrenching my neck. The pearls and beads of coral and silver jangled near my ears as I walked.

Most Mongols consider the wedding to be official once the wedding banquet is over. By that standard, I was now part of Khaidu's family. I still did not accept that; no man in my family had agreed to this marriage. But once Chapar took me to his bed, no one would doubt that I was his wife.

Chapar didn't walk with me. He and the other men stayed near his father, who sat on a wooden bench with a good view of the lake, close to the shore. The women sat behind them, on the gentle, grassy slope. I remembered what Marco had said, to run west. So I carefully found a spot on the edge of the crowd toward the west.

Ai-Jaruk, who always seemed to be keeping an eye on me, stood nearby. She started pulling at the pins that held her formal hat, to take it off, now that the banquet was finished. I, too, tugged at my wedding headdress, which was terribly uncomfortable. A maidservant appeared to help me with it.

"Lady, I am here," she said softly.

With a start, I realized it was Nasreen, dressed like the other servants. I wanted to ask her a hundred questions, but too many other people were nearby, and I could see from her lowered eyes that she did not want to draw attention to herself.

"Did he tell you to meet him by the lake?" she asked quietly as she reached behind my ear to take a pin out of my hair.

I nodded.

Nasreen reached behind my other ear and tugged at a pin there, still whispering. "I know where Temur is. When the show begins, I will go to him, to try to set him free."

I was in awe. How had Nasreen come here? Had she come with Marco? Why would she risk her life trying to set Temur free? I should have thought of rescuing Temur; but a bride cannot easily slip out of her own wedding banquet, or from the after-dinner entertainment. Especially when her new sister-in-law is sitting nearby.

"I should be the one to rescue him," I said.

She tugged at the headdress but it did not come off. "No, Lady. Your mission is in the West. The Khan's letter is in the boat."

She had the letter! I had not thought of it since leaving Almalik, since my capture and imprisonment. So Marco intended to take me to the Far West. I dared to hope.

Two other maidservants appeared, the ones who had helped dress me. They elbowed Nasreen aside and finished removing the awkward wedding headdress.

Nasreen pulled back and got to her feet. Her eyes sparkled with conspiracy. She bowed her head toward me, then walked behind me, back toward the tents. My heart beat hard in my chest. I must get ready. I was glad this wedding del was not tight-fitting, that my boots, though new, were of soft leather and easy to run in.

Whatever Marco and Nasreen were planning, it had to happen before Chapar took me off to his tent to consummate this monstrous marriage. I felt for the medicine packet between my breasts. Perhaps I would not have to use it now, but at least I had it, in case Marco's plan did not work.

I sat down on a blanket my servants spread for me to watch the show in the sky. Ai-Jaruk sat on her own blanket, not far away.

At this late hour, after dusk, the lake looked smooth and black in the moonless night. Not far offshore floated a single, wooden boat, lit by a single lantern. Marco was in it, alone, preparing something.

With a loud boom, the first rocket hissed straight up from the boat. Some women near me gasped at the noise, which sounded like a crack of thunder.

Then, with a second loud crack, high in the sky, it burst into hundreds of tiny flecks of red, in the shape of a grand chrysanthemum, before the flecks began to fall in graceful arcs. Many around me let out a loud "waaaah!" of amazement and delight.

The second one fizzled and fell into the lake. But after a pause, with Marco busy working on the boat, a third rocket boomed, shot straight up, cracked, and broke into a thousand speckles of white and gold.

These fireworks were crude compared to the shows I had seen back home in Khanbalik, but Khaidu's people had never seen fireworks.

The people around me buzzed with enchantment. "How is it possible?" "That cannot really be fire." "Amazing!" As fearful as all Mongols are of thunder and fire, these people could appreciate the artistry of this show.

My heart felt as though it was expanding inside my chest, into a large, soft ball. If Marco could put on such a remarkable display less than a day after arriving in camp, he could do anything. Still, I found myself flexing my leg muscles with tension.

Several of the rockets fizzled into the lake. But many were gorgeous, and the viewers relaxed, leaning back on their arms, chatting in between. Ai-Jaruk sat not far away. I caught her eye. She smiled, as if reassured, then turned to watch for more.

After nine or ten of the fireworks had produced marvelous displays, Khaidu's relatives and supporters seemed relaxed, drunk on airag and sated with roasted meat.

Suddenly, one of Marco's rockets went astray. Instead of shooting straight up and bursting into a parasol of color, it shot low over our heads, buzzing with a menacing whir, so close over my hatless head that I ducked instinctively. It landed a little inland and just west of me, with the loudest boom I have ever heard, setting off a cloud of thick smoke. Everyone screamed at once, including me.

We all jumped up. By instinct, most people began running away from the explosion, toward the east. Ai-Jaruk caught my eye, as if checking on my well-being, then took off with the others.

But I turned my head toward the site of the explosion. I noticed an angry black hole in the earth and the twigs of a small bush burning, right next to a ger. In seconds, I thought, that ger could burst into flames.

I recalled Marco's urgent words: *When others run east, you run west, to the side of the lake.* How could I run into and past that terrifying smoke?

The thunderous explosion had shaken loose my deepest fears. I saw a strip along the edge of the water where I might run past the explosion site. My heart shouted "Danger!" My mind said, "Go toward it. Trust Marco." Fighting my instincts, I turned toward the shore. The smoke was growing thicker, obscuring everything beyond the explosion site. I half fell as my foot shifted in the sandy soil, and I had to regain my balance with my arms. Somewhere back there, where people were running, was Chapar, who would want me that night. I had to escape.

The lake was deep and full of dangerous water, but I headed toward it, into the billowing smoke. I coughed as I ran. The smoke stung my eyes, and I flailed at it, trying to shove it away. I ran faster, hoping to get to the shore as quickly as possible. It was probably only a few seconds, but it felt much longer. Finally, the air cleared, and I could see Marco in the boat, rowing toward the shore, with heavy splashes of the oars, a little further to the west. He was rowing quickly, aiming toward a sheltered spot on the shore just beyond a small grove of trees.

I hiked up my dress, and my long legs stretched out under me, covering the distance with increasing speed. Behind me, I could hear screams, but I shut out the sounds as I raced toward the spot on the shoreline where Marco was headed. It was as if we were two arrows, shot from archers in different spots, aiming at the same deer.

I reached the point shortly before Marco did and stood, watching him row toward me. It is the nature of rowing, I now know, that the rower faces backwards from the direction he is rowing. So I could not see his face as he approached the shore. He turned to see where I was standing. A look of alarm crossed his face.

"Look out!" he shouted.

Suddenly, a thick arm reached around from behind me and pulled me to the ground. My head hit hard on the sand, and I rolled so I faced up.

"Not so fast, you rat-dung." It was Ai-Jaruk, her high-pitched voice squawking with exertion and rage. "Where do you think you are going?" she spat.

I grappled with her arms, straining to push at her. This threw her off balance, giving me enough time to scramble to my knees. Her wrestling expertise worked against me. She grabbed my upper arms and tried to pin me down. While I still had some control of my arms, I snatched the dagger from her waistband. She tried to push me onto my back again, but I shoved my shoulder into her thick breast. I heard Marco shouting.

I did not want to kill her, but I had to stop her. Her grip on my arms tightened. I twisted sharply to get some freedom of movement, then shoved the dagger into the only part of her flesh I could reach— her massive abdomen. Her shriek pierced my eardrum.

"You trash!" she cried out. "You dung!" She loosed her grasp with one hand as she reached for my hand that held the dagger, trying to wrest it from me. I pulled the dagger out, then wielded it again. This time I cut her left hand. She pulled it away.

"Stupid child!" she shouted.

Flailing in pain, she still tried to fight for me. Blood flowed from her hand and side, and her eyes filled with anguish. I just wanted to make her release me. I slashed at her upper leg, but the cut was superficial. Still, she screamed and thrashed, loosening her grip on me.

I jumped to my feet. Marco was there, in the shallow water, shouting. "Come. Get in the boat!"

The water was calm, but it still moved, lapping against the shore. The boat bobbed up and down. I would much rather fight than get on a boat, any day. Still, I did not hesitate. Ai-Jaruk made one last lunge at me, nearly grabbing my ankle, but I had already moved into the water.

A few steps into the lake, I lost my balance and fell, splashing heavily into the cold water. I yelped. Marco steadied me as I stood up. The water was up to my knees. Marco held my elbow as I got in the boat, the first time he had touched me in months.

"Do not fear," he said, in his most reassuring tone.

I sat down, hard, on a wooden plank at the end of the small craft, and it rocked sickeningly. Marco stepped in and pushed off at the same time. Then quickly, expertly, he used an oar to push off from the ground under the shallow water. I dropped the bloody dagger in the bottom of the boat, grasped the wooden sides, and closed my eyes. Ai-Jaruk was screaming, but so were many others. Her wounds, I knew from my experience in battle, were not life-threatening; still, I felt nauseated.

When I opened my eyes, we were pulling away from the shore. Ai-Jaruk was running away, limping and holding her side. Would she alert someone to my escape?

Marco sat facing me, rowing backwards, his face toward the shore.

We were together, alone on the water, heading west.

As the oars slapped against the water, the briny odor of the lake mixed with the wet whiff of Marco's exertion. One curl of hair stuck to his face near his ear. Relief spread through me. I had gone through so much to arrive at this moment, skimming across the water away from my captors, toward an unknown future. Now my escape was in Marco's hands.

The scattered screams onshore swelled into a roar. I turned to look back.

Khaidu's camp had caught fire. Several tents, closest to the lake, were in flames. I gripped the sides of the boat harder and lifted my body to see. A loud gasp escaped my lips, and Marco raised his head to look back at the shore. He stopped rowing.

"Temur!" The word shot out of my throat.

The felt covering of the tents, dry from long hot days, burned quickly. I watched as the two gers closest to the water quickly lost their skin, exposing the bones of the tent, the latticed wood sides and the spokes of the roof. These glowed brightly, then began to crumble. The flames leaped quickly from ger to ger.

"Temur is tied up," I shouted. "He can't run."

"Nasreen went to save him," Marco said. "They should be safe by now."

"She might not get to him. If his tent catches fire..." I could not finish the thought.

Marco turned around, and we both watched in horror. Every person I could see was running away from the angry blaze. Had Nasreen succeeded in her plan to free Temur, while everyone else was watching the fireworks? Might Temur's guards have been distracted by the fire in the sky? Maybe. Maybe not.

How could I escape with Marco across the lake without checking to make sure?

"Is this boat big enough—for Temur and Nasreen?"

Anguish filled Marco's voice. "Yes. I planned to take both of them. But I didn't expect to set a fire. If we go back..." This time Marco didn't dare complete the thought.

I wish I could say that I carefully weighed all the options and considered the implications for my future, for Marco's, for Temur's, for the future of the Empire. But there was no time for that. In my mind, I could see Temur in his cangue, the contraption around his neck, his right hand twisted and tied, his feet tethered to the tent post. That was his punishment for trying to protect me. I remembered the stiff, dead face of his brother, Suren, after the Battle of Vochan. I uttered a cry of anguish.

Marco's hands gripped tighter on the oars, but he did not begin to row again. The boat continued to drift onward.

"I can't leave him," I said, in a quiet, pleading voice.

On the far side of the lake, somehow, some way, lay a future with Marco in the West. The husband of my heart, the object of my devotion—Marco was here now, and he wanted to take me away. Did anyone else matter?

The boat rocked and drifted sideways.

On shore, the glowing skeleton of yet another tent collapsed. Women were wailing, children shrieking. The gers were like dry kindling, catching fire the instant the flame leaped from one to the next. The whole camp was burning down.

Gers, tent poles, wooden bowls, prized bows, quivers of arrows, sleeping furs—all the symbols of my childhood and our Mongol way of life—were burning, burning, burning. The flames were leaping toward the tent of Temur—my cousin, my companion, my competitor, my compatriot.

My face was wet with tears. I looked at Marco, whose hands lay still on the oars. I shook my head. "I'm sorry," I said.

Marco began rowing with one oar only, turning the boat. As he directed the boat back toward shore, his face twisted in agony. I can only imagine what he was thinking: this bold plan of escape, so close to success, was now lost. If Khaidu's men caught him, they would surely execute him for setting their camp on fire.

Specks of red-orange danced on the water splashed up by the oars. As we drew closer to shore, Marco's features blacked out against the terrible brightness of the fire. I picked up Ai-Jaruk's dagger from the floor of the boat.

We reached the shore closer to the camp. I stepped out carefully and waded in, glad to feel the solid ground under my feet.

Marco jumped out, too, holding the rope of the boat.

"Emmajin!" he shouted, stopping my headlong rush.

"If they come for you, get back in the boat and leave without me," I said.

"Emmajin." This time, his voice filled with despair. He had risked it all, and I was running away from him.

"If Nasreen has already freed him, if I can't find them, I'll come back to the boat," I said. *Back to you.*

Anguish contorted his face. I embraced him tightly, pointing my dagger away from him. "Te amo," I said, in apology. I did love him. But I had a higher duty. I had not been able to save my cousin Suren from death on the battlefield. If it wasn't too late, I might be able to save his brother, Temur.

I kissed him, hard, on the lips, my tears mingling with his beard. All I could smell was smoke. "I'll be back," I said. The firelight reflected on his brimming eyes.

I did not look back as I rushed toward the flames. It was far harder than running through the smoke had been a few minutes earlier. The intense heat seared my face, and burning soot flew into my cheeks as I ran. The wooden tent frames crackled as they burned around me. I was alone, running through the now empty camp. Fire roared in my ears. Smoke filled my nose. The felt of a ger, aflame, smells like burning hair. Everyone had left the camp, running east along the narrow lakeside road. From that direction, I could hear a crowd shouting and screaming on the other side of thick smoke, as they tried to escape along the narrow lakeside road.

The image of Temur, burning, writhing in pain, drove me on. I ran between flaming gers, in the smoky, swirling paths between infernos. Running between two fires, in Mongol tradition, purifies a person. But this fire was not purifying but destroying lives.

Remarkably, Khaidu's banquet tent still stood, intact, though the fire was only one tent away. No one was fighting the fire. Not far beyond the big tent stood Temur's. No guards stood watch outside it.

*Perhaps Nasreen has already cut him loose*, I thought. *If his tent is empty, I'll run back to Marco.*

I burst into Temur's prison tent.

Nothing could have prepared me for the scene I saw there.

Through thick smoke inside the ger, I saw the shadowy figures of three people. A large, thick figure—Ai Jaruk—held Nasreen's head in a chokehold, arm around her neck, and brandished a sharp knife. A patch of drying blood marked the spot on her abdomen where I had stabbed her; her left hand did not seem wounded at all. None of her injuries seemed to weaken her.

An even thicker, larger figure, Temur was on his feet—alive! He was still weighed down by the heavy cangue, but his legs and hands were free. I guessed that Nasreen had cut his legs and hands loose, but Ai-Jaruk had interrupted before Nasreen could cut him out of the cangue.

Temur was rushing toward Ai-Jaruk, shouting, "Release her!" Temur grabbed at Nasreen's arms and pulled, but the chokehold just grew tighter. Nasreen's pretty face was contorted into a breathless scream.

Ai-Jaruk looked up at me as I barged in. Her eyes narrowed. "I thought you had left with your red-haired barbarian," she said.

Temur looked at me, too, his eyes registering confusion.

"You spilled my blood. I'll spill yours," Ai-Jaruk said, nodding toward my cousin.

Nasreen twisted toward Ai-Jaruk, attempting to break the hold, but Ai-Jaruk put the tip of the blade to her neck. The maidservant went still, her eyes popping in fear.

"You beast!" Temur yelled. Baring his teeth, he lunged at Ai-Jaruk again, throwing the bulky weight of his cangue at her thick figure. She ducked out of the way, pulling Nasreen and nicking her neck. Temur lost his balance, stumbled and fell.

We were three against one, but Ai-Jaruk held a sharp knife. I had her dagger at my waist, but if I attacked her with it, she could quickly kill Nasreen. This was not the moment for knife combat. I glanced around the tent. Beside me, near a guard's stool next to the door, lay a bow and arrows. Apparently, in fear, the guard had left his weapons behind—what no good guard should ever do. I grabbed the bow with my left hand and an arrow with my right.

Ai-Jaruk was across the tent from me, as far away as she could be, but still too close for a normal bowshot. Howling with pain from the wound I had inflicted, seething with anger, she spit at Temur and attempted to kick him.

"Grovel, you rat!" she cried. Sweat dripped down her forehead in the overheated tent. The light of the fire outside flickered on the inside of the rounded tent walls.

I was furious. No one insults and spits on the heir to the throne. But I chose to keep silent. Moving in slow motion, I fitted the arrow to the bow.

From his spot on the floor where he had fallen, Temur grabbed for Ai-Jaruk's leg but missed. Looking down at him and not at me, Ai-Jaruk shuffled farther back, still holding the knife to Nasreen's neck.

"Which of your girlfriends should I kill first?" she taunted.

As much as I hated her, I did not want to kill Ai-Jaruk. She was a member of the Golden Family, and it was forbidden to kill family members. That was probably the reason she had the knife to Nasreen's neck and not Temur's.

So I decided to aim at Ai-Jaruk's knee. Only one leg was visible behind Nasreen's long brown del. Ai-Jaruk's own white del partially hid her knees, but I could guess its location from where her boot was planted. The smoke in the tent was getting thicker, making it harder to see.

"You're brutes, all of you!" Temur shouted, swinging his fist at her. I could tell that he had seen me aiming at her and knew he had to distract her attention. "Not one of you is worthy of wiping the Great Khan's bottom."

Ai-Jaruk was moving, so I had to predict her direction, but I was trained in this from mounted archery. Still, it was risky. If she shifted the wrong way, my arrow might hit Nasreen instead.

I pulled back on the bow and released the arrow. It whizzed the short distance, across the tent, toward Ai-Jaruk.

My arrow hit the mark, Ai-Jaruk's kneecap.

Ai-Jaruk jerked back in pain. The shock of the hit also caused her arms to jerk back, and the knife cut deeply into Nasreen's neck.

We all screamed. Ai-Jaruk dropped Nasreen's body, which fell, limp, to the ground. Her knife flew to the ground. Ai-Jaruk dropped to her knees, then fell to one side, grasping her knee in pain. Blood spurted out from Nasreen's neck in a gush. I knew, from battle, what that meant: instant death.

Temur reached for Nasreen and pulled her to him. He cradled her in his arms, holding her head and covering her neck with his hand, as if trying to stop her life's blood from bursting out. I had never seen such a tender, anguished look on his face.

Next to me, the tent flap crackled. It had caught fire. We had only moments.

I ran to Ai-Jaruk and grabbed her knife from the ground. Then I rushed behind Temur. The ropes that bound the cangue to his body were barely visible in the smoke.

Battling fear and anger and smoke, I gently pushed his neck forward and held his braid loops to the side. He buried his face in Nasreen's hair and keened. The horsehair rope that bound the branch behind his neck was wound tightly, scratchy and hard to cut. The knife was not as sharp as I expected, so I had to use the sharp tip again and again against the many strands of the rope.

It was too late to rescue Nasreen, but not Temur. I had to work quickly. Ai-Jaruk was pulling the arrow out of her knee, and I knew she would rise again.

Poke. Slice. Poke. Slice. I was so close to Temur, as I cut the rope behind his ear, that I could feel his rapid breathing.

"She came to save me," Temur said, holding Nasreen. Temur's voice quivered with amazement.

My eyes filled with tears. My knife slipped and I cut his braid loop. "Oh!"

His braid began to unravel. As a Mongol man, Temur had never cut his hair from infancy, so this long braid, one of six, represented not only his manhood but his whole life. His hand flew up to the braid, as if trying to hold it in place.

The door flap was crackling. Could I free him and get him out of the ger before the whole tent caught on fire—and before Ai-Jaruk rose up to stop us? Surely she, too, wanted to get out quickly. Would Marco still be there, with his boat, waiting for us?

With one last slice, the rope fell away. I pulled the thick branch away from the back of his neck, and the whole contraption fell off. Temur pushed the cangue away and down, then lifted his head and looked at me, still cradling Nasreen's limp body.

"It's too late," I said. "Let's go."

He lingered one moment longer. Gently, he touched her forehead. Carefully, he laid her body flat on the floor, her head to the north and feet to the south. Then he laid his braid across her neck, to hide the gaping wound. Just as I had covered his brother's battle wound with a scarf.

Flames now engulfed the fabric around the door flap.

"Temur! Come!" I yelped.

I reached for his hand and helped him stand to his full height. He stretched out his arms, celebrating his freedom. Then he reached for me and embraced me. For a moment, I closed my eyes, in relief. He held me a moment longer, putting his forehead on my shoulder in a gesture of overwhelming gratitude. The roar of the fire deafened me, and the stench of smoke blocked my nose.

Still holding her knee, Ai-Jaruk was limping toward the tent flap, trying to get out. Temur released me, and I turned to go.

He followed me out. The sea of smoke was even denser outside, choking me. Ai-Jaruk collapsed in the open space, not far away.

The fire had spread so wide that it formed a barrier, barring our way back to the lake. The only clear escape route was north and east, away from the flames.

"I know of a way," Temur said, "over the mountains." He grabbed my hand and pulled me north, toward the fresh air, toward the mountains, away from the lake.

"Marco has a boat," I said. "He's waiting there, for both of us."

Temur took one look in the direction of the lake, through fire and smoke, and then looked up the mountains. A clear path led that way. "No," he said. Then he began running in that direction, toward safety.

But my feet would not move. I stared into the flames, straining to see Marco, in grave danger now that he had caused this inferno at the heart of Khaidu's power. He had not set the fire deliberately, but Khaidu would not see it that way.

I needed to return to Marco, at the lakeside. Yet, how could I run away from Temur at this moment? My loyalties crashed against each other like two armies that had long been preparing for battle.

"Hurry!" Temur returned and grabbed my arm. "We can't get through that way."

I turned to him, the full anguish of the moment tearing apart my innards. "You go without me," I said. "When you get back, to

Almalik, tell them that the Great Khan is in danger. Khaidu plans to retake Karakorum. You must warn the Khan."

Temur gave me a dazed look. "Are you crazy?" He pulled my arm, dragging me away from the flames. "Hurry!"

Maybe I was crazy. Tears streaked through the soot on my cheeks. "Temur, I can't go with you."

A wave of shock and incredulity registered in his eyes. "Chapar?"

I shook my head, eyes full of misery, unable to explain.

He let go of my arm as if I were diseased. Disgust and betrayal shot through his eyes. Words could not express his horror at the thought that I would free him, then return to Chapar. Yet I could find no words to tell him I had chosen Marco.

"The marriage was against your will," he said. "It was not valid."

Temur. His beard had grown during his captivity, covering his square chin with a light layer of coarse black hair, but otherwise his features were so familiar, so dear. Despite his beard, Temur's distinctive wide-set eyes were the same as those of the little boy I had played with, back in the courtyards of the palace. I had helped set his chubby hands on the arrow the first time he drew a bow.

Temur tugged me back toward my people, the people who had raised me, who had lifted me with their marvelous tales of daring. It was the sour bite of fresh airag, the aroma of roasted meat, the whipping of a horse's mane across my cheeks, the inspiring stories of my forebears, men and women, the hearty shouts of "Good! Good!" What could Marco, in his frail boat, offer me to replace all that?

Temur pulled my arm again. My feet chose to run with him, as if beyond the control of my will. Temur was back in charge.

By contrast, Marco had let me go. Even after all he had done to rescue me, he did not try to control me. Only with Marco had I ever been truly free.

I was doing what I should, leaving Marco behind. What my family expected of me. I hoped he would get in that boat and row hard, to safety. Tears streamed down my face as I ran, with Temur, back toward the Khan, toward my own people, toward the life I had known. Temur assumed that I would run with him, that I belonged to the Khan's family, that I would do what I had been taught to believe was right. My body, accustomed to following him, did.

But my heart began to tear away. Yes, it was vital to warn the Khan. But Temur could do that without me. I had fulfilled that obligation. I no longer wanted to follow orders. I wanted to follow my heart. Besides, I had a higher mission now, to get that letter to the Pope. Wasn't that the right thing to do, too?

North of the camp, not far away, we came to the cliff. Temur seemed to know just where to go. He found a steep trail and started to climb up it.

On the other side of these mountains, I knew, lay the main road, leading east toward Almalik, where the Khan's forces could provide safety.

I climbed up after Temur, using hands as well as feet to push aside prickly bushes. But I turned and looked back, down at the camp below. I could see the lake now, in the eerie light of the fire. The few gers between me and the lake had already burned.

The smoke twisted and shifted. Through a gap, I saw Marco's boat. He had already left the shore but had not gone far yet. There might still be time to reach him.

"Temur!" I shouted to the man on the trail above me, fast disappearing into the mountainside. "Be sure to warn the Great Khan!" I am not sure he even heard me.

I turned back and slid down the hill. My eyes were so full of tears that I could barely see where I was going. At the bottom, I began to run, straight south, toward the lake, past the remains of Khaidu's camp. All the gers had burned to the ground.

A few of Khaidu's men were beginning to return to the camp, perhaps to salvage what they could. But in the darkness and confusion, no one paid attention to me. When I reached the beach, I stumbled.

Marco must have seen me coming, because he rowed his boat closer to shore.

What possessed me to leave behind my people, my cousin, all the brave dark-haired people who dwell in felt tents, to go with a red-bearded foreigner to an uncertain future? I had stopped listening to my mind and listened only to my heart.

Marco pulled the boat to the water's edge and jumped out. I got to my feet and ran to him, splashing in the shallow lake waters. He embraced me with a hard, desperate hug, nearly crushing my ribs. Then he steadied the boat with one hand and held my hand in the other as I climbed in. The boat rocked perilously. I closed my eyes and gripped the sides.

"Nasreen?" he said. "Temur?"

I shook my head, unable to explain just yet.

Marco got in and began rowing with smooth, strong strokes, facing the shore. In the flickering firelight, his face was wet with tears. I touched his cheek.

For once, words seemed to choke in his throat. He looked away, stretching his arms and pulling back on the oars, straining against the water as if it were a sea creature trying to drag us back to danger.

My back was to the shore, and this time I did not turn around. I did not want to see any more of the damage the fire had done. I squeezed my eyes shut and covered my ears, leaning forward into a ball.

Temur's shocked face. The smell of burning flesh. The taste of smoke. The shouts of those who would hold me back, the shouts of Temur, of Ai-Jaruk. The sorrowful face of my mother. The disappointed look of my father. I rocked back and forth on the boat, trying to block out these searing images.

Sternest of all was the frown of disapproval, tinged with betrayal, on the face of the Great Khan. How generous he had been, to allow me, a woman, to join his army. I had wanted nothing more than the honor of spending my life serving him, and here I was, in a boat with Marco. I hoped I could still carry out his mission to the West and win back his favor, but I wasn't sure he could ever forgive me for abandoning Temur and running off with Marco.

I tried to imagine instead Temur, racing up the mountain path, facing off against Khaidu's guards at the pass, pushing past them and plunging down the other side toward the Ili River, toward Almalik and the safety of the Khan's garrison. I could live with this image of him, escaping to freedom. It overpowered the horrible image of Temur tied in the cangue, in a burning ger. *Yes,* I told myself. *I made the right choice.*

# Chapter 19

# Marco and Emmajin:
# In Heaven

Marco:

Like Sindbad the Sailor escaping by boat from monsters, I had to row as fast as possible to save our lives. We had lost precious time. We had to get across the lake before Khaidu's men figured out how to pursue us. Although the Mongols hated boats, they had plenty of Kirghiz servants who could follow us. In the initial chaos of the fire, I could see, everyone seemed more concerned with saving lives and property than with catching the criminal who had started the fire.

My arms strained as I rowed. In the front seat of the boat, Emmajin sat facing down, her head in her hands, shaking with silent sobs.

"Nasreen?" I asked again, later. "Is she all right?"

Anguish creased her lovely face as she looked up at me, wordless with grief.

Nasreen. Gone. A pang pierced me. It couldn't be true.

"Temur?" I asked.

Her cheeks were streaked with tears and she could barely get the words out. "He headed uphill," she said, gesturing vaguely behind her.

I looked up at the mountain that loomed over Khaidu's camp. It seemed too steep to climb, but perhaps a narrow path cut over it. I squinted, scanning the hillside for a solitary figure. Instead, I saw a line of scattered colored dots climbing on a zigzag path. Others, too, must have found this sheer path above the chaos. I sent up a quick prayer that Temur was safe among them, for the sake of Emmajin.

Personally, I had no love for that arrogant prince who had held a dagger to my throat.

Clearly, Emmajin was too distraught to give me details just yet, and I needed to put all my effort into rowing. I prayed that Nasreen was still alive, somehow, and that Temur would escape, but their fate was out of my hands.

Emmajin's sobs abated, but she sat, hunched over, her arms wrapped tightly around her body, as if trying to comfort herself. I wished I could protect her from whatever hellish images were torturing her mind.

Waiting for her return, after she ran off to rescue Temur, had been agony. Watching as each ger caught fire, knowing I had set off that chaos and destruction, was torment. Fearing she would be caught or killed or burned alive was torture. My choice to let her go had fought against every instinct in my body, every urge I had to protect her, every desire to become a hero.

But now here she was, in this boat. She had come back. She had made her choice: me. Wonder washed over me.

*Deo gratias*, I repeated with each stroke of the oars.

The wind picked up, rocking our tiny fishing vessel. I knew that just being on the water was frightening for her, let alone in rough waves. My arms ached from rowing all day, but I could not let up.

Facing the shore as I rowed, I could see the fire in Khaidu's camp swell and spread. Less than an hour after the fire had started, men and women were still screaming and sprinting to the east, to flee the flames by the one road that led out of the camp. But that lakeside lane was slender, squeezed between a cliff and the lake. Were people dying, I thought, burned to death because of my error? Were panicked people funneling onto the narrow cliffside road, where they could not help pushing others into the angry waters of the lake? I had hoped to create a small brush fire as a distraction. I had never intended to burn down the entire camp. My stomach twisted as horrific images ran through my mind. Arson was not valiant.

I tried to push aside these disturbing thoughts by focusing on Emmajin. Here we were, at last, alone together. But she looked ill, in body and at heart.

*Please, God*, I switched to this thought with each stroke of the oar. *Help us.*

Later I switched to the Hail Mary, which I knew in Latin as Ave Maria. The steady rhythm of the familiar prayer gave me both strength and serenity. I had never felt a divine presence the way I felt that night. When life was going well, I seldom thought about my religion, but when I was in trouble, it all came flooding back to me.

Finally, calmer, deep into the night, Emmajin offered to take the oars. I had stopped to rub my sore arms, which were shaking. We switched places, and she learned quickly how to move her arms with long, smooth strokes. Her archer's arms had more strength than mine. I stayed awake, scanning the distant shore for some cove where we might find a safe haven. The crescent moon cast only a little light but the stars shone bright. Later, after a rest, I took back the oars and rowed on.

Miracle of miracles, no boat came after us that night. Still, I knew we had to reach the other side before morning light. Lake Issyk Kul proved larger than I had imagined.

The sky had just begun to lighten when we landed on a far shore. Emmajin awoke when the craft bumped against a rock. I steadied it and helped her out, then tied the boat to a tree root, hidden from view. Emmajin grabbed onto a tree to steady herself; she seemed relieved to stand on solid ground again.

We had made it.

The land there sloped steeply up and was covered with fir trees. We had to scramble up on all fours before we found a relatively flat area where we could sit, under a tree and out of sight.

Feeling safe at last, I sighed and rubbed my arms, sore after a day and a night of rowing. I lay back, sighed heavily, and closed my eyes. I breathed in the fresh scent of evergreen needles and listened to the caw of gulls.

We were alone, Emmajin and I. She was just inches away from me. I had rescued her from Khaidu, from marriage to Chapar, from the horrors of being a prisoner. Someday I would tell this story. But now I was too exhausted to feel happy.

She lay back next to me, silent for a moment. Then she laughed out loud.

I opened my eyes in surprise. It seemed as if the pressure inside her had been bottled up for so long that now it spouted out like a geyser. She tossed her head back, shaking with laughter.

"What? What is it?" I wanted in on the joke.

"Look!" She pointed straight up. I tilted my head back and gazed upward. Overhead, the trunks of fir trees pointed straight toward the sky. "They look like arrows," she said, "but with the feathers at the tip instead of the bottom. Is that Tengri's way of designing an arrow?" That made her laugh more.

Her laughter refreshed me, but I didn't understand what was so funny. I had burned down a camp, perhaps killing dozens. Nasreen was gone. My arms felt as though someone had tied knots inside them.

She laughed until tears flowed. "This was supposed to be my wedding night," she said at last, her eyes closed, her cheeks wet. Her release, I realized, arose from relief.

I propped myself on my elbow and turned to her, on the sloping ground. "Emmajin Beki," I said. She opened her eyes, glistening in the pale morning light. "This is your wedding night." I leaned over and stopped her laughing with a kiss.

Her lips were silky and moist, and her musky fragrance enveloped me. She responded eagerly. We had waited so long and risked so much for this moment.

After a long, Latin kiss, a *bacio*, I drew back and looked in her velvety eyes. "You came back to me."

She smiled sadly. "They will kill us if they find us." She stated this fact as if it did not apply to us. I didn't want to hear it. "So let us not waste a moment." She pulled me to her, rubbing her hands over my sweat-soaked back.

It was the worst place in the world for an embrace—uneven ground, sloping downward, rough with rocks and roots. But we were alone, totally alone for the first time, in a private trysting place, in the wild wood, shielded from any prying eyes. Only the frogs kept us company, with their repetitive refrain: *You did it! You did it! You did it!*

We didn't know if we had minutes, days, or years left together. So we grabbed each minute, greedy for each stroke, each touch, each kiss as only lovers long separated can be.


Emmajin:

After Marco fell asleep, I lay on my back, and I stared upwards, savoring the sweetness of him. This was my moment, and I did not care what dangers I might face in the future because of making this choice. If they recaptured me, if they tortured me, if they killed me, I would always be able to remember this interlude of joy. If I cherished every moment, every caress, every sigh, no one could take them from me.

I breathed in deeply of the fresh fir-scented air, felt the soft bed of fir needles, listened to the chorus of birds: the high chirps and whistles of the finches and chickadees and the low croaks and quacks of the coots and mallards. We were in the Heavenly Mountains, lost in the wilderness, between East and West.

In my father's religion, Buddhism, there is a teaching about the importance of savoring each moment, of being present and enjoying the present. Marco seemed to have the ability to do that. It was an appealing idea, but difficult for me to grasp. I guess I'm more practical and hard-headed than Marco. He seems to live half his life in the floating fantasy of the stories he tells. We Mongols are more grounded.

For more than a year, since meeting Marco, I had been struggling, inside myself. I wanted respect from my people, and I would have achieved that if I had made the choice to return with Temur. That would have been the responsible thing to do. But deep inside, I realized that I wanted something else even more. Marco had sacrificed everything to rescue me. What had I ever done for him? It was my turn now to put him first. Whatever his plan was to get to the West, this time I chose to trust him.

What if I had made the other choice? I could easily imagine that alternative life: climbing with Temur across the mountain, finding a horse, galloping across the plains, along the Ili River, back to the fortress of Almalik. We would have been welcomed with joy. Then we would prepare for war against Khaidu. Temur would relish that. But for me—as much as I had dreamed of the warrior's life, as much as I hated Khaidu and everything he stood for—I didn't want to fight. I snuggled up against Marco's warm, sleeping body. This was where I wanted to be.

Might I be punished for this choice, some day? Possibly. Was I being irresponsible? Yes. But I did not want to ruin the moment with such thoughts. So I cut them off and ran my hand over Marco's firm chest.

Marco's eyes fluttered open. He looked startled at first, then smiled when he saw my face, so close. "Hello, my lady love," he said, with tenderness beyond all measure.

"Is this wrong?" I asked.

His eyebrows drew together and he sat up. "Not at all! You are the bride of my heart." Then he took my hand and kneeled on one knee, facing me and bowing. "Emmajin Beki, Empress of all that is good, will you marry me?" His eyes glowed.

It was so odd, so Marco. "What are you doing?" I asked. A man asking a woman directly, if she would agree to marry him?

I laughed and pulled him up off his knees. Side by side, we sat under a tree overlooking a small ravine. His leg was touching mine. "According to Mongol tradition, I am already married. There was a betrothal and a wedding banquet."

"I thought you told me that a wedding is valid only if both families agree."

"True. No one from my family agreed."

"And Chapar did not take you into his tent."

"Thanks to you! Marco, if he had…" I shuddered.

Marco draped his arm gently over my shoulders. His gentleness, deep and strong, kept me safe from every danger. "In the West," Marco began, with a coy smile, "a marriage is not just a decision between two families. It is a union between a man and a woman before God."

Marco and his strange ideas!      "I don't believe you. The fathers have nothing to say about it?" I liked the feel of his protective arm on my shoulder. I took hold of his hand with both of mine. This kind of intimacy was not common among Mongols, at least to my knowledge. His hand was warm and soft, and I rubbed his palm with my thumb.

"That's the theory," he said. "In reality, the fathers and mothers usually arrange the marriage—because the young men and women often have no way of meeting one another."

"No one thinks of marriage as an alliance between two families?"

"Well, sometimes. Especially among rich families. My parents' marriage was arranged by their parents. My mother told me she objected to the idea of marrying a man who was away traveling so much of the time. But she was young, and she didn't protest loudly enough to make a difference."

"So without the approval of our families, you and I could never marry," I said. At best, I thought, we could only defy their wishes by being together, as we were now.

"How's this for a plan?" Marco said. I looked at him skeptically, but still wanting to believe. "On the way to Venezia, there are many cities with Christian communities. They are Nestorian Christians, with some beliefs that are different from the True Church in Rome. The kind of Christianity your aunt Yurak and her family embrace. They have Christian priests. We could ask one of them to marry us in the church."

"Without our families present?" Now that we were headed west, I knew, we would be cut off from his father and uncle for a long time.

"Since our families could not attend, no one would object. Once we got to the West, it would be considered an official marriage."

This was a strange notion: a wedding without family. What did it matter what some unknown priest did, if neither family agreed? But Marco seemed to think it would work, producing a marriage recognized in Christendom. And it was better than living outside virtue.

I looked around the woods. There were no signs of local villages, let alone towns with churches and priests. How long would we have to wait to marry?

Marco's eyes looked greener than usual—a reflection of the fir trees around us. I could see he had the same idea I had: Neither of us wanted to wait.

"Yes," I said. "I will."

He understood.


Marco:

After months apart, our hunger and thirst for each other was extreme and insatiable. I felt it as vivid anguish, a fever pulsing, throbbing, overflowing the banks of my soul. The crashing of a torrent, the brusque scent of pine, the soar of an eagle, the crispness of fresh mountain air, all heightened our senses as we marveled at the magic of our delight in each other. The earth itself exulted, wildflowers shamelessly flaunted their colors, a finch let loose in song, a bed of pine needles spread itself, all for us.

"I wish we were immortal," she said, rolling onto her back. A smooth underglow shone golden through her skin.

"This moment may be fleeting," I answered, "but it is ours, now."

Staring into the never-ending sky, rimmed by these immense mountains, I felt at one with her and with all God's creation. I marveled that passion could feel so boundless.

Despite all my facility with language, I could find no words adequate to describe the experience. I could not define the ecstasy of her firm body, the delicate curve of her high cheekbones, the utter madness we felt as we reached for each other. Later, the words of my stories came back to my mind, but they seemed insufficient: love, passion, desire, craving, urge, adoration, ardor. When I had told those tales, I had known nothing of true love, of insatiable desire, of the unquenchable thirst to unite. Tristan, Lancelot, Yvain, Erec, all seemed pitiable to me. Surely, they had never experienced true, transcendent love.

We would live in the forest together, heedless and exuberant, just as Tristan and Isolde lived their three years in the woods. Like them, we would live on roots and herbs and game. Like them, we would think only of one another. At last, we both had what we had desired for many months: time together, alone, with no one watching us or trying to keep us apart. No Mongols. No Latins. Just Emmajin and Marco, under the sun, under the stars, in the wilderness, in the Heavenly Mountains.

I chose not to tell Emmajin the end of the story of Tristan and Isolde—which was not a happy one. I knew no story where a couple in love defied the norms of their society and family and found a happy ending. But we were defying the norms of storytelling, creating a happy ending for ourselves.

As the experienced traveler, I led the way. At first, our path seemed obvious. There was no way to go either east or west along the lake, so we had to go up and over. We just needed to cross the mountains, heading to the south, and on the other side find a path leading west. After that, we would have to avoid the main trade routes that Khaidu had blocked. For now, I felt confident that no man controlled this high terrain. At my uncle's insistence, I had brought the golden tablets of safe passage, issued by Khubilai Khan, and they would keep us safe once we reached Persia, which was controlled by Khubilai's brother Hulegu. From then on, it would be a relatively easy journey all the way to Venezia.

But these mountains, the Heavenly Mountains, confounded me. I knew we needed to follow streambeds up, to find a pass, but that proved difficult. Although many rivulets rushed down into the lake, the gorges were too steep to follow for very long. The top of the mountain seemed to be an endless ridge, with cliffs facing the lake. Again and again, we followed a stream up as far as we could, scrambling over rocks, then had to double back down and almost to the lake before moving westward to try to find another stream to follow.

Food was not a problem. At first, not daring to light a fire, we ate orange berries from the buckthorn bush, as well as walnuts and apples from wild trees on the slopes. Nasreen, in her rush, had left her bow and arrows in the boat, so Emmajin could hunt.

"What will we do next?" Emmajin asked in the late afternoon of the second day, as she cut the meat of a rabbit into thin strips and lay them on a rock for the sun to heat. It was a trick she had learned in the army, a way of cooking without a fire.

"We'll head for Rome," I said, sitting on a nearby rock, watching her every movement.

A brief frown crossed her flawless brow. "The Khan's letter to the Pope? Nasreen said she had it."

I smiled and patted my saddlebag. "It's in here. *Deo gratias,* she made a point of getting it before leaving Almalik."

"I'm not sure the Great Khan will want me representing him, after all this."

"Why not? You escaped from bandits. You passed through Khaidu's territory when no one else could."

"Have we passed through Khaidu's territory?"

"Not yet. But we will."

That made her smile. I had never seen her smile so much as she did when free from her family and the army. "And after that?" she asked.

"We'll cross these mountains, then head west, toward the setting sun," I said.

She looked up at the sun, which was clearly not in the direction we had been moving that day.

"I still have some jewels. Once we reach the nearest herder family, we can trade them for horses."

She dipped her hands into the nearby stream to rinse them. "Can we trust the local herders here? Won't they report on us to Khaidu?"

"Nasreen told me the local people, the Kirghiz, despise Khaidu," I said. "Besides, silence is also a commodity that can be bought."

She nodded, looking skeptical as she wiped her hands on her trousers. We were still too high in the mountains to expect to see a herder family.

"And then?"

"Then we will head to Venezia."

She smiled and closed her eyes, as if trying to imagine my beautiful city.

Once back in Italia, I would treat Emmajin as a royal princess, an emissary from the Great Khan. We would not publicize our marriage until later, when we could get the Church of Rome to bless it.

Imagine, I thought—returning home to Venice married to the granddaughter of Khubilai Khan, a royal princess on a mission to the Pope! Some of my relatives might disapprove, not realizing how powerful the Great Khan was. Most non-Latins in Venezia were slaves, especially those who looked different from us.

"I will buy you a fine Mongolian gown and headdress, so that you will appear as royal as possible," I said grandly. "Perhaps your great uncle Hulegu, the Il-Khan would provide proper clothing for you. I'll wager he has heard of your bravery in the Battle of Vochan! He'd enjoy hearing me tell the story of our escape from the evil Khaidu." Between my silver tongue and her letter from the Great Khan, I figured, we could easily carry out our plan.

"No stories now, Marco." She reached out and pulled me up from my rock and then wound her arms around me and laid her cheek on my chest. I could feel every contour of her body pressed against mine.

This forest, early in September, was chilly but dry. Most of the trees were evergreens, though the few with leaves glowed with intense yellows. The nights were cold and we reached out to each other for warmth. During the days it got warmer, but we walked mostly in the shade.

Eventually, we reached high ground, above the tree line. This land was rocky, having lain under snow and ice until summer. But we found meadows covered with grasses and wildflowers. From there, we caught sight of the highest peak of the Heavenly Mountains—Mount Khan Tengri, the King of Heaven. Its majestic cone, a dramatic steep peak, dominated the other snow-capped peaks and shone white with a brilliant light that seemed divine. Surely God could not disapprove of a love as pure as ours.

Above the trees, the sun warmed us. We sat in the sunshine, rubbing each other's arms and legs till we got warm, laughing like children.

It seemed we had fallen off the map of the known world, into a fantasy realm no human had ever seen.

But even there, the mountains kept blocking our path to the west. It seemed that they were directing us to the east, opposite from the way we wanted to go. Again and again, we headed up toward what we thought was a pass, only to meet a boulder or cliff wall. More than once we had to retrace our steps and backtrack down the hill to the meadow, heading eastward again.

Our high spirits began to sag.

To help my lady keep going, I acted as if the road to the West were just over the next mountain range, though I sensed it was much farther away than that. I worked hard to keep my frustration from showing. As we traveled, to keep her mind on positive things, I told her the story of how we would arrive in Christendom. I painted an appealing picture of it, with its kings and queens, knights and ladies, grape wine and dancing parties, soaring cathedrals and winding cobblestone streets. We would visit the Holy Land, meet with the Pope, explain the Khan's good intentions, then race off through grape arbors to meet with the kings and queens of the small kingdoms that made up Christendom.

But Emmajin knew what I was doing. She could see as clearly as I did: We were not moving westward. Even in such high mountains, where the sun is not visible until long after the sky is light, I could see that we were not heading toward the setting sun.

Once in the dark of night Emmajin woke with a start—and told me that the fire had raged in her dream and Temur screamed as his tent burned. I held her tight until she stopped shaking and the horrid images disappeared from her mind.

Why is it that once you have your heart's desire, once you have everything you thought would make you happy, you cannot stay in ecstasy forever?

As days passed and the moon waxed full and then waned, we were both shivering and miserable, longing for shelter, for a decent meal and a deep draft of airag.

One evening, after a particularly sparse meal, Emmajin braided her fingers in mine. We were sitting together under my thickest coat, which held in our anxiety.

"Marco, I still have the sleeping medicine. You never told me why you gave it to me." She pulled out the small leather pouch, which was attached to the rosary beads around her neck. It looked flatter than I remembered, and I wondered if she had used any.

Her face looked strained, as if she had guessed my real reason. Yes, I had considered she might want to use it herself, if she got into a terrible situation. Taking too much of this medicine would bring about eternal sleep. The shaman's mad words had predicted she would meet with danger, and he had proved correct.

"I thought you might need to feed it to someone, to make them sleepy, so you would have time to escape," I said. That was also a reason.

She laughed. "As a matter of fact, that's exactly how I planned to use it: on Chapar, on my wedding night, to keep him away from me."

"In my country," I said, "we have a story about young lovers whose families prevent them from getting married. They decide to kill themselves." I don't know why I brought this up. I was feeling frustrated about losing my way.

Emmajin looked up at the tree branches high above us, as if pondering this story. I chose not to tell her the rest: how the girl and boy both took poison, but only the girl died from it. Then the boy killed himself with a knife. I shuddered.

She shifted her eyes toward my face, as if trying to read my thoughts and emotions. "Well, I still have it. In case we need it." She held it toward me: "Do you want half? Or do you have some of your own?"

I took the leather pouch from her hand. "We are together now," I said. I opened the pouch and dumped the brownish powder on the ground at my feet. Then I stood, and with my boots stomped on the powder and rubbed it into the ground. This felt good.

"Stop! Such expensive medicine!" she said, sounding more like a merchant than my father. "We could sell it someday."

"No," I said, sitting down close to her and taking her hand. "It symbolizes despair and that part of our lives when we were apart. Now that we are together, we don't need it."

She shook her head, as if to say I was foolish, but then smiled and kissed the tips of my fingers. I leaned over and kissed her on the lips. I had let her go, and she had come back to me. At last, she had made her choice.

We had gained what we had long desired. We were together, beyond the confining rules of men, in a safe haven above both East and West.

# Part IV:
# Consequences

# Chapter 20
# Marco: Consequences

As I walked in to face the Great Khan Khubilai, I bowed my head. Guards flanked me, holding my elbows. My hands were tied behind my back. From out of the back of my robe, behind my neck, a stiff board stuck straight up over my head, with my crime written on it in Mongolian script.

My uncle had told me it read 'criminal' in Mongolian. He used the Latin word, *scelestus*. From *scelus,* evil deed. Villainous. Wicked. Abominable.

At this moment of my judgment, my father and uncle walked beside me. They had rushed back to Khanbalik when they heard that I was being taken there to face judgment. Despite our differences, despite my father's disapproval, they were there with me, as my family. If I lived, I promised myself I would never forget their support in this dark hour.

On this, the shortest, darkest day of the year in Twelfth Moon, the monarch was not in his main throne room but in a smaller room, paved with marble, where he attended to lesser matters, such as my life or death. Perhaps he did not want to draw attention to the humiliating scene of punishing a man who had run off with his granddaughter.

At least I was alive. If Khaidu's men had reached us first, they would have killed us on the spot and strung our bodies on trees for the birds to pick. But the Great Khan's men were searching the Heavenly Mountains, too, and they were the ones who found us. They had taken us to the fortress of Almalik, where the commander had immediately packed us off on the long journey back to the capital, Khanbalik. It had taken eighty days—four times longer than the precious twenty days Emmajin and I had spent alone in the mountain wilderness.

Since our capture, Emmajin and I had not been allowed to talk to each other. I had barely even caught sight of her, and I missed her desperately. I hoped she would be at my judgment this day. After one last sight of her, I thought, I could bear anything, even execution. What I could not bear was never to see her again.

Eighty days in a saddle, eighty nights sleeping alone, contemplating your future after being caught *in flagrante delicto*, allows plenty of time for the formation of vivid mental images. I had imagined several fates, including such common forms of execution as beheading, hanging, drowning, and being rolled in a carpet and trampled by horses. The last was reserved for members of the Golden Family, so it seemed less likely. Perhaps I would be dragged through the streets of the city and killed for sport to entertain the citizens, as in Rome in the olden days. Perhaps I would be mutilated. Maimed. Disemboweled. Emasculated. Hanged, drawn and quartered. Burned at the stake. Probably not, though—those were Christian methods. There are distinct disadvantages to having a vivid imagination.

As a granddaughter, Emmajin's life might be spared—although her crime, for a woman, was serious. She belonged, body and soul, to the Golden Family, and she had deserted her cousin in a moment of danger to go off with a foreigner.

I reminded myself, again and again, that I had shown enormous bravery. Stunning boldness. Astounding courage. Valor. Daring. Audacity. Loyalty, even. Daily, hourly, I had practiced my defense. Yet I might not have a chance to speak.

Now, directly before the Khan, at the edge of the carpet at the bottom of the stairs leading up to the dais, the guards let go of my elbows and bade me to kowtow. Head bowed, I dropped to my knees, but with my hands tied behind my back, I could not flatten myself and knock my forehead on the floor as required.

My father and uncle each grabbed one of my arms and helped me to kowtow three times. In this Twelfth Moon, less than a year after this same Khan had lauded me for bringing him medicine to cure his feet, I felt diminished, humiliated, embarrassed, appalled. Walking in, I had noticed that only about twelve men were present, court officials. So my lady would not see me this way. But when would I see her again?

On the third kowtow, they left me, forehead to floor until the Great Khan bade me to rise. Then they helped me to my feet. I stood, head bowed, before the most potent man on earth since Adam.

Torches flickered, and I dared to look up. The Khan of all Khans was leaning back, and both feet were raised on thick silk cushions but did not seem swollen. A good sign. It seemed the dragon-bile medicine I had brought him was still helping. Despite his great bulk, he looked diminished somehow, slumping and less magnificent than I had remembered. Rather than sturdy and imposing, he just looked fat. His hair, in braid loops, was streaked with white. Still, a live tiger was lying near his feet, and it raised its head and stared at me with menacing eyes.

What a contrast to the first time I had met the Khan! A year and a half earlier, my father, uncle, and I had entered the Great Khan's main throne room, kowtowed to show our respect, and enjoyed a warm welcome. My father and uncle had met the Khan on their earlier journey, and they had returned, as promised, bearing oil from the lamp of Jerusalem's Church of the Holy Sepulcher, as the Khan had requested. The Great Khan had complimented my father on what a fine gallant I was, saying, "If this young man live, he will assuredly come to be a person of great worth and ability." I had savored that compliment many times, but now it rang hollow. I had never before thought about the words, *If this young man live.*

But now, trying to look dignified despite the stiff board in my back, my mind could not focus. My tongue stuck to the roof of my mouth. I was, in fact, guilty of what the Khan was about to accuse me of. I loved his granddaughter.

Christendom was safe and would not likely see either the Great Khan's army or any attempt by the Mongols to control it—but not because of my own deeds. Khaidu had prevented the Khan's army from getting to the Far West. But during the journey, some shocking new developments had changed the course of history. Khaidu, infuriated by the burning of his camp, had, as Emmajin suspected, joined forces with the traitor Shirki and ridden off to attack the former Mongol capital, Karakorum. Chapar and Ai-Jaruk had set off with him, headed for the ultimate battle. Nomokhan was still a prisoner, in the Lands of the Golden Horde, but Temur had escaped and was preparing for battle. So Mongols would be fighting Mongols. Civil war had broken out. The Khan's plan to unify all lands under an empire at peace seemed impossible.

From behind the screen, behind the throne, came the sound of footsteps, a flurry of soft leather boots on a wooden floor. I looked up to see who was arriving at the hall in this unusual way. At that moment, Emmajin entered, surrounded by three lady's maids.

I could not help gasping at the glorious sight of her.

Emmajin was dressed as a Mongol royal lady, wearing a tall red headdress studded with rubies and jade, with pearls and silver beads dangling from the sides. It was far more elegant than the ridiculous one Khaidu's people had attached to her head the day of her so-called wedding banquet. By sweeping her hair up into that hat, she had chosen to appear as a royal married lady, not a maiden with braids down her back.

Standing tall in this outfit, Emmajin Beki emanated authority and gravitas, which I knew would help her. She looked stunning and feminine, but also fierce and aloof, proud and untouchable. Clearly, she had made a decision about how to approach this trial before the Khan, and abject apologies would not be part of it. She looked like she knew what she wanted and was ready to fight for it. I just wished I knew what that meant.

In contrast to her bold appearance, her eyes, which found my face immediately, were soft and fond. Her cheeks were rosy, her face more filled out. Even her body seemed thicker and more solid. She must have been given much better food, during the journey, than I had.

*Deo gratias* for this one last opportunity to exchange glances. Now I could bear anything.

Gone was the uncertain, nervous, doubt-filled girl I had met in the gardens of Xanadu eighteen months earlier. Gone was the shamed, humiliated look of Khaidu's prisoner forced to marry her captor's son. Gone, too, was the sweet, soft body that had curled up with me during cold nights in the mountain wilderness.

She did not approach me but took her place, standing, to the side. She glanced at me with concern, and I realized how gaunt I must look to her. I had nearly stopped eating.

A man on my left stepped forward and began to read a proclamation in Mongolian. His words were in formal court language, so it took me a few moments to realize what he was reading. It was the accusation against me.

"This foreigner, this Latin merchant, who goes by the name Marco Polo, has offended the high dignity and solemn reputation of the Golden Family, of the glorious family of the Great Khan Khubilai, descendants of the Great Ancestor Chinggis Khagan, descendants of the wolf and the fallow deer. This foreigner did rescue a princess of the Imperial Family from the clutches of the evil Khaidu, but then, through his own irresponsible actions, he did debase said princess, holding her prisoner for twenty days and refusing to return her to the care of her father's family."

Some of the words, in the formal court language, were hard for me to understand, but it did not seem true. Still, I was not in a position to contradict.

"Therefore we bring this prisoner before the Great Khan Khubilai, to hear Imperial judgment on his actions."

The Mongols did not believe in fair trials, in hearings and witnesses and the weighing of various accounts. I had been brought not for a trial but to hear my punishment. That was clear.

I stood, my head bowed, ready to hear my fate.

"Wait." A deep voice echoed through the marble room. I heard gasps of surprise.

It was Temur, stepping forward to face the Khan. I had not seen him standing among the other men of the court. "I beg for permission to speak in this matter."

Temur looked even taller than the last time I had seen him. With his wide-set eyes and high cheekbones, dressed in a red brocade del, he carried himself like the imperial heir he was. He had matured enormously just in the last six months, since that day, long ago, when we had departed from the capital with the army in Fifth Moon. Emmajin had tried to get an audience with him, to plead to him on my behalf, but Temur had refused to see her.

During our twenty days together, Emmajin had told me the dramatic story of how she and Nasreen had rescued Temur from the cangue. She had described how Temur had held the dying Nasreen in his arms and gently laid her body to rest. So I knew that he had a sentimental side as well as the gruff exterior he had cultivated in the army. I wondered what aspect of Temur we would see this day—and how it would affect my fate.

Temur kowtowed once, then stood before the Khan.

"Grandfather, may I speak?" Temur said.

The Khan made him wait a few minutes, as if to remind us all that he did not need to listen to anyone. No one had the right to influence the Khan of all Khans before he pronounced his judgment.

"Temur, son of Chimkin," the Khan bellowed at last, with an angry edge to his voice. "You know something of this matter. Tell me what happened in the camp of my kinsman, Khaidu."

Temur lifted his chin and spoke in a clear, confident voice. "As you know, our kinsman, Khaidu, held me, your grandson, as a prisoner, restrained by a cangue." A murmur of disapproval rippled among the Khan's men. "That same Khaidu tried to force your granddaughter to marry his son without the approval of anyone in our family." Another murmur. Temur's voice grew louder with each statement. "And as you know, Khaidu gathered his men and, together with the army of the traitor Shirki, they are even now marching toward Karakorum, trying to capture the former Mongol capital, in rebellion against the rightful Khan of all Khans."

"Traitors!" one of the courtiers shouted. "Scoundrels!" shouted another.

"Honored Grandfather, I stand here before you to ask your permission to join the loyal forces that are preparing to prevent these traitors from carrying out their nefarious schemes. All your loyal subjects are eager to band together to stop this evil plot."

Temur, I knew, had been in the army a little over a year, and had recently been promoted to the level of commander of one hundred, at a much younger age than most. The experienced General Bayan, I had heard, was in charge of the forces that were preparing to head to Karakorum to defend the former capital. At age sixteen, what role could Temur expect?

His words seemed to raise the ire of the Khan, who now stood up. Two aides, one on each side, leaped forward to hold his arms and steady him, but he pushed them aside and stood on his own. I had cured his feet, with the rare medicine I brought from Carajan. Had he forgotten?

"That kinsman of mine, Khaidu," the Khan said, his voice shaking with anger, "has brought shame on the Golden Family. His actions dishonor all of us descendants of the Great Ancestor by urging open rebellion and civil war among Mongols. Our sacred legacy is to work together to preserve and expand the Empire of our Ancestors. Tengri, great god of heaven, gave us Mongols the right to rule this Empire, and we dishonor Him by fighting among ourselves. We will put down this rebellion and reunite the Mongols!"

The Khan's men cheered. His criticism of Khaidu made me dare to hope that my judgment might go well, since I had burned down the camp of the enemy. But it might be interpreted that I started the war.

Khubilai Khan looked at Temur and continued. "You, my grandson, do me great honor by this request. Though young, you have endured much suffering at the hands of Khaidu. I hereby promote you to commander of one thousand men!" Most men did not get such an honor until the age of thirty. "You will leave with General Bayan for Karakorum, as soon as he is ready."

Temur dropped to a kowtow, holding his forehead to the floor.

"Rise!" said the Khan, and Temur rose. "Now tell me what you know of this man, the accused, Marco Polo."

I sucked in my breath. Temur had shown no affection for me and often warned Emmajin against me. She had not only defied him but left him, on the hillside above Khaidu's burning camp, to go off with me. What would his testimony be now?

Temur rose and stood tall. He did not look at me, but he glanced at his cousin Emmajin before speaking. "This man, Marco Polo, showed great boldness in daring to enter Khaidu's camp. If he had not, I might still be a prisoner there. Your granddaughter Emmajin would be yoked to Khaidu's son, Chapar, as a fourth wife. If she had, she might have been forced to bear sons who would have made a dual claim to the throne and dare to rebel against you. This man prevented that from happening."

I began to breathe again, a little. This is what I had hoped to say for myself. It sounded much better coming from Temur.

"This Latin storyteller distracted Khaidu's men with a display of fireworks, then sent a servant to unbind me." I pictured Nasreen's laughing face and felt a pang for her. Temur was giving me credit for something Nasreen had chosen to do on her own. "Khaidu's daughter, Ai-Jaruk, tried to stop the servant. My cousin Emmajin then came through the fires to ensure that I was safe. It was she who freed me from the cangue and allowed my escape."

Temur's voice was almost expressionless—not the way a story-teller would tell the story, but full of the dignity of a gruff Mongol soldier. Emmajin seemed to be trying to keep her face stiff and expressionless, too, but I could see, in her eyes, a look of relief.

"O Khan of all Khans," Temur continued, "I learned something in the camp of our kinsman, Khaidu. I saw that the old ways are truly barbarian—mindless slaughter, grasping for power, taking what is not yours, turning against your own people, imprisoning men for personal gain. Now that I have returned to the light of your reign, I can see the benefits of wise rule. Under you, O Great Khan, the Mongols have advanced to a new level, where we set aside grain, where we care for widows and orphans, where we judge people based on their actions."

The Khan's face beamed with pride, mixed with a little sadness. Perhaps he saw the future of the Empire, two generations after his death, in this handsome grandson.

"However," continued Temur, and my breath caught in my throat. "Emmajin Beki did not escape with me, over the mountains, as I expected. This foreigner, this Marco Polo, had arranged a boat, planning to take us both away by water. She chose to go with him rather than with me. That was her decision, and it was a mistake."

His word *mistake* echoed through the small chamber, where everyone stood silent. Temur may have learned about love, in that burning tent, but he would not let sentiment rule his judgments. But he had said it was Emmajin's mistake, not my *crime*.

It was time for me to speak up, to defend Emmajin and her decision. Although I had no right to speak, I began to formulate the words in my head.

At that moment, Emmajin stepped forward, on my right. Exactly as her cousin had done, she kowtowed once and held her head to the floor until her grandfather bade her to rise.

I held my breath again. So many times, Emmajin had said she did not have my gift for speaking, especially in front of others. She had longed for the approval and approbation of her family, especially from her grandfather, the Great Khan. Yet she had tossed that away by choosing to come with me. What could she possibly say now?

Then she astounded me. Instead of taking her place next to her cousin, she stepped back. She came around to my left side and knelt beside me, as a wife would. My heart squeezed tight in my chest. This action seemed too humble for the proud Emmajin I admired. *No!* I thought. *Don't sacrifice yourself. It's too late to save me. Save yourself!* But fear and confusion tied my tongue.

"Rise!" barked the Khan, a second time.

Emmajin stood up and lifted her chin. I could hear her breathe deeply. The hall smelled of incense and leather. A strange serenity emanated from her.

"Emmajin, daughter of Dorji. What have you to say for yourself?" The Khan sounded sad. He smoothed his thin beard and rubbed his cheek.

She smiled up at the old man who was her grandfather, as if aware that he felt the burden of ruling all the people of the world.

She reached for my elbow and helped me to my feet. With a move so swift I barely felt it, she sliced the rope that tied my hands together, so that my hands dropped to my sides. Gently, she pulled the wooden plaque out from the back of my shirt and laid it on the floor. Then she held my arm as we walked to the base of the steps, as close as we could get without mounting to the dais.

Stunned, I could not take my eyes off her, my lady, my soul mate.

"O Khan of all Khans," she began, "O leader of the Mongol Empire, wise ruler of hundreds of thousands of men and women of all nationalities. As you have heard from my cousin Temur, this man is not a criminal but a hero. I beg you to see him as such.

"To me, Marco Polo is more than a hero. That day, amidst the terrible smoke and flames of Khaidu's burning camp, I realized something. Marco Polo is the husband chosen for me by Fate."

My breath caught in my throat. Could this be happening?

"He is the husband of my heart, even if our families have not agreed. I want to spend my life with him. I don't know what that life might look like, but I ask your permission, as head of my family, to marry him."

Her words, spoken in such smooth, sweet tones, seemed unreal. My spirit left my body for a moment and hovered over the two of us, standing side by side, asking the impossible. Instead of execution, I might finally achieve my heart's desire.

The Khan, still standing, wavered, and his two aides caught his elbows to steady him. He frowned down at her, an unmarried girl of his family who dared to choose her own husband, a lowly foreign merchant.

"If this man has taken you as his wife, without my permission, he is guilty as charged," the Khan roared.

Temur spoke up. "I have an announcement."

We all turned toward him with surprise.

Facing the Khan, he continued. "Before I escaped from Khaidu's camp, as the only male relative of the Princess Emmajin, I gave my permission for this marriage, to the Latin Marco Polo."

What? I glanced at Emmajin, who seemed as shocked as I felt. Temur, who hated lies, was lying for us. He had done no such thing as give his permission. I wasn't even sure he had the right to do so, under Mongol customs.

The Khan stared at his grandson in astonishment. It was the first time I had seen him speechless. I watched his face for signs of anger at this insubordination.

But just then Emmajin spoke up. "I, too, have an announcement."

I glanced at her in alarm.

"The next generation is about to begin."

Panic flooded me. What was she saying?

"New life begins in me."

I nearly choked. Of course, this was possible. But I had not anticipated it.

The Khan's mouth closed, and his face went stony.

"You may ask," she continued, "who is the father of this baby, and who is his clan? It is right to ask such questions."

The Khan's massive head tilted to one side and he leaned forward slightly, as if eager to hear. Emmajin had assured me that Chapar had never touched her, but the Khan did not know that.

Beside me, Emmajin took a deep breath as if to calm herself. "One night," she said to the Khan, "a man as yellow as the sun entered my tent though the smoke-hole in the roof. He..."

She glanced at me, with a sparkle in her dark eyes. I did not know this story, which sounded like a traditional Mongolian tale. But I did know the power of stories. She was the storyteller now. Confidence washed over me, like a gentle wave at the seaside.

"He rubbed on my belly," she continued. "The light from this man sank into my womb. Then he left me, crawling out of my tent on the shafts of moonlight."

The Khan frowned as he listened to these words, which seemed lyrical and familiar to the Mongols present. I tried to remember the traditional Mongolian tales I had heard. Was this the story of Alanne the Fair? She was an ancestor of all Mongols.

"Now you know the truth," Emmajin said, as if lying and storytelling were as familiar to her as they were to me. "And you can see that…" She paused, as if listening to a voice inside her head. "You can see that it's a sign." She stood taller and put her hands on her belly. "This babe must be a child of Eternal Heaven."

Voices murmured. The Khan's frown deepened, as if in pain.

She continued. "You asked me once, Great Khan, what I had learned from this foreigner. One thing I now know. We are all sons and daughters of Eternal Heaven. Mongols. Cathayans. Tanguts, Tibetans, Mohammedans, Latins from the Far West. Some men choose to separate and fight, as Khaidu and Shirki are doing on the plains of Karakorum, killing their brothers and cousins. They are the true traitors.

"Or we can live into a larger vision. We can reach out to each other, even those very different, and work together. This is what I choose to do. This man by my side, Marco Polo, this gentle foreigner, has served you well. He risked his life to rescue your grandchildren. He did not force me to go with him on that boat. I chose to trust him.

"Our foremother, Alanne the Fair, showed her sons a bundle of five arrows, unbreakable when bound together, and asked them to work together in unity. Today, the arrows may represent people of different fathers, different clans, different religions, different countries of birth. They may even be of different houses within the Golden Family. But if we are drawn together by a single purpose, no one can break us."

The Khan shifted on his throne, as if ready to speak. But Emmajin had more to say and seemed eager to say it.

"Great Khan, I beg you to consider this child in my belly. This babe is not the child of a clan but a child of Eternal Heaven. He is the symbol of the new Mongol Empire, one that stretches from East to West, an envoy of the future, a sign pointing to that grand vision that only the Khan of all Khans can bring about, a worldwide empire of peace and prosperity.

"The future belongs to children such as this one, in my womb. If Your Majesty continues in his policies, all countries will be united not because of bloody conquest but because of a desire to be part of a well-ruled empire, where all children are valued, according to their merits."

I had thought Emmajin might speak up to beg the Khan to spare my life. But at that moment, it seemed unnecessary. The Khan's small eyes had softened. He gestured for Emmajin to come up the stairs to his side. She took a step forward and nearly lost her balance. I took her arm to steady her and helped her climb the stairs. How had I not noticed the small bump in her belly? At three months, it was not easy to see.

At the top, before the throne, we stopped, arm in arm, face to face with the Khan of all Khans. The Khan reached out his hand, and Emmajin took it. Despite his power, she looked as though she were offering him a gift.

Khubilai regarded her with the concern of a grandfather, not a ruler, but mixed with respect. His broad face glowed, as if relieved that someone had finally seen through the trappings of power and understood the vision he had been fighting for all these years.

"Emmajin," he said, pronouncing it in a way that reminded me that her name was the female form of Temujin, the birth name of their revered Great Ancestor, Chinggis Khan. "You look like your grandmother."

I thought of the Empress Chabi, whose round moonlike face was so different from Emmajin's elegant high cheeks. But Emmajin's face was rounder now. She laughed.

The Khan laughed, too. "If I had wanted to extend kinship to the Latins, I would have sent you off to marry the son of the Pope, not of a merchant."

Then the Great Khan shifted his eyes toward me. His eyes hardened, and I shrank away. Had everyone forgotten, for a moment, that this meeting was to decide my fate?

"Here is my judgment," the Khan said, again speaking in his loud, imperial voice.

The room fell silent.

"I have decided not to execute this man. He may live."

A great weight lifted off my shoulders.

"But a marriage is impossible, unacceptable."

My shoulders tightened again.

"You." He looked directly at Emmajin, with those hardened eyes. "You fought heroically in the Battle of Vochan and suffered as a prisoner in the hands of the traitor Khaidu. You have learned much. But you have shamed the Golden Family by your behavior. I will spare your life, but I hereby send you into exile. You are to spend the rest of your life in Togtoh, at the court of your aunt, Yurak."

I remembered the kind, moonlike face of her aunt Yurak, and the affection with which Emmajin had spoken of her. But my hopes had soared, and this judgment dashed them.

The Khan shifted his narrow eyes toward me.

"As for you, young Latin, son of a merchant, once a storyteller to the Khan. You dared to go where my soldiers could not go, straight into the heart of the enemy's camp. Your fireworks gave a chance to my grandson and granddaughter to escape the clutches of the enemy. You are not a criminal. But you grabbed for yourself what did not, and could never, belong to you. With your reckless behavior, you shamed your father, your uncle, your native land, your Pope, all Christendom."

This was not going well.

"Here is your punishment. You can never return home. Your father and uncle can never return home. I will not permit it."

Hope drained from my body.

"I hereby send you into exile, too. You are to spend the rest of your life in the South, in the southern Chinese city of Yangchow. There you will serve me as I see fit.

"You are never, I repeat never, to see the Princess Emmajin again. On pain of instant execution."

My chest relaxed enough for one normal breath. I would not be executed. But separation from Emmajin would kill me.

Emmajin's fingers gripped tightly on my arm. I looked at her face, which was stricken with grief and crushed hopes. She carried my child in her womb, and I would never see it. She carried my heart in her heart, and I would be empty forever.

But she surprised me, yet again. She released my arm and turned to face me, her back held straight. I instinctively straightened my back as well. Her face transformed from sorrow to joy, and a sparkle lit her dark eyes. "I will enter your tent on a sunbeam, through the smoke-hole in the roof," she said. "I will think of you with each bead of your mother's rosary."

She held out her hand. I took it and kissed the top of it, in the Venetian way.

"I will enter on the shafts of moonlight," I said. "Look for me each night."

I might see her again. Or we might be separated forever. But after our twenty days in the wilderness together, we still had our imaginations—and memories so lovely that we could live on them forever. Not even the Khan of all Khans could take that away from us.

We would live. And we would find a way.

# GLOSSARY

AI-JARUK: Also known by her Mongolian name of Khutulun, daughter of Khaidu. She was famous for defeating her suitors in wrestling. Marco Polo related her dramatic story in his book.

*AIRAG*: Mongolians' favorite alcoholic drink, fermented mare's milk.

ALMALIK: Fortified city on the western edge of the region directly controlled by Khubilai Khan, on the Ili River, near the present-day city of Yining and the border between China and Kazakhstan.

BATTLE OF VOCHAN: A battle between the Mongols and the Burmese. In his book, Marco described the battle, which involved two thousand elephants.

*BEKI:* Mongolian for "princess."

CATHAY: Name used for North China during the thirteenth century; it may be a corruption of the spelling of "Khitai," a group of nomadic people from Manchuria who ruled this part of China from 907 to 1125.

CHABI: Chief wife of Khubilai Khan and a devout Buddhist.

CHIMKIN: Khubilai Khan's second son, who became heir apparent. He died before his father, so he never became Great Khan. Father of Temur.

CHINGGIS KHAN: Known in the West as Genghis Khan, the Mongol leader who conquered much of the known world during his lifetime, 1162 (estimated) to 1227, and founded the Mongol Empire. His birth name was Temujin.

CHRISTENDOM: Europe was known by this name in Marco Polo's era. The word "Europe" was not widely used until centuries later

*DEL*: Mongolian clothing, a long-sleeved robe that crosses over in the front and is secured with a sash at the waist. Worn by men and women in summer and winter.

DORJI: Khubilai Khan's eldest son, who was passed over as heir apparent. Little is known about him. His name is sometimes spelled Jurji. Dorji is a Tibetan Buddhist name.

EMMAJIN: Fictional daughter of Dorji, Khubilai Khan's eldest son. Born in 1260, the year her grandfather became Great Khan. In 1276, she would have been sixteen by today's reckoning but considered seventeen by Chinese and Mongolian reckoning.

*GER*: A round, collapsible Mongolian tent, known in the West as a yurt.

GOLDEN HORDE: The name of the Mongol *khanate* (kingdom) that ruled Russia and nearby lands for nearly three hundred years. The name is believed to have come from the golden, or yellow, colors of the tents and flags used by the Mongols to denote imperial status. The Khans of the Golden Horde were descended from Chinggis Khan's eldest son, Jochi, and were nominally subordinate to the Great Khan, although in reality he had little control over them.

*KHAGAN or KHA'AN*: Mongolian for "emperor," "Great Khan," or "Khan of all Khans." Marco Polo translated this title as "Great Lord of Lords."

KHAIDU: A descendent of Chinggis Khan through his son Ogodei, the second Great Khan. Khaidu believed Ogodei's line should have inherited the right to rule the Empire, so he challenged Khubilai Khan's right to be Great Khan.

*KHAN*: Mongolian for "king," "commander," or "ruler."

KHANBALIK: "Khan's capital" in Mongolian, this city was built by Khubilai Khan to be the capital of the Mongol Empire. It was formerly known as Yenjing, and then as Peking, and is now known as Beijing. Marco Polo called it Cambaluc, a variation on Khanbalik.

*KHATUN*: Mongolian for "queen" or "empress," used for wives of the *khan* or *khagan*.

KHUBILAI KHAN: The fifth Great Khan, born in 1215, who ruled the Mongol Empire from 1260 to his death in 1294. Commonly known in the West as Kubla Khan or Kublai Khan. During his reign, the Mongol Empire reached its greatest size. For details of Khubilai Khan's life, the author found the best source to be *Khubilai Khan: His Life and Times*, by Morris Rossabi.

MAFFEO POLO: Marco Polo's uncle, who traveled to China twice, once with Marco's father only and again with both Marco and his father.

MARCO POLO: A young Venetian who traveled to the capital of the Mongol Empire in China, leaving home in late 1271 and arriving in 1275 at the age of twenty-one. After returning home to Venice in 1295, he wrote a book about his travels, becoming the first European to write about China for a Western audience. Many versions of Marco's book exist; the author relied on *The Travels of Marco Polo: The Complete Yule-Cordier Edition*.

MONGOL EMPIRE: Founded by Chinggis Khan in 1206. At its peak in 1279 the Mongol Empire included all of Mongolia, China, Tibet, Korea, Central Asia, Iran, and Russia. It was the largest contiguous land empire in history. The Mongols ruled China and Iran for about one hundred years, and Mongols continued ruling Russia for about three hundred years.

MONGOLIA: Homeland of the Mongols, now an independent country north of China. In the time of the Mongol Empire, it included parts of China known today as Inner Mongolia.

NICCOLO POLO: Marco Polo's father, who made his first journey to China from 1260 to 1269, and his second journey to China with his son, Marco Polo, from 1271 to 1295. Both times, Niccolo Polo traveled with his brother, Maffeo.

NOMOKHAN: Fourth son of Khubilai Khan, often sent on military missions to pacify the West. In 1276, Nomokhan was captured by treacherous relatives and delivered to the Khan of the Golden Horde in Russia. He was not released until 1284.

POPE: The head of the Christian religion in Rome. When Marco Polo left for China in 1271, the new Pope was Gregory X, whom his father and uncle had befriended earlier, during their travels.

SHIRKI: Sometimes spelled Shiregi, he was a son of the fourth Great Khan, Mongke, who was Khubilai's elder brother. Shirki might have inherited the throne if his father had not died relatively young. In 1276, Shirki betrayed Khubilai Khan and sided with Khaidu in an effort to take control of Karakorum, the original capital of the Mongol Empire. He also seized Khubilai's son Nomokhan.

SUREN: Fictional eldest son of Chimkin, born the same year as Emmajin.

TARA: Buddhist goddess or bodhisattva of compassion, revered by Tibetans and Mongolians.

TEMUR: A son of Chimkin, who later became the sixth Great Khan, ruling from 1294 to 1307.

TENGRI: Mongolian for "Eternal Heaven," or "God."

TOLUI: Chinggis Khan's fourth son, father of Khubilai Khan.

VENEZIA: Italian spelling of Venice.

XANADU: Alternative spelling of Shangdu, the site of Khubilai Khan's summer palace, due north of Khanbalik/Beijing. The name Shangdu means "Upper Capital" in Chinese. Today it is in ruins, located near the town of Duolun in Inner Mongolia. Marco Polo described it in great detail. In the famous poem "Kublai Khan," by Samuel Taylor Coleridge, it was spelled "Xanadu," which is the name most widely used in English.

YELLOW RIVER: Main river in northern China. The Mongols called it Caramoran, meaning "Black River."

YUAN DYNASTY: An era of Chinese history when China was ruled by the Mongols. Khubilai Khan declared the Yuan Dynasty in 1271, eleven years after he became Great Khan of the Mongol Empire. His heirs followed as emperors until the Yuan Dynasty fell in 1368.

# ACKNOWLEDGMENTS

The origins of *Son of Venice* go back to 2001, when I began working on a novel about Marco Polo. I was surprised to learn that he lived in China from the age of 21 to 38, yet he never wrote about any love interest during that time. So I created one for him: Emmajin, fictional granddaughter of Khubilai Khan. Eventually, the novel became Emmajin's story—relating a tale about Marco Polo as seen through the eyes of an Asian woman. The first part of the story of Emmajin and Marco was published by Random House/Delacorte Press in 2011 as *Daughter of Xanadu*. *Son of Venice* continues that story. I rewrote it so that readers could hear both Emmajin's and Marco's perspective.

Many people helped me during the long process of research and writing these two books, and I offer heartfelt thanks to them all. My husband, Paul Yang, suggested the idea of writing a novel about Marco Polo. Week after week, I received input and advice from my writing coach and teacher, Brenda Peterson, and the many in her class who read and commented on the book as it progressed, including Susan Little, Leslie Helm, John Runyan, Mary Matsuda Gruenewald, Donna Sandstrom, Jennifer Haupt, Leigh Calvez, Trip Quillman, J. Kingston Pierce, Liz Gruenfeld, Liz Adams, Laurie Greig, Dan Keusal, Leska Fore, Susan Knox, and Sara Yamasaki.

During the reshaping of this book to become *Son of Venice*, I owe special thanks to fellow writers Trish Lawrence and Carolyn Ossorio, who enlivened it with great ideas and suggestions. At the editing stage, I received crucial input from Susan Little, Carla Jablonski, and Michelle Poploff. I am also grateful to Heidi Francis, who created my author website, and to Kathy Campbell, who designed the beautiful cover. The good-looking young man pictured on the cover as Marco Polo is Andrew Rosenberger, son of my dear cousin Liz.

For information about Marco Polo and the Mongol Empire, I read many books, the most useful of which was *Khubilai Khan: His Life and Times*, by Morris Rossabi. I was also inspired by Jack Weatherford's *The Secret History of the Mongol Queens*, and by his personal endorsement of *Daughter of Xanadu*.

Emmajin is fictional, but many other characters in this book were real. I tried to imagine and recreate them as accurately as historical records would allow. Any mistakes that remain are my own.

# ABOUT THE AUTHOR

DORI JONES YANG spent ten years and sought out faraway places to research this book and its predecessor, *Daughter of Xanadu*. In Mongolia, she drank *airag* in a *ger*, rode camels, and practiced archery. She explored the site of Xanadu, now in ruins, and walked along the walls of Khubilai Khan's palace, which was rebuilt during the Ming Dynasty and became the Forbidden City in Beijing.

Originally from Ohio, she studied history at Princeton, international relations at Johns Hopkins, and Mandarin Chinese in Singapore. She roamed Asia as a foreign correspondent for *Business Week* magazine, based in Hong Kong, for eight years. Her first book, about Starbucks Coffee Company, was translated into ten languages, and her second book, *The Secret Voice of Gina Zhang*, which reveals the inner life of an immigrant girl from China, won two awards. She lives near Seattle with her China-born husband, Paul Yang, who inspired this story of cross-cultural love.

You can find out more about the author on her website, www. dorijonesyang.com.